OPERATION CRISIS

by

Frederick E. Smith

THUNDERCHILD PUBLISHING
Huntsville, Alabama

This is a work of fiction. All of the characters, organizations, and events portrayed in this novel are either products of the author's imagination or are used fictitiously.

OPERATION CRISIS

Published by arrangement with the Frederick E. Smith literary estate.

ISBN-13: 978-1986452335
ISBN-10: 1986452336

Published by Thunderchild Publishing. Find us at
https://ourworlds.net/thunderchild_cms/

Dedication

To:
my cousins Bob and Freda
and
my friends of many years
Mary and Frank Ellis
with love and affection

Acknowledgments

The author wishes to acknowledge his debt to the authors of the following works of reference:

Bekker, *The Luftwaffe War Diaries* (Macdonald)

Adolf Galland, *The First and the Last* (Methuen)

Richard and Saunders, *Royal Air Force 1939-1945* (H.M.S.O.)

Sir C. Webster and N. Franklan, *The Strategic Air Offensive Against Germany 1939-1945* (H.M.S.O.)

Alfred Price, *Instruments of Darkness* (Wm Kimber)

Edward Bishop, *Mosquito — Wooden Wonder*, (Pan/ Ballantine.)

Chapter 1

Frank Adams spotted Davies's private aircraft as he was walking from the Administration Block to his Confessional. It was flying over Bishops Wood towards the airfield and as it made a tight half circle to face the stiff breeze, Adams gained the impression that Davies was in a hurry. As Davies's appearances at Sutton Craddock usually meant trouble of one kind or another, Adams was showing uneasiness as he entered the Nissen hut he used as his Intelligence Office.

At the window Sue Spencer, the slim, attractive officer who was his assistant, noticed his expression and immediately put two and two together. "That's the Air Commodore's plane, isn't it, Frank? Is he expected?"

Adams shook his head. "Not that I'm aware of. I've just seen Henderson and he made no mention of his coming."

He joined the girl at the window. The tiny Miles Master had already touched down and was swinging round to approach the hangars. As it taxied on to the tarmac apron and a couple of mechanics ran towards it, the propeller stopped spinning and a small man dressed in white overalls jumped out. If Adams hadn't already recognised the pilot, the behaviour of the two mechanics and their hasty salutes would have been identification in itself. "It's Davies all right," he said. "I wonder what's brought him here."

Adams wasn't the only airman asking the question. Millburn, one of the Squadron's flight commanders, noticed Davies as he and his navigator walked out of B Flight Crew room. "Uh-uh, look who's arrived! Old trouble-ass himself."

His navigator, a small Welshman, gave a groan. "I thought we'd seen the back of him for a while after that shambles over the Loire."

Millburn grinned. "Maybe he's come to give you a medal. He likes guys who break their legs before a mission."

The Welshman, nicknamed Gabby or The Gremlin by his fellow airman, scowled at the American. "Must you keep on about it? It could have happened to anybody."

"Anybody stupid enough to climb onto the roof of a B-17 hangar and show off like you did: sure it could. What are you going to do the next time? Say you've had too much sex and you're worn out? Come to think of it, you probably are. That's why you're limping like that."

"You should break your bloody leg, Millburn. Then you'd know how much it hurts."

Millburn grinned again. "I've got you taped, boyo. From now on you'll fly, even if you're wearing horn-rimmed glasses, a tourniquet and a truss."

The indignant Welshman was about to reply when he noticed Davies's haste in making for the Administration Block. "He's got some nasty job in mind. Look how fast the little bastard's moving."

"It's that medal he wants to pin on you," Millburn grinned. "He can't wait. Only he's going to pin it on your ass."

Davies's appearance was ringing alarm bells all over the airfield. Mechanics working on the Mosquitoes that were picketed round the base were nudging one another and pointing at the small figure on the tarmac apron. McTyre, an old sweat in oil-soaked overalls working on Millburn's T-Tommy, gave a grunt and turned his lugubrious face to a young armourer. "It's that bastard Davies again. And it means only one thing, mush. Trouble. He's probably goin' to post us to Russia."

Ellis, cherubim-faced and innocent, looked shocked. "He couldn't do that, could he?"

"Davies! Why not? He's sent our bloody kites everywhere else, hasn't he?"

Ellis's troubled young eyes were following the Air Commodore. "Maybe it's just a courtesy call."

McTyre gave a scornful guffaw. "Courtesy? You think the little sod would be moving that fast if he'd just come to say hello? It's trouble, mush. See if I'm not right."

It was true Davies was in a hurry. Overalls flapping round his legs, he ran up the low flight of stairs that led into the Administrative Block and turned down the corridor that led to the C.O.'s office. A G.D. aircraftsman, walking down the corridor in the opposite direction, recognised him and did a tactical side-step into an adjacent room. 'Erks' as young airmen were universally called, were not enthusiastic about encountering Air Commodores face to face.

Laura, the C.O.'s sergeant, was not so lucky. Country bred from Dorset, she was a tall girl with vital statistics that turned the Squadron's younger men glassy-eyed. and its older men reflective. At the moment her arms were piled up with A.P. manuals that Henderson had sent her to collect. As she approached the door of the storeroom which she had deliberately left ajar, the vectors between her and Davies were shortening by the moment.

Reaching the door, the girl used her elbow to open it. Unable to see over the pile of manuals in her arms, she stepped out. At the same moment Davies, with his mind full of the news he was to give Henderson, ran full tilt into her.

The result was a cry, a clatter of books, and a yelp as Davies cannoned off the big girl, lost his footing on the polished canvas and crashed to the floor. About to reprimand her assailant for not keeping his eyes open, the girl recognised him and froze. "Air Commodore! I'm sorry. Are you all right?"

Davies was anything but all right when he realised the girl was still on her feet while he was sprawled ignominiously on the floor. As he sat up, the door of the C.O.'s room was flung open and. Henderson appeared. The big Scot's Highland brogue had never been more conspicuous when he saw Laura bending over the half-winded Davies. "What the hell's going on? What happened?"

Laura turned her dismayed face towards him. "I ran into the Air Commodore, sir. I didn't see him over my pile of books."

Henderson ran forward. "Are you all right, sir?"

Davies climbed painfully and irascibly to his feet. "No, I bloody well aren't all right. This sergeant of yours came out of her office like a bull at a gate. What goes on in this outfit of yours,

Henderson? The last time I came, an aircraftsman nearly tripped me up with a bucket of water. Don't you all like me or something?"

Henderson's eyes were twinkling now although he kept his expression contrite. "I'm sorry, sir. I really am." He turned to the pink-cheeked girl who was picking up the books and pamphlets. "Don't worry about the manuals just now, Laura. Give them to me later."

As the girl apologised again to the Air Commodore, Henderson led him into his office. "I'm sorry, sir, but I didn't know you were here. If you phoned I didn't get your message."

Rubbing a bruised shoulder, Davies was still tetchy. "I didn't phone. But I'll know better the next time, won't I, if it's only to stop your staff attacking me."

This time Henderson allowed himself a grin. "She's very upset about it, sir."

"So she should be. She's a bloody Amazon. You should put her in your gun pits, Henderson. She wouldn't need a gun. She'd knock down Jerries with her bare fists."

With the commotion dying down, Henderson's curiosity over the Air Commodore's visit was growing by the moment. "How did you come, sir? By kite or by car?"

Davies took the chair the Scot offered him. "I flew here," he grunted. "Didn't you hear me?"

"No, sir, I didn't," Henderson confessed. "I've been on the phone to Maintenance for the last hour trying to get some spares they promised me weeks ago."

Mollified, his temper returning as he remembered the reason for his visit, Davies glanced across the office. "Do you still keep that bottle of whisky in your cupboard, Jock?"

It was the last question Henderson expected. Davies was known throughout the Service for his disapproval of daytime drinking. "Yes, sir. For emergencies, of course."

Davies rubbed his shoulder again. "Then let's call it an emergency." Seeing Henderson's expression, his earlier tetchiness returned. "It is four o'clock, damn it. We're not going to lose the war if we have a glass apiece, are we?"

Henderson needed no further persuasion. Walking over to the cupboard, he returned with a half-full bottle of Highland Dew and two glasses. "Say when, sir."

He expected a quick reply but Davies made no comment until the glass was half full. More mystified than ever, the Scot held out his glass. "Cheers, sir."

"Cheers, Jock." Davies took a sip, lit a cigarette, then gave Henderson a grin that made him look like a mischievous elf. "You're wondering what all this is about, aren't you?"

Henderson was never a man to beat about the bush. "If you want it straight, sir, I am."

Davies's laugh announced his temper was completely restored. "Then I'll put you out of your misery, Jock. And when I've finished you'll be on Cloud Nine."

He spoke for less than a minute. During that time Henderson's expression moved through a spectrum of emotions, from delight, to doubt, to hope, and then to scepticism. "Is it possible, sir? Are they sure?"

Davies nodded. "I'd the same doubts myself but now I'm sure they're right because they've checked it from a number of sources."

Henderson swung round and picked up a telephone from his desk. "The boys'll go crazy when they hear it. But first I must let Adams know. He was affected more than most of us."

With a half glass of whisky already inside him, Davies was now in an expansive mood. "Don't do it over the phone, Jock. Bring him into the office first. I want to see his expression when we tell him."

The sudden ring of the blue telephone on Adams' desk made the Intelligence Officer jump even though he was expecting it. He gave Sue a grimace. "I knew it. Here it comes."

Picking up the receiver, Adams heard Henderson's voice. "Hello, Frank? I've got Air Commodore Davies here. He'd like you to come over to my office right away."

Adams' returned the receiver to its hook and sighed at the girl's question. "Yes, they want me over. Davies has something up his sleeve. I could tell as soon as I saw him."

The girl gave a small shudder. "What could it be now?"

Adams sighed again as he made for the door. “He’s never failed to surprise us yet. So why should he this time?”

Adams thoughts on Davies were ambivalent as he made his way to the Administration Block. On the one hand a part of him admired the mercurial Air Commodore whose far-sightedness had seen the need for a special airborne operational unit as far back as 1942 when every front line squadron in the RAF had been screaming for more aircraft. To have won his case and obtained permission to create such a unit had said a great deal about Davies’s personality and perseverance, just as the Squadron’s subsequent successes had been a complete vindication of his beliefs.

But Adams was a complex man, with sensitivity always in conflict with his wartime duties. To him war was an appalling obscenity and while he admired the single-mindedness that allowed Davies to risk his own creation on highly dangerous missions, he also found in it a ruthlessness that he knew he could never employ, even though Adams knew full well that the war against Nazism was one war that had to be won for the sake of mankind everywhere.

Adams’ complexity also showed itself in his feelings towards the young aircrews on the Squadron. Bespectacled, portly of build and in his mid-forties, the Intelligence Officer could hardly have been more unsuitable for aircrew duties, and yet every day of his life he envied the young fliers whose missions over Europe brought hope to its enslaved people. He would have given his right arm to be one of them, and yet he had always believed that no man was less suited temperamentally than himself to fight and kill his fellow men, enemies though they might at present be.

At least, that had been his belief until he had been forced to kill German soldiers to save his young comrades during the Valkyrie mission. That had left a scar on Adams and made him wonder just what sort of man did live beneath his skin. The belief that violence was a permanent disease of man had often made Adams feel ashamed to be a human being. And yet when the time had come he had killed as facilely as any trained soldier.

Such thoughts were plaguing his mind as he hurried towards Henderson’s office. One misgiving was dominant over all. With so many of his friends killed carrying out Davies’s brainchildren, and with the losses incurred during the Squadron’s recent attack on the

Loire bridge still hurting him, Adams was dreading to hear that Davies was planning yet another dangerous operation.

As a result his heart was beating painfully when he tapped on Henderson's office door and then pushed it open. "You wanted to see me, sir?"

Henderson nodded at Davies, who had swivelled round in his chair. "Yes, Frank. As you see, Air Commodore Davies is paying us a visit."

Adams gave the small officer a salute, wishing as always that he didn't feel so awkward and foolish when he carried out the act. There were times when Adams despaired of ever feeling like a military man. "Good afternoon, sir."

Davies returned his salute. "Hello, Frank. Come in and have a drink."

Adams' eyes went wide behind his spectacles. It was difficult enough for him to get used to Davies's familiarity, an accolade earned by his Valkyrian exploits in Norway, but to be invited for a drink by Davies at four o'clock in the afternoon was too much. "I beg your pardon, sir."

"I said have a drink, Frank." Davies turned back to Henderson. "You've got another glass, haven't you? If not, use mine."

Henderson hurried to the cupboard. "No, I've got one." Returning to his desk, he poured out a large whisky and handed it to the bemused Adams. "Here you are, Frank. Knock it back."

By this time Adams' thoughts were on a par with McTyre's, that Davies intended to send them to Russia, Berlin, or Tokyo, and drink was a necessary restorative. He took a cautious sip. "Good luck, sir."

Davies nodded and then grinned at Henderson. "Well! Do you think he's ready for the news?"

Henderson smiled back. "I think we'd better tell him, sir, or his curiosity might give him a hernia."

Davies swivelled round in his chair again. "All right, Adams, get ready for a shock. Moore isn't dead as we all thought. He's alive and well in a German hospital."

Chapter 2

Adams gave a violent start. "He can't be. At least a dozen boys saw him crash into the Loire."

Davies grinned triumphantly. "Just the same, he is. We've had reports from London confirming it."

Adams looked afraid to believe what he was hearing. "But how is it possible, sir? Our crews who saw the crash all said it was unlikely there were any survivors. I've got their reports in my files."

"Just the same, he's alive. Don't forget he crashed into a sand bar in the river. That must have helped to soften the impact."

"But how can London be so certain? Have the Germans confirmed it?"

"They haven't, but it isn't necessary. London gets its information elsewhere." Seeing the effect of the news on Adams, Davies showed unusual consideration. "Take the weight off your legs, Frank. I got a bit of a shock myself when I heard the news."

Adams crossed the room to the typist's empty chair, then turned. "What about his navigator, Hopkinson?"

"We've no news about him," Davies admitted. "Perhaps he was killed or sent to another hospital."

Adams sank down into the chair. "Then Moore's in hospital?"

"Yes. In a surgical unit near Dinant."

"Dinant? But he crashed in the Loire. That's hundreds of miles away."

Davies began to show impatience. "What's the matter with you, Frank? Don't you want to believe he's alive?"

Adams took a deep breath. "There's nothing I want to hear more, sir. It's just it goes against all the reports I've had."

"Your men weren't on the ground, Frank. I'm telling you the Jerries pulled him out of the crash and then flew him up to Dinant."

Here Henderson interrupted. "Why would they do that?"

Davies turned to him. "It seems the military unit at Dinant specialises in bone injuries and damaged limbs in general. From what we hear, Moore sustained more damage to his gammy leg, so it was decided he should be sent there."

Henderson frowned. "That was pretty decent of the Jerries, wasn't it?"

Davies shrugged. "The Luftwaffe aren't the Gestapo, Jock. They've always treated our boys reasonably well once the fighting's over. It's part of the unwritten law. After all, we do the same for them when we take prisoners."

Adams was still needing to know more about Moore's survival. In his years in the RAF, Adams had met many fliers he had admired but, because of his complex nature , he had found difficulty in communicating with them. Most were very young with the black and white concepts of the young, and even fewer wished to discuss the morality and implications of the war in which they found themselves. Yet in the mad world into which the sensitive Adams had been catapulted, there were times when he felt his mind would snap if he could not express his feelings to someone about the deeds of courage, the tragedies, and the obscene waste of young lives that he encountered almost daily.

Some men found such a person in their wives or girl friends, but Adams was not so lucky with his marriage. His wife Valerie, much younger than himself, was a slim woman, with dark, well-groomed hair and a narrow, elegant face. To some she was an attractive, even beautiful woman, and the romantic in Adams had married her without giving second thought to the more uncaring and waspish aspects of her character.

It was true that these had shown up only occasionally during the first eighteen months of their relationship but they had turned from bud into full flower when she discovered the sensitivity and the intellect of the man she had married. Valerie was a woman who admired men who were macho in every sense of the word, and she felt nothing but contempt for a man who put his mind and its concepts on an equal footing to his muscles and his genitals.

Adams' mistake had been to bring her to Sutton Craddock in 1943, where he had found her rooms in The Black Swan. Surrounded by virile young aircrews, she had been in her element, and it had taken the virtual dissolution of the Squadron in the Swartfjord operation to allow Adams to prise her away. She was now living in a flat in London, and with the metropolis full of Americans with money to burn, Adams dared not think how she was spending her time. For that matter, Adams dared not think what life would be like with her after the war.

For these reasons and more, the lonely Adams needed friends, and Sutton Craddock had provided two close ones. One was the homely Yorkshire owner of The Black Swan, Joe Kearns. The other had been Ian Moore, the Squadron Commander. Moore, the son of a wealthy businessman, had been sent to the Squadron after its disastrous losses in the Swartfjord to lift its morale and knit it into an efficient fighting unit again and on both counts he had succeeded spectacularly. In fact, holding the DSO and Bar, the DFC and Bar and the American Legion of Merit Medal, Moore wearing his military uniform had seemed to be the very paradigm of the fighting men with whom Adams found difficulty in relating.

But Adams had soon discovered there was much more to Moore than courage and powers of leadership. To his surprise he had found the good-looking young Squadron Commander was gifted not only with intelligence but also with a high imagination, and Adams had always believed imagination was the biggest handicap a fighting man could labour under. When he had also discovered Moore was quite prepared to discuss the morality of the war in which he was so deeply engaged and even to have philosophical discussions for their own sake, Adams' admiration of the man had been complete and the two men had spent many a night chatting over a drink in the Mess or in their quarters.

All that had ended when Moore's aircraft had been shot down during the Squadron's vital and successful attack on the Langeais bridge during Operation Titan. With Moore such a popular leader, the entire Squadron had gone into mourning and no one was affected more than Adams. To hear the young Squadron Commander was alive was like the release of sunlight into a dark room for Adams, and it took time for him to get used to its brightness.

"Have you any idea how London found out about Moore, sir?" he asked Davies.

Davies gave a terse nod. "I have, but I'm not sure I should tell you."

Henderson, as curious as Adams, came to Adams' support in his usual blunt way. "Frank and I have had to keep our mouths shut plenty of times before, sir. We're not likely to talk now."

Davies frowned. "You don't need to remind me of that, Jock. I'm being careful because there might be much more to this than just Moore's survival. It seems there was a French doctor called Jean Larrouche working in this clinic. The Germans needed him because he was a specialist in bone injuries and some of the Luftwaffe's own casualties are sent there. What they didn't know was that he was working with the Belgian Resistance and sending them any bits and pieces of information he could pick up from the wounded German crews."

"So it was he who found out about Moore?" Henderson asked.

"Right. And he passed on the news to his Resistance contacts."

For a moment Adams became the Intelligence Officer again. "There's one thing I can't understand, sir. We know Moore's importance to us, but to the Resistance he'd just be another pilot. And if the Luftwaffe sent Moore to the clinic, they must have sent other Allied airmen there too. So why should Moore be singled out for this special mention?"

Davies looked surprised. "That's an odd question, Frank. The Squadron's record is the answer. The Resistance know all about us and so Moore got their attention."

It all made sense and yet Adams had the feeling the Air Commodore was holding something back. "I'm sure they know all about the Squadron. But I was talking about an individual pilot. They've never gone to this trouble before over our crews who've been shot down."

"He isn't just anybody, Frank. He is the bloody Squadron Commander." Seeing Adams still looked unconvinced, Davies's tone changed. "It's true the information Moore's giving them might have a little to do with it."

Henderson's ears pricked up. "Information?"

Davies turned to him. "The wounded Jerry aircrews have been making a fuss over him. I don't need to tell you that we're the squadron that's on the top of Jerry's hit list: that Fliegerkorps raid in the spring that nearly wiped us out was proof of that. To Jerry's High Command we're a menace, but to Jerry aircrews we're a glamour squadron. So when our Squadron Commander arrives as a prisoner of war, they make a big fuss of him, much in the way Bader was treated when he was shot down."

"You're saying Moore's been taking advantage of this and pumping the Jerry crews?" Henderson asked.

The watching Adams thought Davies's reply was a little too hearty. "Bang on the button, Jock. Because he can speak German, Moore has played on his popularity and encouraged the German crews to talk about their personal experiences. This has enabled him to find out details such as where their squadrons are based, the numbers of their kites, and so on. All this he passed on to Jean Larrouche once he knew the doctor was working for us."

Henderson grinned. "Trust Ian never to give up. Not even when he's in a prison hospital."

"Right. These bits and pieces about the Jerry squadrons have been useful to us."

In spite of his innocuous appearance and mild manner, Adams could be as tenacious as a dog with a bone if he believed he had not been told the full story. "I'm still puzzled, sir. Did you say this information came from the highest level in London?"

Davies's sudden tetchiness confirmed Adams' growing suspicions. "No, I didn't say that. Why?"

"Because if it did, there must be something more we haven't been told."

Henderson leaned forward. "What are you getting at, Frank?"

"I just can't see Intelligence at the highest level being involved over scraps of information about German squadrons. We obtain them at a much lower level from our contacts all over Europe."

Davies scowled. "I didn't say it had come from the highest level."

"No, sir. But you didn't say it hadn't either. If it has, then surely Moore must be involved in something much more important than squadron details."

With respect for Adams' knowledge of the war within a war, Henderson could not contain his curiosity. "Is he, sir? Or don't you know?"

Davies's short-fused temper began to smoke. "What the hell is this? I came to tell you both about Moore's survival, not to be given the third degree."

Henderson showed contrition. "I'm sorry, sir. It's just that now we know Moore's alive we can't help asking questions about him. If we're out of order, I do apologise."

The handsome apology doused Davies's fuse. His expression betrayed the battle within him. He lit a cigarette, then scowled at Adams. "You're right, Frank, and I suppose it's smart of you to spot it. Moore is up to something else, and because you're both his friends I understand your curiosity. But if I tell you what it is, you'd better keep it to yourselves or I'll have you dropped over Berlin from 30,000 feet."

The big Scot grinned. "Without parachutes of course, sir."

Davies glared at him. "Too bloody true, without parachutes. All right, keep your backsides on your chairs and listen."

As Henderson and Adams leaned forward in anticipation, the distant scream of a drill in one of the hangars could be heard. Davies, an actor to his finger tips, paused until the noise ceased. Then he glanced at Adams. "According to Larrouche, it was the odd behaviour of half a dozen of the highest ranking Jerry officers in the clinic that first awakened his suspicions. This was a week or two before Moore was brought to the clinic. Larrouche noticed their eagerness during the visits of a Luftwaffe Generalmajor and the way they plied him with questions. They also lowered their voices or stopped talking altogether if any of the RAF personnel came near them. It was so unlike their normal behaviour that when Moore was brought in, Larrouche suggested he make a special effort to win their confidence once he was back on his feet."

"This is what Larrouche told the Resistance?" Adams interrupted.

"The bare bones of it, yes. For the rest we've put two and two together. It seemed Moore was up and about in three weeks and he discovered one of the six officers, a chap called Weiner, was more talkative than the rest. So Moore worked on him and, after a few sessions of schnapps, Weiner blurted out one evening that German scientists were the best in the world, something the Allies would soon find out to their cost. Although he was half-pissed, he closed up like a clam when Moore questioned his statement but Moore told Larrouche he felt reasonably certain he'd find out more when his relationship with Weiner developed."

Both men were now showing intense curiosity as Davies continued. "With the Jerry aircrews so excited and secretive, Moore felt it might have something to do with the air war, although of course it could be anything that could win the war for Germany. The only thing he was sure about is that it was something big."

Henderson looked disappointed. "Does that mean we don't know what it is yet?"

Davies shook his head. "No. Not yet."

"So we have to wait and hope that Moore prises it out of Weiner and passes the gen on to Larrouche?"

Davies scowled. "That's what everyone was hoping for until yesterday."

"What happened yesterday, sir?"

Davies' scowl deepened. "The bloody Gestapo picked up Larrouche." As both men started, he went on: "Not for communicating with Moore, but initially for breaking the curfew."

Henderson relaxed. "But surely they won't imprison a valuable surgeon for a little thing like that?"

"It's not that simple, Jock. It seems the Gestapo have got more on him than curfew-breaking. London says that now he's in their hands there's little or no chance of his returning to the hospital."

Henderson shifted uneasily in his chair. "If they break him down — and the bastards always do — won't that mean they'll find out what Moore's been doing?"

"It's a possibility but, as Weiner's hardly likely to admit he's got a loose tongue, the only thing they'd have on Moore would be the bits and pieces about squadron movements. I can't see the Luftwaffe handing him over to the Gestapo for that. Remember the two units hate one another. The only possibility is that Moore might be sent to a higher-security POW camp than he might otherwise have been."

There was a short silence while Henderson and Adams digested all they had heard. Adams was the first to speak. "So the next move is to try to rescue Moore."

Henderson gave a violent start. "Rescue him?"

Adams nodded. "If London believes something big is brewing and that Moore might have found what it is, they'll stop at nothing to get him out or at least to question him."

"Can't Moore use the same channels Larrouche used before he was arrested?" Henderson asked. "He must have some idea who the contacts are."

Davies gave the Scot a scornful look. "Be your age, Jock. Now the Gestapo have got their hands on Larrouche, they'll make that hospital tighter than a bull's arse in fly time. Frank's right. The only way we can get Moore's information — assuming he has any more by this time — is to rescue him after he's been discharged from hospital."

"Do we know how long that will be, sir?" Adams asked.

"Not long. Larrouche did a first class job on his leg so he's expected to be out in two or three weeks. That's when he'll have to be rescued, before he reaches his POW camp."

Henderson's voice was hoarse. "But how?"

Davies shrugged. "How the hell do I know? I suppose London will rely on the Resistance to suggest ways and means. They'll be the ones who'll have to do the job."

"But there'll still be no guarantee Moore has got Weiner to talk."

"There's no guarantee about anything in war, Jock. Everything's full of ifs and buts ... if Moore is right about a secret weapon, if he can find out about it in time, if we can get him out ... it's full of bloody ifs. But we do know Jerry's scientists are among the best in the world, and we also know Moore isn't the sort to cry wolf without reason. As one secret weapon could still win Jerry the war, London has to probe every possibility."

When Henderson didn't reply, Davies went on: "There is one thing in our favour. As far as Weiner is concerned, Moore is a prisoner for the rest of the war, and being who he is, he'll be under tight security. So Weiner won't feel it that dangerous to do a little bragging."

"It's that tight security that worries me," Henderson grunted. "It'll mean a big operation by the Resistance, and if they bungle the job it might put Moore in danger from the Gestapo."

Davies frowned. "What's the matter with you, Jock? Before I came here you thought Moore was dead. Now there's a chance you might have him back before Christmas. So why the doom and gloom about his safety?"

Henderson's problem was his awareness that while the small Air Commodore loved the squadron he had created, he was fully capable of sacrificing the lives of its every member if he believed the war effort demanded it. Past experience had proved that time and again. Conscious that Davies was eyeing him, the Scot pulled himself together. "You're quite right, sir. Thanks for coming and telling us. We appreciate it."

Nodding, Davies glanced at his watch and rose. "I'll be in touch as soon as I hear from London again. In the meantime this is all top secret, so don't even talk to yourselves about it." Reaching the door, he turned back to Henderson. "Do you think I'm safe to go, or will another of your bloody Amazons chop me down?"

Henderson, on his feet like Adams, grinned at him. "They don't hunt in pairs, sir. I think you'll be safe."

Adams' question checked the Air Commodore as he was stepping out into the corridor. "Just one thing, sir. We are allowed to tell the boys that Moore's alive, are we?"

Davies glanced back. "Yes, you can do that. It should bring good business to The Black Swan. But not a word about the rest. Now let me go before Brunhilde has another pass at me."

Henderson waited until the sound of the Air Commodore's brisk footsteps died away before turning to Adams. "What the hell do you make of all that, Frank?"

Adams shook his head. "I'm still trying to ask myself. At the moment I'm just delighted to hear Moore is alive and safe."

Henderson picked up the whisky bottle again. "Amen to that. I'm just hoping nobody cocks things up and puts him into danger again. Those Resistance characters can be pretty ruthless."

Adams shook his head as the Scot offered to fill his glass again. "We'll just have to hope for the best. When are you going to tell the boys?"

Henderson took a swig from his glass, then reached for the phone. "Let's do it now. I'll call 'em all into the Mess."

Adams' voice checked him. "I couldn't borrow your car, could I, sir?"

Henderson looked puzzled. "Yes, if you want. But aren't you going to join me and the boys? There'll be quite a party tonight."

"If you don't mind, I thought I'd drive over and tell Harvey. You remember how hard he took it when he thought Moore had been killed. This news'll put him on Cloud Nine."

Henderson gave a sudden laugh of pleasure. "You're right. I'd forgotten Harvey. It might make the dour old bugger human again. There's Anna too. She'll be just as delighted. Off you go, Frank. I think there's enough petrol in the old bus to get you there and back."

Chapter 3

Adams pulled up the car and switched off the engine. Peering through his side window, he saw a car parked on the opposite side of the road outside a tiny bungalow. Recognising it as Harvey's old bull-nosed Morris, he sank back into his seat.

He wondered why he was not hurrying into the bungalow with his good news. The drive had taken him nearly three hours and with the evening beginning to fade and Harvey's car outside the bungalow it was more than likely that the Yorkshireman's duties for the day were over and he was home.

Although Adams had long given up hope of understanding himself, he wondered if Anna could be the reason for his procrastination. He had long known that Moore had been in love with the courageous German girl and although she had recognised the sterling qualities of Harvey and given him her love, Adams had the intellect to know that love is no more finite than hate, and a woman was fully capable of loving two men at the same time.

Adams believed this was true of Anna Reinhardt and her feelings for Moore. She had chosen Harvey for many reasons, not least because their countries had turned them both into rebels. Anna had become one because of her hatred for Nazism, which had driven her to become an agent against her own people. Harvey was one because his poverty-stricken childhood had embittered him and made him detest the social system that governed his country. In one sense they were two misfits brought together by their mutual misfortunes. Yet Adams was wise enough to know great love affairs had been founded on less.

Not that they lacked other bonds. Since entering the RAF, Adams had come into contact with men and women whose heroism he would never have believed possible in his peacetime days and, along with Ian Moore, Anna Reinhardt and Frank Harvey were two such people. The willingness of Anna to take part in covert operations in Occupied Europe had often made Adams' mind swim at the risks involved. Her fate, as a German, if the Gestapo ever caught her was something Adams found painful even to contemplate. His relief had been profound when the Special Operations Executive had finally decided the dangers were becoming too great and had taken her off their list of agents.

Adams had felt much the same way when Harvey had finally been rested from operations and sent to lend his experience to an Operational Training Unit. A tall, raw-boned Yorkshireman with a face as craggy as his native fells, he had been almost a legend in the Squadron during his days as a Flight Commander. While rumour had it that his scowl could give shingles to young recruits, it was also known and appreciated that no one took greater care of his crews or felt the loss more when combat snatched men from him. In effect, Harvey was a hard man with a soft centre.

He was one of the few survivors from the Swartfjord operation. Although shot down, he had escaped capture and been returned to England by the Norwegian partisans. Given the temporary role of Squadron Commander when the unit was reformed, he had expected the promotion to be confirmed. Instead Ian Moore had been sent in from Pathfinders to take his place and Harvey had been demoted to Flight Commander.

When he had discovered that Moore came from a wealthy family and had attended all the right schools, Harvey's latent bitterness had exploded and for weeks the two men had been at loggerheads. It was only when Anna arrived to take part in the Rhine Maiden operation and began mingling socially with them that the situation had changed. Perceptive and sympathetic, she had used her influence on the two men to show them how much they had in common. The final bonding had come during the Squadron's attack on the Rhine Maiden factory deep in Germany, when Moore had witnessed Harvey's courage and his devotion to his men. Since then, despite being in love with the same girl, the two men had developed a friendship based on personal as well as professional respect.

But war fatigue had been having its effect on them both. Before the last operation, the attack on the Loire bridge, Moore had been finding it difficult to sleep and Harvey was worrying more and more about the risks Anna was taking. Knowing this was affecting his combat reflexes and so putting him in danger, Anna had asked Moore to leave him out of the mission. Although unable to do this, Moore had promised the girl he would see Harvey was stood down afterwards.

It was then that fate had intervened, when the success of the mission had depended on Harvey flying a gauntlet of fire to explode the charges laid beneath the bridge. Knowing it was almost certain suicide, Moore had ordered the reluctant Harvey away and made the attack himself. When he had been shot down and believed killed, Harvey had to be given sedatives on his return to Sutton Craddock. He had known Moore's sacrifice had been made for himself and Anna.

Adams was aware of all this because of a letter Moore had given to him to pass on to Anna in case he did not return. The knowledge had affected him almost as deeply as the stricken Harvey, and his only consolation was the knowledge that Moore's sacrifice had not been in vain. Davies had honoured Moore's last wish by posting Harvey to an OTU where he had at least a chance of surviving the war. With Anna also taken off duty, the two of them were at last living the life together they so richly deserved.

Yet the imaginative and sensitive Adams had always felt the memory of Moore's sacrifice, which had made their happiness possible, would also be the one factor that would shadow it. For this reason he could not understand why he was delaying telling them that Moore was alive.

The roar of engines overhead brought him out of his reverie. A moment later a Mosquito appeared in his windshield and began its descent to the OTU airfield that Adams knew was only a few miles away. The brightness of its recognition lights made Adams glance down at his watch and he saw with surprise that twenty minutes had passed since his arrival. Frowning at the time he had wasted, Adams climbed out of the car, stretched his stiff legs, and made for the bungalow.

He saw it was occupied when he reached the front door. Although like other bungalows along the road the blackout curtains were in place, a chink of light was visible in the small bay window. Feeling his heart thumping hard, Adams rang the door bell.

Almost immediately there was a fusillade of barks and the sound of a dog rushing to the door. Smiling, Adams pushed open the letterbox. "It's all right, Sam. It's me."

The barking changed in tone as the delighted dog began leaping up against the door. A moment more and Adams heard a woman's voice. "What is it, Sam? What's the matter?"

The door opened only a few inches to keep the dog inside. Then there was a cry of pleasure and the door was flung wide open. "Frank! It's you! Oh, how good to see you again."

For the next half minute Adams had to share his attention between the delighted girl and the huge black mongrel who seemed determined to knock him over and to lick him to death. Laughing, breathless, Adams fought his way into a small living room. "He certainly remembers me, doesn't he?"

"Of course he does. He remembers how kind you were to him when Frank was in hospital. But that's enough, Sam. Come over here and sit down."

With the dog reluctantly obeying the girl, Adams was able to pay her more attention. In her mid-twenties, she was a tall, gracefully-built girl with an oval face and grey eyes. With her abundant dark hair swept up in a French roll, and a pearl brooch the only jewellery to set off her green velvet dress, Adams was reminded again what a beautiful and elegant woman she was.

"You're looking wonderful, Anna. You must be very happy."

Although at rest her features were calm and composed, her laugh brought a dimple to her cheek. "I am, Frank. Happier than I can ever remember."

As always her voice with its attractive accent sent a small shiver through Adams. "That's good to hear." He looked round. "But where's Frank? That is his car outside, isn't it?"

"Yes, but we can't always get enough petrol for it. On most days a transport picks him up and brings him back. He is on late today but he should be home soon. He will be so pleased to see you."

"How is he?"

"Oh, he is much better. His stomach wound doesn't bother him anymore and he has put on weight again. But you will see that when he comes home. Meanwhile, take off your coat and sit down. I want to hear everything that has been happening to you. But first, what would you like to drink? I think we have wine. Or would you prefer coffee?"

Adams shrugged off his greatcoat and sat on the sofa. "I'll have coffee if I may. But not right away. I've something very important to tell you."

Her expression changed. Although she looked composed as she sank down beside him, Adams detected a trace of anxiety in her grey eyes, a reminder if he needed one that she and Harvey were still vulnerable to the whims of war. "What is it, Frank? What's happened?"

"It's all right," Adams said quickly. "It's good news. In fact it's splendid news. We heard today that Ian Moore is alive and well."

Her face went very pale. She lifted a hand to her throat as if it had suddenly closed. When her question came it was a mere whisper. "What did you say?"

"Ian is alive and well in a German hospital. Davies told us today."

She shook her head as if to clear it. "But how is that possible? Frank and most of his flight saw him crash."

"Yes, but the sand bar must have softened the impact. And the water prevented a fire. He's alive, Anna. And well enough to be sent to a prisoner of war camp in a few weeks." As her eyes closed, Adams cleared his throat. "You can see why I had to come straight over to tell you."

She took a deep, unsteady breath. Then, with a sob, she threw her arms around him. "Bless you, Frank. You can't imagine what this will mean to us both. It's the only thing that ..."

Although her voice broke and she kissed his cheek instead, she did not need to finish her sentence to Adams. He put an arm around her. "I think I understand. Well, it's over now. Neither of you need to worry about it any longer."

She pressed against him for a moment, then drew back. She gave a little laugh as she wiped a tear from her cheek. "You always were very perceptive, Frank. That's one reason we miss you so much."

The thud of a truck door saved Adams from an answer. As Sam gave a welcoming bark and leapt to his feet, Anna nodded at Adams' question. "That'll be Frank. I'll let you tell him the wonderful news."

She hurried out into the tiny hall with Sam on her heels. The dog's excited barking drowned Harvey's entry, but as a gruff voice shouted for silence, Adams heard Anna's voice. "I've got a lovely surprise for you, Liebling. Frank Adams is here."

Harvey followed her into the room a second later. A tall, powerfully-built man with a face that was all planes and angles, he showed as much pleasure on seeing Adams as his temperament allowed. In the harsh world Harvey had known, a man never allowed his emotions their full rein in case predators took advantage of them. His gruff voice showed the same restraint. "Hello, Frank. How's things?"

Adams, who had risen from the sofa as he entered, wondered why he, at least seventeen years older than the tough Yorkshireman, always felt a raw juvenile beside him. In spite of the evening chill, Harvey was wearing no coat and his faded tunic with its shiny elbows gave evidence of his hundreds of hours in the air. To Adams he was the archetypal fighting man and the Intelligence Officer's inferiority complex did the rest. He tried to hide a wince at the powerful grip of the man's calloused hand. "I'm fine, Frank. How are you? You're looking well."

Harvey cast a glance at the smiling Anna. "I ought to. I'm getting better grub than I did in that Mess of yours. How are things going back there? Has anyone shot Davies down yet?"

Adams hid a smile. The conflict between the irascible Davies and the dour Yorkshireman had been a feature of Harvey's days with the Squadron. Hardly a major briefing had taken place without the Yorkshireman finding some fault in Davies's planning which had brought scowls and dire threats from the small Air Commodore.

Even after Harvey had proved his worth to Davies, the antipathy between the two men had never been resolved, although beneath it Adams knew there was considerable respect. "No, he's still around. He came to the squadron this afternoon. That's why I'm here."

Harvey showed curiosity but before he could speak, Anna broke in. "Listen to what he has to say, Liebling. He has wonderful news for us."

Harvey frowned at Adams. "Go on then. What is it?"

Adams took a deep breath. "It's Ian, Frank. He's alive and well. That's what Davies came to tell us."

In the sudden silence that fell Adams could hear a clock ticking somewhere in the room. Then Harvey's gruff voice drowned it. "What did you say?"

"Ian's alive, Frank. London have confirmed it."

Harvey's laugh was full of scorn. "That's damn well impossible. I saw a tank gunner put a full burst into his kite just as he flew from under the bridge. So did half the squadron. Davies is talking his usual bullshit."

Adams shook his head. "No, it's confirmed, Frank. He's in a clinic in Belgium. The Jerries flew him up there to get attention for his leg. He can't have been badly hurt because he's expected to be released quite soon."

Smiling at Harvey's reaction, Anna caught his arm and hugged him. "Isn't it wonderful news, Liebling?"

For a long moment the tall Yorkshireman did not move. Then, hiding his expression from Adams, he glanced down at Anna. "Haven't we got anything to give Frank? A drop of whisky or something?"

"We've got a bottle of wine."

"Then how about opening it? It's as good a time as any, isn't it?"

Smiling at Adams, Anna hurried out of the room. Giving a grunt, Harvey dropped in an armchair. "So you all believe Ian made it? What about Hoppy?"

"We've no news of him," Adams admitted. "But that might be because he was sent to a different hospital."

Harvey pulled a packet of cigarettes from his tunic and held it out to Adams. Then, remembering Adams was a pipe smoker, he lit a cigarette for himself and blew smoke at the ceiling. "How did Davies get to know all this?"

From now on Adams knew he would have to be careful. "I think word got to the Resistance and they passed it on to London."

"London? Top level stuff? That's a bit unusual, isn't it?"

"Not really," Adams lied. "The Squadron's well known to the Resistance and it's obvious we'd want to hear our Squadron Commander was alive."

Harvey nodded and drew on his cigarette again. "I expect they'll send him to an Interrogation Centre before they stick him in a POW camp?"

"I expect they might, particularly when they know who he is. But I can't see Ian giving anything away, can you?"

Harvey shook his head. In the short silence that followed Adams was thinking that the man's presence seemed to fill the small room. Harvey exhaled smoke again. "How did the lads take the news?"

"I don't know. I left before Pop Henderson told them. But I can guess, can't you?"

Harvey had the Yorkshireman's way of seeming to denigrate the things he admired most. "Aye, I can. If some of us had led 'em into the shit Moore led 'em into, they'd want our guts for garters. But Moore had the knack of getting away with it."

At that moment Anna entered the room carrying a tray with a bottle and three glasses. Harvey rose, took the tray from her, and lowered it on to a small table. "You'll have a glass, Frank?"

Adams hesitated, then nodded. "Just one. I mustn't stay too long."

Harvey grinned as he filled three glasses. "Why? You in a hurry to get back to that party the lads'll be throwing?"

Adams laughed back. "Not really. I've still got a bit of work to finish tonight. But I'll bet Joe Kearns and Maisie are being kept busy."

"You can say that again. Characters like Millburn and Gabby never needed an excuse for a party. This time they've got a good one. They'll blow the roof off that old pub."

Adams was noticing the change in the Yorkshireman's diction since Anna had entered the room. Since entering the RAF

Adams had been fascinated by the two languages servicemen used, one they shared between themselves that was coarse and full of obscenities, and another that gave deference to their families. In the sole company of his kind, Harvey would have said 'buggers like Millburn and Gabby' without thinking twice. But once Adams' news had been assimilated, the Yorkshireman was recalling his second language. Coming from a man who had always called a spade and spade, to Adams his behaviour seemed to underline the respect and devotion he had for the German girl.

Harvey handed glasses round. As he picked up his own and hesitated, Anna slipped an arm into his. "I think we should drink to Ian, don't you, Liebling? To express our happiness that he is alive and well."

Adams did not miss Harvey's look of relief that the girl had saved him from expressing the sentiment. As he raised his glass with the others, Adams knew he had never envied Harvey more.

He stayed another thirty minutes before announcing he would have to leave. Patting Sam, he followed the couple to the front door where Anna kissed him again. "Thank you again for coming, Frank. It was so thoughtful of you and the news has made us very happy."

Although Harvey's crushing handshake said it all, his words were almost non-committal. "Good to see you again, Frank. Give all the lads my regards. Tell 'em I might drop in to see them one of these days."

"You should," Adams told him. "They'd throw another party for you."

Harvey grinned. "Don't give me that, Frank. Most of 'em would he waiting with Tommy guns."

With Anna's laughter still sounding in his ears Adams drove away. With his masked headlights barely able to penetrate the darkness, it was near midnight when he reached Sutton Craddock. By this time a huge moon had cleared the horizon and was beginning to silver the airfield and the slate roof of the pub that stood near its main gates. On an impulse Adams stopped the car opposite and switched off the engine.

For a moment a night breeze, stirring the leaves of the crab apple trees that stood in the pub's front garden, hid other sounds from him. Then, as the breeze died, he heard muffled music and yells of merriment and knew the party Harvey had anticipated was still in full swing. At another time Adams might have joined it: one side of his complex nature liked to share the happiness and successes of the young airmen, just as it often needed to share their pain. But after his encounter with Harvey and Anna, he felt the need to be alone. Starting the engine, he drove into the airfield, acknowledged the challenge and then the salute of the sentry, and parked the car in the transport pool.

He glanced at his watch as he walked out of the wired compound and decided it was too late to begin work now. The squadron was being rested for a couple of days: the job could wait until tomorrow.

As he began walking towards his billet he heard more muffled music and cheers escaping from the Sergeants' Mess. The Black Swan was not the only establishment holding a celebration that night. As he walked past the Mess, with the silvered airfield stretched out before him, Adams knew his mind was too active for sleep. Too many thoughts had been set into motion by the news Davies had brought.

Passing his billet he turned down the perimeter path of the airfield. Soon the sounds of merriment died away, leaving only the sound of his footsteps and the occasional rustle of small animals in the hedges. Beside him a Mosquito looked like a great silver bird asleep on its nest. Used to endless noise and activity, to the cry of orders and the roar of engines, Adams could have imagined a sudden armistice had been called between the warring powers, and the killing was over at last.

His fanciful thoughts were disturbed by the sound of low voices. As he approached the gunpost, with its sinister silhouette of Hispano cannon, the voices went silent and he saw two gunners watching him curiously over the post's parapet. At such moments Adams found the demands and restrictions of his rank an embarrassment. Feeling he ought to make some comment, he wished them a cheery goodnight. He walked on, feeling certain that when he was out of earshot they would share a joke at his familiarity.

His earlier mood returned when he reached the far end of the airfield. With the moon looking like a golden penny over Bishops Wood, and the lucid sky clear all the way to the stars, Adams knew it was one of those nights when the romantic in him could never relate to war. If men had to be idiotic enough to fight and kill one another, so went Adams' whimsical reasoning, at least they could be expected to call a truce when the world itself was having one of its rare moments of tranquillity.

Not for the first time, he wondered what had been said between Harvey and Anna after he had left. Anna had virtually admitted that Moore's suspected death had been the one shadow between her and Harvey, and the Yorkshireman's profound relief at the news had not escaped Adams. With both believing Moore was safe, they could now put to rest the ghost that had haunted them for so long.

At least they could if things stayed that way, Adams thought. If Moore should be killed during a rescue attempt, the shadow would fall over them once again. And even if he were rescued — Adams knew he should not have this thought but it had kept recurring during his journey home — might not his presence bring problems of its own to the couple?

He was certain now this that had been the reason for his delay in telling Anna the good news, although his loyalty to the couple still pooh-poohed the idea. Anna was far too devoted to Harvey, to give him cause for jealousy and Moore had already proved his fidelity to them both. But was Harvey with his poverty-stricken background, exempt from risk? In Adams' eyes, there lay the danger.

A distant drone interrupted his thoughts. As he listened, the drone grew louder. Staring up, Adams saw a winged shadow sweep briefly across the moon. As more heavy bombers destined for a European target followed and the air began to tremble with the pounding of engines, Adams knew his moment of peace had gone. Yet although he sighed, Adams knew that he must not complain: that on the whole it had been a good day. He held to that thought firmly as he walked back across the airfield to his billet.

Chapter 4

The sentry at the tall iron gates of High Elms took a careful look at Davies's credentials before he snapped to attention and waved the staff car through. As the young WAAF driver accelerated up the drive, Henderson, seated with Davies and Adams at the back of the car, peered curiously at the large house they were approaching. "You say you've no idea why Brigadier Simms wants to see us, sir?"

Davies's answer was non-committal. "Not unless it has something to do with Moore."

Henderson shifted uneasily. "You don't think anything's happened to him, do you? It's two weeks since you heard he was alive. Do you think they've already made a rescue attempt?"

The way Davies changed the subject was almost as good as a straightforward order to keep quiet. He motioned at an armed provost sergeant parading across a lawn with a leashed Alsatian dog. "They keep the place well guarded, don't they? I wouldn't fancy my chances breaking in here on a dark night."

As Davies's eyes followed the guard, Henderson gave Adams a look of irritation. Half a minute later the WAAF drove them on to a large courtyard where three other cars were already parked. As Davies jumped out, a young army lieutenant hurried forward and gave him a smart salute. "Air Commodore Davies, sir?"

When Davies nodded, the lieutenant motioned at the huge house. "If you will come this way, sir, Brigadier Simms is waiting for you."

Nodding, Davies turned to his driver, a pretty, pert girl. "We might be some time, Hilary, so you can get out and stretch your legs." He motioned at a provost corporal who was watching her with interest from the far side of the courtyard. "If you ask nicely, that lad might show you round the grounds. Only watch him closely. You can't trust soldiers the way you can trust airmen."

The girl laughed. "I'm not so sure about that, sir. But I'll keep my eyes open."

Grinning, Davies followed the lieutenant up a flight of stone steps. Before following him, Henderson whispered into Adams' ear. "There's something on and he knows all about it. I think it's big, too. That's why he's so bloody cheerful."

The lieutenant led the three men down a corridor, tapped on a door, and opened it. "Air Commodore Davies and his two officers, sir."

The room the three men entered was a huge library with oak-panelled walls. French windows at the far end gave a view of a terrace, a stretch of lawns, and a background of elm trees. But Adams' eyes were on an elderly, slightly-built Army officer with a small military moustache, who rose from a long table that ran down the centre of the room. He acknowledged Davies's salute, then approached him with outstretched hand. Courtesy was Brigadier Simms's hallmark. "Good morning, Davies. Good morning, gentlemen. Welcome back to High Elms. Thank you all for coming so promptly."

Both Henderson and Adams had met Simms before. A Special Operations Executive officer, he had first appeared in their orbit during the Swartfjord mission and since then had been their link man when any new inter-service mission was in the offing. If either man had hoped earlier that they were only attending a routine conference, the Brigadier's presence put an instant end to the thought.

With the losses that every previous SOE mission had caused the Squadron, Adams had often felt he ought to dislike Simms for initiating them. Yet the elderly Brigadier's concern over casualties was so genuine that at times Adams had felt sympathy for him instead of antipathy, an emotion he had never felt for Davies.

Simms' courtesy displayed itself again as he picked up a telephone. "Tea or coffee, gentlemen?"

Davies's eagerness to start proceedings became evident before either Adams or Henderson could reply. "Not just now, sir. I'm sure you'd rather get on with the business in hand."

"Very well, gentlemen. If you'll be seated I'll explain why I asked you over here today. Please smoke if you want to."

Chairs shuffled momentarily on the polished floor as the three men obeyed. Adams tried to hide a nervous cough as the Brigadier walked to the end of the table where a large, half-folded map was lying between four paperweights. He turned to face Davies. "I understand that you've already told your senior officers that Wing-Commander Moore survived his crash, Davies?"

"Yes, sir." The glance Davies gave to Henderson and Adams looked innocuous enough, but both men knew it was a warning. "But so far that's all they do know."

"Quite. Well, gentlemen, you will be glad to hear that London would like your Squadron Commander rescued and brought back to us."

As both Henderson and Adams did their best to look surprised, Simms gave them the explanation they had already heard. "Of course, we don't know that Moore has gained any more information from Weiner," he finished. "We are not even certain that his information is important enough to cause us concern. But before Larrouche was captured, he did tell his contacts that the ZWB were involved in some way and that could be more than significant."

"What's the ZWB?" Henderson asked.

"It's the code-name of Germany's clearing house for reports on secret weapons. If one adds to that Weiner's boast about German scientists being the best in the world, it's easy to see why we are concerned."

As the Brigadier paused, Henderson took the opportunity to ask the question that had been disturbing him and Adams for weeks. "After hearing all this I can understand that you want Moore rescued, sir. But how is this to be done?"

The glance Simms gave Davies convinced Henderson the Air Commodore knew all about SOE's latest plan. "That's why I invited you to High Elms today, Henderson. I want to ask for the co-operation of your squadron."

Henderson gave a start. "My squadron! How can we help to rescue a prisoner of war?"

Nodding, Simms opened up the map and secured its four corners with the paperweights. "If you will join me here, gentlemen, I will show you."

With the curious Adams and Henderson on either side of him, Simms picked up a ruler from the table. "As you will know, before they are put into prisoner of war camps, shot-down aircrews are sent to special German compounds, where teams of experts interrogate them. It is only afterwards that they are sent to POW camps. In Moore's case he has been sent to a centre here, east of Dinant."

"So he is already out of hospital?" Adams interrupted.

"Yes, along with a number of other RAF airmen. He came out yesterday and was driven with the others straight to the compound."

"Then how is anyone going to rescue him?" Henderson asked. "Compounds like that must be well guarded."

"They are, Henderson. The rescue attempt has to be made while Moore's in transit to his POW camp. That's when your squadron enters our plan."

Instantly Henderson looked alarmed. "Are they taking him by train?"

"No. By road convoy."

The Scot relaxed, but only slightly. "I thought for a moment you wanted us to do another train job. Like the one we did for the Americans that turned out such a disaster."

"No, not a train this time, Henderson. This time we want you to attack the road convoy. We need you because ..."

Henderson waited to hear no more. Showing unusual agitation for a man of phlegmatic temperament, he swung round on Davies before Simms could finish his sentence. "Sir, you can't agree to this. You can't have forgotten what happened when we tried to help those Yank prisoners to escape. We killed a dozen or more of them and had every newspaper in America at our throats. You can't risk the same thing happening again."

Davies tried to calm him. "Hang on, Jock. These aren't Americans. They're our own lads and there'll be no newshawk keeping a beady eye on us."

"What consolation will that be if the same thing happens? What if we kill Ian? Our lads' morale would sink to zero. This just won't do, sir. Some other way has to be found."

So far, conscious of the memories the earlier train attack had awakened, Davies had been unusually patient. Now his mood changed. "For Christ's sake, calm down, Jock. You haven't heard the Brigadier out yet. Keep quiet and let him finish."

Sharing Henderson's dismay, Adams feared for a moment that the Scot's resentment would get him into serious trouble. A natural peacemaker, he tried to calm him down. "I'm sure the SOE are as eager as we are to keep Moore safe, sir."

Although the comment earned him a look from Henderson, it allowed Simms to add his own balm to the painful memory. "Believe me, we are, Henderson. For personal as well as professional reasons."

When the Scot did not reply, Simms turned back to the map. "At the moment this is our plan, although we are prepared to modify it if you gentlemen have any better ideas. Our agents in Belgium tell us that convoys from the compound usually take a route through the Ardennes to prison camps in East Germany or Poland. Because of the activity of our fighter-bombers they usually travel at night until they reach the Ardennes, which, as you know, is well wooded."

"You're saying they risk driving by day through the Ardennes?" Adams asked.

"Yes. I suppose they want to keep the roads open at night for more important convoys, like ammunition supplies and troop movements. They rely on the wooded and hilly terrain for protection, as well as the Red Cross markings they use on the trucks carrying their prisoners."

Henderson was breathing heavily. "You're not saying this is where you want us to hit them? In a terrain totally unsuited for low level attack?"

Simms showed no annoyance. "Perhaps everything will be clearer when I've explained our plan. We have to attack the convoy in the Ardennes because it is the only area where our Resistance fighters can assemble and escape before they come under attack themselves. We were hoping they could carry out the operation without the need of air support, but of late the Germans have been providing a flak wagon with each convoy as a precaution against partisan interference, which has become markedly stronger since VE Day. This is why we need you. The partisans believe they can handle the German guards but they cannot bring up the weight of weaponry necessary to subdue a heavily-armoured flak wagon."

Davies glanced at the frowning Henderson. "That's not so bad, is it, Jock? You're not attacking train coaches this time. Your target is the flak wagon and once you've knocked it out you can go home."

Henderson had not given up yet. "We attacked in the Ardennes for the Americans. And look what a cock-up it was."

Davies controlled his impatience only with an effort. "Well, it's not going to be a cock-up this time. When we've ironed out the problems, it's going to go like clockwork."

"But how are you going to iron them out, sir? How are we going to know when the convoy reaches the Ardennes? And even if we find out, how do we catch it in open ground?"

The Brigadier spoke for Davies. "Because of Allied air activity and the high casualty rate of drivers, the Germans have started using foreign workers for non-essential convoys. One of these has been ferrying prisoners for some weeks now and he is providing our agents and the partisans with time-tables and routes. As soon as the prisoners are put into the trucks we shall be told. He'll also keep the partisans advised of the convoy's progress. So we shall know when the convoy reaches the Ardennes. Provided your aircraft are air-tested and ready, the Air Commodore assures me this will give plenty of time for the squadron to take off and reach a suitable rendezvous point."

The Scot was clearly unconvinced. "How do you arrange a rendezvous with so many imponderables? Unlike a train, the convoy might turn off the road somewhere and leave the partisans high and dry."

Simms nodded imperturbably. "In normal terrain that might happen, but there are few road bridges in the Ardennes that will take the weight of a heavy flak wagon. Our agents assure us the convoy will have to take the route they have given us."

"All right, but what about time? Road convoys speed up or slow down for all kinds of reasons. With the help of the driver's information we might arrive at a given co-ordinate at a given time but how can you be sure the convoy won't put a spanner in the works by going too fast or too slow?"

The Brigadier motioned him closer and pointed at a mark on the map. "There is a road bridge here spanning a river bed. The partisans are going to mine it and will blow it up when the convoy is approaching."

Although momentarily checked, Henderson was not finished yet. "Trucks are mobile. They'll simply reverse and find a new route."

"Not when another bridge is blown up behind them, Henderson. They'll be trapped — and they'll be trapped long enough to make good any timing errors that might occur in our planning."

"But surely the trucks will be able to find a way off the road."

"No. The two river beds are too steep and the surrounding woods are quite dense. Besides, you forget the flak wagon. It is far too heavy and cumbersome to drive off the road. And as the commander will guess the convoy is in danger of a partisan attack, the last thing he'll do is leave it unprotected."

As Henderson hesitated, Davies broke in. "It might work, Jock. I know there's a lot that could go wrong but isn't it worth a try? At the best we get Ian out and hear what Jerry's up to. At the worst it's just an abortive operation, because this time the prisoners shouldn't be in any danger if we concentrate on the flak wagon."

"All right, but how are the partisans going to blow up the bridges? Won't they be guarded?"

"Not as far as we know. But if guards are stationed there, the partisans should be able to take care of them. They will be there in considerable numbers."

Henderson was near to defeat. "But if Moore's already in the Interrogation Centre, couldn't he be leaving it at any time?"

"No. Our agents tell us prisoners are kept a minimum of five days and, because of Moore's status, he might be kept a day or two longer. But you are right in thinking we have no time to waste."

Still showing concern, Henderson turned to Davies. "How many aircraft are you thinking of sending, sir?"

"I think eight should be enough. But I want them manned by your best pilots."

"What about air cover?"

Davies waved an impatient hand. "We'll go into all the tactical details later. What I want settled today is the choice of leader. It's a pity Moore's replacement has gone."

Adams knew Davies was talking about John Mitchell, the Pathfinder pilot Davies had sent to the Squadron to take command after Moore's loss. Although he had seemed a fitting man to fill the post, he had been shot down over the Channel during one of the squadron's routine missions ten days before and there had been no further news of him.

Henderson was shaking his head. "I wouldn't have used him for this job. It needs specialist training. Millburn would be my man. In fact he'd have been my squadron commander if you hadn't sent me Mitchell first."

From Davies's expression Adams had the feeling he was relishing the bombshell he was about to drop. "No, I've decided on the man I want. I want Harvey."

Henderson gave a violent start. "What did you say?"

Davies had never looked more like a malicious elf than at that moment. "You going deaf or something, Jock? I said I want Harvey."

"But Harvey's on rest. You put him there yourself. He's finished his third tour of operations."

"So what? Now I want him back. He's the leader I need."

With the antipathy that had always existed between the Air Commodore and the Yorkshireman, Adams was equally amazed. He was also dismayed. "He's only just got over his wounds, sir. And you yourself admitted he deserved a long rest from operations."

Davies turned to him. "I know all that, Frank. But Harvey goes back to the Swartfjord days. He's the most experienced man we have and Jock's right in saying we can't afford to have another cock-up. I want Harvey to lead this operation. What's more, when he hears we're doing it to get Moore back, wild horses won't keep him out of it."

Adams couldn't hold back his comment. "It's going to hurt Anna Reinhardt badly, sir. I saw her only recently and she was over the moon to have Harvey safe from operations."

Davies, who had initially brought the German girl to the squadron and admired her, frowned. "I'm aware of that, Frank. But she's a professional and she'll understand our need." Giving Adams no chance to reply, he turned back to the Brigadier. "Is there anything more you want to discuss, sir, or can these two get back to the station? We'll have to go into top gear if we're to be ready in time."

Simms shook his head. "That's all for the moment, Davies. I'll be in touch as soon as we get more news." Courteous to the last, he turned to the two accompanying officers. "I'm sorry to give you a mission with such unfortunate memories, gentlemen. But I'm sure this one will be successful and will seem worthwhile when you have Moore back with the squadron. Thank you again for coming."

Little was passed between the three men during the ride back to Sutton Craddock. But as Henderson and Adams climbed out of the car at the station gates, the Scot made his last plea through the open car window. "Let Millburn lead the operation, sir. No one knows the low level game better than he does and his men will follow him anywhere."

Davies shook his head impatiently. "I said Harvey and I want Harvey, Jock."

Henderson decided all was fair in love and war. "But he might be a bit rusty by this time. And aren't you forgetting how he always found faults in your tactics during briefings?"

Davies grinned maliciously. "That's one reason I want him. If we forget anything, you can bet your flying boots that bloody-minded Yorkshireman will spot it. Face it, Jock. He's the best chance we have of avoiding a disaster like the last time."

By this time Henderson knew it was hopeless. "Then who's going to tell him?"

"I'll tell him. I'll phone his C.O. today and have him sent to me. Now you two go to the Mess and have a couple of stiff whiskies each. You both look as if you need 'em."

With that Davies tapped Hilary's shoulder and the car accelerated away. The Scot watched it for a moment, then with a groan turned to Adams. "Let's do what the little bastard says. It's the only sense he's spoken all day."

Chapter 5

The white-faced Anna looked as if she had been struck across the face. "How could he do such a thing? He promised you a rest."

Harvey shrugged. "He's an Air Commodore, love. They can do anything they like."

"But you have completed three tours. You have earned the right three times over to come off operations. Didn't you remind him of that?"

"I pointed out he'd been the one who sent me here, if that's what you mean."

"That isn't what I mean. Did you tell him that you had a right to be rested? That it was Ian's wish and he'd agreed to it?"

Lying had never come easily to Harvey. "He knows all that, love. He's known me since the Norwegian days."

"You didn't tell him, did you?" she accused. "And I know why. You wanted to go."

He tried to take her in his arms, but she drew sharply away. "I'm right, aren't I? You were pleased he asked you."

Harvey, who had just arrived back from Group Headquarters, dropped heavily on to the sofa. "What else could I do? He said they needed me for the mission."

"That's ridiculous. What difference will one more pilot make?"

"It's not that simple. He wants someone to lead it and he knows I've had plenty of experience of low level work."

"No more than Millburn and others." With the girl frantic for his safety, her voice attacked him. "Why don't you admit how delighted you are?"

It was never wise to challenge Harvey. His eyes lifted to her white, shocked face. "All right, I am pleased. I'm pleased to take part in an effort to rescue Ian. Does that satisfy you or do you want more?"

With their happiness suddenly in jeopardy, Anna hardly knew what she was saying. "Yes, I do want more. I want to know if this means you're going back on active service again. I want to know if I have to go through all that hell again, waiting to know if you're dead or alive. I want to know what kind of an arrangement you've made with Davies."

"What do you mean — arrangement?"

"Does this all mean you're going back to the Squadron after this raid? I need to know, Frank. I don't want to live in a fool's paradise if that's what's going to happen."

Harvey's outburst came from his own mixed feelings. "How can I say a thing like that? I can't read Davies's mind. If he orders me back, I'll have to go back. That's life in the bloody Services."

"But you have a right to be rested. Will you fight for it? That's what you must tell me."

"Davies knows I've done three tours. I don't have to remind him of that."

"It hasn't stopped him sending you on this mission. So why should it stop him in the future if you don't remind him of his promise?"

With an exclamation Harvey jumped to his feet. "For God's sake, leave it now. I've had a hard day. Let's talk about it later."

Trembling, she put a hand on the back of an armchair to support herself. "That means you are going back, doesn't it? All that hell is going to start over again."

With a curse, Harvey made for the front door. She took a frightened step forward. "Where are you going?"

He answered without looking back. "I've some unfinished jobs to do at the airfield. I might be late. Don't stay up for me."

The slam of the front door seemed to echo throughout the small bungalow. For a long moment the girl did not move. Then she sank down into the armchair and began to sob uncontrollably.

* * *

Back at Sutton Craddock, Henderson was making sure his station was ready in case Davies ordered a sudden briefing and scramble. On his return he had cancelled all passes and given his ground crews orders to ensure all operational Mosquitoes were tuned and airworthy. Wireless mechanics checked radios, armourers tested guns and bomb release gears, fitter engineers checked and ran Merlin engines. Pilots and navigators then gave their machines a strenuous air check before returning to Sutton Craddock and signing the forms 700. The only task left was the arming of the Mosquitoes, but that Henderson could not do until SOE's agents discovered the type of flak wagon the Germans would be using. Nevertheless, Henderson ordered Greenwood, his new Armament Officer, to make sure an adequate supply of 60 lb rockets, 250 SAP bombs, and Hispano cannon ammunition was on hand. Whatever his misgivings about the forthcoming operation, the Scot remained a fully professional airman.

Adams's task on his return had been to retrieve the maps and photographs employed during the earlier operation in case they might prove useful again. Given permission by Henderson to enlist Sue Spencer's help, he was finding the girl's growing silence, as she sifted through files, an embarrassment. The pilot who had killed the Americans had been the girl's fiancé, St. Claire. A shell had struck the wing of his Mosquito at the moment he had fired a rocket, and the projectile had struck one of the wagons containing American prisoners. To make matters worse for the young pilot, he had crashed, and although the Resistance had spirited him away, a girl who had given him shelter had been tortured by the Gestapo and later killed because she would not betray him.

The effect on St. Claire had been traumatic and although he had eventually been returned to England, it had been many weeks before he had lived down his memories and been able to resume his relationship with Sue. It was clear to the sensitive Adams that the photographs were bringing back all her painful memories and he was now wishing he had not involved her in the task.

He tried to make his comment as innocuous as possible. "I can manage now, Sue. You get back to those interrogation reports. Group will be expecting them tomorrow."

She was paging through a filing cabinet. "There should be another file of photographs somewhere. I know we kept them."

"I'll find them, Sue. Leave them to me."

It did not take women long to know Adams, and Sue had worked with him for many months. "Stop worrying about me, Frank. I'm just being stupid. After all, it all came right in the end. And lightning doesn't strike in the same place twice, does it?"

Adams was secretly wishing his years in the RAF gave him more faith in the homily. "Of course it doesn't," he said. "This time it's going to be a big success."

Although the rest of the Squadron had no idea of the task ahead, Henderson's orders had nevertheless convinced every airman that Davies had brought with him a new and dangerous mission. However, with a youthful belief in their personal immortality, some men were more concerned with the cancellation of their liberty leave than with tomorrow's dangers. Gabby was one, showing his disgust as he dropped out of T-Tommy at the Mosquito's picketing bay after its air test. "How the hell am I going to tell Wendy I can't see her tonight?"

Millburn was busy signing his Mosquito's 700. "Phone her, the same way I phoned Betty. They haven't cut the lines yet. Or can't you use a telephone?"

"She hasn't got a bloody telephone," the Welshman scowled.

Millburn grinned as he handed his parachute to a mechanic. "Then send her a carrier pigeon. What could be more romantic than a message dropping in from the skies?"

Gabby was in one of his darker Celtic moods. "It's all right for you, Millburn. There's no competition for the kind of women you date. But Wendy's got every sodding airman in Scarborough chasing after her. If she thinks I've let her down, she might get the huff and go off with that big swaddie sergeant who fancies her."

Millburn gave a guffaw. "You're not telling me she prefers a swaddie to the Swansea Stallion, are you? I thought you were the guy women slavered over. The greatest stud since Casanova. What's been happening, boyo? Hasn't your performance been up to scratch lately?"

Gabby scowled. "You're not funny, Millburn. I've seen you throw some tantrums in your time when they've stopped your pass."

Millburn suddenly slapped his thigh. "Of course. Why didn't I think of it before?"

"Think of what?" Gabby asked suspiciously.

Millburn pointed to a crescent of moon high in the early evening sky. "That's it, isn't it? Gremlins can only do it under a full moon. So you're lucky, boyo. If you saw her tonight and she got passionate, you'd have to run away and hide."

Gabby heard muted laughter from a couple of nearby mechanics. The banter between the two men was legendary on the Squadron. The Welshman scowled. "Why must you talk such bullshit, Millburn?"

"What's the matter? Don't you want the WAAFs to hear? Anyway, why can't you make do with Gwen Thomas tonight? Wasn't it her you once had out on the airfield?"

Gabby's face darkened at the memory. After his going to great lengths to entice the voluptuous Gwen into a dispersal hut, Millburn and friends had dropped a smoke generator down the chimney just as the Welshman had been enjoying the fruits of victory. "That was a filthy trick, Millburn. Only a Yank would do a thing like that."

"We did it for Gwen, boyo. We were worried she might become pregnant and produce a litter of gremlins."

"Funny, funny," Gabby grunted. He jabbed a finger at a Mosquito that was sweeping over them to land. "What do you think all the flap's about? Hasn't Pop said anything to you?"

"Not a word, except we might be given a briefing at any time."

"But you're a Flight Commander. What's the problem? Doesn't he trust you?"

There was no one quicker at ripostes than Millburn. "You're the problem, boyo. Henderson knows you gremlins work for the square heads, so he plays it safe and keeps his cards close to his chest."

Gabby refused to be amused. "Why don't you give us all a break and go and join the Yanks, Millburn? Or won't they have you?"

Millburn grinned as a 25 cwt truck pulled up alongside them. "They might not by this time. They might think you lot have contaminated me. Jump up, you little short-ass, and let's get to the Mess. Talking to gremlins always makes me thirsty."

Although Anna was wide awake when Harvey entered the bedroom, at first the fear of reviving their earlier quarrel made her pretend to be asleep as he undressed in the dark. But although he was never one to harbour a quarrel, his present behaviour as he slipped quietly into the double bed gave her the encouragement she needed. She reached out and touched his arm. "Frank. I must talk to you.'

He turned towards her immediately. "I thought you were asleep."

"I know you did. But I can't sleep on quarrels. I want you to know I do understand why you are going on this operation."

"I've told you why. Because Davies ordered me to."

"No. You've never got over the fact that Ian sacrificed himself for us. This is your way of repaying, isn't it?"

In the silence that followed she knew he was thinking of some way to take sentiment out of his answer. A full ten seconds passed before he shifted restlessly. "Maybe that has a bit to do with it. I don't know."

"It has everything to do with it. But you must remember that our debt is to Ian, not to Davies." When he made no comment, she knew that battle, if it came, was for another day. Instead she changed the subject. "When do you expect to attack the convoy?"

"I haven't any idea. Davies is waiting for a report from his agents. But he'll brief us tomorrow so we'll be ready when the co-ordinates come through. That means I'll be leaving for Sutton Craddock early tomorrow morning."

She sat up sharply. "Tomorrow! Why didn't you tell me?"

"You didn't give me much chance, did you? Anyway, I'll be back in a couple of days."

She made her decision without a second thought. "I'm coming with you. I'll stay in The Black Swan as I did before."

He gave a start. Then his voice struck at her. "You damn well won't. You'll stay here and look after Sam."

Expecting his opposition, she put a hand over his mouth. "Listen to me, Frank. If I stay here, I'll be sitting on the edge of my chair the whole time you're away. But if I go with you, I'll only have to worry from the time your aircraft takes off to the time it comes back. Isn't that much kinder to me?"

He was propped up on his elbows now, his troubled eyes trying to read her expression in the darkness. "You never used to worry like this before."

He could not see the smile she gave. "Perhaps I have more to lose now. But listen who is talking. Ian once told me you sometimes acted like a crazy man when I was over in Europe."

"That was different," he muttered. "You were taking such hellish risks."

"No more than you take when you fly over Germany." Before he could answer, she went on quickly: "Let me come to Sutton Craddock, Frank. It will make it so much easier for me."

Although the curse he muttered under his breath was another protest, his reply told her she had won. "What if they won't have you? That charwoman of theirs hates Kearns taking in visitors."

"Mr Kearns will give me a room if Frank Adams asks him. The two of them are very good friends. Will you please talk to Adams tomorrow?"

As he sighed, she put her arms around him. "I'm sorry about tonight, Liebling. But after all that has happened, it seemed as if the nightmare was beginning again."

To those who had only known Harvey as a tough Flight Commander whose bark could make erks jump out of their skin, the gentleness of his voice would have amazed them. "I know that, lass. I only acted that way because I felt ashamed to tell you. That's how I am sometimes."

She drew his face to her breasts. "I know that," she whispered. "I know you better than you know yourself. And I have never known a braver or finer man."

As always his lovemaking was passionate but gentle. Before the tempestuous sea in which she was floating rose and drowned her, she heard the far-off sound of a passing aircraft. For a moment it held her on the sea's tossing surface and drew her gaze to a storm-swept sky. Then the oncoming wave swept forward and to her relief overwhelmed her.

Chapter 6

The English summer was having one of its unseasonal blips the following morning, reminding locals that autumn was only a few weeks away. There had been a frost during the night and at Sutton Craddock the mechanics out in dispersal huts were wrapping their hands around mugs of hot sweet tea. Aircrews, ordered to breakfast at 6 am and then called by tannoy to attend a briefing, were finding the Operations Room a chilly place as they filed into it. The stoves had only been lit half an hour before and, along with the chill, the air still carried the acrid smell of coke fumes. Men coughed as they took their seats on the rows of benches.

With all crews knowing that Davies was to attend the briefing, the chatter and buzz of conversation was loud that morning. It ended abruptly as a shout brought the assembly to attention. A moment later Davies, followed by Henderson, Adams, Harvey and Greenwood, marched between the ranks of men to a platform at the far end of the room.

All eyes were on Harvey as, along with the other officers, he took a chair in front of the platform. The presence of Davies always brought speculation: the return of Harvey to the squadron made that speculation intense. Aircrews gazed at one another with raised eyebrows as Davies climbed on to the platform and faced them. "All right, men, you can sit down now. In fact, you can smoke if you want to. It'll kill this bloody smell from the stoves."

There were a few nervous laughs, followed by the scratching of matches. Davies gave a grin. "These early morning briefings don't suit you lot, do they?" A firm believer in starting with humour before getting down to the nitty-gritty of his talk, Davies fixed his eyes on a lean Irishman on a front bench. "You, Machin, you look like a dog's dinner this morning. What were you doing last night? Still celebrating your Squadron Commander's survival?"

Machin, one of the squadron's long-surviving members, had a line in cynical humour, as Davies knew full well. "Yes, sur, that's the truth now. Oi always celebrate the survival of my superior officers."

Davies grinned. "I hope you'd do the same for me, Machin."

Machin did not let him down. "Yes, Oi would now. In spite of what y'are, sur, Oi'd still have a drink of stout on yer."

Adams drew in his breath as muted cheers and catcalls were heard. But although Davies blinked, he took it well. "I'll draw comfort from that, Machin. All right, let's get down to business. You've all heard about your Squadron Commander's survival. Now we're going a step further. We're going to help him to escape."

The entire audience gave a start, and a loud hum of curiosity broke out. Davies let it run on for a moment, then lifted a hand. "No, we're not turning into commandos and storming his prisoner of war camp. We're going to do it a much easier way. We're going to work with a crowd of partisans to help him escape from a road convoy that'll soon be taking him into Germany."

A loud hush fell in the room as Davies explained the Squadron's role in the operation. Walking over to a large map of Europe that stood at the rear of the platform, he pointed at Belgium and the Ardennes province. "This is where we will attack. Precisely where I can't say yet: we are still waiting for the co-ordinates from our agents over there. But, as we won't have much time once Moore's convoy is on its way, we have to be airworthy and ready. Any questions so far?"

A hand was raised from a rear bench. "This is the same kind of job we did for the Americans, isn't it, sir?"

Knowing the question had to come, Davies was ready for it. "No, not one little bit. That time it was an armoured train we had to attack, and because of its defences and other factors, it caused us all kinds of problems. This time it's a convoy of unarmed transports stranded between two blown-up bridges. Knock out the one flak wagon and the job's as good as over."

Although Davies had made it sound as easy as falling off a log, the crews' faces and their murmurs of disquiet told him the shadows from the earlier debacle still lay over the Squadron. "All right, I know some of you took part in that operation and I'm fully aware it was a cock-up. But it only happened because of bad luck and the same thing isn't going to happen again. All we have to do is immobilise the flak wagon and the partisans will do the rest. With any luck that means Wing Commander Moore will be back with the squadron before Christmas."

The rows of doubtful faces told Davies the crews remained unconvinced. "Why the hell are you all looking like kids without Christmas presents? You've done a dozen jobs far more difficult than this. Convoy busting is routine stuff these days. Typhoons are doing it all the time."

Another hand rose. "Then why aren't they doing it, sir? Aren't they supposed to be specialists?"

"They're specialists at busting trains and convoys, Brown, but we don't want this convoy busting. We just want its defence immobilising so that the partisans can get Moore and other aircrews out and back to England. That requires the kind of precision attack only you can carry out." Davies, who never missed a chance to boost morale, warmed to his task. "Remember you're an élite squadron and considered the best for special operations of this kind. Also I must point out to you that it's your Squadron Commander we're going to rescue."

This time it was Harvey's hand that rose. "I hope that convoy driver knows what he's doing, sir. Because the timing's going to be incredibly difficult."

Davies was only too aware the Yorkshireman was right. "The partisans seem to have complete confidence in him. And they're more at risk than we are."

Harvey had not finished yet. "I don't expect you know where the flak wagon will be situated?"

"Do you mean where it'll be in relation to the other trucks?"

"Yes, sir."

"No, I can't say that yet. We'll have to wait until the driver or the agents report back to us."

"You do realise its importance? One reason our earlier operation went wrong was because the flak wagons were in the middle of the train."

Davies was beginning to regret ever asking for Harvey's participation. "Of course I realise its bloody importance. But either way you have to prang the wagon, otherwise the partisans won't be able to get close enough to rescue our lads."

With crews exchanging glances, Davies knew Harvey had put his finger on the problem that was worrying all the long-serving crews. A flak wagon at the end of the convoy, although a formidable war machine, could be attacked without too much danger to the other transports if it led or followed them. But one in the centre meant that the slightest deviation of a rocket could imperil the transports both front and aft. To Davies' relief, the Yorkshireman changed his question, instead of pursuing the point. "How are the partisans going to blow up the bridges if a flak wagon's bearing down on them? They can't do it before the convoy arrives or it'll just take another route."

Secretly Davies had had the same thought. "They're going to handle the bridges while we're keeping the flak wagon busy. We haven't been given the full details here, but they seem quite confident they can do the job."

Harvey sounded sceptical. "Let's hope they're right. I suppose there's no danger they'll change their minds and mine the road instead? If they did and anything went wrong with their timing, it could be a disaster for the prisoners."

Davies wondered why the Yorkshireman could bristle his fur even when he was talking good sense. "Of course they won't change their minds," he snapped. "They've given us their plan and they'll stick to it." Relieved when Millburn put up a hand, Davies turned to him. "Yes, Millburn."

"Will you be using the full squadron, sir?"

"No, we don't think that's necessary. Eight kites should be enough, but as we haven't decided on the crews yet, you're all being put into the picture. You'll hear who's going and who isn't soon after this briefing. Needless to say, in case any of the stay-at-homes think about a foray to The Black Swan, the Station will he closed until the operation is over."

As muted groans were heard, Millburn raised his hand again. "How are we to go out, sir?"

"As we're expecting the convoy to reach the Ardennes in daylight, you'll go out at ultra low level to keep below Jerry's radar detectors. You won't have an escort, because that will alert Jerry, but the Banff Wing have agreed to stand by and carry out spoof raids along the Danish and North German coasts. With any luck this should give you a clear run in."

Someone made a sarcastic laugh. Choosing to ignore it, Davies went on: "Once you've spotted the convoy, four of you will make the attack and the other four will make height and give protection. The attack group will carry armour piercing rockets and a 250 SAP bomb apiece. The other four will carry full tanks of cannon shells. On your return you'll be given protection by Spitfires from one of our new bases in France. All other details, except the co-ordinates, will be given to you now by your specialist officers. After that you'll just have to be patient until the green light comes. That's all from me for the moment except to wish you good luck and the safe return of your Squadron Commander."

Leaving Henderson to take his place, Davies stepped down from the platform. Although it was customary for the Station Commander to make the final comments after a briefing, on this occasion Henderson looked faintly embarrassed. "I've only a few things to add before you talk to your specialist officers. The call signs will be as follows: the Squadron's will he Moonglow, the Spitfire escort's will be Flashlight, and the Station's will be Starshell. Your leader will be someone many of you know very well. It will be Flight Lieutenant Harvey."

Most crews now understood the Scot's embarrassment. After the initial outburst of surprise, cheers could be heard. The 'old sweats' among the aircrews, while accepting that Harvey was a strict disciplinarian, were happy enough to balance that against the attention the Yorkshireman gave to the safety of his crews. The members of Millburn's flight, some of them replacements of lost crews, either looked puzzled or indignant at what seemed a slight to their Flight Commander. Fully aware of this, Henderson gave no one an opportunity for reflection. "As you've all heard, we don't know when you'll be scrambled, so after you've seen your specialist officers, stay on your toes. That's all for now."

Exchanging his place on the platform for the Armament Officer, Henderson walked straight over to Millburn who was chatting to Van Breedenkamp, the Squadron's other Flight Commander. Blunt as always, the Scot came straight to the point. "Sorry about this, Millburn, but on this occasion it was decided Harvey was the right man for the job. I'm taking it you'll be happy to serve under him this time."

"Does that mean I'm going on the operation?" the American asked.

"Yes. We're sending our most experienced men. I want you to help me pick 'em after this briefing. You'll go out as second in command, of course."

Millburn shrugged. "I'm happy enough. That is, as long as the Tyke doesn't make me stand to attention before takeoff."

Relieved, Henderson smiled. "I don't think he'll do that."

Millburn's tone changed as his eyes moved to the tall figure of Harvey talking to Greenwood. "Why has he been brought back, sir? He's among the best but we could still have done the job. Isn't it a bit hard on the guy after three tours?"

Full of his own misgivings, Henderson frowned. "How long have you been in the RAF, Millburn? Haven't you learnt yet not to ask questions?"

Quick to put two and two together, Millburn grinned. "Some guys never learn, sir. Do you mind if I go over now and chat to the Tyke? I want to ask him who his tailor is."

Eyes twinkling, Henderson watched the American walk over and tap Harvey on the shoulder. As Harvey's brooding face lightened and the two men exchanged handshakes, Henderson knew that at least one possible problem would not surface. Grateful to Millburn, he went off in search of Davies.

Thanking the taxi driver and putting Sam on his lead, Anna guided the dog along the gravel path of The Black Swan and pressed the door bell. Half a minute later, a stoutly-built man wearing a worn smoking jacket opened the door. Joe Kearns, the landlord and owner, was a man in his middle fifties, with thinning white hair and a countryman's ruddy complexion. His face cleared when he recognised the girl. "Mrs Harvey! I thought it was one of the lads trying to get a drink before opening time."

"Frank Adams did ask you if I could have a room, didn't he?" she asked.

Kearns patted the dog and took her small case from her. "Oh, yes. He phoned me first thing this morning. We've given you the same room you had the last time."

Anna followed him into an oak-panelled hall. Through an open door she could see into the common room of the old inn. Wooden tables, the cross-sections of some huge and ancient tree, stood around its white-washed walls. Like the huge bar that ran almost the full length of the room, the tables had the rich black patina that came from centuries of wood- and tobacco-smoke. Copper ornaments stood around a wide stone hearth and others were pinned to a huge beam that formed a lintel over the bar.

Pushing aside the memories the sight of the bar brought back, the girl followed Kearns up a well-worn staircase into a bedroom that overlooked the airfield. Sparsely furnished, it contained a chair, a double bed, an old mahogany wardrobe, a dressing table, and an ancient wash cabinet complete with water jug and basin. Kearns lowered her case on to the chair. "I think you'll find the bed all right. Maisie gave the sheets and blankets a quick airing after Frank phoned us."

She gave him a smile as she patted Sam. "Thank you. I'm sure everything is fine. It is kind of you to have me at such short notice."

As always Kearns was impressed by the beauty and composure of the German girl. "How long are you expecting to stay, Mrs Harvey? Frank didn't seem to know."

"I'm afraid I'm not sure myself. Do you mind if I let you know later?"

Kearns' hesitation was only momentary. "No. Mrs Billan, our charwoman, grumbles a bit when we take in guests but Maisie can handle her, so that's no problem. You stay as long as you like."

She had moved to the latticed window as he was speaking. Knowing of Adams' friendship with the innkeeper, she motioned at the airfield opposite. "Did Frank say if the Station is closed for the day?"

"He said it might be. We'll know when opening time comes round. There's always a few of the lads sneak out for a pint."

She gave a half smile. "Thank you, Mr Kearns. I do appreciate your helping us out like this."

The innkeeper moved to the door. "Would you like a cup of tea? It won't be any trouble."

"No, thank you. Not at the moment."

"Well, if you change your mind, just give Maisie a shout. Otherwise lunch will be at one o'clock."

The girl turned back to the window as the innkeeper left her. With her bedroom higher than the Station's surrounding fence, she had an almost uninterrupted view of its hangars and the Control Tower as well as the Mosquitoes that ringed the airfield. All seemed to have mechanics working on them, and as she stood there she heard the cough and then the roar of a Merlin engine under test. Although the activity was muted, the girl had the sensation that the airfield was geared to spring into life at any moment.

Opening her case, she took out her clothes and hung them in the wardrobe. As she was sliding the empty case under the bed, there was a tap on the door. "Hello, Miss. Can I come in?"

Maisie appeared in the doorway a moment later. Maisie, Kearns' barmaid, was an institution at Sutton Craddock. Dark-haired, bold featured, generous-natured, with a figure that made airmens' eyes glow like Very lights, she was a girl who had never been known not to run out into the pub garden and wave at the Mosquitoes when they returned after a mission. Weary crews, seeing her buxom figure waving at them, knew another nightmare was over and they were home again.

"Sorry I didn't get a chance to see you downstairs, Miss. But I was down in the cellar sorting out some beer casks. I heard Mr Harvey's come back to the Station. He's not coming back for good, is he? I thought he'd finished with operations, at least for a time."

Anna knew there were few secrets that did not reach Maisie. "So did I," she said. "But it seemed they want him here for a few days. So I thought I'd spend them with him."

"Good idea, Miss. It's nice to have you back." Seeing Sam wagging his tail, Maisie reached down and patted him. "And to have you too, Sam. I like dogs."

Anna noticed the girl hadn't asked the reason for Harvey's recall. Whether it was due to prudence or guesswork she did not know but was grateful not to be called upon to lie. "I don't suppose Mr Harvey has phoned me today, has he?"

"No, Miss. But why don't you phone him? The Station hasn't cut communications yet."

"If he doesn't phone in the next hour, I think I will."

Maisie chatted for a few more minutes then went downstairs at an impatient shout from Kearns. Restless, Anna returned to the window. Half a dozen birds were perched on the crab apple trees, pecking without enthusiasm at the sour fruit. A 25 cwt lorry came speeding down the road from Highgate, drew to a halt at the sentry box, then accelerated towards No. 1 hangar. Three mechanics, jostling one another playfully as they crossed the tarmac apron, were brought to attention by a sergeant, whose yell reached the girl through the closed window. On the surface, Sutton Craddock had never looked more normal. Yet once again the girl thought of a humming generator. Spinning quietly until a switch was thrown and then leaping into dynamic life.

Aware that her knowledge of the forthcoming operation was stimulating her imagination, Anna picked up a book and tried to read. But distant sounds from the airfield kept drawing her back to the window and preventing her from making sense of the words. Finally, remembering Maisie's suggestion, she went downstairs to the oak-panelled hall and picked up the telephone. "Hello. Sutton Craddock airfield? I would like to speak to Squadron Leader Harvey, please."

The WAAF who answered her sounded doubtful. "I'm not sure he's available. But I'll try."

She had to wait for nearly five minutes before Harvey came to the phone. "Hello, is that you, Anna?"

She sighed her relief. "Yes, Frank. I was hoping you might be able to phone me."

"Sorry, love, but it's all go here. Where are you? At The Black Swan?"

“Yes, I got here just after ten thirty. What is the situation? Will you be able to get over today?”

“I doubt it, love. But I’ll come over as soon as I can. Just relax and don’t worry about anything. Promise?”

Conscious how difficult it was for him to talk without giving anything away, she knew she must not keep him on the phone. She hoped her voice disguised her true feelings. “I’m perfectly all right here. Mr Kearns and Maisie are looking after me very well. So you have nothing to worry about.”

He sounded relieved. “That’s my girl. We probably won’t get a chance to talk again today, but I’ll be in touch as soon as I can.” As he paused, she heard an impatient voice addressing him. She heard him answer, then his voice returned to the phone. “I’m sorry, love, but I must go now. See you soon.”

“Good luck, Frank,” was all she dared say before lowering the receiver to its hook. Then, uncertain whether the conversation had made things better or worse for her, she walked slowly back upstairs where Sam, uneasy in his new quarters, showed his relief at seeing her again.

The information for which Davies was waiting came unexpectedly at two-thirty that afternoon. The bell of the teleprinter brought the Duty Officer to his feet. After reading the swiftly-moving paper he first phoned Henderson and then the rest of the officers named on his roster sheet. In turn Henderson phoned Davies who had spent the morning closeted with Harvey and Millburn. “The co-ordinates have come through, sir. Our ETA is 11.15 tomorrow morning.”

Davies sounded surprised. “So soon? We thought they’d be a couple more days at the least interrogating Moore.”

“Perhaps they’ve realised it’s a waste of time,” Henderson suggested.

“I’ll tell you what, Jock. It’s a good job we wasted no time getting ready. What about photographs? Have they mentioned ’em?”

“I haven’t had a chance to see the teletype yet, sir, but my guess is that Benson will already have dispatched a Mossie over the site.”

The teletype proved Henderson to be right. A photo-reconnaissance Mosquito had taken off for the chosen site in the Ardennes and would drop off its photographs at Sutton Craddock later that day. Davies's satisfaction was patent when he met Henderson in the Scot's office. "Everything's going like clockwork so far, Jock. All we have to do now is clobber that flak wagon and Moore ought to be back in time for us to throw him a Christmas party."

Henderson wished he could share the Air Commodore's confidence, as he put a call through to the Navigation Officer. "Let's hope you're right, sir. I take it the boys can be given the co-ordinates now?"

"Not unless you want all communications to be cut. Wait until this evening, Jock. Then we'll go into purdah until the job's finished."

Chapter 7

The early promise of a fine day on the morrow was threatened by a sullen bank of cloud on the eastern horizon. Crews eyed it with mixed feelings. If it turned to rain, the reduced visibility could increase the hazards of their low-level dash to the Ardennes. On the other hand, it reduced the possibility of their being spotted by patrolling enemy fighters.

In other words, like so many other things in wartime, its ultimate effect could not be assessed until the blood-stained profit and loss account was drawn up, Henderson thought as he waited in his office for Davies to arrive. In spite of all the Air Commodore's assurances and arguments, Henderson could not push from his mind the traumas he and his Squadron had suffered after the American rescue attempt, and he could not shake off the fear that something similar might occur today.

With so much to do before takeoff, the squadron had been given an early call that morning. Out on the airfield, mechanics were running through more checks before the eight Mosquitoes were air-tested again. The crews chosen for the mission had enjoyed a breakfast of bacon and eggs, a menu that had brought a wide, white-toothed grin from 'Stan' Baldwin, the lawyer from Barbados who was the Squadron's only black crewman. "Two eggs! Man, this must be some mission. We only got one when we went to Rensburg."

McMaster, a sharp-tongued Londoner whose eggs were over-fried, glanced at West, a pink-cheeked ex-hairdresser from Cheltenham. West was a pilot recruited to the squadron to make up its losses after the TITAN operation. His youthful appearance and profession occasionally drew jokes from some of the squadron's harder cases. "You know what they're for, don't you, West?"

When West shook his head, McMaster leaned forward. "They're the M.O.'s idea. They're to prevent young kids from messing their trousers when the shit starts to fly."

Although West tried to smile, his cheeks turned a deeper pink. Unlike earlier replacements, who had been volunteers from front-line squadrons, attracted by either the fame of 633 Squadron or its special service role, he had come directly from an OTU and so had needed training before being chosen for his first combat mission.

Before 1944, recruits had arrived battle-seasoned and had needed only integrating into the Squadron's special tactics. But by early 1944 this well of reserves had begun to dry up. The reason was threefold. Front-line squadron commanders had become resentful at losing their best men and started to erect barriers. At the same time, as 633 Squadron's fame had spread, so had the news of its casualties, and it was now rumoured to be a suicide unit. A third reason was the massive ground attacks the Allied Air Forces were inflicting on Germany's war machine. At low level, an experienced man was as vulnerable to ground fire as a 'fresher' and as 633 Squadron were specialists in such attacks, seasoned replacements could not keep up with casualties. None of the Flight Commanders liked the situation, because statistics showed that only one in two novice crews survived their first operation. Nevertheless West was not the first recruit from the OTUs, nor would he be the last.

Seeing the youngster's embarrassment, the good-natured Baldwin stepped in quickly. "Say, you could be right there. Only how did you find that out, man? Do eggs work for you too?"

McMaster scowled as laughter broke out along the table. "I notice you've eaten yours fast enough, matey."

Baldwin was nothing if not imperturbable. "That's right. I need all the shit stoppers I can get." He held out his plate. "As you don't need 'em, how about giving me yours?"

As loud laughter ran along the table, McMaster managed a grin and pushed Baldwin's plate aside. "You couldn't eat these, matey. They're too tough for you bloody colonials."

Back in Henderson's office, Davies, all bustle and keenness, had now arrived from his night quarters at High Elms. As he was scrutinising the photographs that Benson had provided, Harvey, Millburn, Adams and the Navigation officer began filing in. Once all were present, Davies wasted no time.

"These are the photographs of the stretch of road you have to find. You'll see there are also photographs of the two bridges. Take a good look at them all before we start briefing the crews."

As the curious men gathered round the desk, Harvey gave a grunt of disapproval. "It looks a damn steep valley. And those trees on either side aren't going to make things any easier."

With the operation close on hand, Davies had decided he would be patient with the tall Yorkshireman. "We can't help the trees. Without them, the partisans wouldn't have any cover."

Harvey picked up a photograph of a bridge. It had two red-pencilled rings drawn over it. "What are these, sir?"

Davies made the admission with reluctance. "The WAAFs at Benson think they're flak posts."

Henderson got in his protest a split second ahead of Harvey. "Flak posts! Nobody mentioned flak posts. I thought the partisans were going to destroy those bridges? What armament do they have? Does anyone know?"

Adams gave the answer. "We think one is a 37 mm post and the other an LMG post. The first bridge has just an LMG."

"So they're both defended?" When Adams nodded, Henderson turned to the frowning Davies. "This changes everything, doesn't it, sir? I can't see the partisans knocking out that second bridge. Not without unacceptable casualties."

Davies tried to hide his discomfort. "No, we'll have to do that. London informed High Elms this morning. The partisans will have a try at the first bridge, however." Seeing Henderson's expression, Davies adopted his most amiable manner. "Don't look so worried, Jock. Your boys have done jobs a dozen times harder than this. After all, they're only small bridges."

Bridges were infamously difficult to destroy from the air. All the Scot's apprehensions were back. "They can't be that small if they'll take a flak wagon. There's no way we can guarantee to blow them up before Jerry's fighters arrive."

Knowing Henderson could be right did nothing to improve Davies's unease. "You don't have to blow the bloody things up. All you need do is knock out the gunners and the partisans will do the rest. That shouldn't take long, should it?"

When no one spoke, Davies turned to Millburn. "Give the job to two of your lads. When they've finished with the gunners they can rejoin you." Seeing that Harvey was about to say something, Davies sharpened his voice. "The job has to be done, so let's stop arguing about it. I want the crews briefed and ready before 09.00 hours in case the green light comes earlier than we expect. So get 'em all in the Briefing Room right away."

While the eight crews detailed for the operation were being briefed, 633 Squadron made its preparations with its customary high efficiency. By 07.30 the Mosquitoes were ready for their air tests. After each aircraft landed and its pilot had signed the necessary forms, last checks were made and then the armourers took over. 60 lb rockets were loaded on to the wings of Harvey's four Mosquitoes and magazines were snapped on to their short-barrelled 20 mm cannon. As a further precaution a time-delayed 250 SAP bomb was hauled into each bomb bay. Two of Millburn's Mosquitoes were armed with 500 lb bombs with time delays and two were given an extra supply of cannon shells to compensate for their lack of rockets. By 08.15 hours the safety pins of bombs and rockets were withdrawn and the aircrafts' bomb doors closed. Eight Mosquitoes, waiting on their dispersal points, became sophisticated and deadly instruments of war.

Meanwhile, the eight crews were collecting their parachutes, revolvers, survival kit, foreign money, and all the other miscellaneous equipment considered essential for men flying over enemy territory. When their rounds were completed, the sixteen men went into their respective Flight Offices and waited for the signal to scramble.

It came at 09.13. As the telephone in each flight office rang, the Station tannoy crackled out its message. Crews grabbed their parachutes and ran out to the transports that skidded to a halt outside their offices. The mission to rescue Moore had begun.

* * *

It was the harsh sound of the Station tannoy that made Anna jump from the bed and run to the window. Until then, she had had no idea when the mission was to begin: communication with the station had been cut off since 23.00 the previous night. Now she could see the frantic activity that had broken out on the airfield. As transports raced around the perimeter track, dropping off crew after crew at each picketing point, mechanics were starting up the engines of their charges. Within seconds of the alarm, the first Merlin gave its characteristic cough and fired. It was followed almost instantly by other throaty coughs as the eight aircraft became alive. As crews swung into them, the roar of engines became deafening as the Mosquitoes moved forward and began assembling on the far side of the airfield.

There was a brief wait until the last aircraft was in position. Then a green Very light soared up from the Control Tower. It was the signal for the foremost Mosquito to thrust forward. Heavy with its load of weapons, it bounced again and again on the runway before breaking free and rising with a crackling roar.

Seeing that its flight path was bringing it towards The Black Swan, and believing Harvey to be the pilot, Anna threw open her window with the intention of waving. Then, afraid the action might distract him, she drew back. As the Mosquito swept over she could clearly see battle scars on its fuselage from some previous engagement, and the sight made her flinch. Then the Mosquito was past her and two others climbing in its wake. The rest followed, orbiting and formatting over the airfield before turning south. She waited at the window until the noise of engines died into an indeterminate hum. Then, hearing a low whimper from Sam, she sank down into a chair and called the dog to her side.

Chapter 8

The eight Mosquitoes flew in two tight echelons down to the South Coast. It had been known for some time that the Germans had long-range radar that could pick up Allied aircraft almost as soon as they left their airfields. However, by flying in tight echelon, light aircraft could merge their images on the enemy's radar screen to make it appear that they were heavy bombers. If before they left England they sank down to ultra low level, they could give the impression they had been only air-testing and had landed again. Five years of war were imposing stratagems on both sides that had been unthinkable in 1939.

The North Sea was having one of its tantrums that morning as Harvey, flying D-Danny, swept over the Suffolk coast and signalled his flight down to sea level. The swell was heavy and an easterly wind was blowing spindrift from crest to crest. As Harvey ordered his flight even lower, spray hissed into spinning propellers and splattered on windshields. Although by this time Mosquito squadrons were famous for their low-level flying, few activities required greater training and concentration. A split-second diversion by a pilot, as his aircraft skimmed like a stone over the hungry waves, could mean collision and almost certain death.

With such concentration necessary by the pilots, surveillance for enemy activity was their navigator's responsibility. Earlier, navigators had hoped the low cloud base would minimise the chance of enemy detection. But in the hours since dawn the clouds had lifted and now made a luminous ceiling some three thousand feet above the sea. To most navigators this represented the worst of two worlds. It not only increased the possibility of detection by patrolling enemy fighters but would allow them to mass unseen before making their attack. Aware of all the permutations, Harvey addressed his new navigator, Carter. His old navigator, Hanson, had been lost during Harvey's absence and Carter, a somewhat superior ex-estate agent, had been offered to him as the best navigator available. "Get up on the seat and watch out for bandits."

Carter looked surprised. "On the seat?"

"Yes. Turn round and kneel on it. You can see up better that way."

With the seat metallic and hard on the knees, Carter made the mistake of arguing. "I can see just as well sitting as I am, sir. And what about flak ships? I won't be able to spot any if I'm facing backwards."

It was then Carter discovered that the stories about Harvey's temper were no rumours. Nor did the fact that the Yorkshireman had to keep his eyes glued to the tossing sea improve it. His shout made the intercom earpieces rattle. "Do as you're bloody well told. Get your knees on that seat and don't move a muscle until I tell you. Otherwise I'll bounce you over the Control Tower when we get back. So move!"

Carter moved. Hastily. As the navigator knelt on the seat and scanned the luminous sky, Harvey prepared for the enemy flak ships he knew they might encounter along their route. With R/T silence strictly imposed all the way to the target, he pulled the Mosquito's nose up a degree and waggled his wings. A pre-set signal, it ordered the superbly trained pilots behind him to fly line astern. When the order was gingerly but precisely carried out, the eight Mosquitoes were strung out like a piece of string and less vulnerable to enemy fire.

Harvey saw only one flak ship as he neared the enemy coast, a distant grey hulk on the horizon. It was too far away to represent an immediate threat but he knew it would already be sending out radio messages for fighter interception. With the possibility in mind, he took the precautions given him by Davies's navigation specialists and swung his Mosquito ten degrees to port, turning back on his original course only when the grey hulk vanished over the horizon. Ten minutes later he saw a long shadow appearing on the horizon and knew it was the enemy coast. As the other crews spotted it, the gap between the Mosquitoes increased. All crews were only too aware that the enemy had guns the entire length of the occupied coastline, and flying over them at low level was a perilous exercise. Waggling his wings again, Harvey turned on his fire-and-safe button and tested his guns. Behind him the seven Mosquitoes moved out of line for a few seconds as each one followed their leader's example and spat jets of fire. The serious business was about to begin.

As the Mosquitoes swung hack into line, Harvey tapped his indignant navigator on the leg and motioned him back into his seat. "We'll be over the coast in a minute. I want you to check our position."

The coast was clearly visible now, a stretch of grassy dunes with occasional summer houses visible between them. It looked innocent enough, but every crew member knew hidden enemy gunners would already be yelling warnings and stripping the covers off their LMGs and multi-barrelled pom-poms.

The dunes were less than a mile away now and growing by the moment. The sea was calmer here and the slipstream of the Mosquitoes was scuffling the water like the wake of ships. As he hugged the water even lower, Harvey caught sight of a fishing boat from the corner of his eye and the oilskinned figure of a man waving. The image came and went in a flash as a roller coaster of beach and sand dunes streaked below his windshield. As he eased back on his control column to leapfrog a dune, a double fork of tracer stabbed upwards and curled past his port wing. A line of black explosions appeared ahead, rocking the aircraft as it flew between them. Then the dunes were cleared and a road and fields appeared ahead.

Relaxing, Harvey glanced at Carter. "Have they all got through?"

Carter was trying to see. "I think so." A moment later: "Yes, they have."

He was right but only just. A piece of shrapnel had ripped a hole a foot long in Temple's port wing and bullets had ricocheted from Millburn's starboard engine cowling. They had brought an alarmed yell from Gabby. "You bloody fool. Didn't you see that LMG?"

Millburn, drenched in sweat as all the crews were, for the Mosquito was a warm aircraft, glared at him. "Of course I saw the goddamned thing. What was I supposed to do? Ask it to leave us alone?"

Gabby glanced uneasily at the inflicted engine. "It's a miracle it didn't take the prop away. Then where would we be?"

"You'd be in a hot place getting hell for your sins, you little binder. Down there they've got a list a mile long ready for you."

"And where do you think you'd be, Millburn?"

Quick to recover, Millburn grinned. "I'd be playing my harp and laughing like hell when they stick the pitchforks up your ass."

Equally resilient, Gabby came back quickly. "There's one thing you wouldn't be getting, Millburn."

"What's that?"

"You wouldn't be getting any nookie. They don't do that up there."

Millburn grinned again. "There's always a first time."

"What, on a cloud?"

Fields and stone hedges were now flowing beneath the Mosquitoes. Aware that the efficient German Observer corps would soon be tracking them, Millburn jerked a thumb at the sky. "Talking about clouds, keep your eyes open. That flak ship will have alerted the bastards."

The danger, Millburn knew, came from the German Third Fighter Division's headquarters at Arnhem-Deelen which controlled the air space they were entering. While it was true that the Banff Wing were carrying out diversionary attacks that morning, the enemy still had substantial reserves and once Arnhem-Deelen was alerted about the eight intruders, it was virtually certain that swarms of Me 109s or Focke-Wulf 190s would be directed to find them.

Harvey, leading the intruders, was having the same thoughts. In truth Harvey had mixed feelings about the operation. While nothing could have prevented his leading the effort to rescue Moore, the Yorkshireman's canny instincts saw too many imponderables in the plan. What if the convoy was delayed for some reason, for road congestion, for a breakdown, or even for something as simple as a burst tyre? What if the bridges couldn't be blocked or destroyed in time to prevent the trucks escaping? What if enemy aircraft arrived in time to upset the entire applecart? What — in Harvey's mind the worst risk of all — what if Moore and his fellow prisoners were killed during the attack?

Harvey was sure there must be other imponderables, but the ones that worried him seemed more than enough. No one wanted Moore back at the squadron more than the Yorkshireman, but at this moment of time, with the Mosquitoes skimming deeper and deeper into enemy-held territory, the risks of failure seemed innumerable. It made one thing certain to Harvey. London must believe the enemy was developing a secret weapon so threatening that it made all the risks worth taking.

Harvey was now flying parallel to the road, its telephone poles blurred by speed. A startled bird, rising from a hedge, struck his right wingtip and was hurled away in a tangle of bone and feathers. A large farmhouse appeared ahead, forcing him to bank to port. The pilots behind him reacted as one man and the line of Mosquitoes curved like a piece of string before straightening again.

Beside Harvey, Carter was examining his maps and giving the Yorkshireman instructions. As a railway line appeared and he was told to follow it, Harvey had to admit grudgingly that the man wasn't a bad navigator.

Namur appeared, a crenulated silhouette on the skyline. Aware the town was well defended, Carter took Harvey around its boundaries. For a minute puffs of smoke disfigured the luminous sky and rocked the Mosquitoes with their explosions. Then buildings and chimneys fell behind and woods and fields returned.

Images came and went to the tense crews. Starlings, feeding in a newly-ploughed field, rose in a startled cloud and divided in panic as the aircraft tore through them. One struck McDonald's bullet-proof windshield and left a red, running stain. Startled cattle reared and bolted at the sudden roar of engines: grass shivered and flattened under the blast of propellers. A woman walking down a country lane ran into the hedge, then, seeing the Mosquitoes' roundels, waved and blew a kiss. Gabby glanced at Millburn. "The Belgian women can't wait for us to arrive, boyo. I wish I was in the bloody army."

Millburn gave a guffaw. "A short-ass like you? You wouldn't make first base. Anyway, the swaddies don't take gremlins."

Gabby scowled. "Funny, funny."

With the plain of Liege well behind, fields began to give way to hills and woods. With summer advanced in the higher ground, dry leaves were torn from the trees and swept away like confetti as the aircraft skimmed over them. For half a minute the Mosquitoes squatted down a major road. A convoy of enemy trucks appeared: carrying ammunition and stores for the front, was Harvey's guess. As the Mosquitoes roared towards them, soldiers leapt off the trucks and dived into ditches. Gabby gave a yell of derision as they sped past. "Pity we can't give 'em a squirt."

A minute later the countryside changed again into pine-covered hills and fast-flowing streams, provoking intense concentration in Harvey as he led the Mosquitoes between the hills or leapt over them like a horseman taking fences. Catching sight of another winding road, he threw a quick glance at Carter. "What's our ETA?"

"Six minutes," Carter told him. "But it might be longer. That flak ship detour wasted a couple of minutes."

Harvey nodded. Five minutes later he addressed Carter again. "Want a better look?"

When the navigator nodded, the Yorkshireman waggled his wings twice and drew back on the control column. His altimeter needle swung up to three hundred, then four hundred feet. "I can't go much higher or their radar'll spot us," he told Carter.

The navigator was searching the roads that ran through the hills. Below, the remaining Mosquitoes had gone into orbit. Carter's voice came again. "I'll need more altitude, skipper."

Harvey cursed but obeyed. Turning north on Carter's instructions, he flew another fifteen seconds before the navigator's triumphant shout rattled his earphones. "There's the convoy, skipper! At ten o'clock."

Gazing down, Harvey saw a distant line of trucks making their way down a narrow strip of road between scabrous hills. "Are you sure?"

Carter was eyeing the road through binoculars. "I think so. The trucks have red-cross markings."

Harvey banked steeply to take a look. As Carter studied the convoy, he gave a start. "The Jerries must have been tipped off. They've got half a company of soldiers down there."

Harvey snatched the binoculars from him and saw he was right. Apart from a huge flak wagon in the van of the long convoy, two trucks bristling with grey-clad soldiers were following in the rear. He thrust back the binoculars. "Are you sure it's the right convoy? It seems a hell of a lot of protection for a couple of dozen prisoners of war."

Carter pointed at two large canvas-covered trucks in the centre of the convoy. "Those middle trucks could be the reason. They're not carrying prisoners, even if they do have red crosses. Jerry's probably moving back some important equipment."

When Harvey still looked doubtful, Carter indicated to a spot a mile ahead of the convoy. "It must be the one, skipper. There's the first bridge. The second should be at the other side of that hill."

Below, sighting the Mosquitoes, the convoy had drawn to a halt at a point where the hills rose steeply on either side. Convinced now that this was his target, and aware that it was safe from attack there, Harvey waggled his wings urgently. Immediately the orbiting Mosquitoes swung away and flew south in line astern. The move had been anticipated during briefing, and Millburn had been instructed to bluff the convoy commander into thinking that his vehicles were not the target.

In the meantime, Harvey swept around the hill and confirmed the existence of a second bridge. The valley was wider here with trees dense on both slopes. There was no sign of partisans among them but as Harvey swept over the trees a light flashed a signal. Carter gave an excited cry. "It's O.K., skipper. They're in position."

Now it's up to the convoy commander, Harvey thought. If he doesn't move in the next few minutes we'll have to abort. We can't arse around running out of gas with half Jerry's air force looking for us. Afraid to circle back in case his own presence alerted the convoy, he had no alternative but to make height, in the hope that Carter could keep an eye on the trucks.

Endeavouring to make his movements look as innocent as possible, he climbed to three thousand feet while Carter tried to keep his binoculars on the convoy. It was not easy. The steep hills kept screening the trucks and Harvey dared not fly closer. Fortunately there was a large iron mine and processing plant west of the valley, and by circling over it he hoped to give the impression it was his target. Although the other aircraft would still be heard by the convoy, as they had not made an attack he could only hope that its commander no longer saw them as a threat.

To the south, Harvey kept catching glimpses of the Mosquitoes orbiting among the hills. He could imagine the crews' thoughts as the minutes passed. They would know his altitude would have given his position away and so every wasted second was adding to their peril. Gritting his teeth, Harvey damned the convoy commander and urged him to drive on.

Carter's voice came as an immense relief. "I think they're moving again, skipper."

"Are you sure?"

A long moment and then: "Yes, they are."

Harvey grabbed the binoculars. He saw the flak wagon had already crossed the first bridge. For a moment, as his Mosquito orbited, he lost the image, but as he came around the circle again he saw the rest of the convoy had also crossed the bridge and was heading for the larger bridge on the far side of the hill.

Harvey, who had already decided that time did not allow the partisans to attack the first bridge, wasted no more time. Putting the Mosquito's nose down, he headed straight for the bridge, at the same time switching on his R/T. "Moonglow leader to Blue Section. Convoy confirmed. Attack second bridge. Go."

The first bridge was already growing in Harvey's windshield. At first it appeared unprotected, but suddenly a double line of tracer squirted out. Seeing it came from the hillside just above the bridge, Harvey gave a grunt of satisfaction and made straight for the gunpit, at the same time yelling at his navigator. "Are you ready?"

Carter nodded. He had already fused the 250 lb bomb and had the bomb tit in his hand. Ignoring the tracer although it lashed out like a deadly whip, Harvey waited until the last moment and then swung in a tight arc parallel to the hillside. "Now!" he shouted.

The bomb was slung down as the Mosquito flashed over the tree tops and then rocketed upwards. As Harvey tried to avoid the tracer that was following him, he was counting ... two, three, four ...

At five, there was a shout from Carter and a huge jolt that threw both men against their safety straps. At the same moment the accurate enemy fire ceased.

Circling, Harvey gazed down. A column of smoke was rising from the hillside and trees were burning where the gun post had been. Other trees had fallen on to the bridge and were blocking it but as he watched, Harvey saw a dozen small dark figures run from the trees to set high explosives beneath it.

Content, Harvey headed for the convoy. As he swept along the valley, a series of explosions rocked D-Danny and puffs of black smoke appeared around her. Although there was chaos on the road below as drivers tried to decide whether to drive on or turn back, the flak wagon gunners remained cool enough to sight on Harvey's lone aircraft.

Ahead, around the hill, Millburn and Machin were already attacking the second bridge. Better defended than the first, its 37 mm battery was built into a concrete bunker. With its crews already alerted by the first sight of the Mosquitoes, their defences were ready and the flak that met the two aircraft was heavy. Machin lost a bomb door before both aircraft released their bombs.

Although their aim was accurate, the bridge itself suffered little damage, as Henderson had feared. However, the attack's main object, to knock out the enemy gunners, was successful and the bomb explosions had hardly died away before partisans could be seen swarming over the bridge and attaching explosives.

To Harvey, now sweeping along the road, it was clear that the partisans would be scattered or killed while working on the bridge unless his Mosquitoes could destroy the flak wagon before it came round the hill. When a shout from the Mosquitoes patrolling above told him the rear bridge had been successfully breached, he knew no other alternative was left to the convoy commander but to press ahead at full speed.

Harvey was just about to order the attack when there was a huge eruption of smoke from the front of the convoy. A second later there was a startled shout from Carter. "They've mined the road, skipper."

Harvey stared down at the cloud of smoke. As it blew away, he saw that the flak wagon, moving at speed towards the second bridge, had missed the mine but the foremost truck had received the full explosion. A shattered, smoking wreck, it was lying on its side with motionless figures in blue uniforms scattered around it.

Harvey's curses were unprintable as he circled over the road. The flak wagon had pulled up short, its commander either reluctant to leave his convoy or afraid of more mines ahead. Up among the Mosquitoes the R/T channel was filled with dismayed shouts from the crews at the sight of dead and dying comrades. Although raging at the waste of life himself and afraid that Moore was one of the casualties, Harvey knew he had to finish the task and get away before the Focke-Wulfs arrived. His shout rattled earphones. "Belt up, you lot! Blue leader, take the flak wagon with me. Usual drill. The rest of you attack the escort but for Christ's sake don't hit the prisoners. Go!"

The battle that followed was swift but bloody. The flak wagon crew knew they were fighting for their lives and their resistance showed it. Automatic weapons lashed out vicious whips of tracer and the wagon's 37 mm threw murderous shells at the Mosquitoes as they prepared to attack.

Back along the convoy the grey-clad soldiers were obeying orders and running for cover among the trees. It was a signal for the hidden partisans to open fire on them. As the German troops hesitated, Mosquitoes came diving down parallel to the convoy and strafed them. Unable to find cover, men tried to run back to their trucks only to be mown down as they ran.

Meanwhile Harvey and Millburn were making certain the flak wagon could not fire on the partisans working on the bridge. Their stratagem was one the squadron had long perfected, their attack coming from both sides to thin out the defensive fire. Diving steeply and slightly obliquely to avoid collision, Millburn had to fly through sheets of LMG fire and Harvey to face the dreaded 37 mm before they were close enough to fire their rockets. As shells bracketed D-Danny and she rocked and bucked under the explosions, Carter's face became a pale, sweating mask.

But both Mosquitoes survived the ordeal and rockets shot forward like luminous lances at the wagon. One struck its cab, a second hit the ground beneath it and flew harmlessly away, a third struck the turret just above the armoured skirt and drove its armour-piercing head into the body of the wagon. Although little damage could be seen from the outside, in fact the steel projectile ricocheted brutally around the inside of the wagon, smashing men and machinery alike. As Millburn climbed away, Gabby reported that all the wagon's guns had stopped firing. A few second later an explosion set the wagon on fire.

Sweating freely, Harvey turned his attention to the convoy. By this time the escorting enemy soldiers had been overcome and partisans could be seen advancing from the woods. Bewildered prisoners of war could also be seen, jumping out warily from their trucks.

Harvey would have given much to find out if Moore was among the survivors but even if it had been possible time was at a premium. Even as he was about to order his men to break off the mission and close in behind him, a shout on the R/T made him stiffen. "Bandits, Moonglow Leader! Bandits at three o'clock!"

Chapter 9

The bandits Van Breedenkamp had sighted were Focke-Wulf 190s with BMW 801 engines, which gave them a slight edge in speed on the versatile Mosquitoes, although their turning circle was not so tight. They were a single flight of a squadron based near Fegelen. For nearly half an hour they had answered call after call from their Controller as members of the Banff wing attacked various targets in Northern Europe. Frustrated by these diversionary sweeps, their Controller had finally picked up an urgent call from the convoy flak wagon and directed them towards the eight Mosquitoes that the Observer Corps had first spotted crossing the coast.

Although their Flight Commander, an ambitious as well as a brave man, saw his flight was outnumbered, he had no intention of waiting until the rest of his Gruppe arrived. Although he knew well enough what a formidable fighter a Mosquito could be, from the fires burning below he believed he was confronting the bomber version of the adaptable aircraft, which often flew unarmed. In his haste and zeal he failed to notice the short-barrelled cannon that 633 Squadron's aircraft carried.

His crews made the same mistake. As Harvey's urgent voice called his Mosquitoes to form a defensive circle and make for the clouds above, the Focke-Wulfs dived from the sky like gannets and picked out their targets.

It was a costly error for one young German pilot. As he dropped on the tail of a Mosquito, ignoring the Mosquito that was covering its tail, a burst of cannon fire smashed into his plane and literally blew it apart. As the huge ball of fire and black smoke exploded before him, Millburn's yell of triumph distorted earphones. "I got one! See that, you guys! I got one."

Taking warning, the Focke-Wulfs' Kettenfuhrer issued new orders and his remaining fighters began to dive, fire, and pull away before they entered the defensive circle. Heavily armed themselves with high-velocity 151 Mauser cannon, they turned the sky around the Mosquitoes into a hell of screaming steel. A cannon shell blew a two foot hole in Killingbeck's starboard wing and another shell shattered the port propeller of Van Breedenkamp's aircraft, forcing the South African pilot to shut off the screaming engine. Harvey, conscious that the defensive circle's manoeuvres were slowing down the Mosquitoes' climb to the clouds, was about to order his men to break off and pick their own adversary when a cool, very English voice made him start. "Hello, Moonglow Leader. This is Flashlight leader. You don't mind us joining the party, do you?"

Glancing up Harvey saw the sleek and graceful shapes of Spitfires already engaging the Focke-Wulfs. His gritty voice disguised his relief. "Not before time, Flashlight leader. Where the hell have you been?"

"We got held up, old boy. Ran into a pack of 109s and had to smack their bottoms before we could get through. But we're here and will look after you. Any damage done?"

"Yes. I've got one crate without a port engine."

"O.K., old son. We'll nurse him home." With the Focke-Wulfs now fully occupied, Harvey was able to fly alongside Van Breedenkamp. "You all right, Van?"

"I'm fine, Frank. The other engine seems O.K."

Harvey nodded and raised his face mask. "Moonglow Leader to Blue Leader. Take 'em home, Millburn. I'm staying with F-Freddy."

There was an immediate protest from the South African. "I'm O.K., Frank. The Spitties are giving me an escort."

It was never Harvey's way to leave a comrade if it could be avoided — a sentiment that had nearly cost him his life more than once — and with Millburn leading the remaining Mosquitoes into the clouds, the Yorkshireman knew they were in good hands. To draw attention away from his behaviour, he threw a crack at the

Spitfire pilot who had appeared above Van Breedenkamp. “You can’t rely on these Brylcreem boys. They’re all wind and piss.”

A chuckle answered him. “Jealousy will get you nowhere, Moonglow Leader. Not everyone can be brave and handsome.”

As Harvey struggled to find an answer to that, the clouds closed around the three aircraft, leaving the valley below to the dead, the dying, and the partisans who were hurrying the surviving prisoners of war into the shelter of the woods.

Sam gave a bark. Anna raised her head from the open book on her knee. “What is it, Sam?”

The dog gave another bark, then rose to its feet. For a moment the girl could hear nothing. Then, as the dog barked yet again and wagged its tail, she heard the far-off sound of aircraft engines. With a cry she ran to the window. As she threw it open the distant hum sounded louder.

The cloud cover had lifted during the morning, but still reached to the horizon. As Anna strained her eyes, tiny specks began to appear beneath it. As she blinked hard and stared again, the specks began to grow wings. Beside her, Sam whimpered and tried to reach up to the open window.

A girl’s shout sounded below. Maisie had now heard the engines and was telling Joe Kearns that the squadron was returning. Across on the airfield a tannoy rasped a message and truck engines began firing. A moment later an ambulance and two fire tenders moved into position.

The specks were clearly aircraft now, and approaching fast. Below, Maisie was already standing at the front gate, ready to give her customary welcome to the returning crews. Patting the excited Sam, Anna leaned from the window and began to count them. One ... two ... three ... four ... five ... six. For a moment her heart stopped, then her mind sought relief. Aircraft could not fly in formation in cloud. The other two would appear shortly.

Reaching Bishops Wood, the six Mosquitoes peeled away and began to orbit the airfield. As each in turn passed over the pub, revealing its battle scars, Anna tried to read its identification letters.

When the last one had completed its orbit and was making preparations to land, her face was pale and strained.

At the gate below, Maisie's quick glance at the bedroom window showed that she too had noticed Harvey's absence. Unlike her normal behaviour, she stayed at the gate until all six aircraft had landed and the sounds of engines had died away. When she finally turned away and walked slowly back into the pub, the act seemed to suggest to the watching Anna that all hope had gone.

For a full minute the German girl felt stunned and panic stricken. Then, calling on all her courage, she pulled away from the window and made her way downstairs. As she entered the hall Maisie appeared. Without a word she ran towards Anna and threw her arms around her.

For a moment neither girl spoke. Then, with a final sympathetic squeeze, Maisie drew back. "It could be anything, luv. He might have had to land at an emergency airfield. And even if he didn't get back he could be a prisoner of war. Don't think the worst yet."

Anna nodded. "May I use the phone? I want to ring the airfield."

"'Course you can, luv, although it might be a bit soon for them to have any news."

Joe Kearns appeared in a doorway as Anna made the call. After a minute she put down the receiver. "It's no use. They haven't restored communications. I'll have to try later."

"Can I get you anything, Mrs Harvey?" Kearns asked. "I've got a bottle of brandy under the counter."

Anna managed a smile. "No, thank you. But I will have a cup of coffee later, if I may."

"Of course you can, lass. You can have anything you like. But try not to worry. We've had scares like this before and they've often been for nought."

There was a muted sound from Sam. The dog had followed Anna downstairs and was looking up at her with brown, puzzled eyes. She managed a laugh as she bent down to pat him. "Poor Sam. He doesn't know what's going on, does he? I'll take him back to my room and give him a biscuit."

As she vanished up the stairs Kearns turned to Maisie. "She's taking it well. I thought she'd be shattered."

Maisie gave a scornful laugh. "She is shattered. But she's been through so much she's learned to hide her feelings."

Kearns shook his head. "They should never have brought Frank back. It was asking for bad luck."

Upstairs Anna had returned to the window. A breeze was stirring the dry leaves of the crab apples and sending a few fluttering to the ground. The sight sent a shiver through her. Maisie's sympathy, although well intended, had emphasised the nature and depth of her fear; she was racked by a dozen emotions.

Among them was anger. Frank had done treble his share of combat operations. He had lived on borrowed time for years. Davies himself had admitted as much and withdrawn him from combat. Yet it had been Davies who had recalled him when at least two men on the squadron were just as fully equipped to lead the mission.

But her anger was not limited to Davies. In the illogical way the mind works when under stress, it was also directed at Harvey. He need not have agreed to Davies' request. If he had refused it, no one would have blamed him. She had begged him not to go, and he had ignored her. Damn him. Damn him for putting his sense of duty before his love for her.

She stood at the window, her beautiful face pale, while emotion fought against emotion. Remorse and guilt followed swiftly on her anger. Frank's reason for accepting the mission had nothing to do with duty, but had been all about friendship and integrity. At the risk of his own life, Ian Moore had given the two of them the chance of a life together. To Frank that meant a debt that must be repaid if the chance ever came. The chance had come and so he had been left with no option. Some men could live with their betrayed consciences but never Frank.

Gazing at the airfield, she tried to remember Maisie's words. The girl was right. There could be other reasons why Frank had not returned. But as she watched the reduced activity on the airfield, with its suggestion the Squadron was resigned to four more casualties, her sense of foreboding grew. Was he dead, the man she had slept with only two nights before and whose strength and warmth had filled her world? Could life be so cruel as to give them the illusion of security after months of fear and separation, only to snatch it away? The knowledge that it could, that human happiness and suffering were mere playthings for the gods, did nothing to lighten her fears.

Maisie's arrival with a cup of coffee turned her from the window. "Here you are, luv. Drink it while it's hot. And try not to worry. I'm sure Frank is all right."

Left alone again, Anna noticed a flavour of brandy as she sipped the coffee: either Kearns or Maisie had decided a little medication could do no harm. As she finished the drink and put it aside she noticed that Sam was lying with his head on his paws and gazing plaintively up at her. Dropping on her knees she began stroking the animal. Her words were to comfort herself as much as the dog. "It's all right, Sam. Your master is coming back. He must come back."

The sound of the telephone downstairs made her pause and listen. She heard Maisie's voice but not what she was saying. Then there was a cry from the foot of the stairs. "Mrs Harvey, it's for you. It's Frank Adams from the airfield."

She flew downstairs and grabbed up the receiver. Her heart was hammering so hard she had to take a long deep breath before she could speak. "Yes, Frank. What is it? What's happened?"

The silence that followed seemed to stretch into minutes for the two onlookers. As Anna's eyes momentarily closed, Maisie winced and moved nearer the girl. Seeing her cheeks grow even paler, Maisie was about to lay a hand on her arm when Anna broke the silence. "Thank you for thinking about me, Frank. I'm very grateful."

She returned the receiver and stood motionless for a moment. Then she turned to the anxious couple and gave them a tight smile. "It's all right. Frank had to land at an emergency landing field with one of his crews who'd received damage. He's on his way back now."

For once, Joe Kearns forgot his Yorkshire phlegm. "Thank God for that, lass."

She turned her grey eyes on the innkeeper. "Yes, it is good news, isn't it? I was beginning to think he was missing."

"It's splendid news, lass. We're both delighted for you."

“Thank you. You’ve both been very kind.” Giving them another smile, the girl moved towards the stairs. “I don’t expect it’ll be long before Frank gets back. So I think I’ll go and change. Come along, Sam. Your master will be home soon.”

They both watched her tall, elegant figure disappear up the staircase. Maisie’s laugh was one of pure delight. “A bit of good news for once. Ain’t that a change? But didn’t she take it all like a trouper?”

Kearns, a widower and a romantic beneath his rough-hewn Yorkshire veneer, shook his head. “She’s one in a million all right. And to think she’s one of the people we’re fighting. None of it makes any sense, does it, lass?”

Chapter 10

Harvey wasted no time orbiting the airfield on his return. Instead he swooped in low and touched down with screaming tyres. Ignoring signals from his crew on D-Danny's hard standing, he revved his engine and sent the Mosquito bounding towards Adams' Confessional. Braking, with a terse comment to Carter, he dropped from the plane and started walking towards the Nissen hut like a bear on the rampage.

The hut was empty but for Davies, Henderson, Adams and Sue Spencer. The rest of the crews had been interrogated and sent off for a meal. Before any of the senior officers could speak, Harvey took the offensive to Davies. "Did Millburn tell you what those damned partisans did?"

With Davies dismayed himself at the news, conflict between the two men was inevitable. "I've heard, yes. But what about some politeness to a higher ranking officer?"

In Harvey's present mood, the presence of the King of England wouldn't have changed his tone. "The bastards mined the road. Didn't London warn you?"

"No, London didn't. They probably didn't know. But that doesn't mean you have to behave like a dog with a sore arse. What's the matter with you?"

A large vein was visible on Harvey's forehead as he fought for control. "Moore might have been in that first truck. If he was, it's ten to one he's dead."

Although sharing the Yorkshireman's feelings, Adams tried to pour oil on troubled waters. "There were two other prisoner of war transports, Frank. We must hope Moore was in one of them."

Harvey swung round on him. "If he was, it's no thanks to the partisans, is it? I felt like strafing the bastards when I saw what they'd done."

With his fears confirmed, Henderson added his own protest. "They should have told us, sir. It was a reckless thing to do."

Davies frowned. "Now don't you start, Jock. They probably did it to delay the flak wagon while they mined the bridge. And then someone fired the charge too late." Then, noticing the expressions of the three men, Davies found the grace to make a concession. "But I agree that we should have been told."

"Too true we should." It was Harvey again. "They've conned us right down the line. They didn't mine that road to give protection to their men on the bridge. That was our job. I think they had another reason."

"What other reason?"

"There were two trucks in the convoy that weren't carrying prisoners. I think they wanted them so much that they took a chance with our men."

Davies was showing curiosity now. "Millburn mentioned two trucks. What do you think they were carrying?"

"I don't know. But I could see the partisans swarming all over them before we left."

"So you think they mined the road as an extra precaution?" Adams asked.

Harvey nodded. "That's how I saw it. To make certain the flak wagon was out of action and the road blocked." As he spoke, Harvey's anger returned. "Then the stupid sods exploded the charge too late and killed our men in the first truck."

Henderson was looking puzzled. "But in that case why did they ask for our help?"

"I suppose they still wanted us to knock out the bridge gunposts. Maybe they weren't certain the mine would disable the flak wagon. Or maybe they felt we ought to be on it because it was our men they were rescuing. Whatever it was, I hope London gives them hell."

The mystery was cooling Davies's temper. "Perhaps I'll find out more when I've spoken to the Brigadier. But in the meantime we've all got to remember that Moore still has a two-thirds chance of survival and of getting back to England."

Harvey eyed him bitterly. "You think that's good enough, sir?"

Davies's testiness returned. "It's better than most chances we get in wartime. So stop bellyaching and go and get your meal. It might bring your temper back. You can give your report to Adams later."

About to reply, Harvey caught Henderson's warning glance. He paused in the doorway. "How long will it be before we hear about Moore, sir?"

"How the hell do I know? A day? A month? Who can say?"

As Harvey nodded and disappeared through the door, Davies swung round on Henderson. "I want you to talk to that character about his manners and his discipline. Otherwise he's going to find himself in serious trouble." Henderson sighed. "I'm very sorry, sir. But he's worried about Moore. They were very close friends."

"For Christ's sake, do you think I don't know that? It's the only reason I'm not having him cashiered."

At that moment Adams remembered. Excusing himself, he ran to the doorway and shouted at Harvey who was making for his aircraft. "Frank! Hold on a minute."

As the Yorkshireman paused, Adams hurried up to him. "I forgot to tell you. I phoned Anna when communications were restored."

Still living with his dismay at the morning's happenings, Harvey looked puzzled. "What for?"

"I told her why you hadn't come back with the others. She had noticed."

Harvey gave a violent start. "Christ, yes. I hadn't thought about that. How was she?"

"I'm sure she'd been worried. But she's all right now."

"Why didn't I think of that? Thanks, Frank. I'd better get over to her right away."

Adams held up a protesting hand. "Not yet. You've still got your report to give me. Davies only needs one more excuse and he'll shoot you straight back to Padgate."

Harvey hesitated. "You are sure Anna's O.K.?"

"Yes. I told her you were quite safe."

The Yorkshireman relaxed. "All right. I'll see you after I've got this kite parked and had a bite to eat. In the meantime, tell the little sod I don't like him around and the sooner he pisses off back to Group Headquarters the better."

Relieved, Adams smiled. "I'll tell him. I know he'll appreciate your advice. See you in half an hour."

Harvey muttered something and stirred in his sleep. Anna, wide awake, turned to look at him. With the moonlight flooding through the uncurtained window and laying a silver pool over the bed, she could see his face clearly. His eyes were twitching and there was sweat on his forehead. As he muttered something again and shifted uneasily, she knew he was having a bad dream or the beginning of a nightmare.

She wondered whether it would be kinder to awaken him or let him sleep. Although so far he had refused to discuss the major details of the operation with her, his appearance on arriving at the inn and his behaviour afterwards had convinced her that something traumatic had happened. Harvey seldom if ever drank in excess when with her, and yet that evening he had drunk more than she could remember.

As a consequence he had fallen asleep almost immediately when they had retired. But now it seemed that alcohol was no longer able to hold some private nightmare at bay.

Unsure of what to do, she watched him as his lips moved again. Touching his shoulder, she found that his pyjamas were damp with sweat. A moment later he gave a sharp cry and jerked upright.

For a moment his eyes were full of his nightmare and showed bewilderment when they turned on her. Then memory returned and his sweating body relaxed. "Sorry, love. I must have been dreaming."

She badly needed to know what had happened that morning. "It must have been a bad dream. You've been talking in your sleep for the last few minutes."

He frowned. "What did I say?"

"I couldn't tell. But you were very upset. What happened this morning, Frank? Something went wrong, didn't it? Don't you think you should tell me?"

He dropped back on his pillow. "We did our job and the partisans got away with our men. What else is there to tell?"

"Something else happened. I know it. Otherwise why were you so upset when you came over here?"

In the silence that followed she heard the distant clang of metal and the scream of an electric drill. Mechanics at the airfield were working late to carry out repairs on the damaged aircraft. "I'll find out, you know," she said when he failed to answer. "I'll get Frank Adams to tell me if you won't. Had it anything to do with Ian?"

He gave a muffled curse, then reached out for a cigarette. He exhaled a cloud of smoke at the ceiling before answering her. "Yes, I suppose so. I'm just hoping he's all right."

Up to that moment she had believed Moore was relatively safe in the hands of the partisans. "Why are you worried? Don't you think he'll get away?"

He exhaled smoke again. "No, it's not that." Reluctantly, in a few brief sentences that omitted most of his part in the operation, he told her about the accident to the truckload of prisoners. "London should have been told what they intended to do. Then we could have pointed out the risks to the prisoners."

The news that Moore might be dead had made her wince and catch her breath and it took her a moment to ask her question. "Were there many prisoners in that first truck?"

"Enough. Perhaps nine to a dozen."

"And you think they were all killed?"

"Not all. Maybe a few survived. But they all looked in a bad way."

She winced again, then laid a hand on his arm. "It wasn't your fault, Frank. You did all you could do."

He blew smoke at the ceiling again. "That's not going to help anybody if Ian's dead, is it?"

She was still coming to terms with the news when he went on: "It was all so unnecessary. We'd been given the job of knocking out the flak wagon, and if they'd left well alone all the prisoners would have been rescued. Instead they mined the road, and this is the result."

Although part of her was still shocked, training from years of war allowed her quick mind to run through the permutations. "Perhaps the two extra trucks were put into the convoy at the last moment, which wouldn't have given the partisans time to contact London. Perhaps the mining was carried out at the last moment."

"What, with the sentries on the bridge watching them?"

"They might have done it during darkness the previous night."

He shifted restlessly. "It's possible, I suppose, but if so, what the hell was in those wagons that's so important?"

"You have told all this to Davies?"

For a moment wry humour entered his voice. "You're not kidding. It's a miracle I'm not in the glass house."

"You didn't blame him, did you?"

"I told him I wasn't too pleased about the operation. He didn't take it too well."

She tried to laugh at his understatement. "If the partisans did it without telling London, Davies is hardly to blame."

He reached out and pinched her cheek. "Don't defend his hare-brained schemes to me. You know what I think about them."

Grateful for his change of mood, she caught his hand and kissed it. "None of this was your fault, so try to forget about it. Try to get some sleep."

As he drew on his cigarette again, she knew how unlikely that was. With the effects of alcohol wearing off, tension was like a coiled spring inside him. She kissed him on the mouth and then drew off her nightgown. As she lay back on the bed, the moonlight made a monochrome picture of her dark hair, shapely breasts and long slender legs. Seeing his eyes on her, she reached out and drew him nearer. As her legs intertwined with his, she felt his desire rising but as he moved to cover her she pushed him gently back. "No, Liebling. You are tired tonight. Let me love you."

For a moment he protested but then his fatigue overcame him. He lay back, staring up at her as she threw a slender leg over him. Bending down she kissed him again and then her shapely body began to move rhythmically to his mounting passion. As he tried to speak, she laid a soft hand over his mouth.

The end came swiftly, his powerful body jerking and spasming. Slipping back beside him, she kissed him again. "Now go to sleep," she whispered. "Think of nothing but that I love you."

In the moonlight his eyes were dark and grateful as he gazed at her. Then they closed and a few seconds later his steady breathing told her he had been released, if only for a while, from his fears.

She lay back and gazed at the dark ceiling. The news about Moore had come as a great shock to her: she had surprised herself by hiding so much of it from Harvey. The knowledge of what it meant made her feel almost ashamed. Surely she did not believe a man of Harvey's character would feel jealous over a friend who might have been killed that day? The very thought seemed unworthy of them both.

Yet the fact she had done it must have its reasons. The more she thought about it, the more the irony denied her sleep. On hearing Moore was alive and there was the possibility of his rescue, Harvey had jumped at the chance to help. He had returned half-sick with the fear Moore might have been killed. Yet if Moore returned to the station and she gave any excessive indication of her relief and affection, might not Harvey's old jealousies return and perhaps imperil the very thing he valued most, her love? That surely was the fear that had prompted her behaviour. There seemed no escape, she thought, from the distortions and tortures inflicted by the emotions on the human mind.

But would Moore return? Not if fate had included him with the other unfortunates on that first truck. Until a few days ago they had all believed him dead and had learned to live with the loss. Then hope had been restored, only to be suspended again. The gods were playing their sadistic tricks once more, she thought, as pain closed her eyes.

But one thought only led to another as the long night wore on. Even if Ian did return, who would lead the squadron? She knew that escaped aircrew prisoners of war were seldom allowed to fly over Europe again. The danger was too great that, if captured a second time, they might reveal under torture the identity of their rescuers. Millburn had temporarily led the squadron after Mitchell's death, and yet Davies had brought Frank back to lead the rescue operation. Did that mean Frank was ear-marked for the post that he had once wanted so much? Were all those days of tension and fear to begin again? Or had this been a one-off mission and would he be given his well-earned rest once more?

Unable to quantify her thoughts and fears, Anna lay awake while the moonlight slid away from the bed and the first light of dawn appeared in the window. It was only then that she fell into a fitful sleep.

Chapter 11

There was no rest for the squadron in the days that followed. The short-winged, stubby V1 rockets that had first appeared over the South of England in early June were now reaching as far as London. Alarmed by the destructive potential of these flying bombs, which was causing a second evacuation of children from the capital, Churchill had ordered all available fighters and fighter-bombers to counter attack the new weapon.

The main targets were the launching rails sited on the Dutch and Belgium coasts. Other options, although less easily attained, were to catch the V1s during their flight over the Channel and destroy them either by cannon fire or by tipping their stubby wings and setting them off in a less harmful direction.

Because the latter options were more suited to Typhoon squadrons, with their massive supercharged engines, 633 Squadron was given the task of attacking the launching sites. Day after day flight after flight was sent out to bomb and strafe the sinister launching rails that pointed towards the English mainland. Here and there men grumbled at a task that seemed more suited to front line squadrons than to an elite group formed for special assignments, yet in his heart every man knew the importance of destroying weapons that were threatening the heartland of his nation.

Nor was the task without its risks. Launching sites were heavily defended and Mosquito after Mosquito returned to Sutton Craddock with battle damage. On the third day of the assault, Mason and Little failed to return. The task was no sinecure, as Millburn and Gabby were reminded on the fourth day of the assault. As T-Tommy began her shallow dive towards the circle of huts that ringed a launching platform, lines of coloured shells suddenly soared up and flashed past the perspex canopy. A second later an explosion made the Mosquito kick like a badly-handed mule. As more exploding shells peppered the sky ahead of the diving T-Tommy, Gabby's yell came over the sound of the screaming engines. "Jesus Christ, watch it, boyo. They're throwing the bloody book at us."

As if to confirm his words, a shell burst directly ahead, cracking the perspex and filling the cockpit with acrid smoke. Gritting his teeth, Millburn held the Mosquito on course through the hail of bullets and shells until the launching rails and huts were large in his sights. Then, yelling at Gabby, he opened fire with his 20 mm cannon. At the same time, Gabby pressed the bomb tit and T-Tommy bounced four times as its 250 GPs fell at one-second intervals.

Although Millburn tried to fox the ground gunners by flying low instead of climbing, bullets still smashed into the back of his armour-plated seat as he banked away and screamed through the side of the cockpit. Then, like heavy doors slamming in an empty house, four explosions sounded and the hail of fire ceased. Seeing dense smoke covering the site, Millburn wiped his sweating face and turned to Gabby. "You O.K.?"

Gabby was looking shattered. "No, I'm bloody not. Do you always have to be the first to go in?"

With the smoke blowing away, Millburn could now see one hut was on fire and the launching rails were bent and twisted. He spoke to the two Mosquitoes circling above him. "O.K. you guys. Finish the job and let's go home."

As the other Mosquitoes, relieved of defensive fire, swooped down to demolish the rest of the site, Millburn turned to Gabby. "How else could we do it? I'm supposed to be the leader. I can't give the job to some other guy, can I?"

The shaken Gabby clearly did not agree. "Why not? Montgomery doesn't lead in the first tank, does he? Churchill doesn't march ahead of his army. So why must we always take the shit?" When Millburn made no reply, Gabby motioned at the pilot's armoured seat. "Do you realise what would have happened to me if it had been my seat instead of yours?"

Although Millburn had been shaken himself by their near escape, his resilience showed in a broad grin. The fact that only pilots' seats were armoured in Mosquitoes was a perpetual source of complaint from navigators and Gabby was no exception. "You'd be down there having those pitchforks stuck up your ass. So aren't you lucky?"

"Lucky? I'm putting in for a transfer when we get back. I want a pilot with something between his ears, not a bloody stupid Yank who wants to be a hero."

"Quit bellyaching, you little punk, and get your maps out. We'll be crossing the coast in five minutes."

While Gabby sullenly obeyed, Millburn switched on his R/T. "O.K. you guys. The job's over. Let's go home."

With German air power mainly concentrated further inland against the daily Allied pounding of troops and communications, the main threat left to Millburn and his flight were the coastal defences. Crossing them safely, Millburn took his crews straight back to Sutton Craddock. There, after giving their reports to Adams, the six men were told they could stand down for the day.

Gabby flung his flying suit into a corner of the hut and dropped on his bed. "Two jobs yesterday and another two today. What do they think we are? Supermen?"

Millburn, who shared the same two-man billet, grinned as he lay back on the other bed. "They're taking you at your word, boyo. Isn't that what you always told Gwen Thomas? She must have spread the word around."

Gabby scowled. "I haven't had a date with Gwen Thomas since you buggered things up for me. I haven't forgotten that, Millburn."

"I'll bet you haven't, boyo. The two of you looked really something when you came prancing out of that hut."

Gabby's scowl deepened. "Why don't you go over to the Yanks, Millburn? Think of the medals you could get. They get one for every op, don't they?"

"Jealousy'll get you nowhere, boyo. The Yanks are doing all right. Remember how they looked after us over Copenhagen? And over the Loire. You're full of sour grapes, kiddo."

"All right, why don't you join 'em? Then I might get a pilot who has a brain between his ears instead of between his legs."

At that moment there was a tap on the door and an MP appeared. Carrying a large parcel he offered it to Millburn. "This was dropped into the guardroom today by an American, sir. It's for you."

As he saluted and left, Millburn examined the parcel curiously. Gabby, now sitting up on his bed, looked equally curious. "What is it? A parcel from a girl friend?"

Millburn shook his head. "I went to see the guys at that Yank airfield near Selby last week. Some of them must have clubbed together and sent it."

"What the hell for? Did you say we didn't feed you or something?"

Millburn was tearing the brown paper from the parcel. A moment later he pulled out a huge carton of cigarettes. "Lucky Strike! Hey, those guys. They remembered what I smoke. And look — two tins of candy. This is really something."

Gabby gave a sniff of envy. "You must have shot them a hell of a line. Poor bloody Yank roughing it with the British. Haven't you any shame?"

Millburn was still digging into the parcel. "Wait a minute. What about this, boyo? What about this?"

Gabby goggled as the tousle-headed American pulled out a pair of transparent tubes and dangled them before him. The Welshman's voice turned hoarse. "They're stockings, aren't they? Girls' stockings. My God."

Millburn gave a triumphant laugh. "That's what they are, boyo. Real silk stockings. Two pairs. You know what girls'll do for these things, don't you?"

"Did you say two pairs?"

"That's right. Two lovely pairs of silk stockings."

Gabby jumped off his bed and held out a supplicating hand. "You're going to give me one pair, aren't you? We've always shared things before."

Millburn snatched the stockings away. "Are you kidding? These are for emergencies. There's always one broad who does as mummy says and shakes her head. One look at these and the battle's over."

"Just one pair," Gabby begged. "I'll give you a quid for them."

"A quid? I wouldn't sell 'em for a hundred. And don't get any ideas about pinching them, you little creep. Or I'll have your guts for garters."

The Welshman watched Millburn put the parcel's contents into his locker and turn the key. "You're mean, Millburn. Mean through and through."

Millburn grinned as he pocketed the key. "That's right. I'm the meanest guy in the RAF. You remember it."

Searching for a way of punishing him, Gabby suddenly found it. "You can't go out for the next couple of nights, can you?"

Millburn frowned. The extra duties involved in his role of Squadron Commander had put a premium on his free evenings. "No. So what?"

"That's what I told Susan. So I said I'd take her to the flicks tomorrow night. I said you wouldn't mind."

Susan was an ash blonde the two men had met for the first time at a dance in Highgate the previous week. Sophisticated, high-spirited, with a figure to match her good looks, she had drawn both men like bees to a honeypot. Millburn's frown deepened. "When did you see Susan?"

"I ran into her in a pub on Monday night. I told her you had to put your duties first but I'd be happy to help out."

Millburn was beginning to smoke. "You're a sneaky little creep, aren't you? You took advantage of this promotion they gave me."

"All's fair in love and war. You've said it yourself often enough."

Millburn glared at him, then shook his head. "You won't get anywhere with Susan. She's too sophisticated. She's used to champagne and caviar, not fish and chips."

"So what? There are restaurants in Highgate, aren't there? And in Scarborough."

"You wouldn't know what to do in a decent restaurant. Anyway, she likes real men, not puny Welsh gremlins."

Gabby smirked. "Haven't you heard what they say about smaller men? I think she has, because she jumped at the chance."

"I don't believe a word you're saying. Susan never gave you a second look at that dance."

"Yes, she did. Only you're so conceited you never noticed. I'm taking her out, Millburn, and I'll lay you odds she goes with me to Bishops Wood after the flicks."

"She might let you spend your money on her but she'll never let you take her necking. Anyway, how do you think you're going to get to Bishops Wood? You're not borrowing my car again."

"I don't need your car. I'm borrowing Lindsay's."

Millburn guffawed. "That little Austin Seven? You're not going to turn her head by taking her out in a baby carriage."

Gabby smirked again. "I don't need an MG to turn a girl's head, Millburn. I'll take her to Bishops Wood and you know what'll happen there."

Seeing the big American rise to his feet, Gabby moved hastily towards the door. "I'm going to the Mess for a drink. Think about Susan and tomorrow night while I'm gone."

He disappeared through the door before Millburn could react. A moment passed and then the American's expression changed. Taking a writing pad from his locker, he began a letter. It appeared a difficult one to write because he tore up two attempts before he was satisfied. Then he sealed it in an envelope, scribbled an address on it, and took it across to his flight office where a young LAC was on duty. "I want you to take this into Highgate on the next transport that goes there, and deliver it to this address. Don't wait for a reply because there won't be one. O.K.?"

The LAC nodded and saluted. As Millburn started the walk back to his billet he noticed a passing mechanic staring at him. It was only then the American realised he was laughing.

To Anna's relief and surprise, Harvey was not included in these V1 raids. With Millburn back in his role as temporary Squadron Commander, Harvey, to his indignation, was told to aid Adams and other specialist officers in defining targets and briefing the crews. Although, since her return to The Black Swan, Anna had not yet met Davies, whom she knew well enough from the Rhine Maiden days, it did seem as if the Air Commodore, after his one aberration, was now keeping his promise to rest the Yorkshireman from combat duties. She wanted to believe it, but at the same time could not understand why Davies was keeping Harvey at the Station. Until the mystery was resolved, in spite of Harvey's protests, she decided to stay on at The Black Swan.

Davies returned to the squadron six days after the attack on the road convoy. Having received a warning of his visit this time, Henderson met him on the steps of the Administration Block. Wearing a white flying suit and walking with haste, Davies had the expression of a man bearing good news. His first cheerful words seemed to confirm it. "What is it, Jock? Are you waiting to escort me past that WAAF of yours?"

Henderson grinned as he steered the diminutive Air Commodore past the closed door of Laura's office. "I thought it might be wise, sir. She seems to like close contact with you."

Davies had a recollection of Laura's vital statistics. "I wouldn't mind close contact with her, Jock, if she wouldn't overplay her hand. I've still got a bloody great bruise on my arse."

It was a remark that added to Henderson's expectancy of good news to come. "It must be her country background, sir. She's probably used to wrestling with big farm labourers."

"I wouldn't be surprised," Davies grunted. "And I wouldn't be surprised if she won, either." As they entered Henderson's office, he nodded at the door. "Shut it, Jock. I've some news for you."

Henderson quickly obeyed. As he turned, Davies, looking like a pleased elf, could conceal his news no longer. "It's all right, Jock. The operation was successful and Moore's alive. London got the news this morning."

The Scot took a deep breath. "Thank the lord for that. When will they get him home?"

"They can't say at the moment. But hopefully it won't be long. Then we might hear what Jerry's up to."

"What about the two trucks Harvey mentioned? The ones that caused the cock-up. Have the partisans said what they were carrying?"

"Yes, we heard that too. They were carrying drugs."

"Drugs?"

"Yes, it seemed that Jerry had captured a large consignment of medical kit including quinine, sulpha drugs and this new wonder drug penicillin and decided at the last minute to send it with the convoy. It explains the partisans' behaviour. They had to make certain of re-capturing the stuff. I also think it's likely they wanted some of it for themselves. So they mined the road during the previous night."

Henderson grinned. "I hope we can tell this to Harvey. It might make him feel less homicidal towards them."

Davies's expression changed. "I'm wondering what to do with that bloody-minded character. How do you feel about returning him to flying duties?" The question clearly worried Henderson. "I'd like to, sir. To be honest he's the best flight commander any CO could have. But he has done more than his share of ops. I think he ought to go back to the OTU. Don't you feel the same way?"

Davies gave a sarcastic grunt. "If you want to know what I feel, I'd like to hand him over to the Jerries. With him arguing with their Luftwaffe Commanders, we'd win the bloody air war in weeks." As Henderson hid a grin, Davies went on: "But I have to admit he's a good man in the air. So I'm keeping my options open at the moment. We don't know what news Moore is bringing us. If it's as serious as London thinks, we might need every experienced man we've got. There's another factor to consider. We don't know yet whether we'll be allowed to use Moore for combat duties."

Henderson nodded. "I wondered about that, sir. Who decides that?"

"It's a directive that comes from the top. So I might have to do some fast footwork if I'm to get him clearance."

Not for the first time Henderson found Davies's enthusiasm bordering on ruthlessness. "Surely Moore should have some say in it. After all, he'd face torture if he was shot down again."

Davies waved an impatient hand. "Of course he'd have a say. But if I know Moore I know what his answer would be."

When the Scot didn't reply, Davies grew impatient. "What's the alternative, Jock? Do you want another outsider bringing in?"

"Why couldn't I go on using Millburn? He's got all the experience we need."

"Millburn's a fine pilot but he's so bloody reckless. You might need a steadier character at the helm if this job turns out to be a big one."

Henderson felt the conversation was leading him down an inevitable path. "You're talking about someone like Harvey, aren't you?"

Davies shrugged. "Now do you see why we must keep him? If I can't get permission for Moore to fly again, we'll have to use him."

Henderson sighed at the brutal facts of war. "So he has to stay with us for the moment?" When Davies nodded, the Scot went on: "I suppose I can tell him that Moore is safe?"

"I don't know about that. Jerry will be looking for the escapees as it is. We don't want 'em pepping up their search if they think Moore's return is all that important."

"Harvey won't talk, sir. The two men are friends."

Davies capitulated with as much grace as possible. "Oh, all right. Tell just Harvey and Adams. We'll break the good news to the rest of the boys when Moore's safely back in England."

At that moment there was the roar of Merlin engines as a Mosquito took off on an air test. Taking a look from the window, Henderson glanced back at Davies. "I suppose we have to continue with these flying bomb raids until we hear more from you, sir?"

"I'm afraid you have, Jock. I know it's a bind for a special service squadron like you to be doing this bread and butter stuff, but we're having to throw in every kite we can to limit the damage. However, if Moore comes back with the news we're expecting, who knows, you might be back on the glamour trail again. Let's hope so."

"Glamour trail" was not exactly the expression Henderson would have used for the exacting missions Davies gave his men, but he made no comment as Davies picked up his cap from the desk. "I'll have to go now, Jock. But I'll be in touch the moment Moore gets back."

Henderson watched the Air Commodore's Miles Master climb into the sky before entering his WAAF's office. "Get hold of Squadron Leader Harvey and Squadron Leader Adams for me, will you, Laura? Tell them I want them in my office right away."

Chapter 12

The tiny Austin Seven bumped and rocked along the rutted foresters' path, its headlight swinging wildly among the surrounding trees. The blond, nubile girl in sweater and skirt who was seated alongside Gabby gave a cry of complaint as she clung to her seat. "Where on earth are you taking me?"

Gabby patted her knee. "Not much further, love."

"But why must we go so far?"

"You'll see in a minute."

The path swung to the right. As it straightened, the car headlights illuminated a stretch of grass by the roadside. Satisfied, Gabby drove on to it and switched off the engine and headlights, leaving the wood in faint moonlight. Before he could speak, the girl turned towards him. "What's so special about this place?"

Gabby put a finger to his lips. "It's the nightingale."

"The what?"

"The nightingale. It sings here almost every night."

Susan, with a distinct upper-class accent, gave a titter of amusement. "There aren't any nightingales in these parts, you silly man. Wherever did you get that idea from?"

Gabby was fast realising he would need to adapt his usual patter for this girl. Sliding a casual arm around her, he grinned. "I didn't really think you'd fall for it. You're something special, Susan. You really are. Millburn thought the same."

From Susan's sudden interest Gabby inwardly cursed his mistake.

"Tommy's very good looking, isn't he? Did you say he's your pilot?"

Gabby decided he was doing Millburn no favours tonight. "Yes, and a bloody bad one at that. I've got to keep an eye on him all the time."

"But aren't pilots in charge of aeroplanes?"

"Pilots? You're joking. It's the navigators who're in charge. We do everything: tell the pilots where to go, identify the targets, drop the bombs ... The pilots are only drivers. And Millburn's a lousy driver at that."

"I still think he's very good looking."

Gabby scowled. "He's a show off, like all Americans."

"But I like Americans. They're polite and generous."

"You're kidding. Millburn isn't generous. He wouldn't even lend me his car tonight."

The girl's eyes twinkled. "Perhaps he didn't want you to take me out."

"No, he's just mean, that's all. You'd do well to keep clear of him." Deciding that was more than enough of Millburn, Gabby tightened his arm around her shoulders. "You know something? I couldn't keep my eyes off you at that dance."

"Couldn't you?" she said. "Really?"

Gabby took a tentative nibble of her neck. "Really. I even dreamed about you that night."

"You did? What did you dream?"

"I saw you dancing before me and didn't want to wake up. You know why?"

She shook her head. Gabby kissed her neck again and when she offered no resistance, decided his next move was on. "You hadn't any clothes on. Not a stitch."

"No clothes on? Gabby! You do have naughty dreams, don't you?"

"You looked gorgeous. That's when I knew I had to see you again."

"What — without any clothes on?"

Deciding the omens were excellent, Gabby slid his hand up her tight-fitting jumper to the back of her bra. "I've had the same dream every night since. And it's driving me crazy. You're so beautiful."

"Am I now?"

"No question about it. You're the most beautiful girl I've ever met." Although her bra was tight and he was working with only one hand, Gabby managed to unloosen the strap. As she gave a muted giggle, he turned and tried to pull off her sweater. For a moment she resisted him, then she allowed him to remove both sweater and bra.

"You're in luck tonight, aren't you?" she said.

With her charms exposed, Gabby was in no mood for small talk. As his lips sank between voluptuous hills of flesh, his voice took on a muffled sound. "I said you were gorgeous, didn't I?"

She laughed again, then began to struggle as his weight bore down on her. "Be careful. You're heavy. And something's sticking into my back."

Experience had taught Gabby to be prepared for all emergencies. Coming up for air, he dragged a blanket and an Air Force ground sheet from the rear seats and spread them out on the grass. "Why not be comfortable? The car's too small."

Amused, she climbed out. "So that's why you came here? I knew you were up to something, Johnnie Gabriel."

Eyes glinting like a stoat after a rabbit, Gabby followed her to the blanket. "Isn't that better? Now you can relax and enjoy yourself."

She laughed and lay back. "You're pretty sure of yourself, aren't you?"

With her half-naked body stretched out before him, Gabby felt enough time had been wasted. Throwing himself on top of the girl, he tried to remove her skirt and knickers. As he struggled, she caught his hand. "Just a minute. What are you up to now?"

Panting with passion by this time, Gabby muttered a curse as her skirt caught around her hips. "I want to see you like I saw you in my dream. Won't you give me a hand?"

"Is that all you want? Just to look at me?"

"Of course it is."

She gave a wriggle and the skirt slid down to her knees. The Welshman gave a final tug and both skirt and knickers came free. With eyes glowing like star shells, he dropped back on the girl, only for her to give a gasp of pain. "Why are you keeping your clothes on? Your buttons are hurting me."

With a muttered curse, Gabby sat up and tore off his jacket, kicked off his shoes, and slid off his trousers. As he flung himself back on the girl, she gave a sigh of pleasure. "That's better. You know, I really do like you, Gabby."

Gabby was too busy trying to solve the problem of a pair of tightly-locked legs to reply. As he struggled, she sighed again. "It's going to be wonderful when we're married, isn't it, darling?"

Gabby was too far gone to make sense of her words. "Don't talk, love. Just lie back and enjoy yourself."

"But I want to talk. I want to know how many children you would like."

This time the panting Gabby paused. "What was that?"

"I asked how many children you would like when we're married."

"Married? What are you talking about?"

"You are going to marry me, aren't you? You must now you've done this to me."

"Done what to you?"

"Ripped all my clothes off." Susan wriggled voluptuously beneath the startled Welshman. "I don't mind, darling. I don't mind one little bit. But you must marry me now. My brothers won't let me be compromised."

Gabby had the eerie feeling that suddenly this was a different girl to the one he had taken to the cinema. "I didn't know you had any brothers."

"Oh, yes. I've got four. Two in the Army, stationed in York, and the other two on Daddy's farm. Tony's there. He's the biggest. He's six foot four and very jealous of men who try to tamper with me. Tony has a terrible temper."

Dismay was now taking a heavy toll of Gabby's passion. "I haven't tampered with you. I've just taken you to the flicks and then for a ride."

"And then torn off my clothes. I don't know how things are in Wales, darling, but here that's called tampering."

With alarm bells ringing loudly in his ears, Gabby rose and began searching for his trousers. Susan looked disappointed. "You needn't get dressed, darling. It's all right as long as you're going to marry me."

Certain now that he had a screwball on his hands, Gabby was cursing his luck. "People don't get married just because they've had a bit of necking," he muttered. "You'd better get dressed and I'll take you home."

The girl sat upright. "Perhaps people don't in Wales. But in my family a girl doesn't give herself to a man unless he's made a commitment. And if he rapes her, he hasn't any choice."

Gabby gave a startled yelp. "Rape? What the hell are you talking about now?"

"You've raped me. Didn't you tear off all my clothes?"

"No, I damn well didn't. You helped me to take them off. And then wouldn't let me do anything."

"But you tried, didn't you? Isn't that the same as rape?"

"Of course it isn't. I didn't get near you."

"That's not what my brothers will believe."

By this time Gabby had a hearty dislike of her brothers. "Who cares what they believe? To hell with your brothers."

With an exclamation she leapt to her feet and snatched up her clothes. "That does it. It's easy to be brave now but wait until they get hold of you. Tony nearly killed a man once for just touching me."

"Sod Tony," Gabby muttered, buttoning up his trousers.

"I'll tell him you said that."

Realising he was only adding fuel to the flames, Gabby tried to control himself. Although believing she was psychologically unbalanced, he was also painfully aware that his sexual advances seemed to be the cause of her present behaviour. Which meant that if he couldn't find some way of calming her down, he was likely to find himself in police custody. Struggling to find a way, he said the first thing that came into his head. "In any case I couldn't marry you. I'm married already."

Her gasp of horror told him he could have said nothing worse. "That's awful! That's terrible! A married man and yet you raped me. When I tell that to Tony he really will go berserk."

"But I didn't rape you," Gabby yelled. "I didn't do anything."

"How can you say that after all that happened? Daddy always said I mustn't trust the RAF." A picture of outraged virtue, Susan pulled on her sweater and climbed into the car. As the dismayed Gabby climbed in after her, she began to cry. "I'm so ashamed. I thought you were a nice man and I could trust you. Now I feel awful."

Gabby gritted his teeth. "I'm taking you home."

"You'd better, Johnnie Gabriel. Right away. I can't wait to tell my brothers what you've done."

Gabby remembered little about the drive back to Highgate except that every now and then the girl would turn on him and issue new threats about his fate at the hands of her brothers. As he drew up at the end of the drive that ran to her house, she stared at him indignantly. "Why are you stopping here?"

"Go home, Susan," Gabby pleaded. "Please."

She jumped from the car. "You're afraid of facing my family, aren't you? Well, you should be. They'll never rest until they find you and punish you for what you've done."

With that she began marching down the drive. The incredulous Gabby sat watching her for a moment. Then, as she entered the house, he remembered his peril. Swinging the Austin round, he made for Sutton Craddock as if the entire Luftwaffe was on his tail.

Chapter 13

The roar of engines made the models of enemy aircraft dangling from the Intelligence Office ceiling tremble and sway. The noise brought Harvey to a window. He stood there until the last of the Mosquitoes was airborne, then turned back to Adams who was seated at a long table down the centre of the Nissen hut. "How long do you think they'll keep us on these raids, Frank?"

Adams glanced up. "It's my guess we'll be on them until Moore gets back. Always assuming he has any important news for us."

Frowning, Harvey dropped on the bench alongside him. "Doesn't it seem a bit far-fetched to you that he'd hear anything about secret weapons from Jerry aircrews?"

Adams, an inveterate pipe smoker, pulled out his pouch before replying. "I don't know. You have to remember that to the Jerries this is a famous squadron. So the capture of its Squadron Commander would be quite an event. Aircrews have always shown respect for one another and Ian would be a hero to them in much the same way that Bader was. So it's quite possible that one or two of them might have gossiped to him, if only to show off their own importance. After all, they'd never imagine he might escape."

Harvey nodded. "I can accept that, but I can't see Jerry allowing his aircrews any detailed knowledge of secret weapons. When have we been told anything about ours? It's too bloody dangerous in case we're shot down. So why should Jerry aircrews be any different?"

With his pipe bowl now filled, Adams applied a match. "In general terms it doesn't work that way, Frank. It's scraps of information our people work on. A bit here, a bit there — it's rather like assembling a jigsaw. The main factor is getting the first hint of a new weapon. Once that's known, agents can start hunting for the missing pieces."

"And they're hoping Ian might have a hint of what that weapon is?"

Adams pressed down on a rising flake of tobacco. "In this case it's just possible that he might have more than a hint. From what I can gather, there were some high ranking Air Force officers in the hospital with him. They might have had more information than the average aircrew. London's certainly gone to enough trouble to get him back."

Harvey glanced round to assure himself that Sue Spencer had not yet returned to the hut. "What's going to happen to him once he is back, Frank?"

Adams took the pipe from his mouth. "Do you mean what'll happen to his flying career?"

"Yes. They can't let him fly against the Jerries again. So what'll happen to him?"

Adams shook his head. "I've no idea. They might send him on a recruitment drive. Or they might send him to the Far East to fly against the Japs."

"The hell with that. Ian's done too much already. He needs a long rest."

So do you all, Adams was thinking. You and Moore were showing the strain before Operation Titan. Even Machin and Van Breedenkamp are showing it sometimes and they joined the squadron long after you. Adams returned the pipe to his mouth. "I've no idea. I honestly haven't. I suppose it rests with Davies. He seems to be able to break all the rules as far as this squadron is concerned."

Harvey's opinion of the small Air Commodore was expressed in a grunt of disgust. "You know what Anna's thinking, don't you?"

"I can guess," Adams said. "She's thinking that Davies is keeping you here to lead the squadron in case we have a big job coming up."

Harvey gave a wry grin. "Right on the button. She's giving me hell for not requesting a move back to the OTU . "

"I don't blame her," Adams said. "Nobody has earned a rest more than you. For that matter, what about her? What about the risks she took? Don't you think she needs a rest from worry too?"

Harvey scowled. "I know all that. That's why I want her to go back to the bungalow. But she won't go unless I do."

"Of course she won't. That's why you're wrong in not putting in your request."

The Yorkshireman ignored Adams' reproach. "Go and see her some time, will you, Frank? She likes talking to you."

"Of course. I'll give her a ring. What room is she in?"

"The front one. The one Hilde and Valerie used when they were here."

Adams drew on his pipe. "That seems a long time ago, Frank."

"Only a hundred years," Harvey said. "How is Valerie these days?"

Adams pressed another flake of tobacco carefully down before replying. A loyal man, he had never sought comfort by sharing his personal problems with his colleagues. But Harvey went back to the old days when Valerie had stayed at The Black Swan, and the Yorkshireman had witnessed her behaviour first hand. Harvey was an old confidant and one who, Adams had discovered, was totally trustworthy. "She seems all right. But then she would be, wouldn't she, with London full of Americans with money to burn."

"What will you do when the war's over, Frank? Will you go back to her?"

Adams shrugged. "I suppose so. I can't help thinking the war might be to blame. It does strange things to all of us. But when is it going to end? Sometimes I think it'll go on forever."

Harvey was wondering if he could be so forgiving himself. "Will you go back to your old job too?"

"I won't have any option. But it'll be hard to settle down after all this."

Harvey gave a harsh laugh. "You can say that again."

Remembering the Yorkshireman had been a builder's clerk before the war, Adams trod carefully. "Didn't Ian promise you a job in his firm after the war?"

"Something like that."

"Now we know he's alive, you'll take it, won't you? Knowing Ian, it's sure to be a good one."

Harvey was silent a moment, then rose from the bench. "How the hell could I take his job, Frank? I'd feel dependent on him day and night."

"That's stupid. Ian isn't that sort of man."

"Maybe not, but I am."

Adams surprised himself by his own frankness. "You can't afford that sort of Northern pride any longer. You've got Anna to think about now."

"You think I don't know that?" The sudden roar of a Merlin under test drowned the Yorkshireman's resentment and brought a wry grin to his craggy features. "What the hell are we going on about, Frank? We'll probably all be six feet under the soil before this bloody war is over."

Millburn gave his thick, dark hair a final brush and donned his cap. Setting it at a jaunty angle, he crossed the billet to the bed where Gabby was lying and gave the Welshman a wink. "At last, boyo. Freedom until dawn."

Gabby raised a dispirited head. "Dawn?"

"The privileges of rank, kiddo. But what's the matter with you? You sick or something?"

"No. I just don't feel like going out tonight, that's all."

"Why not? Did Susan turn you down? I told you she would."

Gabby gave him a look of dislike. "Well, she didn't. I took her to the flicks and to Bishops Wood afterwards."

"Then what's wrong? Wouldn't she let you have your wicked way with her? Did she tell you she preferred big husky Americans?"

"No, she didn't. She had her clothes off so fast I couldn't keep up with her."

"Then what happened? Couldn't you make it?" Gabby scowled. Until now, fearing Millburn's hilarity and the chance of the story spreading round the Squadron, he had managed to keep the night's happenings to himself. But now his need to talk proved too much. "She's not what you think, Millburn. She's a nut case.

Everything was going fine until I got her down on the blanket and got her clothes off. Then she went all funny."

Millburn sat down on the edge of his bed. "Funny? What's that in English? Coy? Giggly? Hysterical?"

"No. Just crazy. She suddenly said we had to get married. When I told her not to be so bloody silly, she started going on about rape and what her brothers would do to me when they found out."

"Rape! Did you rape her?"

"Of course I didn't. She seemed keener than I was until she went queer. After that it was a shambles. She accused me of just about everything in the book."

"So what did you do?"

"I got her home as fast as I could. But it made no difference. She said she was going to tell her family I'd raped her and that I'd better watch out. One brother is a big bastard and she says he'll beat the hell out of me the next time I leave camp."

Millburn's grin had been broadening as he listened. Now he let out a loud guffaw. "So it's happened at last. The Swansea Stallion has got his come-uppance. Serve you right, you little creep, for stealing a date with her. I'll bct shc only did it to punish you."

About to protest, Gabby suddenly sat up on his elbows. "You think that's what she did?"

"What else? No dame's as crazy as that. She didn't fancy you, so she gave you the short straw and you fell for it."

Gabby decided this was a time to be very cunning. "I never thought of that. You could be right. Are you seeing her again?"

Millburn grinned. "Why? Do you want me to?"

Gabby did his best to sound casual. "It's up to you. But she did sound as if she'd got a crush on you. If your guess is right, you could be on to a good thing there."

"I am right, boyo. I'll bet those silk stockings to a pair of your old socks that with me she'll lie back and coo like a dove."

"Then you're going to see her?"

"Yeah, I said I'd give her a ring tonight. Stop worrying, kid. Go into the Mess and have a beer. Leave it to me to bust her bluff wide open."

Gabby sighed. "I hope you're right. But good luck, anyway."

Adjusting his cap again, Millburn opened the billet door. "It won't be luck, boyo. It'll just be good old Yankee charm. See you."

The billet door closed. Grinning all over his face, Gabby dropped back on his bed and hugged himself.

At the same time that Millburn's old MG was climbing up the hill to Highgate, a large Army staff car with masked headlights was driving past London towards the Great North Road. Two men occupied the back seats. One was Brigadier Simms and the other a much younger man in civilian clothes. As the car rounded a corner and a vivid flash appeared on the horizon, Simms pointed a finger. "Another V1. They're coming over night and day now."

The younger man had a voice that was very English, pleasant, cultured and somewhat laconic. "There's a rocket too, isn't there? Something called a V2?"

"Yes, we had the first of those a few days ago. It's causing a great deal of concern because it gives no warning."

"I suppose there's no defence against it?"

"That's correct. We can at least attack the V1 sites by aircraft, as your boys have been doing recently, and we also have a chance of destroying them when they're airborne. But there's nothing we can do against a rocket dropping from the sky. We've heard a rumour for a long time that the Nazis are working hard on secret weapons, and this V2 confirms it. That is why London pricked up its ears when your reports came through."

"I couldn't be sure, of course, whether Weiner was exaggerating, or even pulling my leg, but it seemed good sense to play safe."

"You were absolutely right, my boy. We've reason to think the Germans are working on dozens of new projects and it's imperative we get some idea of what we might have to face. At the same time, I hope our Intelligence section didn't grill you too enthusiastically on your return."

Moore laughed. "I can't deny they were enthusiastic, sir. But they did allow me a few hours sleep."

"I'm glad to hear it." Then the Brigadier's tone changed. "But I was deeply sorry to hear what happened to your colleagues. Were many killed?"

"I was whisked away so quickly that it's hard to say. But I know there were at least fifteen men in the truck."

The older man winced. "That was a tragedy. Davies told me your colleague, Harvey, was very upset."

Moore turned sharply towards the Brigadier. "Harvey didn't fly on the operation, did he?"

"I understand so. That's why he was so distressed he saw the truck being blown up."

"Davies shouldn't have allowed him to take part. It was agreed after Operation Titan that Harvey should be taken off combat operations."

Realising he had sailed into troubled waters, Simms steered the conversation into a smoother channel. "I suspect there will be quite a celebration when you arrive back at the squadron, although I doubt if anyone will expect you back so soon."

Moore made no reply. Although agreeably surprised to be returning to his squadron, he was also aware of the directive that forbade escaped prisoners of war to fly over Europe again. As a consequence, he could see no role for himself in a squadron whose sole purpose was to attack and harass the enemy.

He wondered if the Brigadier knew, but decided against asking him. Simms was a courteous old soldier, but no one knew better than Moore that he was also a man who kept his cards close to his chest. He, Moore, would have to wait and hope that Henderson or Davies could throw more light on his return.

The masked headlights of the car were barely reaching the wet road ahead. Trees, brushed by the faint light, loomed up out of the darkness and disappeared. As the car reached the crest of a hill, another vivid flash lit up the night sky. Watching the crimson glow that followed it, Moore was reminded of the Brigadier's words about secret weapons. Were these two only the first, he wondered, and had Weiner told the truth in hinting there were greater threats yet to come?

* * *

With the Squadron still pounding the rocket sites, the crews had another early call the following morning. Gabby, who hated early rising, was busy shaving when Millburn returned from his night pass, and for a moment he forgot his problems with Susan. "What bloody time is this to get back? You forgotten I've got to fly with you? I don't want a pilot who can't tell 109s from Spitties."

Millburn grinned and feigned a yawn. "Sometimes it's worth it, boyo. Like last night."

It was then that Gabby remembered his traumas. "What happened?"

Grinning, Millburn dropped on his bed. "Everything happened. Didn't I tell you she liked Americans?"

Gabby gave an impatient growl. "Sod Americans. What did you do?"

"I didn't take her to the Salvation Army, if that's what you mean. I took her to the same place as you did."

Gabby's voice turned hoarse. "And then?"

"And then we floated into paradise, my little Welsh gremlin. Arm in arm."

Gabby's teeth gritted. "I don't believe you. You're lying, Millburn."

Millburn grinned expansively. "Do I look like a guy who was frustrated? Or like a runt I know who's terrified of leaving camp in case he gets made into meatballs? I had nookie all night and had to tear myself away this morning. That's the straight, honest truth of it."

Gabby dropped weakly into a chair. "Then I don't get it. It makes no sense."

"It's like I told you, boyo. Some guys have it and others haven't."

"Bullshit," Gabby muttered. Then his face brightened. "I've got it! She's schizophrenic. She acts differently on different nights. That's it. Why didn't I think of that before?"

Millburn's grin turned into a scowl of disgust. "You little phoney. You tried to set me up last night, didn't you? You hoped she'd put her brothers on me and let you off the hook."

The Welshman's expression betrayed him. "You said she might have acted that way because she didn't fancy me. I thought you might be right."

"That's a laugh. The Swansea Stallion having doubts about himself? You hoped to frame me, you little sonofabitch."

Gabby was too shaken to deny it. "Did she say anything about me?"

"A hell of a lot. She said you'd tried to rape her and all four brothers want your guts for garters."

The Welshman groaned. "Didn't you try to put in a good word for me? I'd have done it for you."

Millburn grinned wickedly. "No. I told her you'd been raping girls ever since they sent you here and if you were put down it would be the best thing for every girl in Highgate."

Gabby was aghast. "You're a bastard, Millburn. A bastard through and through."

The American suddenly began to roar with laughter. Gabby stared at him bitterly. "What's so funny?"

"Your face, boyo. You look so bloody scared."

"You'd be scared if you had four big zombies wanting your blood."

"But they don't, kiddo. It's just been a gag."

Gabby gaped at him. "A what'?"

"I sent her a letter asking her to do it. I thought you deserved it for being so sneaky."

The Welshman's face was a study of disbelief. "I don't believe you. Nobody could act that well. She even let me take all her clothes off."

"So what? I asked her to make it look real."

"No girl would go that far. What's your game now, Millburn? What're you trying to do to me?"

The American was laughing so hard there were tears pouring down his cheeks. "She's an actress up on holiday from London. Didn't I tell you that? And by the sound of it she's a hell of a good actress."

For a moment Gabby was crushed by the enormity of the deception. Then fury rallied him. "That's the dirtiest thing you've ever done to me, Millburn. Do you know I've wasted two nights worrying about those brothers?"

"I know you have, boyo. And I've wetted my pants watching you." As Gabby glared round for something to throw, the American put up a hand and backed away. "Stay calm, my little gremlin. Remember we have a job to do in Hunland in a couple of hours."

Gabby was breathing fire. "I'll lose you over there, Millburn. I will, so help me."

As the American laughed again and began to change his clothes, Gabby's curiosity overcame his fury. "I still don't see how you persuaded a girl to go that far for you. What did you offer her? Your bloody car?"

Grinning, Millburn walked over to his locker and pulled out a pair of flimsy tubes. "Only one pair left, boyo, but it was worth it. Didn't I always say a girl'll do anything for silk stockings?"

Chapter 14

Dawn was still over an hour away when Henderson's scrambler telephone rang. The Scot was a heavy sleeper, and the impatient jangling took some time to waken him. Muttering a curse, he swung his legs out of bed and groped his way to the light switch. Then he grabbed up the receiver. "Yes. Henderson here. What is it?"

A familiar voice answered him. "Christ, Jock, what's taken you so long? You got that WAAF in bed with you?"

Henderson gave an inward groan. "No, sir. I wish I had. What can I do for you?"

"I want you and Adams to come over to High Elms this morning. At 10.00 hours sharp."

Henderson wondered irritably why Davies needed to give him such an order in the middle of the night. "At 10.00 hours, sir?"

"That's it. On the dot. Bye."

The Scot replaced the receiver, crossed the room, and flopped down on his bed. Although he had a room in Officers' Quarters, Henderson had become so accustomed to Davies's eccentricities that when the Air Commodore was in the vicinity he had a bed brought into his office. As he yawned, scratched himself, and sank back, the Scot was glad of his foresight, although he reflected that the hassle might be avoided if he had a scrambler telephone installed in his proper quarters.

He wondered again why Davies had phoned him at such an ungodly hour. Not that such behaviour in itself was unusual: Davies often had a blind spot where the comfort of his junior officers was concerned. But, terse though the order had been, the Scot thought he had detected a note of suppressed excitement in the small Air Commodore's voice.

He wondered if it could mean Moore was back. It was possible, he thought, but highly unlikely. Normally it took months before the Resistance movements could get escapees back to England. On the other hand, as everyone seemed so keen to find out what Moore knew, fingers might have been pulled out to speed up his return.

With one thought leading to another, Henderson's hopes of getting more sleep receded. He glanced at his watch. 04.55. Only an hour before the general squadron call that would begin another day of maximum effort against the V1 sites. A professional airman, Henderson was often unable to decide which he preferred, the everyday chores of war that resulted in steady but less crippling casualties or the specialised tasks that, while allowing more rest between operations, often devastated his squadron. In the way the mind has of introducing quirky humour at such moments, he was reminded of a saying of his old Edinburgh grandfather: "You win some and you lose some, laddie. That's the way of the world."

Henderson fidgeted and tossed about in his bed for another thirty minutes. Then he cursed and walked over to the telephone. Why the hell should he be the only one to lose sleep wondering what Davies was up to? He picked up his duty telephone. "This is the C.O. I want you to send a message to Squadron Leader Adams. Ask him to come over to my office at his earliest convenience. Yes, of course I know what the bloody time is. Do it right away."

Autumn announced its nearness that morning, draping the countryside in a grey fog that grounded flying for the day. To the imaginative Adams, curious to know why he and Henderson were being called to High Elms, the tall trees on either side of the front gate looked like ghostly sentinels as the fog swirled and billowed around them.

It was evident that tight security was the order of the day as soon as their car was allowed through the gates. Guard dogs were being paraded around the lawns and the RAF car was stopped twice for security checks before it was allowed to drive on to the forecourt.

As it stopped, Henderson pointed at a large American automobile parked alongside three other cars. "See that, Frank? Staines is here."

Adams was as curious as the Scot. "Then it must be something big."

Loss of sleep was making Henderson irritable. "Yes, but what? Why hasn't Davies given us a clue?"

"Perhaps Ian is back," Adams suggested.

"Then why couldn't Davies tell me when he phoned? It can't be that big a secret, can it?"

As they climbed from the car, a young Provost captain waved from the top of the steps and then hurried down towards them. As the two men waited, smoke from a nearby bonfire gave the morning air the scent of autumn. In the elms that surrounded the grounds, rooks were heard cawing angrily as if some intruder had settled among them. As Henderson was about to make some further comment, the young captain came to attention before them. "Group Captain Henderson?" As the Scot nodded and returned the salute, the captain led them towards the steps. "The Brigadier and Air Commodore are in the library, sir."

"Is General Staines with them?" Henderson asked.

The captain hesitated as if being asked a state secret. In the end he was noncommittal. "I think he might be, sir."

With some ceremony the two men were led into the library and announced. "Group Captain Henderson and Squadron Leader Adams, gentlemen."

Adams would have recognised Staines at once, even if he hadn't been wearing the uniform of an American Air Force general. Two hundred and ten pounds in his socks, Ed Staines had once played football for West Point, and the years that had passed since those days showed more in his spiky grey hair and leathery face than in his granite hard body. But even without such identifiable features, Adams would have recognised him for the huge cigar he held in a tobacco-stained hand. Massive Havanas were Staines's trademark and Adams had never seen him without one.

But at that moment neither Adams nor Henderson were giving much attention to the American or to the slighter figures of Davies and Simms alongside him. Their eyes were on the young man in RAF uniform who had risen to his feet at their entry. Medium in height and build, with a fresh complexion and wavy fair hair, he bore a small puckered scar on his right cheek. Now back in uniform, Moore wore the ribbon of the Victoria Cross and the American Legion of Merit Medal among the many other lesser medals for valour beneath his RAF brevet.

Henderson was the first to speak. "Ian! So you *are* back. How the hell did you do it so quickly?"

Moore saluted him and then moved forward to take his outstretched hand. "Hello, sir. It's a long story. Perhaps I can tell it to you later." He turned to Adams. "Hello, Frank. How are things with you?"

For Adams it was a reunion with an old and valued friend. As their hands clasped and held, he could only hope he did not sound too emotional. "It's good to see you again, Ian. It didn't seem likely a few weeks ago."

Moore smiled. "Yes. I'm lucky, aren't I? It's certainly good to be back."

The three officers at the table were smiling as they watched the reunion. Then, deciding enough sentiment had been displayed for one morning, Davies called the assembly to order. "All right. You've had your hugs and kisses. Now if you'll come and sit down, the Brigadier will explain why he wanted you here this morning."

The three men moved to the table. Adams, a perceptive as well as a sensitive man, noticed how much more pronounced Moore's limp had become since the Loire mission. When the three men were seated, the Brigadier moved to the head of the table.

Although Davies was patently eager to get proceedings started, Simms's old-world courtesy insisted first on a tribute to Moore. "Before we begin our business, gentlemen, I must offer my congratulations to Wing Commander Moore on his escape from captivity. We all know the debt we owe him for his past leadership, and I for one am delighted and relieved that he is back to help us again. Welcome back, Wing Commander."

A rumble of 'hear hears' ran round the table, none being louder than the one from Staines. "Attaboy, Moore. It's great to have you back."

With the acknowledgement made, Simms's voice changed in tone. "However, life has a way of mixing its blessings, and this is no exception. I've called you here because of the somewhat startling news that Moore has brought back with him. As this news might affect our American allies too, I got in touch immediately with General Staines. Agreeing with me that the matter needs our full attention, he has been kind enough to attend this conference in person."

Staines gave a terse nod. Prone to straying thoughts in moments of high drama, Adams was thinking that if the American exhaled much more smoke from his Havana, the men grouped around the table might be unable to see one another. Then Simms's voice drew back his attention.

"I don't need to tell you gentlemen that modern war is as much about science as about conflict. Although so far we have managed to breach Hitler's coastal defences and liberated much of France, that is only because we have so far been able to keep abreast of the enemy's scientific achievements. But it doesn't mean the war is won yet. The Germans are a gifted, scientific people: the V1s and V2s that are now hitting Southern towns and London are proof of that. If they could produce more secret weapons of that kind, we might quickly find our roles reversed again. Our decoding teams at Bletchley Park do keep picking up hints of new weapons under research: a long-range gun, a super rocket, more efficient bombs, a new type of submarine, and a host of new aircraft. However, until last month we hadn't been able to substantiate any of these snippets, and so we were powerless to do anything about them. But now, for the first time, we believe we have some positive details about a new weapon — and just possibly a location. That's why I asked you all here today."

Henderson could keep his curiosity under check no longer. "Is this the information Moore has brought back?"

"Yes. The wounded German aircrews did chatter to Moore, and although the information they gave him was limited, we are hoping it might be enough for us to locate and perhaps even eliminate one enemy threat." The Brigadier glanced at Moore. "Perhaps you will take over now, Wing Commander?"

Nodding, Moore took the elderly soldier's place at the head of the table. Watching him, Adams was reminded of the many aircrew briefings he had attended in the past. When Moore had been off stage, the briefings had been routine, but the moment he had walked forward the atmosphere had changed. The man had a natural presence, a charisma that drew and held one's attention. From Staines's expression, even the hard-bitten American could feel it.

"I understand from the Brigadier that you've all been told what happened in the military hospital, so I won't go over all that again. I'll just say that during the weeks I was there I managed to squeeze bits and pieces of information from the German crews, particularly from a pilot called Weiner. He liked his tipple, and as the crews kept offering me bottles of schnapps, I was able to keep him happy."

Staines grinned. "You mean you kept getting him drunk?"

Moore gave his light, pleasant laugh. "Fortunately he liked chatting to me about aerial tactics, and by giving him bits of useless information and plenty of schnapps I think sometimes got him to forget that I was on the other side."

"This was after Larrouche was arrested?" Davies asked.

"Unfortunately, yes. It meant I'd lost my link to London but, from what I'd heard already, the project seemed so extraordinary and threatening that it seemed good sense to go on finding out all I could."

"Amen to that," Staines muttered. Moore's eyes moved to Henderson and Adams. "I must stress this is only my conclusion. But from all I heard I believe the Germans will soon have a fighter/bomber that will be at least a hundred and fifty and possibly two hundred miles an hour faster than anything we can put into the sky."

Henderson gave a start, then a grunt of dismay. "An aircraft? Two hundred miles an hour faster?"

"That's what I believe is being developed."

Adams, who had shown less surprise than the Scot, broke in at this point. "Our people have known for some time the Germans are working on a fighter with a new type of engine, Ian. But everyone doubts they'll get enough made to have any decisive effect on the war."

Moore nodded. "I know. Time is their problem. None of the German crews I spoke to thought that fighter would be ready in time. But if I've put the snippets together correctly, the one they are so excited about could be coming off the production line in hundreds by the New Year or even earlier."

Adams was still looking sceptical. "But how can they produce a new aircraft so quickly? It'll need factories, new tools — an immense amount of technical preparation. Even if they worked like slaves, I can't see they could possibly produce enough aircraft in numbers until 1946 or even later."

At this point the Brigadier rose to his feet. "I wonder if I might answer that, Wing Commander?" As Moore nodded Simms took his place at the head of the table.

"The answer, gentlemen, lies in the long-held German emphasis on air power. For years, their Air Force received far more resources than their other services. Much of this research investment came from German business concerns who stood to make huge profits from the production and sale of successful aircraft and weaponry, and in the initial stages of this war their confidence seemed justified. It is true that the Luftwaffe is on the defensive now, but it is still seen by the public and the military alike as the one arm that can save Germany from defeat. As a result an enormous amount of research and development is still being carried out, as the introduction of the V1s and V2s proves."

Adams nodded. "Yes, sir, I accept that, but with all the will in the world I don't see how a new, highly sophisticated aircraft can be produced so quickly. Unless of course it has been developed for a long time without our knowing it."

Davies was secretly wishing the elderly Brigadier would get to the point. Irritated by Adams's scepticism, which he felt was holding up the issue, he could contain himself no longer. "For Christ's sake, Frank, forget that bloody intelligence training of yours and listen. The Brigadier hasn't finished yet."

Abashed, Adams was about to apologise when he received a smile from the Brigadier. "You are quite right, Squadron Leader. It would be impossible for the Germans to produce a brand new aircraft so quickly."

Adams avoided Davies's glare. "Then what does it mean? How can this fast aircraft be produced?"

"Supposing the Germans managed to adapt one of their standard aircraft to travel at near-sonic speed. Wouldn't that speed up production?"

Adams suddenly understood. "It would make all the difference in the world. Provided it was possible, that is."

"From what Moore has told us, we believe they have found a way. Moreover, we suspect their research is far advanced."

Henderson was listening in deepening dismay. "Do we know what type of kite they're working on, Ian?"

Moore shook his head. "I couldn't find that out from the snippets I got from Weiner. But as both aircraft have already been produced in many variations, my guess is it's either a Junkers or a Heinkel."

Staines' gravelly voice checked Henderson's reply. "So you guys see now why I've left an Air Force to take care of itself for a day. If the Heinies can adapt one of their ships to go at that speed, they could use it both as a fighter and a bomber and we wouldn't be able to do a goddam thing about it. You couldn't stop 'em bombing the hell out of the U.K., and my B-17s would go down like ducks in a shooting gallery."

There was a brief silence while Henderson and Adams digested what they'd heard. With Adams now inhibited by Davies's chastisement, he was grateful for Henderson asking the next question. "Did Weiner give you any idea where the research was being carried out, Ian?"

"Not directly. But more than once I overheard the name Buchansee when the crews were talking among themselves. Wiener dropped the name once, but sobered up quickly when I tried to pump him. I could be wrong, but that's the first place I'd check on."

"Buchansee? That's Rhine Maiden country," Staines said. "Deep into Bavaria with all those forests, where that German agent of yours, Anna Reinhardt, operated. Wasn't she born in those parts?"

"In Munich," Davies told him.

"Didn't you once tell me she used to take tourists round the province before the war?"

Aware of what Staines might be leading up to, Moore broke in quickly. "If the research is being carried out there, it won't be any help to know what things were like before the war. The centre will be too well hidden for that."

To Moore's relief, Staines did not pursue the point. "Yeah, I guess the Krauts will have done a first class job, as they did with those Rhine Maiden rockets. So what's our next move?"

"I think we first should establish that Weiner wasn't being very clever and giving me false information."

"You think that's possible?" Staines asked.

"I don't think it's likely," Moore admitted. "As he had no idea I was going to be rescued, it wouldn't have had much point. But we have to start somewhere."

"So what does it mean? Recce ships over the Buchansee?"

Davies, whose sharp eyes had been darting from one speaker to another, settled on Simms. "Do you agree with that, sir?"

The Brigadier nodded. "Yes. As Moore rightly says, we have to start somewhere."

"All right, I'll get on to Benson and ask them to send a photo/recce kite right away. Unless you'd like your boys to do it?" Davies asked Staines.

The American shrugged. "No, we're in the same war. Your boys will do fine."

"I've a better idea," Moore said. "Why don't I go?" He smiled. "I've got a personal investment in Buchansee."

Henderson beat Simms's protest by a short head. "Are you out of your mind? You can't fly over Jerryland. You've just come back from there."

"I'd go over at high level, sir. There wouldn't be any risk."

"No!" Henderson said. "Absolutely and positively no. We use Benson. That's what the unit is for."

Agreeing, Davies glanced at Simms. "Is that all for now, sir?"

"I think so, Davies. But I would like Wing Commander Moore to stay behind. The General and I still have a few questions to ask him."

Davies caught the eye of Henderson and Adams. As the three men saluted Staines and prepared to leave, the big American grinned at Davies and held out a huge Havana. "Take one with you, Davies. They soften the edges and help the world go round."

Davies tried to hide a shudder. "No thanks, sir."

"C'mon, Davies. Have one. They're good for the libido."

Davies, who had not liked to refuse at an earlier meeting for fear of being thought chicken , decided the time was past for reckless courage. "The last one damn nearly destroyed my libido, sir. Another might finish it off for good."

Staines let out a roar of laughter. "You don't say? You must have a back to front metabolism, Davies. Does anyone else want a pick-up?" When nobody took his offer, Staines grinned and returned the airship to his pocket. "I guess I'll never figure out you Limeys."

Davies managed to hold his smile until the three of them were outside. Then his testy self returned. "Why the hell must he always be shoving his damned poisonous cigars at me?"

Henderson winked at Adams. "The Americans are very generous, sir."

"Generous be damned," Davies grunted. "He just knows they make me puke. Come on. Let's get back to the airfield. I want to get in touch with Benson this afternoon."

Chapter 15

Henderson took Moore's glass and topped it up with another dram of Highland Dew. Then he offered the bottle to Adams and Harvey. The Yorkshireman took it, filled his glass, and then turned to Adams. "What about you, Frank?"

Adams shuddered and shook his head. Never able to take much hard liquor, he was already afraid he had gone over his limit. "No, thanks. I'll be seeing green-eyed gremlins if I have any more."

Harvey grinned. "I've been seeing 'em for years. And they haven't done me any harm."

The four men were seated in Henderson's office. Delighted by the return of his ace pilot, Henderson had practically ordered Moore and Adams to join him for a celebratory drink after their return from High Elms. Aware of the friendship between the two men, he had also invited Harvey. Although the Yorkshireman seldom displayed his feelings where other men were concerned, this was one occasion when his pleasure could not be disguised, although Harvey had done his very best. "So you're back, are you? What was it, Ian? Did they think you'd be more useful to 'em over here?"

Moore had laughed as their hands clasped. "What else? I wasn't doing them much good eating their food, was I?"

With a few drams of Highland Dew inside him, Henderson was finding it all very satisfying. Overhearing Adams's remark about gremlins, he grinned back. "Talking about the wee bastards, there'll be a few flying around The Black Swan tonight. Millburn and Gabby are organising a party for Ian." He turned to Moore. "You'll be getting your invitation when the boys get back. Don't forget to take your flak jacket with you. It could be that kind of a party. Millburn and Gabby haven't changed much since you were with us."

Moore laughed. "I didn't think they would. After all, it isn't that long."

It was a remark that provided Adams with the lead he needed. "How did they get you back so quickly, Ian?"

From the silence that fell it was clear Adams was not the only curious one. Moore took a cigarette from Harvey and lit it before replying. "It wasn't like the old days when escapees had to work their way across Europe and get out through Spain or Portugal. All the partisans had to do was get me into liberated France. Mind you, we had a bit of trouble in the beginning. Jerry dropped a plane full of paratroops in the woods behind us and we had a skirmish with them before we got away. We also had a hold up for over a week when a safe house was raided. But after that I was passed from group to group until they got me to our troops in France. Luckily they'd almost reached the Belgium frontier by that time. So really it was a piece of cake."

With more than his ration of whisky within him, the imaginative Adams was making flesh and blood out of the young pilot's bare-boned understatements. A vicious fight with hard-nosed paratroopers in the forests ... Taking refuge in 'safe' houses that might at any moment be raided ... Hungry and tired, facing torture if captured.... Just a piece of cake.

"Were there others with you?" Henderson asked.

"Yes. There were six in our group."

"Did they all get back so quickly?"

"I don't know. As soon as I was delivered to our troops, I was whisked away and flown back to England."

Henderson was showing respect for Simms's planning. "I never realised the SOE could pull so many strings. So what's the score now? Has Davies given you any idea what his plans are for you?"

Moore gave him a wry smile. "Not yet. Although I know what I'd like."

The Scot scowled. "Well, you're not getting what you'd like. With Sod's Law operating the way it does, you'd be shot down on your first operation and dropped right into the hands of the Gestapo. So that's something you can forget."

At that moment Henderson's internal phone rang. He spoke into it for a moment, then glanced back at the three men. "Sorry but I'm going to have to break it up now. But if nothing goes wrong, I'll try to get over to the party tonight." Catching sight of the second bottle of Highland Dew which was still half full, the Scot overcame his native caution. "If you want to take that bottle over with you to A Flight office, I don't think I'll notice."

Adams started to rise, only to feel the floor move disturbingly beneath his feet. Harvey gave Moore a wink. "What's wrong, Frank? Is that ankle giving way again?"

Adams took off his spectacles and wiped them. "Yes, it does sometimes. But it's all right once I start walking on it."

"Good man. But we're right behind you if it goes again."

Adams returned his glasses to his nose and glanced at Harvey with some reproach. "It won't. It's perfectly all right now."

With that he walked with dignity to the door. Grinning at Henderson, Harvey picked up the half-full bottle of whisky before joining Moore and Adams in the corridor outside. "Let's finish this bottle in The Black Swan. I have to take Ian over or Anna will skin me alive."

"Have you told her Ian's back?" Adams asked.

"Yes. I phoned her fifteen minutes ago. Just long enough for her to put her war paint on."

Although Adams was fully aware that he had no real part in Moore's reunion with the married couple, it was the Yorkshireman's last remark that overcame his hesitation. An interest in his friends' personal affairs was a part of Adams' complex nature and although his better side censured him for his curiosity, Henderson's whisky had weakened his resistance. "As flying's scrubbed for the day, I suppose I could come over for a few minutes," he said, despising himself for the excuse.

Harvey slapped him across the shoulders. "Course you could. Come on. She's expecting us."

* * *

Harvey tapped on the bedroom door. "Anna! Are you dressed? I've got someone here you know."

Adams, standing behind the two pilots, saw Anna appear in the doorway little more than a second later. He saw her face was pale as Harvey playfully pushed Moore towards her. "Ian! Oh, Ian, how good it is to see you again!" To Adams she appeared to hesitate for a moment before she flung her arms around the young pilot.

Moore's good looking face was almost as pale as her own as she kissed him. "Hello, Anna. I hadn't expected to see you so soon. I didn't know you were staying here."

Giving Adams a welcoming smile, she drew both men into the room. "Yes, I wanted to be with Frank. Let me look at you, Ian. Do you know you've lost weight? And what about your leg? Frank said you've had a bone injury."

"My leg's fine. I'm as good as new. You're looking wonderful, Anna. Marriage obviously agrees with you."

Adams saw her colour slightly as she glanced at Harvey. "Perhaps that is because Frank looks after me so well. He spoils me, you know."

"So he should. He's a lucky man."

Harvey gave a grunt. "You wouldn't say that if you'd heard her a few weeks ago. She played hell with me for coming back to the Squadron."

"I don't blame her," Moore said. "Davies promised you a rest. He should have kept his word."

Anna pointed an accusing finger at the Yorkshireman. "You see. Ian agrees with me. So never argue with me again."

Harvey gave his craggy grin. "Stop ganging up on me." He indicated the bottle of whisky he was carrying. "Have we four glasses, love?"

Smiling at Moore, she ran to the door. "I'll go and get some. Sit down, all of you. I won't be long." Adams hesitated, then sat on the double bed. He was thinking that in all the time he had known the German girl he had never seen her anything else but self-controlled. Yet to him she seemed slightly flustered since greeting Moore. He wondered if Harvey had noticed it.

She returned a couple of minutes later and tried to take the bottle from Harvey. "Let me pour for you, Liebling."

Harvey shook his head and crossed over to the dressing table. "Not a chance. We want man-sized drinks today. Put 'em down here and I'll handle it."

Laughing she obeyed, taking the glasses from Harvey as he poured. Watching the grace of her movements as she walked across the room to Moore, Adams thought again what a beautiful woman she was. As she handed Moore a half-filled glass, Adams could have sworn her hand remained in touch with him a split second longer than the occasion demanded.

She gave a toast to Moore a moment later. "To Ian. To your return, which has made us all so very, very happy."

It was all natural and normal, Adams told himself, and if she kept smiling at Moore during the half hour that followed it was only because they were friends and she was showing her relief at his return from the dead. There was nothing in it to arouse Harvey's jealousy, nor did Adams think the Yorkshireman's behaviour gave any indication of it. His fears were all in his own mind, he told himself, and when a gossiping rebel voice kept whispering that he was being naive and refusing to see the signs of danger, Adams chastised himself for allowing drink to disfigure his judgement.

Chapter 16

The library at High Elms was cold that morning. The old-fashioned central heating had not yet overcome the early chill and Davies was wishing he had slipped on a pullover beneath his tunic as he pushed a pile of photographs towards Simms. "Nothing, I'm afraid, sir," he admitted.

The Brigadier showed his disappointment. "You've had them examined by experts?"

"Naturally. Even Babington Smith has looked at them. And the answer's the same. Just the village of Buchansee and few hamlets with a railway linking them, surrounding woods, a lake and a couple of small islands. Oh, yes, and a saw mill. Nothing they find in the least suspicious."

Simms glanced down at the enlarged prints. "These were taken by a Benson crew?"

"Yes, sir. Experts in their field."

Simms sighed. "Well, it was only a shot in the dark. Moore did say he heard the name used out of context. It could be anything, perhaps even a place where air crews are sent to convalesce."

Davies was aware the elderly brigadier could be right. Yet knowing Moore better than Simms, he could not eliminate Buchansee yet. "Photographs or not, I know Moore wouldn't have given us the name unless he believed the possibility existed. He's too aware of what might be involved."

"It's a pity we couldn't have another word with him now we have these photographs. He is still on leave, isn't he?"

Although Simms' voice was as bland and courteous as always, Davies could not escape the feeling he was receiving a gentle reprimand. “I had to give him a fortnight’s leave, sir. His mother was recently widowed, and naturally wanted to see him after all that’s happened.”

“Yes, of course. When is he due back?”

“In a week’s time. Next Monday, I believe.”

In the short silence that followed, Davies could hear a telephone ringing somewhere in the large house. As the ringing ceased, he reached out for the photographs again. “There is one thing, although it doesn’t show on these photos. Benson said the crew saw an airfield about thirty miles from the village.”

“Are you suggesting it has a purpose there?”

Davies shrugged. “It might have.”

Simms frowned. “But what? There weren’t any large buildings on the field, were there?”

“No. Only the usual hangars.”

“Then I don’t see where there could be a connection. Unless, of course, the planes stationed there are to protect a nearby research centre. Is that what you’re suggesting?”

“I don’t know what I’m suggesting, sir,” Davies confessed. “I know we’ve nothing but circumstantial evidence and, God knows, that’s flimsy enough. But Moore is no fool, and he wouldn’t give us information without considering the implications carefully.”

Simms nodded. “I’m convinced that he’s right about this new aircraft. I wouldn’t have contacted General Staines otherwise. It’s the location of the research centre that’s the problem. We must give our agents something to work on, and these photographs don’t offer the slightest promise.”

Davies couldn’t refute the SOE officer’s argument and yet a rebel cell in his mind would not dismiss Buchansee. “The trouble with these Bavarian forests is that they can hide anything. Remember how cleverly Jerry hid that research plant at Ruhpolding. It only came under suspicion because of the railway running towards it, and even then we couldn’t be sure until our agents found there was a high-security ring around the plant. Couldn’t this be much the same?”

Simms shrugged. “It could be, but then so could any other village in Bavaria or Austria that’s surrounded by forests.”

"Except Buchansee is the only name we've got," Davies reminded him.

Simms rose from the table and walked towards the large French window that overlooked the gardens. Outside a cobweb, stretching from a flower pot to a nearby step, looked like silver filigree in the sunlight. "What does all this add up to, Davies? That you'd like agents to investigate the forests round Buchansee?"

Davies hesitated. "It's not my job to make suggestions to the SOE, sir."

"I know that, Davies. But what's your personal view?"

"Personally I don't see we've any choice. If Moore's right and Jerry's well advanced on adapting a standard aircraft, then we haven't a minute to lose. So until something better comes along, it seems to me we have to play any hand we've got."

Simms stood gazing out of the window a moment longer. Then he gave a shrug of assent. "I can't fault your reasoning, Davies. Very well. I'll recommend to London that agents go to Buchansee as soon as possible."

"What about General Staines, sir?"

"I'll tell him when I give him the result of these photographs. He's already asked me to keep in close touch. He's as concerned as we are about Moore's news."

Davies was thinking Staines wasn't the only man worried as he walked out on the chilly forecourt. If agents found nothing around Buchansee he was going to find it hard to face Simms when their report arrived. Seeing his WAAF driver chatting to a young officer, Davies released his misgivings in a shout that sent rooks clattering from the nearby elms. "Hilary, stop fooling about and get into the car. I want to be at Sutton Craddock in twenty minutes."

The sound of the steam train took on a sterner note as it hauled its freight wagons and passenger coaches higher into the Bavarian hills. In the growing dusk outside, the dense woods that flanked the track were creeping slowly past. In the first of the three passenger coaches two men in German local defence uniforms were seated side by side. One, Hausmann, was middle aged and burly. The other, Meyer, was a taller man in his early forties.

The coach was half filled with a mixture of workmen, soldiers and countrywomen. Midway down its length four soldiers were drinking and playing cards. As the train rocked over an uneven section of the track, a soldier let out a loud curse and his bottle of beer slid off the table and crashed to the floor Hausmann nudged Meyer's arm. "We'll be in Buchansee in a couple of minutes."

Meyer nodded and gazed at the coach window. In the shaded blue light he could see a reflection of Hausmann's weather-beaten face. Beyond the reflection the dense woods could be seen sweeping up a steep hillside. Then the hillside fell away and the train began to slow down. Half a minute later the track widened and cranes and trucks appeared alongside.

It was a signal for the workmen in the coach to rise and collect their effects from the racks above. As a siding slid into view and the train jerked to a halt, they jumped out and disappeared into the dusk. Hausmann leaned towards Meyer again, keeping his voice low. "Workmen at the saw mill. They're not part of our brief."

Meyer, as gaunt and sardonic in appearance as Hausmann was burly, nodded. "I didn't think they were. How big is Buchansee?"

"From what I can gather it's quite small. It's mainly a junction for the saw mill and timber yard. The train brings in felled logs and trucks take them to the mill. So the village has only got a few dozen cottages for workers and a shop or two."

As if to confirm his words, the train jolted as wagons were detached and shunted towards the waiting cranes. Meyer half rose in his seat and gazed down the coach. With the workmen gone, the only other travellers in the coach were the soldiers and countrywomen and all were too far away to overhear their conversation. Relaxing, he dropped back alongside Hausmann. "So you don't think we need worry about this part of Buchansee?"

Hausmann shrugged his burly shoulders. "I don't think so. The saw mill's only a kilometre from the lake and the photographs London took show fire breaks among the woods on the far side. So there isn't room for a research or development centre between the mill and the lake."

"So what's your plan?"

"The first thing is to take a look at the airfield and see if there's anything unusual going on there. Then we'll go into Nurnbach, twenty miles down the line. If there are scientists and test pilots around, that's where they'll go for their booze and their women. If we run into any, at least we'll know London's on the right track."

Meyer glanced down at their civil defence uniforms. "Let's hope the local police aren't keen types. I haven't that much faith in these documents they've given us. The last time I showed my medically unfit papers they damn nearly took me to a doctor."

"We'll be all right," Hausmann said. "We've got away with it before. And the Bavarians are easier-going people than our own kind."

"Amen to that," Meyer muttered. "All right, suppose the airfield is clear but we find scientists in Nurnbach. What then?"

Hausmann sighed. "We start combing the woods. What else can we do?"

Glancing at the trees, shrouded in damp evening mist, that were now sweeping past the train, Meyer gave his sardonic grin. "You're going to find that fun, aren't you?"

Hausmann, who suffered from arthritis, hid a shudder. "Don't even think about it yet. Let's just play it by ear."

Chapter 17

Davies looked disappointed. "Are they sure of that?"

"Not absolutely sure," Simms told him. "The woods are very extensive, as you know. But our agents feel there would be more security guards in the area if a research or production centre was based there. If you remember, it was the tight security in the Ruhpolding valley that gave us our first indication of the plant there. There is nothing like that in or around Buchansee."

"What about the airfield? Has that been looked at yet?"

"Yes. It seems to be slightly larger than we thought but still contains only one squadron of Focke-Wulfs. It has one unusual feature: a hangar that remained closed during the three days our agents kept up their surveillance. But what relevance that can have to our enquiry I can't imagine. According to our agents, it is quite a small hangar and therefore couldn't possibly be what we are looking for."

Davies, whose ears had pricked up at the news, turned to Moore who, recently back from leave, was sharing the High Elms library with himself and Simms. "Have you any views on that, Moore?"

"Not really, sir. I agree it's unusual to keep a hangar closed for three days. But we do close ours now and then to keep our boys warm, although I wouldn't have thought it was cold enough yet. But perhaps it is in Bavaria."

Disappointed again, Davies turned back to the Brigadier. "And they haven't spotted anything else unusual? No military personnel, or civilians who're out of place in a country district like Buchansee?"

"That is the only other comment the agents have made," Simms said. "There do seem to be a quite a number of high-ranking officers and well-dressed civilians in Nurnbach. All on good terms and sharing the same cafés and clubs."

Davies showed immediate interest. "Doesn't that suggest a research establishment of some kind in the area?"

"But where? Nurnbach is twenty miles from Buchansee. A research establishment could well be twenty miles in the other direction. Nurnbach is quite a large town with good entertainment facilities. So men could travel a long way to enjoy them."

Davies knew Simms was right. He turned again to Moore. "Tell us about Buchansee again. Why you felt it was connected with this new aircraft project?"

"I heard the name when half a dozen of them were talking to the Major General one day. As I guessed they were discussing some secret weapon, it seemed reasonable to assume there was a connection. At another time Weiner mentioned the name when he was bragging about secret weapons and closed up like a clam when I mentioned it myself. So it did seem possible that the name had significance."

Davies frowned. "But it was all conjecture on your part?"

It was never Moore's way to avoid implied criticism. "I thought I made that very clear at our earlier meeting, sir. I heard the name mentioned in the context of this new aircraft and repeated the name to you and the Brigadier. But I never made the definite claim that the research centre was at Buchansee."

Davies waved an impatient hand. "All right, all right. I'm not saying you did. But as it's the only name we have, we had to investigate it." He glanced at Simms. "How long will London keep your agents there, sir?"

"They won't give up yet, Davies. As you rightly say, it's our only lead."

Davies shifted restlessly. "If they could only get to those officers or civilians. If they were technicians and scientists, at least we'd know we were on the right track."

At that moment there was the sound of a buzzer, and a red light appeared over the library door. Excusing himself, the Brigadier went out, leaving the two men alone at the table. Davies gave a grunt of frustration. "What the hell are we going to do, Moore? You don't think it's possible the whole thing was an elaborate hoax, do you?"

"Nothing's impossible, sir, but there'd seem to be little point unless they were planning to have me rescued and returned to England." Moore's sensitive face showed wry amusement. "Certainly those paratroopers didn't give me that impression."

Davies scowled. "I'd forgotten about them. But how are we going to find this plant if Simms' agents have failed?"

"Has General Staines been in touch recently?"

"Christ, yes. He's on the scrambler to Simms every day. He's as worried as we are."

Simms returned a couple of minutes later. In spite of his urbane manner, his appearance suggested concern as he addressed the two men. "That was London, gentlemen. They have just received a radio message from one of our operators in Bavaria. An aircraft has been seen flying at great speed over Chiemsee. You will remember that's another lake in Bavaria."

Davies's voice turned hoarse with excitement. "Did that come from one of your agents at Buchansee?"

"No. But isn't that irrelevant? The plane could have flown from anywhere in Bavaria. The radio operator thinks that, from its manoeuvres, it might have been on a test flight."

"So it's true," Davies muttered. "Jerry has done it. But how and where?"

"London is going to instruct our agents to re-double their efforts. But Bavaria is a huge province, so we mustn't expect results too soon."

"The point is, how long can we wait? If Jerry can get this kite flying in numbers, we won't have an Air Force by next spring. And neither will the Yanks. We have to speed things up somehow." As he spoke, Davies gave a sudden start that brought curious glances from the other men.

"Have you an idea, Davies?" Simms asked.

Davies pulled himself together. "Not really. Just a thought, that was all." To subdue further speculation, he rose to his feet. "If there's nothing more to discuss, sir, Moore and I will get back to Group. If you have any more news, I know you'll be in touch."

* * *

Hausmann leaned across the table and offered Meyer a cigarette. "Take a look across the road when I give you a light," he muttered. "At the party coming out of that restaurant."

The two men were sitting outside a small cafe in Nurnbach. Late summer had momentarily halted its swift march into autumn and the small town was bathed in sunshine.

Meyer accepted the match, drew in smoke, and then casually glanced across the road. To disguise his faint start, he took a sip from his tankard of beer before meeting Hausmann's eyes. "Colonel von Haldenberg," he murmured. "So he didn't die with Von Lowerherz at Ruhpolding."

Hausmann's glance moved back at the party of high-ranking officers, well-dressed civilians, and giggling girls who had emerged from a restaurant opposite and were making towards three large staff cars parked nearby. "Obviously not. He was probably out whoring when the attack was made."

The object of their interest was a tall, slim man in his early forties with two schlager scars on his cheeks. Arrogant in his bearing, a tall attractive girl on his arm, he was making his way along the pavement as if the local townsfolk did not exist. Reaching the leading staff car, he waited for his chauffeur to open the rear door. Then, stepping inside, he drew the girl in after him. As the rest of the party disappeared into the cars, Hausmann let out his breath. "Von Haldenberg! It has to mean something. Or why would he be in a small Bavarian town with a party of civilians?"

Not all the girls who had emerged from the restaurant went off in the cars. Two, looking sullen and disappointed, were muttering to one another on the opposite pavement. As one turned and walked away and the other crossed the road, Hausmann glanced at Meyer. "Shall we chance it?"

"It's risky," Meyer said.

Hausmann gave a wry grin. "Nothing risked, nothing won. And she does look fed up. Go on. You're the glamour boy."

The girl, slim, blond, and wearing high heels, was almost level with their table by this time. Although she had a pretty face, it was clouded by resentment and temper. Giving Hausmann a look, Meyer rose and confronted her. "Hello. Would you like a drink?"

The girl stared at him sullenly. She had a local accent. "Do I know you?"

Meyer grinned. "Not yet. But I'm worth getting to know."

She tossed her head. "You've got plenty of cheek, haven't you?"

"I've plenty of everything. Why don't you do yourself a favour and find out?"

She gave a derisive laugh. "God, you really think you're something, don't you? Who the hell are you anyway?"

Meyer indicated the table where Hausmann was innocently sipping his beer. "Why don't you have a drink and find out? It won't cost you anything?"

Her eyes took in his sardonic face and lean body. Then she gave a shrug of indifference. "I suppose I can waste a few minutes. Who's your friend?"

Interested spectators smiled at one another as Meyer led the girl to the table. "My colleague," he corrected. "We're in business together. What's your name?"

"Inga. Inga Muller. What's yours?"

"Call me Carl." Meyer waved a hand at Hausmann. "Meet Gunter Neumann."

Giving Hausmann the briefest of nods, Inga sank into the chair Meyer held out for her. "I haven't seen you around here before. Why aren't you in the Army?"

"We've been in the Army. Now we're timber merchants. Gunter and I are directors."

Inga sniffed. "You don't look like directors. Why're you wearing those uniforms?"

Meyer waved a waiter towards them. "There's still a war on. Didn't you know?"

"I'll have a beer," Inga told the waiter. She turned back to Meyer. "You could have fooled me about the war. The bloody officers who come here don't seem to have heard of it."

Meyer decided he couldn't have had a better opening. "We saw you with a bunch of them across the road. Why didn't you go with them?"

She took the cigarette he offered her and sullenly inhaled smoke. "I didn't want to go."

"Why? Didn't you like where they were going?"

"Not particularly."

"Where were they going?" Meyer grinned. "The Russian Front?"

Inga gave another sarcastic laugh. "That'll be the day. That sort don't get their arses shot off fighting. They leave it to mugs like my brothers."

"You've got brothers in the Army?" Hausmann broke in.

She nodded moodily and inhaled smoke again. "Three of 'em. And one's gone already."

"Killed?"

"Yes. This July. In France."

Hausmann sighed in sympathy. "You're right. It's the man in the street who takes all the stick. Officers like that keep their noses clean. Do you see them often?"

"Now and then."

"Where do they come from? The airfield?"

"No. At least I don't think so."

"Don't you know?"

The girl shook her head. "No. They don't talk about their work. I don't think they dare."

"Why is that?"

"I think they're all scared of that colonel. Von Haldenberg. The one with the scars on his face."

Meyer was sharing Hausmann's disappointment. "He looks an arrogant one."

The girl took a long sip of her beer. "You should talk to the girls about him."

"Why? What does he do?"

"He's a bastard, like the rest of his kind. He treats girls like muck." Then, remembering where she was, the girl checked herself. "Anyway, why are you two so interested in them?"

Hausmann kicked Meyer's foot under the table. "That kind have money and influence. We might do business if we could meet them."

The girl ground out her cigarette under her shoe. "Well, you won't meet 'em through me. I've had enough of the bastards. I'd rather have my regulars." She glanced at her wrist watch and then at Meyer. "I have to go. Thanks for the drink."

Meyer rose with her. "What about another drink some time?"

"Why? Are you staying here?"

"For a few more days. Maybe longer."

She pulled a notebook from her handbag and scribbled an address on it. "You can get me here during the daytime. But not at nights. Bye-bye."

Meyer sank back into his chair as she tip-tapped away along the pavement on her high heels. "I felt sure she'd know where they came from. What a bloody waste of time."

Hausmann shook his head. "Not altogether. London was playing it by ear before but now we can tell them one important thing is confirmed."

"What's that?"

"Von Haldenberg often comes into town. That means there must be a development centre round here, or he wouldn't be involved. That leaves only one thing."

Meyer gave his sardonic grin. "Don't tell me. Let me guess. Someone has to find out where it is."

Chapter 18

The Brigadier opened the file and laid it before Staines. "Von Haldenberg! Like Colonel von Lowerherz, he studied with distinction at Heidelberg University. He then went into the aircraft industry and soon became one of Germany's leading designers. At the outbreak of war he was drafted into the Heereswaffenamt Prufwesen — known as the Wa Pruf — an organisation designed specifically for the testing and improvement of weapons. From the Wa Pruf he was transferred into a section known as Waffen Forschungs — Wa F for short — which was set up to develop modifications of weapons proved valid by its parent organisation. It was there he probably met von Lowerherz who was working on the Rhine Maiden weapon. However, von Haldenberg's speciality remains aircraft design and London have no doubt that his brilliance has led to a number of the Luftwaffe's recent innovations."

Staines removed the cigar from his mouth. His leathery face was showing respect for the SOE Officer's dissertation. "How do you people know so much about these guys?"

Simms allowed himself a smile. "Know thine enemy, General. We have files on most of their researchers and scientists, just as they probably have files on ours. Of course, most of the information was gathered before the war."

There was a sound like sandpaper on wood as Staines rubbed his chin. "Yeah, I suppose so. I guess our people do the same." He picked up the file, studied it for a moment, then dropped it back on the table. "So you feel this guy's presence in Nurnbach more or less confirms Moore's suspicions?"

"I feel it must, sir. It's not as if he has been there for only a few days. Our agents believe he is stationed in the area, which can only mean Moore is right."

"But your agents still don't know where?"

"No. It seems the security is watertight at the moment. But, as you were told, a plane flying at very high speed was seen over the area."

Staines was on familiar ground now. He glanced at Davies, Adams and Moore, the only other men attending the meeting. "That doesn't mean much. If a ship can fly that fast it could appear almost anywhere in Krautland. And as Bavaria and Austria are about as far from us as they can get, that's where they'd do their testing."

With his throat tickling from smoke, Davies was secretly wishing the American would put out his damned cigar. "That's true, sir, but if von Haldenberg has been seen in Nurnbach it does appear the pieces are starting to fall into place."

"There's that closed hangar at the airfield too," Adams suggested. "Perhaps that's where they keep this experimental aircraft."

The big American gave Adams a look of approval. "You think they might be test-flying from there? Yeah, that's possible, Adams. I like that."

Seeing Davies also showing his approval, the flushed Adams was compelled to protest. "It wasn't just my idea. Ian and I were discussing it before we came over this morning."

There was a twinkle in Staines's eyes as he glanced at Moore. "You guys want to get together more often. Maybe we'd win the war more quickly." He turned back to Simms. "O. K. Let's assume for the moment the goddam centre is in the area. What's our next move? To pour more agents in?"

"I wouldn't advise that, sir. The problem with saturating the area with agents is that sooner or later the enemy will find one, and then his security will be tightened even further."

Staines drew on his huge cigar. "For Christ's sake, Simms, how tight is tight? He's got us running around in circles as it is. I'm worried about my ships. If the Krauts are already test-flying, they could be in mass production in three months. Maybe less."

Davies broke in before the elderly soldier could answer. "We need someone who knows the district very well. Have you thought about Anna Reinhardt?" Adams felt as if an electric shock had passed through him. Moore gave a violent start and then made an immediate protest. "We can't use Anna, sir."

Davies swung round. "Why not?"

"She was withdrawn because it was felt the Gestapo had identified her. If she went back she could be in great danger."

Adams, as shocked as Moore, added his protest. "It is out of the question, sir. You told her yourself she wouldn't be used again."

Guilt turned Davies aggressive. "I can change my mind, can't I? What the hell is it with you two? Have you both fallen for her or something?"

Adams had never seen Moore oppose a suggestion so passionately. "You promised her yourself, sir. And you promised Harvey. You can't go back on your word to them."

Two red spots appeared in Davies' cheeks. "Don't tell me what I can and can't do, Moore. Remember who you're talking to."

Moore's voice went very cold. "I remember very well who I'm talking to, sir. And because of your rank, I don't see how you can break your word to a girl who has risked her life so many times for us."

"Who the hell said I was going to break my word? I want to ask her if she'll go. That's all."

"If you ask her, she'll agree. You know that."

Staines, whose eyes had been moving from one to the other, lifted a nicotine-stained hand. "Hold it, you guys. Let's take it quietly. What's your point, Davies? That the girl can find out things your other agents can't?"

"It's possible. She knows the district and has a relation in Nurnbach. In addition, she's an attractive woman. Remember how she helped us in the Rhine Maiden affair."

Adams winced when he thought what the Rhine Maiden affair had cost the girl and Harvey. Moore's interruption told him the pilot had the same thoughts. "That affair nearly killed Harvey, sir."

"Yes, but it also destroyed the threat of those proximity-fused rockets." Conscious he was on the defensive, Davies modified his tone. "For God's sake, Moore, I hate the idea of her going back as much as you do. But think what's at stake here. If Jerry gets these modified kites in numbers, we could lose hundreds and perhaps thousands of aircrew. Worse than that, we might even lose the war."

The old war chestnut to which there was no answer, Adams was thinking bitterly. Could the saving of one life be justified if it meant the deaths of thousands? Needing to support Moore, he added his own conviction. "Anna will agree if she is asked, sir. She's that kind of a person."

Davies eyed him for a moment, then turned to Simms. "What would you like me to do, sir? Drop the idea or talk to her?"

Knowing the Brigadier's sensitivity, Adams held the hope for the moment that he would shake his head. But Adams had forgotten the elderly officer's professionalism. "I don't like the idea any more than you, Davies, but if you feel it might work, then you must ask her."

Davies turned to Staines. "And you, sir?"

Staines shrugged his huge shoulders. "I've got my B-17s to think about. So if you think she can help, you go ahead."

He had barely finished speaking when Moore jumped to his feet and limped toward the library door. Hesitating but feeling a moral obligation to support Moore, Adams gave a quick salute and followed him, goose pimples running down his back in the expectation of a furious outburst from Davies.

The outburst nearly came but was prevented by Simms laying a hand on Davies's arm until Moore and Adams had disappeared outside. Staines, astonished by such a display of British passion, broke the silence with a loud laugh. "I never thought I'd see you Britishers getting het up this way. Maybe we'll win the war after all."

Davies, free to talk now, felt the need to explain. "They admire the girl, sir. And so do I. So I'm not looking forward to asking her."

The Brigadier's voice was full of sympathy. "They'll understand that when tempers cool, Davies. In the meantime, while the General is here, we'd better decide how to brief the girl if she agrees to go."

"She'll go," Davies said moodily. "As Adams said, that's the kind of girl she is."

* * *

The Black Swan was closed when Davies's staff car drew up outside it the following morning. Although Joe Kearns, aided by an understanding constabulary, seldom kept to opening hours when the Squadron was off duty, the mornings were invariably quiet and this morning was no exception.

Davies hid a shiver as he climbed from the car. Although a pale sun was shining, a cold wind was rustling the dried leaves of the crab apple trees and a sullen bank of cloud on the northern horizon hinted rain was not far away.

Telling his WAAF driver he might be some time, Davies walked up the private path to the front porch. Finding the oak door locked, he swung down the heavy iron knocker. A few seconds later a bolt was withdrawn and Maisie appeared in the doorway. The sweater she was wearing, and the short apron tied beneath it, accentuated her large breasts. Although she had met Davies often enough, Maisie's feminine instincts never failed to be triggered automatically when a man in uniform entered her sphere. Despite Davies's age and the knowledge that he was highly unlikely to engage in an extra-marital relationship, Maisie could not help touching her hair and giving her most alluring smile. "Good morning, sir. Come inside. I'll tell Mrs Harvey you're here."

As Davies entered the hall he caught a glimpse of Joe Kearns. Wearing braces and an open-necked shirt, the innkeeper was polishing glasses behind the bar. Seeing Davies, he called a greeting. "Good morning, sir. How are you? We haven't seen you for a long time."

"No, I've been busy. Is it all right if Mrs Harvey and I use your private lounge?"

"Of course, sir. Help yourself."

Seeing Maisie run upstairs, Davies drew nearer the innkeeper. "There's no one else here this morning, is there?"

Although curious, Kearns was quick to understand. "No one, sir. Anyway, if you keep the door closed no one can hear you."

Thanking him, Davies entered the private lounge. The room was familiar to him, with its oak-panelled walls and blackened beams supporting a low, whitewashed ceiling. An old grandfather clock stood in one corner. Opposite was an alcove with a mullioned window. With dust motes floating in the pale sunlight and thick stone walls resisting sounds from the airfield, the atmosphere was that of a bygone age.

For a moment Davies considered discarding his greatcoat, then, seeing the fire was unlit, decided against it. As he was about to walk over to the alcove, Anna entered the room. With her dark hair resting on her shoulders, she was wearing a simple, slim-fitting dress with only a cameo brooch as jewellery. Although Davies was not prone to such speculation, the Adam in him had to confess he had never seen her look more beautiful.

Smiling, she approached him with outstretched hand. "Hello, Arthur. It is good to see you again."

Although her composed features showed nothing but pleasure, Davies wondered what her real thoughts could be when all their previous meetings had led her into great danger. "Hello, Anna. Thanks for seeing me so quickly."

She indicated the seat in the alcove. "Can I get you a cup of tea or coffee?"

Davies could not decide whether he wanted to get the business over quickly or whether he wanted to procrastinate. "No, thanks. Perhaps later." Although he seldom smoked, he drew out a cigarette case from his greatcoat pocket. "Will you have one?"

She shook her head. "No, thank you. I'm trying to get Frank to stop. He smokes far too much."

Aware that his behaviour was betraying him, Davies struck a match. "They all do. It's the job, I suppose."

"I'm sure it is. Combat flying is such a strain, isn't it?"

Hypersensitive that morning, Davies wondered if she was giving him a reprimand for ordering Harvey back to the Squadron. At the same time he was grateful to her for giving him the opening he needed. "I had to bring him back, Anna. It was imperative that Moore escaped."

"Yes," she said quietly. "I do realise that."

"Does that mean Frank has told you why?"

There was the faintest challenge in her grey eyes as they met his own. "We have total trust in one another, Arthur. And I am not likely to talk to others, am I?"

Although in Davies' eyes, Harvey's behaviour was a breach of security, for once he was glad of it. Rising, he went to the door and opened it. Seeing the hall outside was empty, he closed the door again and returned to the alcove. He drew on his cigarette before meeting the eyes of the silent girl. "Then you know what's worrying us. We have to locate the site of that research centre before the Germans go into full scale production."

"You have not found it yet?"

"No. But we're sure it's in the Buchansee district." Forgetting his cigarette, Davies told her about von Haldenberg. "We can't see any other reason why he would be stationed there."

The tick of the grandfather clock suddenly sounded loud in the silence that followed. Davies found he was holding his breath as he saw Anna give a sad, rueful smile. "So you want me to go? Isn't that why you are here?"

Although not surprised at the girl's perception, Davies was grateful for it. "Yes, it is. I know it could be dangerous for you but we're getting nowhere as things stand and time is so important."

She gave a small shake of her head, less a refusal than a protest at the inequity of life. "You do realise how Frank would take this? He would think it a total betrayal."

Davies shifted uncomfortably. "I know that. I've already had Moore and Adams telling me what a scoundrel I am. But, Anna, what else can I do? If the Nazis get this aircraft into production, every Allied airman will be in danger. That includes Frank."

She gave a low, bitter laugh. "You're not blackmailing me, are you, Arthur?"

Davies cursed himself for the slip. "Of course I'm not."

"Yet you broke your word and ordered him back into combat only a few weeks ago."

"I've explained why. We had to get Moore out. But I haven't used him again since, have I?"

Another silence fell. Then she held out her hand. "Give me a cigarette, please."

As Davies held out his case, she said quietly: "You do realise what Frank's reaction would be?"

Davies knew only too well. The blast of a 1000 lb bomb would be easier to contain. "Would he have to know?"

A crease appeared between her smooth eyebrows. "He is my husband. Doesn't that give him a right to know what I am doing?"

"I'm not denying that. But this is a special case. If you tell him he's sure to object. Wouldn't that make things very difficult for you?"

"It would. And if I saw it was going to break his heart, I probably wouldn't go. You have only seen his hard crust, Arthur. Underneath there is a fine and very sensitive man. Rightly or wrongly, he feels I have done enough for the Allied cause."

Davies frowned. "I can't deny he's right. But this is an emergency. With your parents in England, couldn't you use them as an excuse for going away? Couldn't you say one of them is ill?"

For a moment her voice turned cold. "I see you've thought this out very carefully."

Davies had seldom felt less comfortable. "I've had no choice, Anna. But don't think I'm enjoying it."

The tick of the grandfather clock sounded loud again as she rose and gazed from the mullioned window. Feeling his fingers suddenly burn from his forgotten cigarette, Davies bit back a curse and stubbed the butt into an ashtray. As he sat back Anna turned to him. "What will happen if the location of this research centre is discovered? Will you use your Squadron to attack it, as you did in Rhine Maiden?"

"That depends on the circumstances. We might have to use our heavies, B-17s or Lancasters. It's impossible to say at this point."

"I understand that. But if I agree to do this and you do use your Squadron, you must make me a solemn promise that you will not order or allow Frank to take part in it."

Davies took a deep breath. "Of course I'll promise."

"And you will keep your word this time?"

"I've promised you, haven't I? Yes, of course I'll keep my word."

For a long moment her grey eyes gazed down and searched his face. "Very well," she said quietly. "On that condition I will go. But Frank mustn't know anything about it until I am over there." As she turned sharply back to the window, Davies had to strain to hear her words. "I couldn't bear his pain, you see."

Davies winced. Not for the first time he wished that all human emotion, and particularly that between men and women, could be put into suspension until the war was over. "So what will you do? Use your parents as I suggested?"

"Yes. I will see to that. When do you want to brief me?"

"I'd like to do it this afternoon at High Elms. We'll send a car for you at 14.00 hours. I'll see you are back here before Harvey comes off duty."

"And when will you send me over?"

"The Brigadier will need to alert his agents to expect you. And depending where they have to take you, Tempsford will need the right weather conditions. But I'd like you at Tempsford tomorrow evening."

She gave a faint start. "Tomorrow? That doesn't leave us long, does it?"

"I realise that. But we are pressed for time, Anna."

Recovering her composure, the girl moved away from the window. "In that case I'd better start getting ready. I'll see you this afternoon."

Davies remembered no more until he was outside the inn. The sun had disappeared behind the bank of clouds and a drizzle was threatening heavier rain to come. Cursing under his breath, Davies wondered why the damned weather always seemed to augment a man's most depressing moods. Deciding it was yet another aspect of Sod's Law, he turned up his greatcoat collar and hurried back down the path to his car.

Harvey showed surprise. "I didn't know your mother wasn't well."

"I didn't know myself until Father phoned me today," Anna told him. "I think I might have to go to them for a few days. Father never was any good at cooking or doing things in the home."

Harvey made a quick decision. "I'll come with you. They owe me a few days leave."

She hoped her sudden concern did not show. "Surely you can't get away so quickly?"

"Why not? The weather's grounded us."

"But that won't last. It might clear up at any time."

Harvey shrugged. "So what? I'm not a pilot any longer. I'm just a damned dogsbody. Nobody would miss me."

She realised that to argue further would raise his suspicions. She would have to ask Davies for help. "It would be nice if we could get away for a few days, wouldn't it?" she said, hating her deceit.

"Then let's do it. When do you want to leave?"

"I said I'd phone Father tomorrow to see how Mother is. If she's no better I'll look up the train times."

"All right. Let me know as soon as you can. I'll need a bit of time to arrange it with the C.O." Hearing laughter from the bar downstairs, Harvey glanced at the bedroom door. "What do you want to do? Join the boys for a drink?"

It was the last thing she wanted. "I'd rather not. I don't feel in the mood for company tonight."

He drew her towards him. "You're not going to be ill too, are you?"

She smiled and kissed him. "Of course not. I'd just rather be alone with you tonight, that's all."

Clearly delighted by her admission, he tightened his arms around her. "That makes two of us. What shall we do? Play bridge?"

She laughed as his lips ran down her neck to her shoulders. "Not unless you stop doing that."

He grinned. "But I like doing it. It's the next best thing to flying that I know."

She pretended to smack his face. "So I come second, do I? I'll remember that in the future, Frank Harvey."

His expression changed as he gazed at her. "You wouldn't come second to the moon and the stars. Why are you so damned beautiful?"

Suddenly her eyes swam with tears. "You mustn't love me so much, Liebling. You mustn't."

He showed instant concern. "What's the matter, love?"

She quickly brushed her eyes. "Nothing. I just worry about you sometimes. I don't want you ever to be badly hurt if anything were to happen to me."

He frowned. "What could happen to you?"

She managed to laugh. "Nothing, you silly man. But when you love somebody as I love you, you think of things like that."

"You're not sick, are you? There isn't something you haven't told me?"

"Of course I'm not. Look at me. Did you ever see such a healthy woman?"

She felt him slowly relax. "You're sure there's nothing wrong?"

"I've told you there isn't. I was just being silly. I meant that I love you so much I wouldn't want you ever to be hurt. That was all."

He took her face between his two hands. "If I ever lost you, the world would end for me. So you take care of yourself. Promise?"

She had to swallow before she could speak. The reminder that this big, powerful man was a hostage to her promise to Davies brought her a surge of panic. By some mysterious metastasis it also turned her love for him into an intense desire. "Of course I promise. There is nothing wrong with me, so stop getting silly ideas."

He laughed as she began to unbutton his tunic, convincing her she had allayed his suspicions. "What're you doing? I thought you wanted to play bridge."

Her lips caressed his cheeks and neck. "Don't talk," she whispered. "Just make love to me."

Her desire was like a fire, striving to fuse their bodies together before life tore them apart. Although her love for him had always allowed her freedom, it had faced certain restrictions because of his puritanical background. Tonight she allowed him no restraint. Her body became an altar of desire that demanded his total devotion. After their climax, when their shuddering bodies finally sank back, she took his face in her hands. "I love you, Frank. Never, never, forget that I love you."

In the semi-darkness she could see his puzzled eyes. "What is it, love? Please tell me."

"Tell you what?"

"I don't know. But you seem different tonight." She made herself laugh. "Are you saying I've never loved you properly before'?"

He frowned. "Of course I'm not. But you seem more ... more intense. You must have noticed it."

She leaned forward and kissed him. "Perhaps that's because every time I see you I love you more. Now think about that and go to sleep, you silly man."

He was soon asleep but Anna lay listening to the rain outside and the wind in the eaves. She knew this might be their last night together, and her loneliness was a black demon that offered her nothing but pain and despair.

Chapter 19

The following morning, after Harvey had left for the airfield, Anna took the local bus into Highgate. There she made two phone calls, one to the airfield and the other to High Elms, where, unknown to Harvey, she had attended her briefing the previous afternoon. To her relief she was put on to Davies almost immediately. "Frank wants to go with me to my parents. You'll have to do something to stop him."

"I'll see to that," Davies told her. "Will you be ready to leave this evening?"

With security in mind she was careful not to mention Tempsford by name. "Do you still want me to go so soon?"

"Yes. They've been alerted. I don't know when they'll be able to accommodate you but the sooner you're there the better."

"You won't forget Frank, will you? He's determined to go with me."

Davies sounded grimly confident. "Don't worry about Frank. I'll speak to the airfield right away."

Replacing the receiver, she glanced at her watch. Ten minutes later she entered a small tea room in the High Street, an old-fashioned place with copper ornaments, linen tablecloths and lace curtains. Finding it half empty, she took a table and ordered tea. Then she waited.

Moore entered the cafe half an hour later. Despite the adverse weather, he was wearing no greatcoat and his good looks, decorations, and limp drew the attention of every woman in the tea room, although he looked oblivious of it as he crossed the floor. A close observer would have noticed he was showing concern but he hid it well as he approached Anna's table. "Hello, Anna. Sorry I'm late."

She looked relieved. "I was afraid something had happened after I phoned you."

He dropped into a chair opposite her. "No, I just had a few problems to sort out. Nothing very serious."

"It's good of you to come, Ian. I do appreciate it."

His eyes were taking in her appearance. Since the time he had escorted her to Tempsford to fly back into Gestapo-infested Europe, Moore had known she was the girl he had been searching for all his life. Sitting opposite her now, he knew nothing had changed. "It was no hardship, Anna. I think you know that."

Unsure what to say, she was relieved when a waitress approached them. Moore nodded at the teapot and empty cup on the table. "More tea? And what about scones? I seem to remember they serve them here."

Smiling, she knew he was referring to the time before Operation Titan when, in that same café, she had begged him not to take Harvey on the mission. "I think they still do," she said. "Shall we have some?"

As the waitress moved away with their order, Anna glanced round the tea room. "I've always liked it here. I find it so very English."

"I remember you saying something similar the last time. You said it all seemed so cosy and sane."

She gave an uncertain laugh. "You remember that too?"

He was watching her closely. "Yes. We were making small talk before we began talking about Harvey."

One of her slim hands began toying nervously with an ashtray on the table. "I was wrong to ask those things, Ian. I realise it now."

He shrugged. "I don't see why. You knew his nerves were bad."

"Yes, but it wasn't fair of me to ask. You couldn't do it for one and not for the others."

"I certainly couldn't do it for Frank," Moore said. "He'd have half-killed me if I'd tried. Do you remember what you said to me?

You said that Frank is different to most men in that he accepts the penalties love brings and tries to honour them."

Her eyes widened. "Did I say that?"

"Yes, and it's something I've never forgotten. If Frank hadn't gone and any of his crews had been killed, he would have felt personally responsible. Frank's the most protective flight commander I've ever known."

She wished he had not reminded her of it. "Yet he seemed to adapt to life at the OTU."

"That's different. He'd done the job by that time and been ordered to rest. There was no longer a call on that conscience of his."

"Except for what you did for us, Ian," she said quietly. "He never got over that. You offered your life for us. How can we ever repay you for a thing like that?"

To Moore's relief the waitress arrived at that moment. "There's no cream, miss, but I did get you a pot of jam."

"Thank you. That'll do very nicely." As the waitress left and Anna began pouring the tea, Moore smiled at her. "Let's stop talking all this nonsense, shall we? Tell me instead what happened between you and Davies." She gave a start, then lowered the teapot and sank back into her chair. "Then you know about it?"

"I was at the meeting when Davies suggested using you. And he phoned this morning telling me to make Frank Duty Officer from 08.00 hours to 08.00 hours tomorrow. It didn't require a genius to put two and two together. What did you tell Davies?"

She glanced round, saw that no one appeared to be listening, then met his eyes again. "I said yes, Ian. I hadn't any choice."

He gave a groan, an exclamation of anger and resentment. "Of course you had a choice. You should have told him to keep his damned promises. What about Frank? Didn't you think about him?"

She flinched at his accusation. "It's Frank I wanted to see you about. I couldn't tell him or he'd go crazy. So I've let him think my mother is ill and I have to go to her."

"What use is that? In twenty-four hours he'll want to know why you haven't phoned him."

She tried to calm him. "That's why I asked to see you. I want you to tell him after I've gone. You're his best friend. If anyone can make him understand, you can."

"Anna, he'll go berserk. He'll want to kill Davies. And I wouldn't blame him."

She had never seen his good looking face contain so much anger and bitterness. "Please, Ian," she begged. "Do it for me. There's only you or Frank Adams I can ask."

He shook his head slowly as his accusing eyes met her own. "You're a fool, Anna. You could be throwing away your happiness and Frank's too. Damn Davies for asking you."

Fighting back her tears, she reached out her hand across the table. "Do it for me, Ian, please. I know it's going to hurt Frank so much. Please talk to him and explain why I had to go."

He looked down at her long, slender hand that was clasping his own and knew he could never analyse the emotions he felt at that moment. "I'll talk to him, Anna. You know that. But when?"

Her hand tightened in gratitude. "Leave it for a day or two. Until he starts worrying why I haven't been in touch. But do it gently, Ian. Try to make him understand."

He opened his mouth to reply, then decided against it. "When are you leaving?"

"Tonight. Arthur is sending a car for me."

"Then you won't see Frank again before you leave?" When she shook her head, he went on: "Would you like me to give him a couple of hours off at lunch time? I can arrange it."

She wondered if it were wise but the temptation was too strong. "Will you? I'll be careful what I say."

"You'd better be. Or he'll run off with you and end up being court-martialled for desertion."

Although grateful to him for his touch of humour, she was only too aware that Harvey's reaction would be drastic. Before she could reply, Moore glanced at his watch and gave a rueful grimace. "I'm afraid I'll have to get back. Are you staying in town or can I give you a lift?"

She wondered why she hesitated. "Thank you. There isn't another bus for half an hour."

Little was said between them on their way back to Sutton Craddock but as he drew up the car outside The Black Swan he turned and took her hand. "As I'm not going to see you again before you go, you must do something for me. Something very important.

You must promise not to take one unnecessary risk while over there. You were withdrawn because it was said the Gestapo knew about you." For a moment his anger returned. "That's why it's monstrous you're going back. So for God's sake be careful. Promise me that."

She cleared her throat. "I promise. But you mustn't worry like this."

He gave a half-laugh. "Mustn't worry. Don't you realise ..." Unable or afraid to finish his sentence, he reached out and drew her towards him.

She made no effort to break away. Responding to his kisses at that moment seemed as natural as breathing. When she finally drew away she saw his face was pale. "I must go now, Ian. God bless you and thank you for everything."

He tried to speak as she climbed from the car but emotion choked him. Although he avoided glancing at her, she saw moisture in his eyes as he started the engine.

She stood watching the car swing into the main gates of the airfield before she turned away. With her own eyes wet with tears she was grateful that no one saw her enter the inn.

Wiping her cheeks, she climbed the narrow stairs to the landing. As she reached it, she saw her bedroom door was ajar. As she pushed it open and entered, she saw Harvey sitting on the bed facing her. Beside him Sam lay on the carpet. As the dog saw her and leapt to its feet, Harvey's harsh voice ordered him down. The girl's heart was beating painfully as Harvey turned back to her. As he jerked a calloused thumb at the window, he sounded as if he were keeping himself under control only with a massive effort. "That was a pretty scene outside. Where did he take you?"

She tried to keep her voice casual. "I've been in a tea room in Highgate. I asked Ian to meet me there."

"I know. You phoned him this morning, didn't you?"

She took off her coat, still trying to talk as if their relationship was normal. "Yes. How did you know that?"

He leaned forward. "Because I damn well tried to phone you from the airfield to tell you I'd been put on duty for twenty-four hours. When I couldn't get you, the switchboard operator told me you'd phoned Moore only a few minutes earlier. Why didn't you tell me you intended seeing him this morning?"

She felt sudden panic on realising she couldn't give him a reasonable excuse of any kind. "As I was in Highgate and he's just come back from Germany, I thought it would be nice to invite him for a cup of tea. After all, we are old friends."

His laugh of disgust made her only too aware how lame her excuse sounded. "I suppose that explains why he made me Duty Officer today. Just to keep me from seeing the two of you in a tea room."

Her panic grew as she realised almost everything she and Moore had done would seem highly suspicious without the true reason being given. She crossed over to him and tried to take his hand. When he snatched it away her distress grew. "Please, Frank, we've done nothing wrong. I swear it."

It was then the storm burst. Cursing, he jumped up from the bed, startling Sam who ran to the other side of the bedroom. "I saw the two of you only five minutes ago in his bloody car. Kissing and cuddling as if you'd never stop. Is that the way old friends behave?"

She was very frightened now. "I was just glad to see him back. I couldn't help remembering what he once did for us. But for him I might never have seen you again."

It was a mistake. A vein was swelling on his forehead. "So that's it. You feel in his debt. Only I didn't get the impression just now that you hated paying it."

She gave a gasp of shock. "You can't believe that. You know Ian's not that kind of a man."

He was not listening to her. "A lot of things are clearer now. I understand better what happened last night."

"Last night? I don't understand."

His huge body was shaking with emotion. "It was guilt, wasn't it? Guilt and a way of hiding the truth from me."

She felt as if her entire world was coming apart. "You can't believe that. I love you, Frank. All I was doing was showing my love."

"You mean you were showing your guilt. But, Christ, you were good. I see now why you were a good agent. You'd fool that little bastard Hitler himself."

She felt as if he had struck her across the face. Trembling, she sank down on the bed. "Frank, what's happening to us?"

He snatched his cap from a chair. “I’ll tell you what’s happening. Moore was always your blue-eyed boy, with his education and his money. I was useful while you thought he was dead, but now he’s returned it’s back to square one again.” He walked to the door. “You’ve just reminded me I’m in his debt. So what do you want me to do? Let him move in here?”

She felt almost in shock. “Where are you going?”

“I’m going back to the airfield. At least I’m some use there.”

She ran forward. “You can’t go yet. We can’t part like this.”

He pushed her back. “Go to your mother,” he said. “Or is that just an excuse to see Moore again’?”

She felt tears trickling down her face. “Frank, don’t do this. I’ve never betrayed you. I swear I haven’t.”

His jealousy was beyond argument or reason. “I saw you both in that car. You’ve lied to me. So why the hell should I believe you?”

She knew that only the truth would convince him, and the temptation to tell it was overwhelming until she realised that in this mood he would not only seek out Davies but almost certainly break all security rules as well. If he did that, and the operation was imperilled as a result, Davies was ruthless enough to destroy him. “Trust me, Frank. I’ve never betrayed you. Just trust me.”

She could see the yearning as well as the torment in his eyes and she longed to comfort him even while his tongue whipped her. “I did trust you. And look where it’s landed me. Go to your mother or wherever you’re going and we’ll talk about it later.”

With that he turned and ran down the stairs. As she stood at the door, Sam gave a whimper and came to her side. With her world falling apart, the dog’s devotion seemed to emphasise rather than diminish her loneliness. Dropping on the bed, she sobbed as if her heart would break.

Chapter 20

The night wind, rustling the tall firs, had a lonely and apprehensive sound. Hausmann gave a shiver as it penetrated the roof of the deserted woodcutter's cottage and sent a cold draught round his legs. As the flame of the shaded paraffin lamp flickered, he glanced at a wiry, middle-aged man who was sitting cross-legged on the floor alongside him. "You pick some cheerful places for us, Anton. Is this the warmest you could find?"

The man, who was crouched over a portable radio and had a phone pressed to one ear, grinned cheerfully at him. "You've got walls and a roof. So what are you bellyaching about?"

Hausmann, who along with Meyer was stretched out on the bare wooden floor, gave a grunt of disgust. "How the hell do you sit like that? Don't your legs ache?"

Anton looked surprised at the question. "No. Should they?"

Hausmann, whose arthritis was playing up, scowled. "Yes, they bloody well should. No one of your age has a right to sit like that."

Anton winked at Meyer. "You mean not after they've turned eighty?"

Cheeky sod, Hausmann thought. About to make a comment to Meyer, he checked himself as Anton lifted a warning hand and pressed the phones closer to his ears. After a few seconds he snatched up a pencil and glanced at the two alerted men. "It's Jean Poix in France. He's got an urgent message for us."

As the wind outside abated for a moment, the two tense agents could hear the thin, shrill sound of Morse from Anton's earphones. As he scribbled the message on a pad, the other two men glanced at one another apprehensively and moved to his elbow. After two minutes Anton reached out for the transmitter key and tapped out an acknowledgement. He then switched off the radio set and hurried to a corner of the bare room where he moved a loose brick from the wall. Picking out a sheet of paper, he moved back to his radio and began de-coding the message. Thirty seconds later he gave a start and turned to the waiting men. "You're not going to believe this. Lorenz is coming back."

Meyer gave a gasp of shock, then cursed. "She can't. It's bloody suicide."

Anton spat on to the bare floor. "Just the same, she is. Those bastards in London must be more ruthless than our lot over here." He paused. "Unless they've decided this new scare is worth the risk."

Meyer, who had a soft spot for Anna, cursed again. "Nothing's worth a risk like that."

Hausmann, although initially as shocked as his companions, was now looking thoughtful. "Perhaps it's not as dangerous as all that. After all, we are out in the sticks here. The police aren't so likely to have a record of her."

"It's not the police," Meyer said. "It's the Gestapo. They've got their slimy tentacles everywhere."

Anton broke into their conversation with some malice. "You'd better hope they haven't, because you two have been given the job of helping her when she arrives."

Hausmann winced. "When is that?"

"As soon as they can get her over to France. Then she'll be passed on from group to group until she arrives here. You're to meet her in Nurnbach."

"Where?" Meyer asked.

"They'll let me know later. There's a hell of a lot of planning involved in getting her here. But they're doing it fast, so things must be urgent."

"When do you think you'll hear?" Meyer asked.

Anton shrugged as he began packing away his portable radio. "I don't know. I have to tune in every four hours, which isn't going to be easy. But I'll be in touch as soon as I've got definite news. Now help me clean things up. If there is a research establishment around here, they might have D/F facilities." He grinned at

Hausmann as he rose to return the code book to its hiding place. "Meyer and I'll take down the aerial outside. You'd better stay out of the cold as long as possible, you poor old sod."

Scowling at him, Hausmann waited until the two men had left the cottage before blowing out the small paraffin lamp. He then removed a blanket from the only window before joining the men outside who were pulling down the aerial from the roof. When all was stored away, the three men shouldered their packs and started down a firebreak between the tall firs. As they came to the crest of a shallow hill, Buchansee lake could be seen in the far distance, glinting like steel in the half-light of a new moon. Anton motioned at the clear sky. "If the weather's like this over France, it won't be long before they bring her over."

The three of them parted as they reached a crossroads in the woods, Anton taking a path to a local hamlet and Hausmann and Meyer the road to Nurnbach. The two men had barely covered half a mile when Hausmann halted. "Listen!"

Thinking he had heard the approach of a car or an Army transport, Meyer was about to take cover in the flanking trees when Hausmann checked him. "No, there's nothing coming. Just listen."

Obeying him, Meyer could now hear a far-off wailing sound that grew in volume as he listened. He stared at Hausmann. "What is it?"

Hausmann hushed him. The noise now sounded like an animal in agony, a scream that went on and on as if the creature was being tortured by a sadist. It lasted for perhaps five minutes before the scream faded into a hushed silence.

Hausmann turned to Meyer, who looked startled. "It can't have been an animal. No animal could have kept up a scream like that for so long. Where do you think it came from?"

Meyer made a gesture at the wooded hills that surrounded them. "Who can say? Echoes travel a long way and go in circles in these parts." Catching sight of Hausmann's expression, he gave a start. "You don't think it could have anything to do with this research centre London's looking for, do you?"

Hausmann frowned. "I can't see how. If it was anything mechanical, it sounded more like the scream of an engine. And they're not looking for an engine plant."

"Perhaps they should be," Meyer suggested.

Hausmann shook his head. "Not unless they're hopelessly off the scent. But let's ask around and find out if the locals have heard it before. If they have, we'd better let London know." Turning, he gazed down the road that disappeared into the trees ahead. "How many more miles have we to go?"

"Only two. Perhaps two and a half." Meyer grinned at Hausmann's expression. "Never mind. In a few days we'll have Lorenz to look after. Then our troubles will really begin."

It was typical of Hausmann that he was thinking more about the walk back to their quarters than the horrors of Gestapo capture and interrogation. As he started forwards and his arthritic leg gave a twinge, he gave a groan. "What makes you think they haven't started already?"

Harvey made no attempt to knock on Moore's billet door. He threw it open and went in like an infuriated bull determined to gore everyone in sight.

Moore was seated at a small desk writing a letter. Although for a moment he showed annoyance at the rudeness of the intrusion, his expression modified on seeing who the intruder was. "Hello, Frank. You look upset. What's the problem?"

Upset was an understatement. The Yorkshireman's face was as black as a fell in a thunderstorm. "Don't tell me you don't know, Moore. Where's Anna?"

Believing he understood, Moore lowered his pen to the desk. "Why don't you take a seat, Frank?"

"I don't want a bloody seat. I want to know what the hell's going on between the two of you."

A line appeared between Moore's eyebrows. "Going on? I don't follow."

"Don't act the innocent with me, Moore. I saw the two of you in the car yesterday. Anna said there was nothing between you and I decided afterwards to believe her and let things drift. But now ..." Harvey almost choked in his rage. "Christ, although I said it to her, I never believed she'd do a thing like this to me."

Moore rose to his feet. "What are you talking about? What's happened?"

"Are you saying you don't know?"

"Isn't that obvious? You're accusing me of something and you haven't told me yet what it is. So pull yourself together and tell me."

The glowering Harvey took a step forward. "You made me Duty Officer so there was no chance of my seeing you together. Then you took her out for the morning and afterwards sat necking her outside the pub in your car. I know you did because I saw you from our bedroom window."

"Yes, I saw Anna in a café yesterday morning. And then I brought her back to the inn. That was all."

"All? What about the two of you in the car?"

"We were only saying goodbye, Frank. After all, we are old friends."

Harvey took another step forward. For a moment it looked as if he were about to strike the Squadron Commander. "You're a liar, Moore. I found that out this morning. As Anna hasn't contacted me, I've just phoned her parents. Her mother's never been ill and Anna isn't there. So it's all been a pack of lies and she's waiting somewhere for you." Harvey nearly choked again. "Who thought of it, Moore? You or her?"

Moore's face had paled at the accusation. Now, understanding the Yorkshireman's suspicions, he controlled his temper. "It's not what you think, Frank. If you'll sit down I'll explain everything."

"I'll bet you can, you bastard. Liars like you usually can."

Moore decided there was only one way to handle the situation. His voice turned cold and authoritative. "Sit down and listen to me. That's an order."

"Go to hell, Moore."

"Sit down or I'll have you put under arrest for insubordination and for abusing a senior officer. I mean it, Harvey."

Although Harvey still did not obey, his voice suggested that ingrained discipline was bringing back some of his self-control. "Don't think your rank's going to help you, Moore. Not where Anna and I are concerned. I'll kill you if you break up our marriage."

Seeing there was no way to soften the blow, Moore took a deep breath. "I'm not seeing Anna, Frank. It's more than likely she's in France by this time."

Harvey looked as if he'd been struck by a bullet. "What did you say?"

"If you sit down and listen I'll explain."

This time Harvey sank into a chair. As he stared at Moore, the young Squadron Commander went over to a small cabinet by his bedside and poured out half a glass of whisky. As Harvey hesitated, then took it, Moore noticed that the Yorkshireman's hands were trembling. "I'm sorry you have to go through all this, Frank. But Anna asked me not to tell you until you found out yourself that she wasn't with her parents."

From the fear in Harvey's eyes, Moore knew he had already guessed the truth. "What's been going on, Ian?"

"It's this damned secret aircraft that's got everyone in a panic. We think the centre is in Bavaria but we can't find out where. So Anna volunteered to go. But she knew what would happen if she told you, so she had to invent this story about her parents. And because we are old friends, she asked me to break it to you when the right time came."

Harvey looked shattered. He lifted his glass and drank twice before his shocked face gazed back at Moore. "Didn't she realise how dangerous it would be?"

"Of course she did. We all tried to stop her."

Like the removal of a tourniquet that allows blood to flow again, the full implication of the news was now reaching the Yorkshireman. "All? Someone must have asked her to go. Who was it? Was it Davies?"

Feeling as if he were sliding the safety pin from a fused bomb, Moore nodded. "I suppose he felt the threat justified it. For that matter so did Simms and General Staines."

"Never mind the others. It was Davies' idea, wasn't it?" When Moore did not reply, liquid suddenly spurted over the Yorkshireman's tunic as the glass in his big hand shattered. His chair clattered to the floor as he leapt to his feet. "The bastard," he choked. "He promised her. He promised us both."

Moore grabbed his arm. "I know how you feel. I felt the same way. Frank Adams and I walked out on him. But I suppose he felt the threat was so great that the risk had to be taken."

Harvey was not listening. His powerful body was trembling with shock and hatred. "The bastard promised us. And she promised me. God Almighty, is there anyone in this world you can trust?"

Afraid for him, Moore picked up the chair and tried to ease him back into it. "Try not to take it too hard, Frank. She's come back safely before."

Harvey was still not listening. "Where did she go to? Tempsford?"

"Yes."

"Then maybe she hasn't gone yet. Maybe I can catch her."

Moore grabbed his arm again. "You know you can't do that. They'd never allow it. And it would only distress her if she found out. In any case, it's almost certain she's gone already. They don't need to fly her out to a secret landing strip now. She's probably been flown to Normandy and passed on from there."

The Yorkshireman's failure to resist was an admission that he knew Moore was right. "She should have told me, Ian. For Christ's sake, I'm her husband." His cry was a mixture of anger and pain. "What if those Gestapo bastards get hold of her? Didn't she think about that?"

"I'm sure she thought of everything," Moore said quietly. "But in the end she felt it her duty to go."

"Duty? To a sod like Davies? To a bloody unfeeling world that one day won't even remember her name? What duty, for Christ's sake?"

With his hand on the Yorkshireman's arm, Moore could feel the sweat soaking through his tunic. "She was thinking about us, Frank. She knows a kite like that could shoot us down like clay pigeons."

With a groan, Harvey sank down on the chair and buried his face in his hands. Blood from his cut hand was trickling through his fingers. Moore's thoughts were painful as he gazed down. This was the man who had faced a hundred dangers without flinching. Now he was being brutally punished for loving too well. Damning the war and its soulless demands on human emotions, Moore filled another glass with whisky and returned it to the stricken man. "Drink it, Frank. All of it."

Harvey lifted his swollen eyes. Blood was smeared over his sweating face. For a moment he seemed about to refuse. Then he cursed, took the glass and drained it. Moore filled it again and pushed it back into his hand. Fifteen minutes later he guided the Yorkshireman to his own bed and laid a blanket over him. As Harvey groaned and rolled over, his right arm swung down from the bed. Seeing a drop of blood fall to the floor, Moore took the man's big hand and gently opened it. Wincing at the depth of the cut, he debated calling in the M.O. Instead, knowing his man, he took one of his own handkerchiefs and bound it tightly round the injury. Then, lighting a cigarette, he returned to his desk and sat in silence with his thoughts.

Chapter 21

Hausmann's whisper carried only across the cafe table. "Do you see her?"

Across the street two German staff cars had halted outside the restaurant and four couples were emerging. Meyer drew deeply on his cigarette as he nodded. "Ja, I see her. The girl's a miracle worker."

Hausmann was watching the tall uniformed von Haldenberg helping the elegant figure of Anna from a car. As the couple made for the restaurant entrance, with von Haldenberg holding the girl's arm possessively, Meyer expressed his fears. "With her looks, getting him interested at that party she gatecrashed the other night was one thing. But how the hell is she going to get away from him?"

"She won't be thinking in those terms yet," Hausmann said. "She'll only want to get away when she's got all the information she needs. That could be days or weeks."

Meyer watched the couple disappear into the restaurant, followed by the other laughing officers and girls. "If all we hear about Haldenberg is right, he's not going to wait weeks before getting his hands on her."

Hausmann, the older man, did his best to hide his irritation at Meyer's concern over the girl's sexual problems. "Lorenz is a highly experienced agent and knows what she's doing. I'm more worried what we're going to do if someone spots who she is."

Anna, the object of their concern, was at that moment being escorted to a private table within the restaurant. Every table contained a vase of flowers and a candelabra, and waiters moved unobtrusively between them with trays of food or pushing iced tubs of German champagne. Romano's in Nurnbach was doing its very best to ape its bigger brothers in Munich by trying to make its distinguished clients forget how badly the war was going for the Fatherland. "Does this table suit you, fräulein?"

The question drew Anna's attention back to von Haldenberg. The tall officer, as urbane to attractive women as he was arrogant to his subordinates, had pushed aside a waiter who was about to perform the service and was offering her a chair. As she nodded and sat down, his hand brushed her bare shoulder as he glanced round at the abashed waiter. "Send champagne, Hans. The best in the house." As the waiter hurried off, the officer sank into the chair opposite her. "So, you were able to get away from your aunt and relatives this evening, fräulein. Did it prove difficult?"

She smiled at him. "Not when I told them who had invited me out to dinner."

He looked amused. "Are you saying they have heard of me?"

"Of course. Who has not heard of the famous Colonel von Haldenberg, who has designed so many splendid aircraft for the Fatherland?"

This time he laughed. "You are flattering me, fräulein. I doubt if many of our good Bavarian citizens know much about aircraft. Now, if it were beer or cream cakes it would be a different matter."

Anna laughed with him. "You are quite right. They didn't know about you personally but like most people in Nurnbach they had heard that a number of high-ranking officers were in the town, and when I said their Commanding Officer had invited me to dinner they were most impressed."

His pale blue eyes were running over her as she spoke. She was wearing a white, off-the-shoulder gown with a deep décolletage that set off to perfection her dark hair and superb figure. With the candlelight giving an extra gloss to her flawless complexion, von Haldenberg was wondering what good fairy had brought this paragon to Nurnbach.

She gave an embarrassed laugh. "What are you looking at?"

"I'm admiring both you and your dress, fräulein. A man does not see many beautiful and well-dressed women these days. Did you bring the dress to Nurnbach with you?" She almost lied and then thought again. After her arrival in Nurnbach she had spent two days searching through the shops for such a dress, and so it was possible one of the good-time girls he or his colleagues entertained might have seen it earlier. It had cost her a sizeable proportion of the Reichmarks London had sent with her but it had served its purpose two nights ago in helping to draw von Haldenberg's attention. "No, I bought it here," she told him.

His eyebrows lifted. "I had no idea such dresses could still be obtained in Germany. You surprise me."

"Anything can still be obtained in Germany if one pays enough for it, Colonel."

It was a remark that could be taken in half a dozen ways but, from the look he gave her, he had taken it as a veiled promise. "I'm delighted to hear it, fräulein." He glanced round with some distaste at the tables of laughing officers and giggling girls. "Although, since I was posted here, there have been times when I've had my doubts."

It was the opening she needed. "Have you been here long, Colonel?"

He made a moue of disgust. "Over six months."

"Six months. That is a long time."

"Too long, fräulein. There are times when I think these forests will smother me." To her disappointment he changed the conversation. "But let us talk about you. Why have you come to Nurnbach? Is it the bombing that has driven you here?"

She lowered her eyes and answered quietly as if in pain from the reminder. "Yes. The bombing was very bad in Stuttgart. It killed my mother, and my father insisted I came here to escape it. He didn't want another of his children killed."

"Another child? You have lost a sister or a brother too?"

She nodded. "My brother, who was a pilot, was killed when trying to stop the Americans and the British bombing our cities." She drew in a shuddering breath. "God, how I hate those terror fliers. If only we had some way of stopping them. But every day, it seems, there are more and more of them."

At that moment their champagne arrived. Von Haldenberg tasted it and then stared up at the waiter, a small man with a pronounced limp. "Is this the best you have?"

The man looked frightened. "I'm afraid it is, Herr Colonel. We cannot get French champagne any longer."

Haldenberg frowned at him and then made a terse gesture for the wine to be poured. As the waiter limped away, Haldenberg held out his glass to touch her own. "To you, fräulein. The most beautiful woman I have seen since coming to Nurnbach."

She laughed. "Only in Nurnbach, Colonel? I would have thought a flatterer like you could do better than that."

He smiled back at her. "I wanted to say Munich and Berlin too, fräulein, but was afraid you might think I was overstating my case."

He was good, she thought. And handsome, with his lean, scarred soldier's face and immaculate uniform. It was his eyes that betrayed him. As pale as gun-metal and as pitiless. Not for the first time, Anna wondered how she would be able to escape from him after making so many implied promises. Then she pushed the thought aside. That problem would come later. Tonight she must try to discover why a designer with his skills should have been brought six months ago to this country town in the heart of Bavaria.

Wondering how she was going to draw the conversation back to his work, she was glad of the interruption when a waiter took their orders for dinner. When he left their table she motioned at the wings on Haldenberg's tunic. "I see you are a pilot, Colonel. Do you do much flying these days?"

"Do you mean in combat?" When she nodded, he went on: "Sadly, no. They will not allow it unless I am flying for test purposes. They seem to think I am more use to them on the ground."

"You mean in your role as a designer?"

"Yes. Design moves swiftly in wartime. Our job is to keep up with the enemy and surpass him if we can."

"Are we doing that, Colonel?"

"I like to think so. In fact I'm sure we are." Then, as if remembering himself, he reached for the champagne bottle. "But we must keep the war at bay tonight. Give me your glass."

Disappointed again, she allowed him to top up her glass and then watched him fill his empty one. Acutely aware that it was unlikely she would ever get a better opportunity to interrogate him, and noticing how quickly he drank, she lightened the conversation and encouraged him to order another bottle of champagne. By the time he was halfway through it, she felt it safe to steer the conversation back to himself and gave a sigh of envy. "It must be wonderful to be an aircraft designer at a time like this. Do you realise how lucky you are?"

Her admiration obviously pleased him. "I suppose it has its compensations, fräulein. Although until tonight they had escaped me."

"Heidi," she said. "Please call me Heidi."

Although his lips smiled appreciatingly, his pale eyes, suffused with alcohol, said other things. "I've been wondering when I might have that privilege, Heidi. So you appreciate my work, do you?"

She felt she had never acted better than at that moment. "Oh, yes. More than you can believe. If God could give me one wish, I would be a fighter pilot in combat against the British and the Americans. I would shoot them down with a song in my heart. But to do that our Luftwaffe must have superior aircraft and sufficient numbers of them. If designers like you can provide them, it will save our country."

Her fervour had clearly impressed him. "You do hate the terror fliers, don't you?"

"Hate them?" she said fiercely. "I would pull them down from the skies with my bare hands if I could, and then burn them at the stake. But every day there are more and more of them. Isn't there anything to be done before it's too late?"

As his glazed eyes searched her face, she wondered if she had gone too far. He drew out a gold cigarette case and offered it to her. When he lit both their cigarettes and still made no comment, she believed her ploy had failed. Then he exhaled smoke and reached out for her hand. "Stop worrying, Heidi. The British and the Americans are going to get the shock of their lives very soon."

Her heart leapt at his words. Then, remembering her role, she gazed at him wide-eyed. "What does that mean? Are you working on a new fighter?"

He had not drunk enough to forget the need for caution and kept his voice low. "Yes. Something that the enemy can't possibly match. When it comes into production, it will shoot them from the skies like as many pheasants."

With the emotion she was feeling at this confession, it was not difficult to squeeze his hand in excitement. "But will there be enough of them? We need hundreds, if not thousands, if we are to win the war."

His nod was full of confidence. "There'll be enough."

"How can you be sure of that?"

"Because we are not building an entirely new aircraft but adapting an old one. That way we save years on plant and development."

So Ian was right, she thought, with mounting excitement. "But how can you be sure your fighter will do all these things?"

Alcohol exaggerated his pride of achievement. "We've already flown a prototype. And it was a great success."

Showing delight, she felt her next question innocent enough in the circumstances. "That's wonderful news. But then why are you here? Shouldn't you be where all this research and development is being done?"

He laughed. "I am where the research is being done, Heidi. We are doing everything here."

Her heart was racing now but she made herself look disappointed. "I thought for a moment you were serious. There's no research centre in Nurnbach. Even I know that."

He made an impatient gesture. "I didn't say it was in the town."

"Then where is it?" When he frowned and shook his head, she withdrew her hand from his. "I'm not sure whether you are saying all this to comfort me, Colonel, or just to play a joke but after what has happened to my family, but I don't think it is in very good taste. There is nothing around here, or my friends and relatives would have heard of it."

She was never to know whether he would have told her the centre's location or not. As he drew deeply on his cigarette, a sudden silence fell in the restaurant. Gazing round she saw two men, one wearing a leather coat, had entered the restaurant and were standing at its entrance. As she watched them, one pointed at her table and they began hurrying towards it.

She felt as if a dagger of ice had pierced her heart as they drew nearer. Noticing her expression, von Haldenberg swung round and showed anger as they halted beside the table. "What do you want?"

The leather-coated man held out an identity card to him. His voice sounded like sandpaper on metal. "You are Colonel von Haldenberg?"

"Yes, I am. What do you want?"

"We have come to arrest your friend." The man made a gesture to his smaller companion, who took the arm of the white-faced girl.

Haldenberg leapt to his feet. "What the hell are you doing? Don't you know my position here?"

"We know all about you, Colonel, and we also know everything about the girl. She is a spy working for the enemy."

No man had ever sobered more quickly than the stunned Haldenberg. "You've made some mistake. The girl's German and visiting relations in the town."

"She is a German all right, but also a traitor working for the British. Her task was to interrogate you and find out all she could about your present work." The man pointed contemptuously at the champagne bucket on the table. "From all appearances she has been carrying out her duties very successfully."

Still incredulous, Haldenberg tried to bluff his way out. "I shall report this to your superiors. You are insulting both me and my guest."

The taller man's voice had the cutting edge of a razor. "You can report whatever you like, Colonel. But when we have interrogated this lady and found out what you have told her, my guess is that you will be very lucky to avoid interrogation yourself." Nodding at his colleague, he turned to the girl. "Come along, fräulein. We have to be in Munich before dawn."

Leaving the white-faced Haldenberg standing like a statue at the table, Anna was led towards the restaurant doors while officers and girls at the surrounding tables gaped at her. Numbed by the suddenness of it all, she was unable to take in the full implications of her arrest. Only one thought rose and screamed in her mind. It was

Harvey's agony when he learned she was in the hands of the Gestapo.

Chapter 22

Dusk was falling outside and although there was a dim light shining through the cafe windows, the tables on the pavement were in semi-darkness. Seeing the two men still sitting at a table, an elderly woman approached them. "Sorry, but we're closing now."

Hausmann turned to her and put on his best smile. "Do you mind if we stay out here a little longer? My friend and I only met today and we've much to talk about."

The woman eyed him, then collected their empty beer mugs from the table. "You can stay here as long as you like. But don't expect any service."

Hausmann hid a breath of relief. "Thank you, mein Frau." He indicated the brightening moonglow over a distant mountain. "It looks like being a pleasant evening."

The woman swept a dustcloth over the table. "Too pleasant perhaps. Let's just hope it doesn't bring out the terror fliers."

Hausmann laughed. "There's nothing here for them to bomb. It's the big cities they're after."

"Those brutes will bomb anything. Some bombs fell near my sister in Prien last week and there's nothing around her but cows and sheep."

"It can't last, mein Frau. The Führer will soon find a way of stopping them."

The woman eyed him again, then gave a sniff of contempt. "The Führer promised they'd never drop a single bomb on the Fatherland. If you ask me, too many promises have been made to us and never kept."

Meyer winked his approval at Hausmann as she disappeared into the cafe. Both men had noticed how confidence in Hitler was diminishing by the day as the Allies drove deeper into Europe. Meyer held his question back until an elderly couple walked past. "How long do you intend staying here? Until they leave the restaurant?"

Hausmann nodded. "I want to see if Lorenz manages to get away from von Haldenberg. If she does, we'll tail her until she's back home with her aunt."

Meyer scowled. "I can't see him letting her get away."

"She's managed it before. Don't forget she's making him think she's a high class pick up. The more she plays hard to get, the more he'll want to see her."

As the men fell silent, muted music could be heard from the blacked-out restaurant opposite. To the east the moon had now cleared the mountain tops and was silvering the pavements. Although most townsfolk were keeping off the streets, now and then a soldier on leave with his girlfriend would pass the table, their low voices exchanging the age-old comments of lovers.

Hausmann was about to offer Meyer another cigarette when a car, speeding past them, made both men turn. With petrol desperately scarce in Germany, both men knew it almost certainly belonged to military or political officers. They watched its tail lights turn off the road a couple of hundred metres from the restaurant and then heard the engine switch off. Meyer glanced back at Hausmann. "Who was that?"

Hausmann tried to hide his unease. "Perhaps another officer visiting his girlfriend. They seem as randy as rabbits in this town."

Thirty seconds passed and then the couple heard rapid footsteps coming up the road. A moment later they saw two men, one in a leather coat and the other in a civilian suit, pause outside the restaurant and then enter it. Meyer's voice sounded hoarse and strained. "Gestapo?"

Hausmann was feeling a hot, burning sensation in his chest. "They could be. Did you bring your pistol with you?"

Meyer nodded tightly. "Yes, but what's our move if they arrest Lorenz? We can't start shooting or we'll have every soldier in the town on our backs."

Hausmann wished his heart would quieten down. "We'll have to play it by ear. Wait and see what happens."

The next few minutes were the longest either man had known. The music that started up again seemed to accentuate the silence and to tighten the tension. The moonlight was now shining down the opposite pavement although the restaurant doors were still in shadow. As the two men watched with bated breath, an inside light flickered as the doors opened and then closed. A moment later Meyer gave a strangled curse. "We were right. They are Gestapo."

The moonlight showed the two men escorting Anna from the restaurant. Given no time to collect her coat, she was plainly visible in her white dress. Too intelligent to struggle futilely with her captors, she was walking calmly along the pavement between them, although each had a hand on her arm. Meyer turned his shocked face to Hausmann. "We've got to try something. We can't leave her to those bastards."

Hausmann was trying to calm his frantic mind. "As she's a girl, they might have come alone. Let's follow them and see. Pretend we've had a few drinks, but for God's sake make it look natural."

They rose from the table and crossed the road. By this time the two Gestapo agents and Anna were some forty metres ahead of them. A soldier and his girl, walking in the opposite direction, paused and then moved nervously aside as the trio passed them. Nudging Meyer, Hausmann increased his pace until they were no more than twenty steps away. As the leather-coated man glanced back, Hausmann laughed aloud and broke into a drunken song. As Meyer joined him, the second Gestapo agent turned and shouted at them to be silent.

Hausmann shouted back and began singing again. The leather-coated man said something to his colleague who shrugged and this time ignored the disturbance. As they approached a street corner, an elderly couple shrank into a darkened doorway: fear of the Gestapo in Germany was now as prevalent in the countryside as in the cities. Another ten paces and the two men and Anna disappeared down the side street.

Hausmann paused for a moment. "We'll have to try to get her away, no matter who else is in the car. Are you ready?"

In the moonlight Meyer's lean face looked both pale and determined. "I'm ready."

Hausmann wished his heart would slow its frantic pounding. "Then let's go."

They rounded the corner and saw a single car parked twenty metres down the shadowy street. The man in the leather coat was opening the rear door and his colleague was pushing Anna towards it. Hausmann's whisper was full of relief. "I think they're alone."

The first Gestapo agent had now seen them and shouted for them to halt. Laughing and lurching forward, Hausmann came alongside him. "I like your taste in girls, matey. Can you find a couple more like her for us?"

He received a violent push. "Get on your way, you drunken fool. Get away before we arrest you too."

For a big man Hausmann moved quickly. Jerking out the pistol concealed in his trouser pocket, he leapt forward and smashed the butt into the man's face, jerking his head back and dropping him in a heap on the pavement. Seeing the leather-coated agent swinging round and grabbing for his coat pocket, Hausmann yelled a warning to Meyer, who leapt forward and grappled with him. As the agent shouted for help Hausmann struck at his head from behind. Although the blow was only a glancing one, it weakened his resistance, enabling Hausmann to strike again. This time the man's knees buckled and he fell stunned alongside his colleague.

Gasping for air as if he had run a marathon, Hausmann turned to the car. "Lorenz! Are you all right?"

The white-faced girl, who had moved to help them when their attack came, sank back into the car. "Yes. But hurry. Before you are seen."

Still gasping for breath, Hausmann turned to Meyer who was staring down at the two unconscious men. "Get the car keys and then shoot them!"

Anna started. "Is that necessary?"

"Shoot them," Hausmann panted, seeing Meyer's hesitation. "They know us now and they know Lorenz. If they live we'll never get her away."

It was the girl's peril that swung the scales for Meyer. As Hausmann cursed and was about to push him away, the younger man began fumbling in the agent's pockets. Drawing out a bunch of keys he, threw them at Hausmann. "All right. You get the car started."

As Hausmann jumped into the car and switched on the engine, Meyer knelt down and put the pistol to the temple of the leather-coated man. Seeing his intention, Anna gave a cry of protest and jumped from the car to stop him. Pushing her back, Meyer pulled the trigger. As the sound echoed across the street, he did the same to the other agent. Then he pushed the shocked girl back into the car and leapt in after her. A moment later, as townsfolk began running out of their shuttered houses, the car accelerated away with a scream of tyres, roared through the awakened town, and disappeared into the forest beyond.

Adams looked horrified. "Are you saying the Gestapo arrested her?"

Davies nodded. "Apparently while she was talking to von Haldenberg."

"That's terrible news. Harvey will go crazy when he hears."

"No one's going to tell him, Frank. At least not yet." Although he did his best, Davies could not disguise his relief. "Two of SOE's German agents managed to get her away."

The shocked Adams wondered why Davies couldn't have given him the better news first. "When? Before or after they interrogated her?"

"Before, although details are scarce at the moment. London's main concern was finding out how much she'd picked up about the project from von Haldenberg."

Adams could believe that. In his view the longer the war lasted, the more inhumane and brutal both sides were becoming. "But she is safe? She has got away?"

"She isn't out of Germany yet, if that's what you mean. But she is with the Resistance again and with any luck she ought to be all right."

Adams began to feel better. "When do you intend telling Harvey, sir?"

Davies frowned. "I'm not telling him a thing yet and neither will you. I've had enough of him behaving like a rutting bull in a pot shop. We'll tell him when we know she's safely back in France." Before Adams could protest, Davies became his old sarcastic self again. "Do you mind if we talk about the business in hand now?"

The two men were back in the library at High Elms, where Adams had been ordered to attend that morning. The Brigadier had been present but been called to his scrambler telephone a couple of minutes ago. It was only then that Adams had heard about Anna's near disaster. "Fm sorry, sir. But you know how we all feel about Anna."

Davies's scowl hid his own admiration for the girl. "You and Moore made it clear enough last month. If I had the sense of a cretin I'd have had the two of you before a court martial."

The Brigadier's entry saved Adams a reply. "Sorry, gentleman, but that was London again. I'm afraid our earlier intelligence was correct. Mrs Harvey did establish that there is an aircraft research establishment somewhere around Buchansee, but she was arrested before she could find out its exact location."

Adams could not help his bitter comment. "So she faced all that danger for nothing."

"Don't be stupid, Frank." The sharp complaint came from Davies. "Before she went we wondered if we could be chasing a red herring. Now we know for certain the site's there, we can concentrate on finding it."

With Anna no longer able to operate in the area, Adams was wondering what options were left. "Haven't we any clues at all?"

Simms motioned Adams to examine photographs of the Buchansee district that were spread out on the library table. "For a while we thought we had one. Mrs Harvey apparently found out from some of the locals that a small contingent of soldiers are replaced every few days on this island. They sail from a small jetty on the southern side of the lake."

Adams gazed down at a photograph of the lake. The Brigadier was pointing at the smaller of its two islands. "What would they be doing there? The island's far too small to hold a research establishment, isn't it?"

"Precisely. It can't be more than fifty metres from end to end. And although we've had it photographed twice and put our experts on examining the prints, they can find nothing of any significance."

Examining the other photographs Simms had pulled out from a pile, Adams saw he was right. Trees and bushes covered the entire island. "On the other hand, why would they put a garrison on the island? How many soldiers are involved?"

"No more than a dozen at the most." At Adams' puzzled expression, Simms nodded. "Exactly. If there were something of importance there, why only a dozen men?"

"Could it be something simple, like a rest camp?" Simms sighed. "I suppose it could be, although it seems a strange place to house solders on leave."

Davies's interjection explained to Adams at last why he had been called to High Elms. "Now we know this establishment is somewhere in the vicinity of Buchansee or Nurnbach, we're going to subject the area to intensive reconnaissance. I've arranged with Benson to send out aircraft as often as the weather permits, to see if one day we can catch Jerry with his trousers down and spot transports coming or going to the site. We'll have our photo experts working on them, of course, but I'm going to have copies made so that you can examine them too. In the past you've spotted things the rest of us have missed, so I'm giving you the chance again. Only keep it to yourself. Jerry's going to get touchy enough when he sees our kites flying around there: we don't want any careless talk to add to his suspicions."

Adams was wondering what he had done to earn such a tribute. "I'll do my best, sir, although I doubt if I'll be able to detect things the others haven't seen."

Looking sorry he had been so fulsome with his praise, Davies was quick to make amends. "I doubt it too," he grunted. "But in the mess we're in, we haven't much to lose, have we?"

Chapter 23

The weather changed the very next day. Depressions born over the turbulent Atlantic began queuing up over the Western Approaches and in turn swung with malicious joy over the British isles. Travelling in a lower trajectory and on a wider front than common-or-garden variety depressions, they completed Davies's frustration by reaching deep into Europe and laying clouds and drizzle over Bavaria and Austria. With Benson's weather planes reporting Buchansee reconnaissances a waste of time, Davies called on Millburn and Gabby to try their luck, but even that intrepid couple could find nothing to photograph over their target but dark and towering clouds.

To make matters worse, heavy gales swept Britain on the eighth day, making grounded American crews understand why their forebears had fled for warmer climes across the ocean. The same gales swept across Europe, ripping off roof tiles and uprooting trees. With Benson refusing to send any type of plane off the ground until conditions improved, Davies's frustration grew.

It was ten days before the weather men reported an autumn high pressure belt establishing itself over central Europe. The moment he received the news, Davies swung into action. Discovering Benson were still quibbling over the weather conditions, a mood no doubt influenced by his repeated and irritable demands for action, the small Air Commodore lost patience. While mechanics were ordered to service the P/R Mosquito, Millburn and Gabby were told their services were required yet again.

The Mosquito yawed, then steadied. Millburn, looking huge in his pressurised waistcoat, airtight mask, and flying suit, glanced at Gabby, who was similarly dressed. "That's about her limit, boyo."

The Mosquito, code-named Z for Zebra, had been climbing steadily since leaving Sutton Craddock. Passing first through the turbulent layers of air in the troposphere where all the variations of weather occur, Z-Zebra was now almost in the stratosphere and her airfoils were faltering in the rarefied air. Below, Europe looked like a green, wrinkled tablecloth. Above, the sky was a pitiless blue with the sun a blinding, molten ball.

With yellow haloes round her spinning propellers, Z-Zebra droned on, her exhaust gases streaming out behind her like railroad tracks. For camouflage her topside had been painted in uneven strips of brown and green and her underside was a bright cerulean blue. Specially adapted, she had a transparent nose with an F.53 camera. Used solely for reconnaissance purposes, she was stripped to the buff and carried no armament of any kind.

In the unpressurised cabin, the two men were already experiencing the discomforts of high-level flight. The cold was intense, instruments kept blurring before their eyes, and as Z-Zebra droned on a sensation of remoteness affected them. The normal roar of the two Merlins was reduced to a muffled sound as if reaching them through a thick blanket. Hearing Gabby's distant, muffled voice and unable to make sense of it, Millburn swallowed to clear his ears. "What did you say?"

"I said at last the bloody wind is dropping. It was playing hell with my navigation."

"Does that mean you're going to find Buchansee?"

"I hope so."

"What does that mean — you hope so? From this height you can damn nearly see the Kremlin."

"Then what's your problem, Millburn? If it's that easy, why am I here?"

"I've never known why, you little short ass. It's just your bloody RAF that makes me drag you along."

"You're all wind and piss, Millburn. If it wasn't for me the Jerries would have been feeding you sauerkraut back in '42."

Although banter was their habit, both men were using it that day to combat the deadening effects of high altitude flying. Nor did it indicate a lack of professionalism. The couple's efficiency and dedication were never in question, as any long-term member of the squadron would testify.

Both men were wondering if they had been spotted yet. To the German Observer Corps they would be soundless and invisible, but if radar had picked them up their survival would depend on the Mosquito's ability to fly higher than German fighters.

The minutes droned past. Below roads could be seen lying across the countryside like pieces of string. Smoke hazes betrayed the location of towns and cities and, as Z-Zebra penetrated deeper into the enemy heartland, the higher mounds of mountains appeared. As dark patches of forest showed between and over them, Millburn addressed his intercom again. "How much longer? Or are you asleep?"

Gabby sounded indignant. "No, I'm not. Ten minutes to ETA. Maybe a minute or two more."

Millburn could now see pools of silver appearing between the wooded mountains. About to address Gabby again, he noticed a low film of stratocirrus cloud ahead. "You see that cloud? It's not going to fog our plates, is it?"

"I can't tell yet. We'll have to wait and see."

Under Gabby's instructions, Z-Zebra swung two degrees to starboard. Below the mountains rose higher and the woods became dark green carpets. Another minute and Gabby pointed ahead. "There it is. Buchansee."

Millburn gazed curiously down. Although everything was diminished by altitude, he saw a large lake surrounded by high hills and dense woods. "Are you sure that's it?"

"It has to be. Adams said it had two islands, a railway that looped south of it, and a sawmill. That smudge of haze must be the mill. We're O.K."

Through his smoked glasses, Millburn could see the Welshman was right but he also saw something else. Although it was flimsy enough to be transparent, the tenuous film of cloud he had noticed earlier lay right across the lake and its surrounding woods. The high pressure area that had stretched almost from the British

Isles had come to an end over their objective. Millburn cursed at this manifestation of Sod's Law. "There's also that damned cloud. Slap over everything. Will it fog your plates?"

Gabby was squinting through his camera. "I'll tell you in a minute." Then: "I think it will. But I'll take a few shots just in case."

Millburn waited until he had finished before asking his question. "How high do you reckon that cloud is?"

"I'd say around eighteen thousand."

"That's my guess. How do you feel? Are you game to risk it?"

In the short silence that followed Millburn knew what the Welshman was thinking. It had been known for some time that the Germans were using nitrous oxide in their engines to boost their rate of climb. If the Mosquito had already been spotted, enemy fighters would be leaping up from the nearby airfield like as many sharks from the sea bed. If any were the latest Focke-Wulfs and had nitrous oxide, they could well reach the cloud before Z-Zebra could take its photographs and escape.

It was a point of principle for Gabby to give his agreement with the least possible grace. "I suppose you'll do it whether I agree or not?"

Knowing his man, Millburn grinned. "That's right, boyo. Here we go."

Z-Zebra tilted a wing and went slicing down. As the air became denser and her airfoils began to vibrate, both men watched the altimeter needle. 36,000 ... 32,000 ... 28,000 ... 26,000 ... 24,000 ... the protesting scream of engines and airfoils forced Millburn to throttle back a couple of notches. Below, the rucked tablecloth was turning into a vast expense of wooded mountains interspersed by lakes. As the first tenuous wisps of cloud brushed past the cupola, Millburn eased back on the control column. "You've got two minutes. Not a second more."

Once beneath the film of cloud, Z-Zebra went into orbit as Gabby began taking his photographs. Sweating freely now, Millburn stared down at the vast panorama, knowing that the Mosquito would now be silhouetted against the cloud above. He glanced at his watch. "You've got thirty more seconds. Then we're getting the hell out of here."

Fifteen more seconds passed and then Gabby gave a yell of alarm. "Bandits, Millburn! Focke-Wulfs. Nine o'clock low."

Feeling his heart giving an explosive jolt, Millburn stared down. For a moment he could see nothing but dark trees. Then he sighted the fighters: two winged objects no larger than wasps but fast making height towards them. Ramming his throttles through the gate, he pulled back on the control column. "That's it. Forget the job and get back up here."

Gabby, his face pale, joined him a few seconds later. He was gripping a pair of binoculars. "What do you think? Can we out climb the bastards?"

Millburn's eyes were on the altimeter. "We'll soon find out, won't we?"

Z-Zebra's engines were screaming their protest as the altimeter slowly registered their climb. For a moment, wisps of cloud swept past its cupola, then Z-Zebra broke out into the bright sunlight. Tearing off his smoked glasses, Millburn grabbed the binoculars and searched for the fighters. For thirty seconds the cloud hid them. Then they broke through and the American saw that Gabby was right: they were Focke-Wulfs. That meant they could reach 20,000 feet very quickly, although after that their power curve would begin to fall away. But then so would their own, Millburn thought. He decided the outcome could well rest on whether or not the fighters were equipped with nitrous oxide.

For the next few minutes the distance between hunters and hunted remained constant. It was only when Z-Zebra began to yaw and falter that the Focke-Wulfs began to close. Gabby glanced anxiously at Millburn. "Is that it?"

Millburn grimly eased the control column forward. "That's it. She's reached her ceiling."

Below, like triumphant hunters seeing their prey was exhausted, the two Focke-Wulfs were still climbing fast. In the brilliant sunlight they could now be seen clearly without binoculars: their short wings, long transparent cupolas, and huge radial engines making them look like huge and deadly insects. After another minute had passed, they were less than fifteen hundred feet below and behind Z-Zebra. As Gabby stared back, the leading pilot fired an experimental burst. Lines of cannon tracer soared up, only to arc and fall away before reaching the Mosquito. At the same time the Focke-Wulf swung crazily under the massive recoil.

Gritting his teeth, Millburn tried to coax more height from Z-Zebra but as she yawed perilously he desisted, fearing she might stall and bring him down within range of the fighters. He turned his perspiring face to Gabby. "What do you think? Are the bastards going to make it?"

"Christ knows," Gabby muttered. "They're trying hard enough."

The deadly chase continued across the cruel sky. Although now as unstable as Z-Zebra, the Focke-Wulfs managed to claw their way to the same altitude and then tried to close the gap. As Gabby gazed back, he could see them yawing and weaving as their pilots did everything in their power to come into range. At one moment he believed they were succeeding, in the next he tried to comfort himself with the hope that the gap was being sustained. Now and again one pilot or the other would fire a burst, searching for Z-Zebra's fuel tanks or the flesh of her crew. When a chain of cannon shells ripped the rarefied air below the Mosquito's starboard wing, both men were certain the range was closing. It was only when Gabby let out a relieved shout that the tension slackened. "The bugger's spinning down, Millburn! It's the effect of his cannon."

Millburn saw he was right. The recoil of multiple cannon had taken their effect in the rarefied air and sent the Focke-Wulf slithering down out of control. But one heavily-armed fighter was left and its pilot showed no sign of allowing his quarry to escape.

It was not a fitting situation for Millburn. Had Z-Zebra been armed, the aggressive American would have spun round and engaged the fighter without question. As things were, he could only keep control of himself and hope his two engines would carry them to safety.

His hope was realised when the mountains and lakes of Bavaria were well behind them. Suddenly he found Z-Zebra more stable, and by nursing his controls he was able to coax another thousand feet of altitude out of her. Behind him the chasing Focke-Wulf tried to follow, only to falter, dip a wing, and begin spinning down. Gabby let out a yell of relief. "The bastard's had it. What happened, boyo?"

Millburn patted the control column affectionately. “The old girl did us proud. She suddenly woke up and started flying.”

Relief allowed Gabby the luxury of a grumble. “Not before bloody time. Are you sure there wasn’t something you forgot to do before? Like using only one engine?”

“Stop talking out of your trousers, you little short ass. Get your eyes on your map and let’s get back home.”

Davies walked to a window of Adams’ ‘Confessional’ and gazed impatiently out. “What the hell are they doing? It doesn’t take all this time to develop photographs, does it?”

Henderson, the only other officer present other than Adams, tried to calm him. “Millburn only got back thirty minutes ago, sir. And there was cloud over the target. Perhaps that’s causing a problem.” Davies turned moodily and walked back to the long table where the other two men were seated. “Let’s hope not. We’ve lost enough time as it is with all this lousy weather.” He turned to Adams. “You say Millburn went down below the cloud?”

“Yes, sir. He took a big chance. In fact it’s something of a miracle the two Focke-Wulfs didn’t get them.”

Although his mind was on other things, Davies had enough grace to give credit where credit was due. “I agree. It was a damn good show and I’m going to recommend both of ’em for a bar to their DFCs. But from all you said, they weren’t under the cloud for very long. Could they have got decent photographs in that time?”

“They couldn’t have got many,” Adams admitted. “I suppose we’ll just have to hope the ones they took came out well.”

Davies frowned and paced back to the window. “At least they were taken from a lower altitude than the others. Let’s hope to Christ they show something this time or I don’t know what our next move can be.”

Glancing at Henderson, Adams ventured a question. “The Brigadier’s agents haven’t come up with anything else, then, sir?”

“Not a thing,” Davies muttered. “From all I can gather, they’re still on the run.”

“Does that include Anna?”

Davies scowled. "I suppose it must." He swung back to the window. "Where the hell are those photographs? Give 'em a ring, Adams, and tell them to get their fingers out."

Adams was saved from the act by a sharp tap on the door. A moment later a breathless WAAF appeared carrying a tin box. Davies' bark made her jump as if her bottom had been pinched. "You've taken your time, haven't you?"

"I'm sorry, sir. but we have been as quick as possible."

"How have they come out?"

"A few are clouded, sir. But others are quite good. We've enlarged the better ones."

Davies took the box from her. "All right. Off you go."

As the girl saluted and hurried out, Davies laid the box before Adams. "Here you are, Frank. Find something this time or they'll make me a bloody erk."

Adams, who already had earlier photographs of Buchansee spread out on the table before him, lifted out a series of wet prints, sandwiched between plates of glass, from the tin box and tried to match them. With Davies peering over his shoulder, he found the exercise difficult. When he moved one photograph three times, the small Air Commodore's voice turned liverish. "What's the problem, Frank? You need a new pair of glasses?"

The perspiring Adams wished Henderson would do something to distract him. "The photographs are taken from different heights, sir. And we've far fewer this time. So it's not easy to pair them off."

Although Davies grunted something, he allowed Adams to complete his task without further interruption, although his sharp eyes scrutinised every print the Intelligence Officer lifted from the box. By the time Adams had completed the task, Davies gave a groan of disappointment. "There isn't a thing, is there? Not one damn thing different from the others."

Adams adjusted his spectacles. "It doesn't look like it, sir. But first I'd like to examine the new prints under magnification."

As Adams produced a large lens and began running it over the prints, Davies sank down heavily on the bench alongside Henderson. "What the hell do we do now, Jock? We've discovered for certain the Jerries have a plant there and yet we're as far off as ever from finding out where. I've never been so frustrated in my bloody life."

Davies was the most positive character he had met, and Henderson was thinking that nothing he could have said could have stressed the seriousness of the situation more. He was wondering how best to reply when Adams gave an excited exclamation. "Wait a minute. There might be something here."

In a second both men were crowded behind him. Davies' voice was hoarse. "What is it, Frank?"

Adams pointed to a spot on one of the latest enlarged photographs. "There! See that small oblong among the trees. It looks different from the original photograph."

Pushing Henderson aside, Davies squinted through the huge lens. "Where?"

Adams pointed with his finger again. "See. It's a different colour."

Davies sounded disappointed. "Couldn't that be a few trees blown down by the wind?"

"No. They'd look different. In any case, why would only those trees blow over? They'd be sheltered by the others. And look at that dark circle. That's got no connection with trees."

Davies stared down again, then looked up at the excited Adams. "Then what do you think it is?"

Followed by the small officer's impatient eyes, Adams went to the door of the Intelligence Office to make certain there was no one outside. Then, returning to the table, he gave his interpretation of the tiny patch. When he finished Henderson gave a grunt of disbelief. "All that from what might only be a fault in the print? You can't be serious, Frank."

Adams turned to him. "It's only a guess, sir. But I think it's possible."

Both men turned to Davies whose eyes had opened wide at Adams' theory. He stared back at them and then suddenly let out a laugh of triumph. "By God, Frank, I think you might have cracked it. It's the only thing that makes sense. Well done. Bloody marvellous, in fact."

Henderson stared at him. "You surely can't believe it, sir?"

"I do believe it, Jock. Jerry's a clever bastard and he's done things just as clever before. What about Rhine Maiden? Remember how long we searched for that factory?"

"Yes, but that was different, sir."

"Only in degree, Jock. Only in degree." Davies turned his shining, sparrow-like eyes on Adams again. "Bloody marvellous, Frank. I'm proud of you."

His euphoria was alarming Adams. "It's only a guess, sir. I'd like Babington Smith's unit to give their opinion before things go any further."

Davies swung round on Henderson. "That's no problem. Jock will send a motor cyclist with prints right away. In the meantime I'm going to have a talk with 618 Squadron about borrowing their B.IVs again."

It was difficult to decide who showed greater alarm at this statement, Adams or Henderson, but the Scot got his protest in first. "Sir, it's all supposition at the moment. You can't make all these changes and throw all these spanners into the works until we're sure what we're doing."

"I think he's right, sir," Adams added. "Apart from consulting the Photo-Intelligence people, I'd suggest we carry out another recce while the weather lasts. If things are back to normal tomorrow, then at least we'll know it's not a false alarm."

Davies smacked a fist into his palm. "That's it! If they carry out repairs right away, we know we're on to something. You're on bloody good form today, aren't you, Frank? What are you taking? Monkey glands?"

When the embarrassed Adams did not reply, Davies turned to Henderson. Although he had scowled at the Scot's frankness, it had served to bring him down to earth. "All right, Jock. Maybe I am jumping the gun a little but don't blame me. This is the first ray of hope we've had."

Mollified, Henderson nodded. "I do realise that, sir. What do you want me to do? Send Millburn and Gabriel out again tomorrow."

"No, they've done their whack. Let Benson do it. I'll get on to them right away."

Adams broke in here. "Ask them to try to take their photographs at the same time Millburn and Gabby did, sir. Then the angle of sunlight and shadows will be the same."

"Good thinking, Frank. How long will it take to get an opinion from Babington Smith's unit?"

Adams hesitated. "Tomorrow at the earliest if we ask them to make it urgent and use a fast dispatch rider. Perhaps by tomorrow afternoon."

"Good. Then get on to it, both of you. I want an opinion from them no later than 16.00 hours. In the meantime I'll see Benson gets new prints for us." Davies glanced at his watch, then made for the door. "I'll be staying at High Elms overnight. As soon as you get an opinion from Photographic Intelligence and those new prints, phone me and come there. All right?"

When both men nodded, Davies paused at the door. With every movement betraying his excitement, he had never looked more like an animated elf. "It's looking good at last. If we're right, we've got some busy days ahead of us."

With that he threw open the door and went out. Henderson gave a groan as his image hurried past the window. "What the hell have you done, Frank? If Photo Intelligence get the same idea, it's going to be hell here, particularly if he wants to use those damned B.IVs again."

Adams was beginning to wonder himself what he had started. "He'll have no option if the job's what I fear it might be."

The Scot gave another groan and rose heavily from his seat. "I'm going to my office. I need a dram. Are you coming?"

Adams shook his head. "No, thanks, sir. I'd better get on right away with Photo Intelligence."

Staines ran a hand through his spiky hair as he gazed down at the photographs. "Are you sure about this, Davies? It all sounds mighty far-fetched to me."

Davies had no option but to be honest. "We can't be one hundred per cent certain, sir, because our agents haven't been able to get near the place. But our Photo-Intelligence unit believes we are right and the fact Jerry has repaired his camouflage so smartly suggests he's hiding something very important."

Staines shook his head. "If you're right, it's been a hell of a project."

"It's massively important to them, sir. And they might have used slave labour."

The big American nodded. "True. But you're asking me to provide a cover of expensive B-17s for you, and that means I have to convince Spaatz they're not going out on a wild goose chase. I take it you can't do the job without them? You couldn't manage with just an escort of long range Mustangs?"

"If we have to go out without B-17s we will," Davies told him. "But there's one important reason why we shouldn't. We don't know what security Jerry's got there. If he gets too early a warning, he might be able to come up with all kinds of tricks to keep us out. Whereas if a box of B-17s could give us radar cover, as they did during Operation Rhine Maiden, we might catch Jerry with his trousers down."

Staines took a drag on his huge cigar before replying. "Spaatz will never give us as many B-17s as we used the last time. Not while they're helping our armies by pounding the Krauts' defence positions and supply lines. That's for sure."

"We don't need that many," Davies pointed out. "Just enough to hide our radar pattern from their receivers." When Staines hesitated, Davies went on: "It's vitally important, sir. If Jerry finishes his research and gets his findings out to his factories, we're all going to pay a hell of a price."

Staines frowned. "You don't have to convince me of that, Davies. My job is to convince Spaatz we're not making a mountain out of a molehill. After all, what have I to show him? A small speck on a photograph."

"You've got everything von Haldenberg told Anna. In his own words he said that the research was being carried out."

"Yes, but where? He never told her that, did he? And that's the issue here. I have to convince Spaatz of something I find hard to believe myself."

"Excuse me, Davies, but there is one thing you haven't yet mentioned." The quiet interruption came from Brigadier Simms who was sharing the library at High Elms with the two men. "You haven't told the general about the noise our agents heard."

Davies gave a violent start, then struck his forehead with his hand. He gave Simms a rueful look. "I'm forgetting to talk about wood for bloody trees. Perhaps you'll handle that, sir."

Simms nodded and turned to Staines. "Two of our agents heard a loud, high-pitched scream one night when out in the woods near Buchansee. Later Anna discovered from her aunt that local foresters have heard the sound for months. No one has been able to identify it but when my unit got word of it our Scientific Advice Group was asked to give an opinion in the light of our earlier suspicions. We received that opinion only yesterday."

Staines was all attention now. "Go on. What was it?"

Simms told him. When he finished the big American looked astonished. "You're kidding, Simms. You have to be."

"No, sir. It was a consensus of opinion from all the scientists involved. Do you see now how it fits in with everything we've believed so far?"

Staines was still digesting what he had heard. "It's clever," he muttered. "Diabolically clever."

Simms shrugged. "They are very clever people. We've always known that."

Davies was trying to analyse the American's expression. "What do you think, sir? Will that convince General Spaatz?"

Staines heaved his bulk from his chair. "It would convince me, Davies. By the Lord Harry it would. I think you can take it you'll get your B-17s and a Mustang escort to boot."

Chapter 24

An armed RAF corporal stepped out on the road and signalled the staff car to halt. As the WAAF driver obeyed, Davies leaned his head from the rear window and held out a pass. The corporal glanced at it, saluted, and waved the car on. Settling back in his seat, Davies turned to Henderson and Adams, who were seated alongside him. "We've put a safety net right around the field to keep away sightseers. At all costs Jerry mustn't know we're on to him or he'll slam the door in our faces."

The car was stopped a second time before it was allowed to drive through a farm gate into a large grassy field. As Adams climbed out, he saw there were two cranes positioned by opposite hedges with crews of soldiers standing beside them. Wondering about the purpose of the cranes, Adams realised they had been used to position two parallel lines of steel poles standing in the centre of the field. Stretched out across the top of the poles was a length of camouflaged netting. The width of the netting was about thirty feet, the height from the ground approximately that of a tall tree.

Seeing Davies was talking to an RAF Regiment sergeant with an R/T set strapped on his back, Henderson turned to Adams, his voice low. "Isn't this all a bit premature, Frank? Even if Photo-Intelligence did agree with you, surely it's still only supposition."

While the self-critical Adams seldom had full confidence in his ideas, he had considerably more faith in Babington Smith's unit. "They do have a great deal of experience in analysing photographs, sir. And from the speed with which Jerry has made his repairs, he must have something important to hide. When you put all the bits and pieces together, it does make sense."

Although the Scot's expression suggested otherwise, he made no further comment. Instead he indicated the contraption in the centre of the field. "I'm not happy about this idea of Davies'. If that netting doesn't give away easily, Ian could go straight into the deck."

On this issue Adams found it easy to concur. "I tried to talk Ian out of it, but he insisted it was his responsibility."

Henderson scowled. "I ought to have forbidden him to fly, but after he volunteered Davies insisted he was the right man for the job."

Adams sighed. "I suppose Ian feels that as he won't be allowed to fly on the operation, he has to do something to help. It's stupid, but that's Ian."

At that moment the two men heard the Army sergeant talking into his microphone. Davies listened for a moment, then came bustling round the side of the car. "Moore's on his way and should be here in a couple of minutes." Full of energy and enthusiasm, he turned to Adams. "I hope the Scots don't hold us up too long, Frank. Whom did you say you'd contacted?"

"Just about every Scottish agency there is," Adams told him. "They all said it was a difficult request but they'd do everything they could to find a suitable place."

"You did say it was urgent?"

"Yes, of course."

"Keep at 'em, Frank. We'll be swopping our Mossies over for B.IVs next week. We can't waste a moment once the swop's made."

The distant drone of Merlin engines made all three men start and turn. As a speck turned into a sleek Mosquito flying only a few hundred feet above the fields, Henderson's uneasy murmur sounded loud in the sudden silence. "I hope to Christ this is going to work."

Davies motioned to the sergeant with the radio to join them. "It will work, Jock. Relax."

A metallic voice emerged from the radio. Nodding at the sergeant, Davies took the microphone. "Hello, Ian. Davies speaking. Everything's ready here, but take your time."

Conscious of the danger involved, the breathless Adams was unable to hear Moore's reply. Instead he watched the Mosquito roar over the field and do a climbing turn to starboard. As it levelled out he saw its bomb doors open and a grappling hook fall out and dangle on a length of cable. As the slipstream swept it beneath the Mosquito's tail, Davies addressed the microphone again. "Give it more cable, Ian. You want the hook well behind you."

Adams watched the cable extend another ten feet. The hook was now behind the Mosquito and about twenty feet beneath it. Davies lifted the microphone again. "That's about it, Ian. Whenever you're ready."

Every man present had his eyes fixed on the Mosquito as it did a final orbit and then sank down to tree top height. Chatter died as it came racing towards the field once more. Beside Adams, Davies was fidgeting like a marionette on strings. "Up a bit, Ian. Up another ten feet or so."

The Mosquito's nose rose slightly as it roared towards the netting. Beneath it Adams could see the long grass in the field bending like green waves in its slipstream. A second more and the Mosquito passed in a blur of speed over the netting. As it banked away Adams could feel the buffeting of air from its powerful engines.

Davies gave a low curse before addressing Moore again. "My fault, Ian. You were a few feet too high. Give it a moment and try again."

The sound of Merlins faded. On the field, soldiers relaxed and began lighting cigarettes. Henderson, who had been as rigid as a statue throughout the exercise, now released his breath. "I don't like it, sir. If that hook catches on a pole or the netting doesn't give easily, he could end up as a pile of burning wreckage."

Knowing he was right did nothing to improve Davies's temper. "Stop bellyaching, Jock. What alternative do we have?"

Unable to answer that, the big Scot turned away. More anxious than either man, Adams was listening to the distant drone of engines. As it grew louder, the radio crackled again. Davies listened, then addressed both men. "He's going to give it more cable this time."

With his throat dry, with nothing to say, Adams watched the second approach of the Mosquito. As it flashed over the distant hedge, he saw the grappling hook was a few feet lower than before.

Seeing it miss the hedge by only a few feet, Adams flinched, believing Moore was flying too low. Instead the Mosquito's nose lifted before she reached the poles, allowing the hook to swing down into the netting. As the netting tore away and followed the Mosquito upwards like some dark billowing cloak, the aircraft swayed perilously for a moment, bringing a choking curse from Henderson. Then, with screaming engines, it began climbing steeply away. At the same time, as the cable was released, the netting fluttered to the ground like some huge misshapen parachute.

Cheers could be heard from the soldiers by the cranes. Davies, who had been watching the Mosquito's progress through binoculars, now grabbed the microphone. "Well done, Ian! A first class job! We'll see you back at the airfield." Handing the microphone back to the sergeant, he turned exultantly towards Henderson. "It worked, Jock. So that's one hurdle out of the way."

Henderson looked less convinced. "It worked under peacetime conditions, sir. It could be a different matter when a load of flak's coming up."

Davies was in too good a mood to lose his patience. "You can't help being a pessimist, Jock, can you?. It's that bloody Highland weather of yours. Let's get back to the airfield and hear what Moore has to say." He glanced at the sergeant alongside him. "Tell 'em all to keep everything as it is. I'll be sending more Mossies here in the next day or two."

Moore shook his head. "No, sir. It's out of the question."

Davies looked shocked. "But why? You did it perfectly."

"You're wrong, sir. I nearly crashed. The netting offers too much drag. I almost lost control before I could release it. There's another point too. The Germans might be using longer lengths of netting."

Davies conveniently ignored his last point. "But you didn't lose control. Surely it only needs practice to learn when to release the cable."

Adams, who with Henderson and Sue Spencer, was sharing the 'Confessional' with the two men, saw Moore hesitate and knew why. The young Squadron Commander was far too modest to add that there were few pilots with his razor sharp reflexes and flying abilities. Instead Moore choose a less personal approach. "How will the men get that practice, sir? You'll lose half the squadron on the first run."

Davies's disappointment showed in his frown. "I can't accept that, Ian. This is an élite squadron, with some of the best pilots in the RAF on its books. So how can you say they can't do it?"

To Adams' relief, Henderson made the point Moore could not. "Sir, that's true, but at the same time we all know Moore is the best pilot we have. If he nearly crashed, we're bound to have casualties. Don't you feel we ought to accept his judgement?"

The glare Henderson received nearly lifted the service cap from his head. "This is what you wanted to hear, isn't it, Jock? I've never claimed it was a brilliant idea — in fact I'm aware it's pure bloody Heath Robinson — but after spending three days thinking about it, it's the best we've come up with. So if you've any better ideas, you let me have 'em now."

Henderson looked duly abashed. "I'm sorry, sir. It's just I have to think about my crews' safety. If Ian says it's too dangerous, I have to believe him."

To Adams' relief, Davies took the apology with reasonably good grace. "Fair enough. But you have to see it from a wider aspect. If we don't stop Jerry producing these new planes, we're going to lose more than a few pilots and crews. We might lose the air war itself. So we have to find a way of removing Jerry's camouflage."

Henderson sighed. "Put that way, I suppose we've no choice. But I think we ought to ask for volunteers, don't you?"

Davies hesitated, then held up his hands in a frustrated gesture. "Hang on, Jock, hang on. I don't want to lose crews in practice any more than you do. So I'm willing to keep it as a last resort and have another try at finding something better. One way or another, we have to get rid of Jerry's camouflage netting before we can hit him where it hurts. So give me some ideas."

Silence fell in the Nissen hut. It was broken by Sue Spencer's shy and diffident question. "Would anyone like a cup of tea?"

Adams was about to quieten her when Davies nodded. "Good idea. What about the rest of you?"

When everyone nodded, Sue filled a kettle and then lit a gas ring. Watching her, Adams gave a sudden start. "That's it! Fire!"

Everyone stared at him. "What did you say?" Davies asked.

"Fire," Adams said excitedly. "Camouflage netting's made of rope. We could burn it away."

Davies's eyes opened wide, then he leapt to his feet. "My God, he's done it again! That's it! We burn the bloody stuff away." He swung round on Adams. "That's a brilliant idea, Frank. Brilliant!"

Although Henderson had given a start at the suggestion, his Scottish phlegm refused to share Davies' euphoria. "It's a good idea, but won't it need to be done from the ground?"

Davies checked himself. "Couldn't we drop incendiaries on it?"

"We could, but they'd drop straight through or only burn away small patches."

Davies frowned. "Yes, I suppose they would." He turned back to Adams. "Come on, Frank. You're the gen man. How would you handle it?"

Moore broke in here. "We need an incendiary spray. To drench the netting and then ignite it."

Davies's eyes shone again. He smacked a fist into his palm. "That's it. We spray the full length and then burn it away. Bingo!"

Even Henderson was showing interest now. "I like it better than the hook idea. We could use our SCIs to deliver it." He glanced at Adams. "But is such a spray available?"

"I don't know of one," Adams admitted. "But the Armament Officer might know of something."

"It'll need to be highly inflammable," Moore said. "Particularly if there has been recent rain. We'd also need special incendiaries to fire it."

Davies interrupted the discussion. "Never mind the details. I'll get in touch with our boffins right away. They're sure to come up with something." He beamed at Adams. "The main thing is the method, and thanks to Frank we've got it. Now, thank God, we can go full steam ahead. I want the crews briefed on their exercises first thing tomorrow morning. That way they'll be ready when the B.IVs arrive."

"They're going to be more than curious, sir," Henderson said. "How much can we tell them?"

"If you mean about their target, not a word. If Jerry gets the slightest hint that we're on to him, he might slam the door as tight as a Scotsman's purse." As Henderson blinked, Davies went on: "Let the boys believe they're going to block a road or railway tunnel. Something important, like the Simplon. That should keep 'em happy, shouldn't it?"

"The Simplon's in Switzerland, sir," Adams said.

His correction brought a glare from Davies. "Then find one in bloody Germany. You've got maps and charts, haven't you?"

Abashed, Adams was grateful for Moore's question. "I take it I can take part in these exercises, sir?"

Seeing Henderson about to protest, Davies checked him. "Yes, as we're practising over the U.K. I'd like you to take overall charge. While you're free to do it your way, I'd suggest you take the boys out in three flights with Harvey in charge of one and Millburn another."

Moore had started at Davies's mention of the Yorkshireman. "I hope that doesn't mean you intend using Harvey on the actual operation, sir?"

Respect Moore as he did, Davies was not a man to have his motives questioned. "It means what I said, Moore. At the moment he's doing nothing but sitting on his arse smoking cigarettes. He can make himself useful by giving his old flight some important training. All right?"

Moore could see there was no point in carrying his objection further. "How much is he allowed to know, sir?"

"No more than the rest of your men. Nor is Millburn. There are too many of us in the know already for my liking. So if Harvey starts any of his bloodyminded nonsense, put the boot in quick. I want the entire squadron to believe we're going on a tunnel-busting operation. Not one thing more."

Chapter 25

From his vantage point on the hill ridge Adams pointed at the flight of Mosquitoes flying over the Scottish mountains. “Is that Harvey’s flight?”

Alongside him Henderson had his binoculars trained on the aircraft. “Yes. All six of them.”

“Are they all carrying a full load?”

Henderson nodded again, then glanced at Adams. “What’s the matter with you, Frank? Has the Scotch mist got in your eyes?”

Adams began polishing his spectacles apologetically. “I’ve always had the same problem when using binoculars. I can’t decide whether to keep my glasses on or take them off. Sometimes if I remove them, I can’t adjust the binoculars enough to get things into focus.”

Henderson exchanged binoculars with him. “Try these. They’ve a bigger adjustment.”

Adams tried them and saw the Scot was right as the six B.IV Mosquitoes sprang into focus. The difference in their shape to the standard Mosquito was apparent even at that range, a shape that Adams had heard Baldwin call ‘vaguely pregnant’. It was a comment Adams could appreciate, for with their bomb bays half cut away to make room for the Highball bombs that Barnes Wallis had recently invented, the Mosquitoes did appear to be carrying more than their normal share of ordinance.

Not that the B.IVs were new to anyone in the Squadron except the latest recruits. They had been borrowed from 618 Squadron for Operation Titan, the 633 Squadron attack on the important Loire bridge during the Allied Invasion of Europe.

Equipped with multiple ejector exhaust stubs to compensate for the drag of the Highballs, they and their cylindrical weapon had originally been intended for shipping strikes. Then it had been realised that the Allies had more shipping to lose than the Germans, once the enemy learned the secret of Highball, and so the B.IVs and their bombs had been withdrawn from service. It had taken the high importance of the Loire bridge to rescind that directive, but once the bridge had been destroyed both planes and bombs had gone back to 618 Squadron to wait until they could be used against Japanese shipping.

So this mysterious operation they were training for had to be as important as the Loire Bridge, Harvey reasoned as he led his flight towards the target Adams had obtained for them. Davies had given the impression it was some important German rail tunnel the Allies wanted to seal off, and on the face of it that made sense. The Highball, with its ability to bounce forward along a road or rail track, was the only weapon that could penetrate a tunnel before exploding and thus cause maximum damage. And for practice they were using a disused Scottish rail tunnel.

And yet the more Harvey thought about it, the more certain he was that Davies was playing the fox again and disguising his intentions from his men. He, Harvey, knew from his work with Adams that Millburn and Gabby had been sent to photograph Buchansee and as far as he knew there were no important tunnels in that part of Bavaria. Everything suggested to the Yorkshireman that the present training had something to do with the research establishment, although why Highballs should be involved remained a mystery to him. If the research centre had been located, surely the answer was to send in a heavy force of Lancasters or B-17s, and blow the site to hell.

Not that any of this lessened Harvey's determination to give his men the best training possible. Although his anger with Davies for using Anna was smouldering as deeply as ever, the thought that she might be involved in some way was more than enough to heighten his resolve. If he could not help her directly, by God he would do his best to make certain the operation was a success.

He had shown this determination during the last three days. As soon as Adams had found a suitable tunnel, he and Moore had flown out to reconnoitre it.

Although it was the best target Adams could obtain, it was not to the liking of either pilot. Set at the end of an ever deepening cutting, it ran through a scabrous hill ridge that rose five hundred feet above the disused railway track. On returning to Sutton Craddock, Moore had given Davies his opinion. “I don’t like it, sir. The walls of the cutting will force us to release the bombs early unless we delay our climb until the last minute. And that could he very dangerous.”

Davies, who had already visited the tunnel and had similar thoughts, scowled. “What choice have I got, Ian? Scotland isn’t full of disused railway tunnels. We were damn lucky to find this one.”

“I appreciate that, sir. I think the best thing is for me to try it first. Then I’ll be able to give a better assessment.”

Davies had given a glance Harvey’s way. “Why must it be you every time? You’ve other men in your squadron, haven’t you?”

Harvey hadn’t needed the hint. “I’ll go, Ian. You can keep a watch on me and see where my Highball goes.”

Satisfied, Davies was turning away when Moore shook his head. “I’m in charge, Frank. That means it’s my baby.”

In spite of the argument that followed, to Davies’s disgust Moore would not give way. So the following morning both pilots had flown out carrying one inert Highball apiece.

For Harvey, flying above the tunnel, the next fifteen minutes had been painful as he had watched Moore attempting to gauge the correct height of entry into the cutting and the right moment to pull out. Moore’s first attempt, using no bombs, had almost been a disaster. Leaving his break-off point too late, he had avoided collision with the hill by the narrowest of margins. As Harvey watched his Mosquito clawing its way up the steep ridge, his big hands had been white on the control column. Afraid his voice might disturb Moore’s concentration, he had waited until the Mosquito was safely clear before addressing his R/T. “For Christ’s sake, Ian. Are you all right?”

Moore sounded only slightly shaken. “Yes, I’m fine. I’ll try it again in a few minutes.”

Harvey already had D-Danny's nose down. "No, it's my turn. I'll try my bomb and see what happens."

The hills and mountains tilted and then steadied as Harvey's Mosquito went plunging down. Levelling it off, Harvey addressed Carter, his navigator. "Start a Highball spinning. Now."

As the navigator obeyed, Harvey could feel a vibration as an air vent opened and the Highball began its forward spin. Waiting until the rev counter registered 500 rpm, Harvey glanced at the navigator. "Now the master and selector switches."

Carter, new to the procedure, nodded and clicked down both switches.

"Now keep your eye on the sight," Harvey ordered, indicating the Highball bombsight situated on the windshield. "When I yell 'bomb', press the release button. You got that?"

As Carter swallowed and nodded, Harvey swung towards the distant cutting and lowered D-Danny until the bushes below were bowing under the slipstream of its propellers. In seconds the banks on either side of the disused track closed in and began to heighten as the Mosquito raced into the cutting. Concentrating on the dark hole of the tunnel ahead, Harvey only vaguely heard Moore's warning. "Watch it, Frank. Don't leave it too late."

With the tunnel and the hill racing towards him with terrifying intent, Harvey's mind was a computer estimating speed and range. As the tunnel filled the sight bar on the bombsight he yelled 'bomb.' The moment he felt the Mosquito lighten, he heaved back on the control column.

For one endless moment he believed he had waited too long, as the moss-covered ridge leapt at him. As he heaved the column further back, the reeling hillside went grey before his eyes as g-forces drove blood from his brain. With its engines screaming their protest and its rivets popping with the strain, D-Danny clawed its way upwards. With his mind still numbed, Harvey only knew he was out of danger when Moore's voice came back into his earphones. "You left it too late, Frank. How's your kite?"

"She seems all right. What happened to the bomb?"

"It hit the side of the tunnel. But it was a near miss."

"Did you take notice where we released it?"

"Yes. I've got it marked. From the speed it was still travelling, I think we can pull the release point back another fifty yards. That'll give the boys a better safety margin. What about your airspeed?"

"I was doing 290. I think we should reduce it to 270."

"O. K. I'll make my run now. Keep an eye on my bomb and where I release it."

At that point Harvey had remembered his navigator. "How are you feeling, lad?"

Carter had looked green but had managed a smile. "I'm all right, sir. Although I did think we'd had it for a moment."

Harvey had felt he owed the young man a little magnanimity. "So did I, lad. But you handled it well."

Carter had looked almost stunned by the praise. "Thank you, sir. I'm sorry we missed the tunnel but we'll do better next time."

This had happened five days ago. The following morning Moore and Harvey had driven up to Scotland and had huge white markers painted on both sides of the cutting to tell crews the right moment to release their Highballs. On the third day both men and Millburn had taken out their flights to begin the training.

They had carried no practice bombs on this first trip. Highballs needed hardened steel casings to avoid breaking up on impact and they were still in short supply. The crews' first mission was to practise flying through the cutting and leaping from it before colliding with the hill range.

Even so, the results had been alarming. Although no aircraft had crashed, Mosquitoes had been shooting out of the cutting like corks from bottles, with the airwaves full of warnings and curses. To Harvey, a veteran of the Swartfjord days, it had reminded him of the Squadron's rehearsals for its target in the Black Fjord. "And just as bloody dangerous," he told Moore.

Highballs had been introduced only on the fourth day and even then rationed to one per aircraft. With the pilots' need to concentrate on the tunnel entrance ahead, the risk of collision had grown in proportion, and although the white markers alongside the cutting minimised the risks, still many a crewman believed his last moment had come.

Inevitably, rumours about the forthcoming operation were flying around the squadron like swifts on a summer day. Jock Smith, one of Millburn's pilots, was certain it was the Simplon tunnel. "Makes sense, doesn't it? The bloody Swiss are selling arms to Jerry on the quiet. So we're going to bung up the tunnel, frustrate the Swiss, and leave Jerry with only bows and arrows to shoot at us."

McDonald of Harvey's flight, a quiet young man who liked reading, had other views. "Everyone knows Jerry's getting short of fuel. I think we're after his oil. Don't they say he stores it in caves?"

Paget, a pink-cheeked Post Office worker from Kent, had a wilder variation on the same theme. "I think we're going for one of Jerry's coal mines. You know, the ones with open entrances."

Purcell, a young cricket lover, gained a number of adherents with his theory. "It's Jerry's submarine pens. They're bomb proof from above but Highballs could bounce into their entrances and blow 'em to hell."

But Larkin had the best liked theory of all. "You guys are all talking out of your trousers. Why the hell have Millburn and Gabby been taking photographs of Bavaria? We're going for Hitler's Eagles' nest. We'll wait until he's in bed with Eva Braun and then put our bombs right through his bedroom window. That'll teach the bugger to keep his pants on."

During this time, residing in an ancient hotel some ten miles from the tunnel, Davies, Henderson and Adams had stayed in Scotland to assess the exercises. It had been noticeable to the two junior officers that Davies was losing his earlier enthusiasm as the days passed and by the fifth day he seemed positively depressed. An explanation for it came that morning when the three men were having breakfast. "It's not going well, Jock. Do you realise we've only landed one Highball in that tunnel so far? And that under ideal conditions."

No one was quicker than Henderson to defend his crews. "Give them a chance, sir. They've only had one bomb each to practise with."

"I know that. But we've used sixteen crews and a number of them have used Highballs before. Moreover, Moore and Harvey made it easier for them by giving them a marking point. They're not going to get that kind of help over the target."

"I still say they'll do better with more practise, sir. One run-in with a bomb just isn't enough."

Davies's gloomy reply made the Scot start. "I can't give 'em any more practice, Jock. Today's their last day."

"But why?"

"There aren't any more practice bombs. And I'm told there won't be any for at least three weeks. Perhaps even four."

"Can't we wait for them?"

"How the hell can we wait, Jock? The prototypes are already flying. That means Jerry might be rounding off his experiments. If he is and the results go out to all his aircraft factories, it won't matter whether we blow this establishment to hell or not. It'll he too late."

"But what about the spray and the incendiaries?"

"The boffins sorted them out a couple of days ago. We can have them at any time."

Adams asked the question Henderson seemed loath to ask. "So what's the next step, sir?"

Davies took a sip of coffee and pulled a face at its sourness. "We go as soon as we can. But first I want to see what happens this morning with two Highballs per man."

"Does that mean the Americans are ready to give us B-17 cover?"

"Yes. Staines has convinced Spaatz we're right about the target. So a box of Forts are waiting for the green light."

Henderson's expression betrayed the responsibility he was feeling. "You're saying it's up to us now, sir?"

"That's the position, Jock. So let's hope the boys get their fingers out this morning."

Adams was reflecting on this breakfast conversation as he watched the first aircraft of Harvey's flight peel off to begin its run through the cutting. From his vantage point where the hill ridge swung south, he could just see the tunnel entrance below. As the Mosquito sped into the cutting he felt his muscles tighten. For a few seconds the plane vanished. Then, as it reappeared, climbing steeply for height, he saw a cylindrical object like a thick coin bounding along the old railway track. As it disappeared into the dark tunnel, Henderson gave a shout of relief. "Well done."

"That's better, Jock." As both men turned, they saw Davies, followed by a radio operator, approaching them. "Who was the pilot?"

"Machin, sir," Henderson told him.

"You are keeping notes of everything?"

Henderson held up the pad in his hand. Nodding, Davies turned his attention back to the cutting. A second Mosquito had come diving down and was about to vanish into it. Following the plane's imaginary passage with his eyes, Adams saw its Highball bound into view and ricochet with a shower of sparks from a rock face near the tunnel entrance. As the Mosquito clawed for height he heard Davies' grunt of disappointment.

Mosquito after Mosquito followed. By the time Harvey came diving down only one hit had been registered. Aware of it, Harvey delayed a full second longer than the others before releasing his Highball and sent it bounding slap into the centre of the tunnel.

Henderson turned to Davies. "One third hits, sir. We can't hope for better than that, can we?"

Davies was watching Harvey's Mosquito rocketing up the face of the ridge. "He cut it too bloody fine," he muttered. Then he turned to Henderson. "It's only one out of six, Jock. You're forgetting I can't use Harvey."

Millburn's flight was the next to arrive. Radford scored a hit, as did Allister. From the sergeant's radio, Adams heard Millburn's metallic voice. "O.K., West. Your turn. Down you go."

Adams watched the youngster's Mosquito come diving down. It appeared to enter the cutting at the correct height and the Highball it released vanished into the tunnel. But just as Adams was about to shout his approval, he heard one of its engines cut. It picked up two seconds later but it was too late. As the Mosquito reached the crest of the hill ridge, its port wing dropped and struck a rocky outcrop. Instantly it went into a crazy cartwheel that flung it a hundred yards along the ridge. As it came to a stop there was a dull explosion. A moment later a huge billowing cloud of fire hid it from sight.

Adams heard someone cry out "Oh, my God," and then realised it was himself. He started to run forward, only for

Henderson to catch his arm and drag him back. "It's no use, Frank. There's nothing you can do. The rescue crew will take care of it."

Alongside them Davies was looking pale but grim-faced. Motioning to the startled sergeant, he took the microphone from him. "Millburn, I want all your men to drop their second bomb. Get them moving right away."

Adams could not hold back his protest. "Shouldn't they be given a little time first, sir?"

Davies ignored him, turning to Henderson instead. "After they've finished, I want you to phone the Adjutant and tell him to shut down the Station and cut all communications. We can't afford any careless talk about this."

"They have all been sworn to secrecy, sir," Henderson said.

"I know that, but there's always someone who gets maudlin in his cups. If Jerry got any word of this he might get suspicious. In any case I've decided to go as soon we get the live Highballs delivered and Staines and I agree on our rendezvous.

Henderson took a deep breath. "When will that be, sir?"

The tight snap in Davies's reply told its own story. "As soon as possible. Two days at the most. I want to get this damned job over and finished with." He swung round on the shaken Adams. "We'll brief the crews tomorrow. So talk to our specialist officers when we get back and get your own bits and pieces together."

Adams could not answer him. He was thinking of the pink-faced West and his colleague being reduced into a pile of cinders in the inferno along the ridge, and felt he was going to be sick.

Chapter 26

Davies entered Henderson's office at 08.05 hours the following day. "Morning, Jock. I hear the Highballs arrived yesterday."

Henderson was thinking he could have waited until he'd had his morning coffee. "Yes, sir. Before we got back from Scotland."

"Good." Davies indicated the chair behind the Scot's desk. "Sit down, Jock. I've something to tell you.

Looking surprised and not a little apprehensive, Henderson obeyed. Davies selected a chair from the other two available and drew it towards the desk. He gave the Scot a somewhat rueful grin. "You ready for a shock?"

"Not at this time of the day, sir. But I've the feeling you're going to give me one. What is it?"

"I'm putting Moore in charge of this operation. I thought I ought to tell you before the briefing."

Henderson nearly shot out of his chair. "You can't do that, sir. He's an ex-prisoner. There's a special directive about ex-prisoners."

"I know all about the directive, Jock. But in this case I've no option." Seeing Henderson about to explode in protest, Davies held up a hand. "I've got special permission. So don't throw the book at me."

"But why, sir? If he's shot down, the Gestapo will get him. And they'll stop at nothing to find out who his rescuers were. You can't put him under that kind of risk."

"I've not ordered him to go. He's volunteered."

"Of course he'd volunteer. He's that kind of man. But it's not fair to force him into a choice." The big Scot's face was pale with anger. "I must put in the strongest possible protest, sir."

"Fair enough, Jock. I'll see your protest is recorded. But now you tell me who else we could put in charge of the operation."

Harvey's name was on the tip of Henderson's tongue when he remembered. Davies saw his hesitation and nodded. "You were going to say Harvey, weren't you? If I used him you'd all jump on me for breaking my promise."

"Then what about Millburn? Or Van Breedenkamp?"

"Good men, both of them, but not to lead this operation. It's too complex, Jock. And it's too damned important. I need Moore as I've never needed him before. Can't you see that?"

Henderson shook his head. "I can only see the risk, sir. And to be honest I don't think you'll feel very happy if he's shot down and has to face torture."

Davies gave him a look, then walked to the window and gazed out. It was a full ten seconds before he spoke. "Wartime decisions aren't always easy to make, Jock. And sometimes there is a heavy price to pay for them. Don't make it harder by reminding me."

This was a Davies Henderson had seldom seen before, and almost to his surprise he felt sympathy diluting his bitterness. It was a relief when one of his phones rang. "Yes, Greenwood. Yes, we'll be using Light Series Carriers for the incendiaries. Don't forget the briefing has been put forward to 10.00 hours. I want all specialist officers there. Bye."

Harvey found Moore out on the airfield supervising an inspection on A-Apple, the Squadron Commander's Mosquito. The grim-faced Yorkshireman came to the point without preamble. "Ian, you can't do it. It's bloody madness."

Moore gave a glance at his maintenance crew and led him out of earshot. "What's the problem, Frank?"

"You know well enough. Adams has just told me what Davies is doing. You can't let him get away with it. Refuse to go. You're within your rights."

Moore shook his head. "You've got it wrong, Frank. He didn't order me to go. I volunteered."

Harvey's laugh was pure disgust. "Don't give me that, Ian. He told you in as many words how much he needed you and then left the rest to you. I know that little sod's ways too well."

"I know all about Davies, Frank, but to be fair to him he does need me this time."

As always Harvey did not mince words. "Why? You're not the only bloody airman who can lead a squadron of Mossies. I led 'em to get you out of prison. Why can't I lead 'em on this job?"

"You could, but aren't you forgetting he promised to give you a break from ops? You can't blame him for keeping his promise."

Harvey needed to hear nothing more. "Then that's easily put right. I'll tell him I let him off his promise and the problem's solved."

Moore grabbed his arm as he was turning away. "No, Frank. Things are better this way. They really are."

For a moment Harvey's latent inferiority complex came to the surface. "Why? Don't you think I can do the job just as well? Don't forget I've been with this outfit since it was created and I was its bloody Squadron Commander for a while until you took over. So what's the big problem?"

"It's nothing to do with your skills, Frank. Of course you could handle it as well. But you're on rest now and you've Anna to think about."

If anything Harvey's face darkened. "I am thinking about Anna. I'm not a fool, Ian. Even if Davies has only seen fit to give Millburn and me bits and pieces about the operation, it's obvious enough she's involved. That's another reason I want to be part of it."

"Leave it, Frank," Moore begged. "Leave things as they are."

Harvey's doggedness had never been more pronounced. "Have you thought what will happen to you if you're shot down and captured again? The Gestapo will butcher you to find out who helped you escape."

"You're looking on the black side, Frank."

"Am I? Maybe that's because I was brought up in a different world to you. In my world you expect the worst because nine times out of ten that was what you bloody well got."

Moore winced. The Yorkshireman concealing his harsh background to all but his closest friends, and no confession could have expressed his fears for Moore more vividly. "Frank, don't think I don't appreciate your offer. But I've promised Davies I'll do the job and I can't walk out on him now. So stop worrying about me."

With Harvey friends were friends and you took care of them in any way you could. His huge frame was trembling with frustration. "You're a fool, Moore. A bloody stupid fool."

Moore smiled. "I'm sure you're right. Now go into the Mess and have a beer. I'll join you in a few minutes."

Harvey made no reply. Muttering a curse, he swung round and walked away. Moore watched him for a moment, a tall angry figure making for Adams' office, then sighed and returned to A-Apple.

As always when an operation involving Davies was concerned, there was a certain nervousness in the Operation Room that morning. The conversation between the seated crews was on a higher level than usual as their eyes kept moving to a large cloth-covered mound that stood on a table before the platform on which half a dozen specialist officers were seated. Nervous laughs kept breaking out and matches scratching. The smoke from dozens of cigarettes, drifting upwards to form a layer of mist beneath the ceiling, made the hanging models of German aircraft look as if they were flying through high-level cloud.

All the Squadron's crews were present. Their Flight Commanders, Millburn and Van Breedenkamp, occupied the first row of benches. Although a supernumerary on the operation, Harvey was also seated alongside them, an indication that however their temperaments might clash, Davies was fully aware of the value of the Yorkshireman's experience and advice. Moore, in his role of Squadron Commander, was seated at a table on the platform along with Adams and the rest of the Station's specialist officers.

A sudden loud bark cut off the buzz of conversation. "ATTENTION!" Benches rumbled on the floor as the entire complement rose to its feet. A moment later Davies, followed by Henderson, appeared and marched towards the platform. As the two men mounted it, the stentorian voice bellowed out again. "AT EASE!" Bert the Bastard, the Station Warrant Officer, was in good voice that morning.

Men sank back on their benches. With a nod at Henderson, Davies walked forward on the platform. In the style he always adopted at briefings, he sounded relaxed and jaunty. "Here we are again, gentlemen. I see from your faces that you're all glad to see me."

A low groan was followed by a hoarse whisper: "Like hell we are." As a gasp followed, Davies used the interruption to his advantage. "There's someone who knows I always bring good tidings. That's good. I like to be popular."

The laughter that followed brought an easing of tension. Satisfied, Davies made a last concession. "Those of you who are hiding fags under the benches can bring 'em out now. You've got permission to smoke."

As matches scratched again, Davies got down to business. "As you can all guess, I've got a special job for you. However, it's not the one I think most of you expect. How many of you took part in Operation Rhine Maiden?"

Watching the scene from the back of the platform, Adams winced when he saw less than half the crews put up their hands, an indication of the losses the Squadron had incurred in the months that followed. From Davies's pause, Adams had the impression the small Air Commodore was equally dismayed, although if it were so, Davies hid his feelings well. "Good. Then you old sweats know all about Jerry's cleverness in hiding his factories from our bombing campaign. We've run into the same problem again: that's why I've had you all clowning about in Scotland for the last week."

A dismayed voice muttered: "Not bloody Bavaria again?"

Once again Davies used the interruption to his advantage. "What's wrong with Bavaria, Machin? The girls are plump and the beer's marvellous."

A wave of shock had run round the room at the name. A 'fresher's hand rose from the muttering crews. "Surely Bavaria's too far for us, isn't it, sir?"

Aware that the younger members of the squadron might need encouragement, Davies used the technique he had used when briefing the crews for their earlier Bavarian mission. "Why do you think that, lad? You'll be carrying drop tanks. And we'll provide plenty of support for you. Remember you're a member of an élite squadron with a record no other unit in the RAF can match. So what's so surprising about a daylight raid into Bavaria?"

A ripple of nervous laughter was mixed with a gasp of shock. "Did you say a daylight raid, sir?"

Davies decided he'd been patient enough. "I know it sounds a little hairy, but if you'd all shut up and listen to me you'd find out we've covered every contingency. Let me first tell you what you're going to destroy."

With his audience hushed and attentive now, Davies told them about the German research establishment and its aims. "I don't need to tell you what it means if Jerry can produce such kites quickly. Even your Mossies wouldn't have a hope in hell beside planes that could fly two hundred miles an hour faster. So it's imperative this establishment is destroyed."

The buzz of excitement came back a full octave higher as Davies paused. It checked when Van Breedenkamp put up a hand. "What kite are they adapting, sir?"

"We don't know," Davies confessed. "But it'll obviously be one of their more versatile types. Possibly Junkers or Heinkels."

The South African was showing the puzzlement common to the rest of the crews. "You've told us what Jerry's doing, sir, but not where he's doing it. What's the purpose of using B.IV Mossies? Is the factory inside a tunnel?"

To gain the maximum effect, Davies had been awaiting the question. Grinning, he held up a hand. "The question you've all wanted to ask. All right, Van, I'll tell you. The establishment you're going to destroy is underneath a bloody great Bavarian lake."

If a bombshell had been dropped in the middle of the room it couldn't have caused greater consternation. Forgetting their discipline, men either laughed their disbelief or shouted their protest.

Even Harvey and Millburn could be seen arguing with one another. Seeing Henderson was rising to quell the hubbub, Davies waved him back, waited until the sound died down, then advanced to the very edge of the platform, his grin wicked.

"That's woken you all up, hasn't it? Yes, it's under one end of a lake. When you think of it, it makes sense. If Jerry can't escape our bombing by hiding his factories under trees and heavy camouflage, he hides 'em beneath a lake. Mind you, it's not a deep lake, as most Bavarian lakes are. In fact, its relative shallowness helped to confirm our suspicions, because our geologists assure us it's the one lake in Bavaria that makes the project technically feasible."

Another puzzled hand rose. "But if it's under a lake, how do we destroy the project, sir?"

Davies grinned again. "A piece of cake, lad." With the agility of a man half his age, Davies jumped down from the platform and walked to the cloth covered mound on the table. "Come round here, all of you, and take a gander at this."

When the breathless crews had surrounded the table, Davies drew off the cloth to show a large, three dimensional, plaster-of-Paris model of Buchansee lake and its surrounding hills and mountains. "I want you all to study every detail of this model until you can see it with your eyes closed. You've got all this afternoon and evening to do it, so you'll have no excuses when you see the real thing. But firstly I want you to take a careful look at this sawmill. This is the key to Jerry's secret establishment. It's enabling him to bring in scientists and technicians dressed as sawmill-workers, and equally enabling him to bring in and take out technical equipment hidden in railway wagons ostensibly carrying timber. Because of this, he hasn't had any need to employ a security cordon. As security guards usually give away the location of a secret establishment, this was what prevented our agents locating it. It was only when the recent gales blew away a section of the camouflage netting that covers the road to its entrance that our sharp-eyed Station Intelligence officer guessed what it might mean. Since then our Photo Intelligence unit has confirmed his suspicions."

As Davies paused to give him an approving glance, Adams realised he was being rewarded for his recent spurt of ideas. As

Henderson grinned at him, Davies turned back to the astonished crews. “The camouflaged track runs from the saw mill to the entrance of the establishment, which in its early stages is a large tunnel. Let me show you.” Leaning forward Davies lifted a small oblong section from the mock trees that lay between the saw mill and the lake. “There you are. There’s the track and there’s the tunnel entrance. Our job is to roll our Highballs into that entrance. With any luck they’ll explode inside and up will go the new aircraft, Uncle Tom Cobley and all.”

A babble of excited voices and questions followed. Davies held up a hand. “I’ll answer your questions in a moment. First take a look at these small islands. Although there is nothing to show from the air, we heard the first one has a small garrison of troops. It seemed to make no sense until we discovered the establishment lies below it. Then the penny dropped. The island must contain an air vent down to the establishment, so we might have to bomb it too. Now have you any questions?”

A small forest of hands rose. Davies pointed at one. “What’s your question, Millburn?”

“The one I guess you must have had, sir. We can’t drop our Highballs until we can see the tunnel. So how do we get rid of the netting?”

Davies grinned. “We burn it away.”

“But how, sir?”

Davies told him. Quelling the excited chatter that followed, he pointed at Harvey. “What’s your bleat, Harvey?”

“Does the entrance have doors, sir?”

“We don’t know,” Davies confessed.

“Then what if it has and they shut ’em while we’re burning away the netting?”

Davies wondered what mad foolishness had encouraged him to bring in Harvey for the briefing. “We’ll have to hope our Highballs will break through it.”

“What if they don’t?”

“Then we’ll just have to come back home and suck our thumbs, won’t we?” Davies snapped. “But our experts don’t think it’s likely. An underground plant will need another air supply, so doors would be pointless as long as the camouflage outside was good."

Another hand rose. "Who'll he carrying the incendiaries and who the bombs, sir?"

"B and C Flight will have the Highballs, as they did during the exercises. Some kites of A Flight will be carrying the incendiary equipment and perhaps bombs for the island. But you'll get all the tactical details when your Squadron Commander addresses you."

Millburn raised a hand again. "Who is our Squadron Commander, sir?"

Davies glanced back at the platform. "The same officer who has led you through the recent exercises. Wing Commander Moore."

More astonished voices were heard. One gruff voice could be heard above the others. "Aye, and it's a bloody disgrace."

Davies glared at Harvey. About to order him from the Operations Room, he then realised the act would only inflame the situation further. "I know this is a surprise to some of you because of Wing Commander Moore's recent escape, but because of the importance of the operation, he has been given a special dispensation to fly over Germany again. My guess is you'll be happy to have him leading you."

Adams saw there was no doubt of that. The old sweats had total faith in the young Squadron Commander and the recruits hero-worshipped him. Adams could feel a noticeable drop in tension as Davies climbed back on the platform. "That's all I have to say for the moment. Go back to your seats now while Wing Commander Moore briefs you. You can look at the model again later."

Crews filed back to their benches while Davies indicated Moore to take his place. The respect the crews felt for the young Squadron Commander was quickly evident in the hush that followed. In the easy style that was his hallmark, Moore walked to the front of the platform and addressed the rows of intent men. "Right, chaps. This is how we're going to do it. We're going to use our full complement of sixteen Mossies and fly out in three sections. If Bavaria seems a long way away to some of you, don't worry, we're not going alone. For a start, the Banff Wing will be providing plenty of diversionary sweeps. In addition, the Yanks are going to provide us with a box of B-17s who'll be flying at their normal cruising height and we'll be stationed five thousand feet above them. This will give us radar cover, as it did in Rhine Maiden, and with any luck Jerry won't cotton on to us until we're almost over the target. After we break away, the Yanks will carry on and drop a few more bombs on Jerry's Messerschmitt factory at Regensberg. So nothing will be wasted. All right so far?"

A hand rose. "Is that all the cover we're getting, skipper?"

"No. The Yanks are also giving us a Mustang escort." As a groan went up, Moore put up a hand. "If you're moaning about Yanks being used, don't. As many of you know, they've escorted us before and done a first class job. Believe me, we'll be well looked after."

Millburn raised a hand. "What do we do if the Forts are attacked?"

"I'm afraid we don't do anything, Tommy. As you know, we did get the B.IVs adapted to take three Brownings, but we must keep all our ammunition in case we need it later. So no one ..." Moore kept his gaze on the American a second longer than necessary.

"No one goes down if they're attacked. The Yanks understand this and the only help they expect is from their own escort. Any more questions before I give the order of battle?"

A fresher raised a hand. "If the establishment's under the lake, sir, how will we know when it's destroyed?"

The question prompted another from Larkin. "Also, how many bombs is it going to take, skipper?"

Davies answered both questions from the back of the platform. "It all depends what precautions Jerry's got down there, such as explosion barriers and the like. But unless he's tunnelled to a great depth, which isn't likely, our boffins don't think it'll take more than three or four bombs to burst open the roof and let the water flood in. When you see signs of that, you'll know the job is finished."

When no more questions came, Moore went on to explain the sequence of attack. "McMaster and Pulford of A Flight are going to do the incendiary job. McMaster will fly the length of the track to the tunnel entrance and spray it with SCIs. Pulford will follow with the incendiaries. If all goes well and the netting is on fire, the two of them will go on and bomb the island. Of course, if the netting doesn't burn the first time, they have to repeat the procedure.

"In the meantime I'll be up aloft doing my Master of Ceremonies job. Along with the rest of my flight, I'll be carrying two Highballs so we can add our contribution if necessary. The other two flights will attack the entrance in numerical order. Hopefully, one attack by each of you should be enough but if it isn't you'll go in again in the same sequence. Between your attacks you'll orbit the target under the instructions of your Flight Commanders."

A hand rose. "What will the Yanks be doing during this time, skipper?"

"The B-17s will be far away by now bombing Regensburg. But the Mustangs will be giving you cover in case Jerry takes umbrage to what we're doing and starts to interfere."

"What time-delays will the Highballs be carrying, skipper?"

Moore's nod showed his appreciation of Millburn's question. "We've had a few problems over that, Tommy. We don't want them exploding on their way to the tunnel and yet we can't afford too long a gap between each attack. Finally we've settled on a fifteen-second delay." Moore's eyes moved from Millburn to the rows of intent faces. "As some of the Highballs are sure to explode outside the tunnel, that means your attacks should follow at twenty second intervals. No sooner or you could go up with the bedroom curtains."

Another hand rose. "How will your crews find the netting, skipper? Won't the forest all look the same if the netting's been replaced?"

"A good point, Allister. But if you examine the model again, you'll see the track is bang slap in the middle of a shallow valley. Hopefully that should be a great help to us."

"Nobody's mentioned flak yet." The gruff comment came from Harvey. "Have the photographs shown any gun posts?"

"No, but that doesn't mean there aren't any: they could be concealed beneath camouflage netting. If there are any, my guess is they'll be on the hillsides on either side of the track." Moore's smile took all the danger out of the situation. "No doubt they'll wake up when we start spraying the netting. So navigators keep your eyes open and mark their positions. Any more questions?"

Machin asked the last question. "When do we go, skipper?"

"I can't say at the moment, Paddy. It depends on the Yanks although it'll almost certainly be tomorrow. So I want the kites air-tested and all of you ready from 06.00 hours onwards. You'll be given the co-ordinates of your rendezvous with the B-17s from the navigation officer as soon as he gets them." When no one asked a further question, Moore nodded. "Right, that's it. See your executive officers now and get all the technical details you can, although you might have to wait until tomorrow to get the latest met report. And then study the model again. It's important you know every tree, hollow and hillside before we go."

Seeing Moore glance at him, Henderson had his customary last word with his crews. "We're calling the job Operation Crisis. Your Squadron call sign will be Barracuda. Major Dent, your Escort Leader's, will be Gettysburg, and our Station here will be Waterloo. The code word you'll send back when the centre's destroyed will be Maelstrom. As your skipper has told you, you'll almost certainly be going out tomorrow and possibly before noon, so tuck into your breakfasts. As for tonight, although I don't want any heavy drinking, I'm allowing the bars to be open from 19.00 hours to 21.00 hours."

A muted cheer sounded from the rear of the assembly. Henderson grinned. "Don't get too excited, Machin. There'll be a ration per man of only two pints apiece. After that I want you all tucked away warm and cosy in bed."

It was nearly two hours before the crews filed out with their notebooks and photographs. Seeing Davies was about to follow them, Adams hurried forward. "Sir, there's one thing I don't understand. You or the Brigadier mentioned at a briefing that your agents had heard a strange screaming sound in the vicinity of Buchansee. Did you ever find out what it was?"

Davies checked his stride. "Haven't I told you yet?"

"No, sir. And it's been niggling at me."

Davies grinned. "Apart from the shallowness of the lake, that's the other thing that gave the game away to our scientists and made them certain Jerry was working beneath it. Apparently he originally made his wind tunnels by pumping the air from them and then letting atmospheric pressure pour back and do the rest. But recently he had a new idea, to let water pressure drive high-speed turbines. Intelligence believes he originally intended to build a tunnel from a water reservoir high up in the mountains down to his turbines. But by having his wind tunnels beneath a lake, the job's half done for him."

Adams' jaw dropped. "So that was the scream? Water rushing down through pipes and driving turbines."

"That's the score, Frank. Modern war isn't just heaving bricks at one another, is it?"

No, Adams thought. Not for the first time, he was stunned by the size and ingenuity of the German project. His reaction was typical of Adams. If only mankind could harness such enthusiasm and energy in the search for peace, he thought, what a paradise the world could become.

Chapter 27

For all the crews detailed to fly on the operation, the rest of the day was something of an ordeal. Although they were able to fill up their time during the afternoon by supervising the servicing of their aircraft and running over all details of the operation with their pilots or navigators, the evening was less easy to handle. Aircrews always disliked delays. Emotions, and they included fear, could sustain a man for a few hours and once he was airborne, self-preservation, adrenalin, and the complexity of the task itself took over. But a lengthy delay without these compensatory factors left men restless and often irritable.

Knowing all this, Henderson made certain that his cooks provided a first class meal that evening. Then, after consulting Moore, he relented his earlier order and told the Adjutant to issue three beer coupons per man. Although this was a welcome concession, it did little but wet the throats of hardened drinkers like Machin and Larkin and it still left long fretful hours to be endured after the bars closed.

Crews filled these hours in different ways according to their temperaments. Four old sweats, the stringy New Zealander Larkin, Paddy Machin, 'Stan' Baldwin, and Van Breedenkamp began a cut-throat poker game with the sky the limit. "After all, mon," Baldwin said in his deep sonorous voice, "There isn't much point in leaving a guy's dough to the sweepers, is there?"

Other men found different ways of passing the time. Purcell discovered another cricket lover in one of the 'freshers', a young navigator named Johnson from Margate, and the two of them found solace in arguing about the respective merits of Yorkshire C.C. and

Kent C.C. McDonald retired early to his billet and began reading a much-thumbed pirated edition of *Lady Chatterley's Lover.* Jock Smith and Killingbeck played one another almost to exhaustion at table tennis and Temple wrote yet another letter to his mother. Men did this and that in their efforts to forget tomorrow, until weariness finally took over and they fell into a fitful sleep.

Morning, with its early call and order to air test their Mosquitoes, kept the men from dwelling too much on the task ahead, but the sight of the B.IVs being armed with the live Highballs was soon a vivid reminder. Used to the graceful configuration of their Mosquitoes, crews found something almost offensive in the sight of the twin crescents protruding from the B.IVs' bomb bays. Millburn's comment that the Swansea Stallion didn't seem satisfied with just making the local girls pregnant brought laughter from the crews, if not from the indignant Gabby. But after a second briefing by their Flight Commanders and orders to collect their parachutes so they would be ready when the green light came, the men's mood changed. Acutely aware of the importance and the perils of the forthcoming operation, they wanted to go and get it over. Instead they now had to hang around like fighter pilots waiting for a scramble, and they found the effect wearing on the nerves.

During this time Staines had arrived at the airfield. He had telephoned Davies the previous evening to say that because of the involvement of his B-17s and Mustangs, he wanted to be at Sutton Craddock during the operation. This was possible because for the Rhine Maiden operation a telephone had been connected directly from the Station's Operations Room to the Texan's USAAF Headquarters.

Davies was delighted with his request. He knew it would be a benefit to him during the present operation because although 633 Squadron had of necessity to fly out under radio silence, the Americans in the B-17s and Mustangs would need no such protection once they were attacked, and so Staines would be able to provide a running commentary on the battle. At the same time nothing could have emphasised more to Mosquito crews the importance of their mission than the sight of the Texan's huge staff car entering the Station's gates. Rumours flew and darted around the airfield like autumn leaves in a turbulent wind. "It's blooming

Eisenhower 'imself," McTyre told his young assistant as the two of them struggled with chilled hands to fit .303 ammunition belts into a Mosquito. "Now d'you see what an important outfit we are?"

Ellis's innocent eyes were wide. "Do you think he's brought Churchill with him too?"

"I wouldn't be surprised, mate. That car's big enough to bring along the whole bloody War Cabinet."

It was 11.30 hours before the Navigation Officer received the American co-ordinates and the time of rendezvous. Estimating a time for take-off, he gave it to the three Flight Commanders who in turn briefed their restless crews. They would scramble at 12.00 hours sharp.

Relieved the suspense was over at last, men left the Flight Offices to make their last preparations. Most went to their billets to collect their parachutes and eat the lunches already packed for them. Moore was among them. After emptying his pockets of any incriminatory items and climbing into his flying gear, he was giving a final look at his notes when Harvey appeared in the doorway. "Can you spare a minute, Ian?"

Turning, Moore saw that Harvey was wearing his flying suit. "Hello, Frank. But why are you kitted up like that?"

Harvey stepped inside the billet. He was carrying a cardboard file. "Davies has asked me to fly some documents to Benson. I wondered if you'd take a quick look at one of them."

A frown crossed Moore's good-looking face. "I'm pushed for time, Frank. We're due off in a few minutes. Has it anything to do with this operation?"

"It could have. That's why I'd like you to take a look at it."

Looking more puzzled than ever, Moore reached out for the sheet of paper Harvey had taken from the file. At the same moment Harvey hit him flush on the jaw. As Moore's eyes glazed, Harvey struck him again. This time the young Squadron Commander's knees buckled and he fell heavily, his head striking the floor.

Wincing, Harvey picked him up, laid him on the bed and felt for his pulse. Showing relief when he found it steady, he fumbled into Moore's flying suit and pulled out the syringe of morphine that crews carried in case of serious injury to themselves or their navigators. Glancing round at the closed door, he pulled back

Moore's sleeve and injected the drug into his arm. Sweating freely, he checked Moore's pulse again, dropped an envelope on the bed, then picked up his parachute. With a last anxious glance at the unconscious man, he closed the billet door and hurried round the back of the billets to A Flight offices. There he kept out of sight for a couple of minutes until a 25 cwt transport arrived to take the flight crews to their dispersed Mosquitoes. Seeing the men hesitating and knowing they were enquiring about their missing leader, he then hurried forward to join them. His gruff voice brooked no argument. "It's O.K. You can get in. The skipper's been taken ill and I've been put in command."

As a chatter of concern broke out among the crews, Harvey indicated the transport. "I said get in. We're due off in five minutes. Move."

Although looking puzzled, men began throwing their parachutes into the truck and jumping in after them. Larkin however, the only old sweat in A Flight, stood his ground. "What the hell's going on, Frank? Moore was all right half an hour ago."

"Well he's not all right now. He's caught a bug of some kind and been vomiting his heart out. So jump in and let's get going."

"I don't get it, Frank. I thought you were grounded."

"I was until Moore was taken ill. It seems he's not been feeling well for days: that's why Davies insisted I went to the briefings. A bloody good job, the way things have turned out." Harvey jerked a thumb at the transport. "Hurry it up, Jim. We can't keep the Yanks waiting."

Still looking puzzled but finding no reason to refuse the order, Larkin allowed one of the crewmen to haul him aboard. Breathing more easily, Harvey jumped into the cab alongside the driver. "Move it, lad. As fast as you can."

The transport sped round the circular track, dropping crew after crew at their respective aircraft. As it reached A- Apple and he jumped down, Harvey tried to compose Martin, the young navigator who had been flying with Moore during the recent exercises. "It's all right, lad. I know the job as well as your skipper. We'll be O.K."

With Harvey's reputation as a hard taskmaster a byword in the squadron, Martin was looking more than apprehensive. "Is our role going to be the same, sir?"

Harvey pushed him towards A-Apple. "Exactly the same, lad. Don't worry. It'll work out fine."

Back at the Control Tower, Davies was inviting Staines to join him on the outside balcony, where Henderson and Adams were already watching the ordered activity. As the two men stepped out into a chilly, blustery wind, they could hear Merlin engines firing all over the airfield. A couple of minutes later a sergeant came out on the balcony and fired a green Very light. It was the signal for A-Apple to roll forward and taxi to the end of the north-south runway.

There it swung round and paused for a moment like an animal scenting quarry. Then, as the Controller gave it clearance, its Merlins thundered out and it began moving forward, faster and faster but still earthbound as the two huge bombs in its belly held it down. As it bounced and bounced and the trees of Bishops Wood drew nearer, Adams felt his muscles tightening. He relaxed a couple of seconds later as A-Apple bounced for the last time and then soared triumphantly into the cloudy sky.

The rest of the Mosquitoes followed in rapid succession. When the last one broke free of the runway, Staines glanced at his watch. "12.05, Davies. That's pretty smart."

Above, the Mosquitoes were orbiting the field in preparation to dividing into three flights. As Davies's eyes followed them, a corporal appeared on the balcony and ran up to Davies. "Can you come inside, please, sir? It's urgent."

Giving Henderson a puzzled glance, Davies followed the corporal. As he entered the Control Room the Flight Controller turned from his microphone. "Sir, did you replace Wing Commander Moore with Squadron Leader Harvey just before take-off?"

Davies gave a violent start. "What was that?"

"I think Squadron Leader Harvey is flying A-Apple, sir. I believed I recognised his voice before take-off and now I'm sure of it."

Davies pushed him away from the microphone. "Barracuda Leader! This is Waterloo! Acknowledge me!"

There was no reply. Davies tried again, then swung back on the Controller. "Are you sure?"

"Yes, sir. Quite sure."

Looking dazed by the news, Davies turned to Henderson who had followed him into the room. "What the hell's going on? What's happened to Moore? Send someone to find out."

At that moment a young WAAF entered the tower and ran up to Henderson. "Sir. Wing Commander Moore's been found unconscious in his billet."

Davies leapt in the air as if a dog had bitten him. "What?"

"It seems he's been drugged, sir. At least that's what the M.O. says."

"Drugged!" Davies choked. "God Almighty."

"There's also a letter for Squadron Leader Adams, sir. I've brought it with me."

Davies thrust the letter at the startled Adams. "Read it. Quickly, man!"

Adams ripped open the envelope and pulled out a single sheet of paper. "It's from Harvey, sir. He asks me to take care of his dog. It's over at the inn at the moment."

"His dog! Then Harvey's planned it all. Oh, my God."

Staines, who had only just entered the Control Room, was looking bewildered. "What the problem, Davies?"

Davies told him. Staines' huge eyebrows rose to the peak of his service cap. "You saying Harvey's knocked out your Squadron Commander and taken charge of the operation?"

"That's the way it seems, sir."

If he had heard that Churchill had taken over the Presidency of the United States, the Texan could not have looked more astonished. "This has happened to your outfit, Davies? An élite squadron? A guy jumps into a ship and takes over the role of Flight Leader? Where the hell's your security and what action are you going to take?"

Davies had never felt so shocked and impotent in his life. "I was going to ask you that, sir."

"You'll have to bring 'em back. And I'll have to explain to Spaatz why I've put fifty B-17s and Christ knows how many Mustangs on an abortive mission. Sonofabitch, I'll be back in the States next week wearing a bowler hat."

Seeing that Davies was for once lost for words, Henderson took a deep breath. "Sir, I don't think you need do that. Harvey is a first class leader. Don't forget he led the operation to rescue Moore. And he attended all the briefings. I don't think it'll make much difference to the operation."

"You can say that about a guy who's just drugged your Squadron Commander and hijacked one of your ships? I don't think I'm hearing right, Henderson."

Davies, a born survivor, saw Henderson had offered him a lifeline and he snatched at it with both hands. "That is true, sir. He was our Squadron Commander not that long ago."

"And yet you brought in Moore to take his place? You had to have a reason, Davies. What was it?"

After what Harvey had done, Davies was not unaware of the irony of his defence. "It had nothing to do with his flying skill or his leadership."

"Then what had it to do with?"

Davies winced. "It was thought his background wasn't right for the position."

"His background?" Staines' voice was scathing. "Jesus Christ. You British. I thought we were fighting a war for human rights." His eyes moved from Davies to Henderson. "What are you both saying? That he has a chance of pulling it off?"

When both men nodded, Staines turned for the door. "You'd better be right or the USAAF and the RAF are going to have a bigger war than the one we're having already. I'm going to contact my two Flight Commanders before they get in R/T range of the Krauts. They've both worked with Moore and have a right to know who they'll be dealing with now."

As his angry footsteps descended the stairs, Davies could not hold back one resentful jab. "That was a load of crap. He doesn't want to cancel it any more than we do." Then he turned to Adams with a groan. "Why did Harvey do it, Frank?"

Adams sighed. "As I see it, for two compulsive reasons, sir. One because Anna's involved and he couldn't sit here and do nothing. Two, because he's never got over what Moore did for him in Operation Titan and he couldn't bear the thought of Moore being shot down and tortured. He probably saw this as a way of paying his debt. Harvey's that kind of man."

Davies stared at him. "Are you blaming me for sending Moore, Frank?"

"I'm answering your question, sir. You did ask me to."

By this time Davies looked as if he had expended all the emotion his small wiry body could contain. "Yes, I suppose I did. But aren't all these feelings going to upset his judgement and make him cock up the operation?"

"I don't think so. The very thing he's done shows how dedicated he is. He'll want it to succeed for Anna's sake."

Davies turned to the window in time to see the last specks that were Mosquitoes disappearing into the distance. "Let's hope so, Frank. Otherwise High Command will crucify us all."

Chapter 28

Peering down through his smoked goggles, Harvey was wondering when the German fighter attack would come. In the past the enemy controllers had waited until Allied fighter escorts had reached their operational range and been forced to turn back. But with the new Mustang powered by Rolls Royce, fighter cover could extend all the way to the target. As a consequence there was little point in enemy fighters delaying their strike.

Harvey was certain they would already be airborne. The German monitoring service would have guessed from the B-17s' assembly point that their target was in central or southern Europe and fighter groups would have been moved to airfields east of Odenstein. With the B-17s now approaching Germany's old border, controllers would be scrambling them and directing them on an interception course. The only question left was where that interception would take place.

Watching the box of B-17s emitting condensation trails from their wingtips, Harvey was reminded of the Rhine Maiden operation in which all the aircraft involved had suffered so grievously. The same ugly black mushrooms of flak were bursting among the Fortresses and similar casualties were being incurred. As Harvey watched, a B-17 received a direct hit by an 88 mm shell on its starboard engine. Yawing wildly, it caused its neighbouring Fortresses to swing away as it lurched across the formation. A burst of flame erupted from its tanks, then the wing ripped away as if the plane were a child's toy. Harvey saw the white puffs of only five parachutes before the asymmetrical remains of the huge bomber disappeared into the clouds below. With his radio tuned to the

Americans' frequency, Harvey heard a calm voice order the B-17s to close ranks again.

Yet there were major differences, as Harvey knew well. On the earlier mission to Bavaria there had been a veritable armada of B-17s. Today there were only 50. They were enough to screen the high level Mosquitoes from radar detection, but only if Harvey and his Flight Commanders exercised the utmost caution in holding station directly above them.

The other difference was the American fighter escort, a comfort to B-17 and Mosquito crews alike. From the height the Mosquitoes were flying, the Mustangs looked like wasps humming around a dense flock of birds. They were led by Major Dent, a likeable stocky New Yorker whom Harvey had met in person more than once. Although not prone to eulogise anybody, in particular his allies, Harvey had to admit Dent was a courageous and capable officer. He and his Wing had escorted them on a number of operations and even on Harvey's exacting terms had met all expectations. Indeed, although it is doubtful if he would have admitted it, the Yorkshireman was finding comfort in the presence of Dent's wing of fighters.

Not for the first time, Harvey wondered what was happening back at Sutton Craddock. He had not been surprised when no order to abort had been made: he had felt certain all along that when all the commotion had died down, both Davies and Staines would realise the operation could not be cancelled. With the invasion of Europe causing massive demands on aircraft, both men would know it was highly unlikely they would be given a second chance of American support in the near future. The attack on the German establishment had to be made now or the inevitable recriminations and quarrels would make a second attempt too late.

What would happen to him if he survived the mission was a thought Harvey kept pushing aside. Although he believed Davies had been grievously at fault in allowing Moore to lead the mission, the Yorkshireman had no illusions that the Air Commodore would forgive and forget. With the grim humour characteristic of Harvey, he was grateful the days of hanging, drawing and quartering were over. Otherwise he could see pieces of himself dangling from the flagpole at Sutton Craddock.

Martin's voice broke into his thoughts. "Bandits, skipper. Attacking the Yanks."

Harvey spotted them immediately, mixed *gruppen* of Me 109s and Focke-Wulfs silhouetted against the clouds below. Ignoring the Mustangs, they were sweeping in like packs of wolves attacking a herd of reindeer. At 2000 metres' range, their 21 cm rockets could be seen lancing out in long trails of smoke. At 900 metres the tracer from their cannon wove cotton like threads among the B-17s. As the air waves filled with shouts of warning, the enemy fighters dived beneath the oncoming Fortresses and swung violently away to avoid the fire from their ventral and side gun positions.

The sky was laced with tracer now as the B-17 gunners returned fire with their .5 Brownings. One Fortress, hit by a rocket, reeled like a blinded animal across the formation before turning over and plunging down into the clouds. Another was pouring black smoke from an engine but remained in station. Analysing the enemy tactics, Dent was now issuing orders to his Mustangs and they were diving down to intercept the aggressive Germans. Soon the sky was like a huge fish tank in which dozens of tiger fish were snapping about with ferocious jaws and tearing one another to pieces.

In T-Tommy, heading B Flight, Gabby was also remembering Rhine Maiden and the torment Millburn had suffered in seeing his compatriots under attack while he, under orders, had to remain a passive onlooker. "You're not getting any ideas, are you, Millburn'?"

The American gave him a glare. "Belt up, you little sonofabitch."

There were times when even Gabby knew teasing was not the order of the day. "Those Mustangs are doing a great job, boyo. I've seen three bandits go down already."

Millburn scowled. "We could take more if they'd given us a free rein."

Gabby made no attempt to argue with him. "Let's just hope none of them spot us up here. Or there might be a reception committee waiting for us at Buchansee."

Ahead, Harvey was having the same thought. Like the rest of his crews, he could only hope the enemy fighters were too occupied to notice the cloud of specks above them. As the fight below raged on, he could hear the sounds of battle on the radio channel.

"Keep your formation, Red Three. Close up tighter."

"Focke-Wulf, Johnnie! Nine o'clock high."

"I got one, skipper! A 109. See him, you guys! At three o'clock."

Like their British counterparts in the Battle of Britain, the Germany pilots were exhibiting the same desperate courage as the B-17s drove deeper into their homeland. Their fighters could now be seen plunging into the centre of the bomber formation where the fire-power of the Fortresses was interlocked and massive. One Focke-Wulf, hit by at least twenty heavy machine guns, blew up in a huge oily burst of flame . Another had its fuselage cut in half as if a giant knife had sliced through it. Yet another collided with a B-17 and the welded wreckage went spiralling down like a giant sycamore seed. With more than one Mustang ablaze or its pilot blown to bloody fragments by cannon fire, the sky from 12,000 feet up to 22,000 feet was a giant slaughterhouse of men and machines.

The carnage only ceased when the German pilots ran out of ammunition and had to withdraw. Although it was a signal for flak to start bursting around the B-17s again, some of the younger crews believed their ordeal was over. The older hands, knowing better, dragged out fresh ammunition boxes, reloaded their guns, and waited.

Back in the Operations Room at Sutton Craddock, Adams was watching Davies with some concern. Twice within the last fifteen minutes the small Air Commodore had jumped from his chair and begun pacing up and down beneath the large map of Europe. Now his fingers were drumming on the long bench where he, Staines, and the Signals corporal were sitting, the American with his telephone and the corporal with the radio that would eventually receive messages from Harvey when wireless silence was broken.

Staines, with an unlit cigar in his mouth and the phone receiver to his ear, had been receiving intelligence from his headquarters about the B-17s since the German fighter attack had begun, and the losses he reported to Davies and the other officers had done nothing to lighten their tension. Along with Adams and Henderson, Brigadier Simms was present. Simms had arrived only a few minutes after the squadron had flown off on its mission and Adams had expected the frail Brigadier to be shocked on receiving the news about Harvey. Instead Simms had taken the news calmly. How much of this was due to the soldier's natural self-control and how much to a surprising confidence in Harvey's abilities, Adams did not know, but it certainly seemed from appearances that Davies was more in need of comfort than the elderly Brigadier.

With Staines' telephone silent for the moment, the sound of Davies' drumming fingers was loud in the room. Seeing Staines frowning at the small Air Commodore, Adams felt he ought to say something to divert the American's attention. "Our boys will be breaking off soon, won't they, sir?"

The big Texan nodded. "Any time now, Adams. Let's just hope the Krauts haven't spotted them yet."

Amen to that, Adams thought. By far the most imaginative man in the room, he had inwardly winced every time Staines had announced the loss of another B-17 or Mustang. To Adams they were not aircraft, they were young men cut down in the flower of their youth, and he could almost feel their pain as bullets ripped into them or fire entered their lungs. With such imaginative power, Adams never understood why he hated the age and poor eyesight that kept him from flying with such men and perhaps suffering their fate.

A faint metallic voice in Staines' earphones made every man in the room lean forward. Fifteen seconds later Staines gave an exclamation and swung round. "That's it! Separation. Your guys are on their way."

"What about the escort?" Simms asked.

"Dent's divided them," Staines told him. "Two thirds stay with the B-17s. Dent's taking the rest to Buchansee." His eyes switched to Davies. "Now it's up to that maverick of yours. Let's hope to Christ he knows what he's doing."

Davies opened his mouth, then closed it again. As Staines put a light to his cigar, Davies jumped up and began pacing beneath the map again. Seeing Staines' eyes following him, Adams was relieved when Simms asked a further question. "When will they break radio silence?"

Henderson, doing his best to hide his nervousness beneath his Scottish phlegm, gave the answer. "Moore was given permission to switch on once they broke away from the Americans. But I don't know if Harvey's aware of that. He might wait until they're over the target. As the range of R/T is limited, it's something we can't know. We'll have to wait for a W/T transmission."

In the fresh silence that fell, broken only by Davies's restless pacing, Adams' imagination took him to the Mosquitoes and to Buchansee. Dry-mouthed crews sighting the saw mill and wondering if they would be able to identify the camouflaged track that led from it ... Pilots asking navigators if they could see any flak posts ... Navigators sharing their anxious search for the enemy fighters they knew must arrive soon ... Below them the shining lake and its islands, the railroad link, the great green woods, all revolving slowly as the crews waited to make their attack. Like a moving film in his mind, Adams could see it all and the tension within him tightened by the minute.

In fact, knowing the efficiency of his crews, Harvey only broke R/T silence when all three flights were orbiting the lake. "Barracuda Leader to all sections. Drop your tanks and test your guns. Now."

Drop tanks went toppling earthward and flame spat from the nose of every Mosquito as the crews obeyed the order. Their earphones crackled again a few seconds later. "Barracuda Leader. Red Section orbit at 4.000. Blue Section orbit at 5,000. Green Section orbit at 6,000. Go."

Mosquitoes dived or rose according to their status until there were three tiers orbiting the lake at different heights. Harvey's voice came again. "Keep your eyes open for fighters and for gun posts. Red Section stay in orbit until you get further orders." Then: "Barracuda Leader to Gettysburg Leader. Are you still with us?"

An American voice answered. "Am giving you high cover. Barracuda Leader. Wouldn't miss the tea party for worlds. O.K.?"

It was a moment Harvey wished he had Moore's gift for light-hearted repartee. "Thanks, Gettysburg Leader. The party's starting now."

As Harvey's voice ceased, A-Apple could he seen diving towards the saw mill. Gabby turned to Millburn. "The tyke's doing all right so far."

Millburn was watching A-Apple level off west of the saw mill and then bank towards it. "He's going to do a dummy run to see where the flak posts are. You have to hand it to the guy. He always leads from the front."

With its camouflage, A-Apple was difficult to see as it raced at low level into the shallow wooded valley that led to the saw mill. Conscious that each of them would soon be making the same run, crews stared down to see what flak response there was. When no tell-tale puffs of smoke appeared and A-Apple came shooting up from the lake unscathed, men were jubilant. "They've been so bloody sure of themselves they haven't bothered to build any flak posts," Gabby chortled. "It's going to be a piece of cake."

The Welshman could not have been more wrong. Nothing could have underlined the importance the Germans placed on their research establishment more than the firepower they had brought in to protect it, even though the chance of an air attack seemed unlikely. Everything from multiple-barrelled pom-poms to LMGs were sited on the hills on both sides of the valley, all heavily camouflaged to avoid awakening the suspicion of prowling Allied aircraft. Since receiving warning about the sudden appearance of the Mosquitoes, their gunners were now on full alert.

At the same time that few if any of the gunners believed the underground cavern could be the target for light bombers, for how could bombs penetrate a lake? The officer in charge decided at the worst it could only be a reconnaissance and issued orders for no one to fire yet and so bring attention to the fact that his guns had something important to defend.

This order had stayed in force while A-Apple had made its dummy run. But when the Mosquito had followed the hidden track right to the mouth of the tunnel, gunners found it hard to believe blind chance had guided it there. Nevertheless their officer, confident in the effectiveness of the camouflage and unable to imagine what damage light bombers could do, decided to hold fire a little longer until the Mosquitoes played their hand.

That hand was about to be played as Harvey's voice rasped on the R/T. "Barracuda Leader to Red Three. Try to follow my track. Down you go."

Red Three was McMaster and Green carrying the incendiary spray. Dropping a wing McMaster dived down to tree top height and headed towards the shallow valley, unaware that dozens of eyes were following F-Freddy from the flanking hillsides. As he swept over the saw mill, McMaster nodded to Green who jerked a lever on the dashboard. Immediately a plume of yellow spray ejected from a long cylinder fitted in the Mosquito's bomb bay. Smoke Curtain Installations, a nom-de-guerre for an instrument designed to carry poison gas if the need ever arose, had been utilised by the Squadron's armourers to deliver the incendiary spray, and from the broad mantle it was delivering it seemed ideally suited to the task.

The effect on the hidden gunners was dramatic. Believing they were being sprayed with mustard gas, NCOs yelled at their men to don their gas masks and then open fire. Gunners dragged their masks over their frightened faces and then tore away the camouflaged netting that concealed their guns. Before McMaster and Green had reached the lake, the first vengeful shells were reaching after them.

As startled voices filled the radio channel, Millburn gave Gabby a look of disgust. "What did you say it was? A piece of cake?"

The two hillsides were now alive with smoke and flashes as the gunners, believing the RAF was breaking the Geneva Convention, fired at every aircraft that came within range. Harvey, wishing he carried an SCI himself, addressed Pulford and Clark. "Your turn, Red Four. Red Two, join me in giving Red Four cover."

Three Mosquitoes dived down to the tree tops. Pulford took the centre of the valley and began pouring out yellow spray while Harvey and Larkin diverted and harassed the gunners on their respective hillsides. From above, the Mosquitoes looked like toys being pierced by dozens of red-hot pins as they raced towards the lake. Pulford was perhaps two hundred yards from it when a 37 mm shell burst through the cockpit floor and exploded. With nothing but mangled flesh and bone to fly it, the Mosquito rolled over like a gaffed fish and crashed in a ball of fire among the trees.

Sweating freely, with LMG bullet holes in both wings, Harvey climbed steeply away. To his left he could see Larkin's aircraft climbing after him. Giving himself time to recover and to think, he went into orbit with the rest of his section and gazed down. The yellow spray delivered by McMaster had now settled on the netting and the trees around it, staining the floor of the shallow valley. Harvey's voice was almost apologetic when he addressed McMaster again. "Red Three, it's time to drop your incendiaries. Keep as much to the centre of the valley as you can. We'll give you cover again. Off you go."

A thousand feet above, Millburn glanced at Gabby, then addressed Harvey. "Blue Leader to Barracuda. We're coming down to help you."

Harvey's bark made the earphones crackle. "No! You stay where you are, Millburn."

"Piss off," the American muttered. "Blue Two, come with me. The rest of you stay in orbit."

Ignoring Harvey's incensed orders, Millburn and Machin dived down after the three Mosquitoes of Red Section. As Harvey and his men grouped west of the saw mill, Millburn went point blank for the guns. Although lightly armed with only .303 Brownings, he cut down a LMG post and scattered the crew of a 37 mm battery before McMaster entered the valley with his twin escort.

Although the four harassing Mosquitoes diverted some of the flak, the gunners had recognised their main threat by this time and McMaster was subjected to intense fire as he began dropping his incendiaries. Flying behind his port quarter, Harvey could see blobs of fire appearing on the yellow curtain below. As they spread rapidly he let out a yell of triumph to his navigator. "It's working, lad! It's bloody well working!"

The cry of triumph died in his throat as McMaster's Mosquito suddenly faltered. It steadied for a moment and the small incendiaries continued falling until the plane was no more than fifty yards from the lake. Then it swung blindly to the left and crashed into the trees. A few seconds later its tanks exploded. The sharp tongue of McMaster would not tease young recruits again.

The triumphant gunners now turned their fury on the four escorting Mosquitoes, forcing them to break to port and starboard. Keeping at tree top-level until out of range, Harvey climbed back into orbit to view the situation. At first he could see little for the smoke that was pouring up from the valley. Then a gust of wind veered it away to show the burning netting had collapsed and was smouldering on the track that led to the tunnel. Gratified, Harvey took the binoculars from his navigator and gazed down again, only for his satisfaction to turn into dismay. To be certain he was right, he ignored the flak and flew over the valley again. Only then did he turn to Martin. "Get in touch with Waterloo. I want you to send them this message."

Chapter 29

Every man in the Operations Room started at the sudden blip of Morse, but no one moved faster than Davies. He was at the side of the Signals corporal before the man could pick up his pencil. "Is it them? Barracuda?"

The corporal was trying to decipher the faint blips. "Yes, sir. It's them."

"What's happening? What do they say?"

Henderson, who had reached the radio set only a length behind Davies, took his arm. "Give him a chance, sir."

Remembering himself, Davies scowled but allowed the corporal to write down the message. After thirty seconds his impatience overcame him. "What the hell's Harvey doing? Writing a bloody book?"

Staines, who along with Simms and Adams was showing the same intense interest, moved along the bench towards them. "What's the hold-up? Aren't they there yet?"

Davies motioned him to be quiet, an impertinence after his own conduct that at any other time would have brought a grin from Henderson. Shaking his head, Staines joined the others in watching the corporal scribbling on a note pad. The moment the blips ceased, Davies snatched the sheet of paper from him. Adams, breathless with suspense by this time, watched his excited face turn from anticipation to dismay. "Well," Staines demanded. "What's happened?"

Davies handed the slip of paper to Simms, then turned to him. "It's the netting, sir. The last stretch to the tunnel wasn't sufficiently drenched because our second Mosquito was shot down before reaching it. That left only one aircraft to drop incendiaries and it was also shot down halfway along the track."

"Sonofabitch, the flak must be heavy," Staines muttered.

"According to Harvey it's intense." Davies glanced at Simms. "That's what we didn't reckon with. We ought to have sent out two more Mossies with incendiaries."

Staines' gravelly voice cut off the Brigadier's reply. "So the tunnel entrance isn't exposed. Your bombs can't find it. Is that how things stand?"

Watching Davies, Adams thought he had never seen the Air Commodore look more dejected. "I'm afraid that's it, sir."

The silence that followed was full of disappointment, dismay and silent recriminations. Then Staines cursed and turned to his telephone. "I'll pass the news on to my HQ. If Dent and his guys are giving high cover they might not know what's happening."

Although the elderly Brigadier looked as dismayed as Davies, he put a comforting hand on Davies' arm as the Air Commodore turned to the Signals corporal. "Send this message to Barracuda Leader. Tell him to abort the mission and to return home."

Harvey's earphones crackled while his navigator was tapping his message to Sutton Craddock. "Frank, all the netting hasn't burned away. What do you want to do?"

Harvey's bark was more at the perversity of life than at Millburn. "Do you think I don't know? Give me a minute, for Christ's sake."

"O.K. but remember Dent's guys. They'll have to keep an eye on their fuel."

Harvey was only too aware of that. As he stared down at the smoking valley the radio blipped back Davies' reply. A moment later, Martin glanced at him. "It's Waterloo, skipper. They're telling us to abort."

Harvey gritted his teeth. Abort. Failure. Disgrace upon disgrace. But, worst of all, a betrayal of Anna. Sweating with frustration, with every cell in his body rebelling against the order, he glanced down again at the valley. A moment later he gave a start. Christ, yes. It might just work. And if it didn't, what was lost? Without further hesitation he put down A-Apple's nose and at the same time addressed his crews. "Red Section and Blue Section, come down and cover me. Now."

Diving down, he levelled off two miles west of the lake and gave more instructions to his escort. Then he swept round and made for the smoking valley.

Although the Mosquitoes on his flanks took some of the flak as he entered the valley, the fire was still murderous as the smouldering netting swept beneath him. As shells swirled past the perspex canopy, Harvey saw from the corner of his eye that Martin was crouched almost into a ball on his seat.

But there was no time for comforting words. Hugging the smoking ground, Harvey could see the intact netting leaping towards him, a shadowy underpass that allowed no glimpse of the tunnel entrance at its far end. His urgent shout brought Martin to life. "Get ready, lad. Ready ... ready ... now!"

A-Apple bucked like a startled horse as a Highball fell and bounded forward. At the same time Harvey heaved back on the control column and sent the Mosquito rocketed upwards. Ignoring the chains of shells following him, he was counting: "Four ... five ... six ... seven ... When he reached fifteen he feared his Highball had bounded past the hidden entrance and disappeared impotently into the lake. But just as he was preparing to make the run again, a fireball burst from the hidden track, rocking A-Apple in its blast. For a moment smoke hid the scene, then Millburn's yell came over the R/T. "You did it, Frank! There's the goddam entrance."

Harvey saw the American was right. Before releasing his Highball, he had guessed there would be a substantial supporting flange around the tunnel entrance and had gambled on his Highball not shooting away after striking it. The result was all that he had hoped for. The blast had blown away most of the final stretch of netting and what was left was now being devoured by fire. The target was revealed at last: a yawning dark tunnel framed by massive stonework.

To his immense relief Harvey could see no doors that could seal its entrance. Knowing the importance of time, he wasted not a moment. "There's your target, Red Two. Red Five and Blue section follow at twenty second intervals. I repeat, twenty seconds."

As Larkin dived down, an American voice held Harvey's attention. "Barracuda Leader, you're doing a great job down there, but the flak's too heavy. I'm sending down half a dozen ships to lend a hand."

Aware the Mustangs had cannon against his Mosquitoes' Brownings, Harvey knew he needed the offer. "Thanks, Gettysburg Leader. But keep your eyes open for bandits. They're already overdue."

With the need now to control the attack, Harvey went into a tight circle and watched the aircraft he had dispatched launch their attacks into the smoke-filled valley. Although Larkin, under orders, waited until the six Mustangs began harassing the guns, he still drew heavy fire. The Highball Harvey had launched had at last explained to the enemy the Mosquitoes' purpose and NCOs were yelling at their crews to ignore the diversionary attacks and concentrate on the Mosquitoes.

Although not every gunner obeyed, the gauntlet the Mosquitoes had to run was laced with flame and steel. Larkin got through without serious damage but his Highball bounded off line, ricocheted from the stonework and exploded harmlessly on the shore of the lake. Millburn, the next to go, pressed home his attack with his usual reckless courage, but at the moment Gabby released a Highball, a bursting shell threw T-Tommy off line and the bomb bounded off the track into the flanking trees. As Millburn climbed away, an explosion hurled tree trunks like matchsticks into the air.

It proved an unfortunate accident. One tree trunk fell back on the track and lay across it some fifty yards from the tunnel entrance. As Blue Two made his attack, his Highball struck the trunk, bounced high in the air, and disappeared among the trees before exploding. As Blue Two tried to fight his way through the murderous flak, a 37 mm shell exploded in his starboard fuel tanks. Like a toy aflame, the Mosquito soared into the air under its own volition, then dropped in a ball of fire into the lake. Purcell would not see Yorkshire win the cricket championship again.

As the watching Harvey cursed, Martin turned to him. "Shouldn't I be sending details to Waterloo, skipper?"

"Were you supposed to?"

"I think Davies wanted them. Once radio silence was broken."

Harvey's voice was bitter as he saw yet another Mosquito of Millburn's flight reel away from the smoking valley, only to crash into the southern hillside. "Then you'd better get on with it, hadn't you, before we run out of bloody aircraft."

As the blips came again, Henderson flinched. His anxious eyes watched the Signals Corporal turn to Davies. "Another aircraft down, sir."

Davies, who had leapt to his feet like an excited elf on hearing of Harvey's success in clearing the track, was subdued again as the news came through of the squadron's losses. Before he could reply, Henderson exploded. "This is madness, sir. I'm losing my squadron over there. And for what? We haven't got one single bomb in the tunnel yet."

Davies tried to calm him. "They're carrying two apiece. There's plenty of time."

"There aren't plenty of aircraft, sir. I've already lost twenty per cent of my strength. If things go on like this it's going to be another Swartfjord disaster."

About to answer him, Davies decided against it and turned to Staines instead. "The flak's the problem. A steady run's needed to launch these Highballs accurately and the flak will be making it difficult for the crews."

Staines rubbed a hand over his bristly chin. "I suppose I could order more of my ships down, but that could leave all the guys exposed when the Krauts arrive."

Davies kept his eyes averted from Henderson. "Leave it a while longer, sir. We must get a bomb in there sooner or later."

The bomb Davies was hoping for bounded into the tunnel just after Martin tapped out his last message. It was delivered by Van

Breedenkamp who, in spite of the hail of bullets and shells, kept his eyes tightly locked on the dark entrance and refused to flinch even when a shell took half his rudder assembly away. The Highball his navigator released bounded over the felled tree, bounded a second time twenty yards from the tunnel, and then launched itself into the darkness inside. The South African's yell of triumph rattled the earphones of every crewman in the sky, and pilots awaiting their ordeal swung away to view the result, not a few praying their run into the valley of death would be unnecessary.

Fifteen seconds passed, twenty seconds passed, thirty seconds passed and when no tell-tale plug of fire and smoke came belching from the tunnel, the crews knew the worst. Sod's law was operating again. The one Highball that had penetrated the tunnel had not exploded.

It had not been the first. One Mosquito of Millburn's section had released a dud too, which had ricocheted from the battered stonework and smashed harmlessly into the surrounding trees. But to be so near success and yet so far was demoralising, as the disappointed voices on the radio channel made clear.

Although sickened himself, Harvey knew the requirements of leadership demanded an upbeat reaction.

"Well done, Van. You've showed it can be done. Go on, Green Two. Put another in."

But although the next four Mosquitoes of Green Section did their best, no further Highball bounded into the tunnel. With the irrelevant thoughts men get during moments of high drama, Harvey was reminded of a childhood game of soccer he had once played. Every shot he or his colleagues had made at goal failed to score as if the goalposts were protected by an invisible wall. Yet when their opponents had finally managed to launch an attack, they had scored with their first shot.

Fuming at the losses and frustrated by the misses, Harvey became aware of a new problem as he gazed down. Although the stonework surrounding the tunnel was massive and most of the Highballs reaching it had ricocheted away before exploding, it had received the blast from a few bombs and stones and concrete slabs were littering the floor at its base. If many more bombs exploded there, the tunnel entrance could be blocked or at least narrowed, so making the task of penetration even more difficult.

Below, the Mustangs were still attacking the flak posts with courage and determination. From A-Apple the scene was pure surrealism with coloured shells and tracer soaring in all directions from the crimson smoke and Mustangs swooping up and diving like as many falcons. As Harvey circled above he saw the last aircraft of Van Breedenkamp's section make its attack. It was manned by two young Australians, Mann and Kemp, whom Harvey himself had advised and trained during Anna's absence. In spite of the harassment of the Mustangs, J-Jenny received its baptism of fire before it even entered the valley. Whips of coloured shells lashed towards it and forks of tracer stabbed its slim body with murderous intent. For a moment it seemed to falter, bringing a groan from Harvey. Then it steadied and entered the valley. As black bursts appeared around it, Harvey saw its Highball fall and bound forward. For a moment it disappeared into the smoke, then the Yorkshireman caught sight of it again, an object no bigger than a penny, leaping along the smouldering valley floor. It bounced for a last time, then, like a stone hurled into an open mouth, it disappeared into the tunnel.

Harvey gave a triumphant yell. "Well done, lads. Bloody well done."

His shout died in his throat a moment later. A pom-pom crew situated near the tunnel entrance had been following the Mosquito's flight along the valley and as it came opposite them they opened up with a point-blank barrage of automatic fire. Almost blown apart by the explosions, J-Jenny rolled over in a tangle of wood and flesh and exploded among the trees.

Although the loss of his crews was torturing Harvey, he was professional enough to continue counting. As he reached fourteen, a great plug of smoke and fire burst out of the tunnel entrance. A moment later the radio channel was swamped by triumphant shouts, with Millburn's cry the loudest among them. "That's it, Frank. Right up the bastard's arse hole."

But Harvey was watching the lake. Sullen beneath the clouds that had gathered over it, it was showing no disturbance of any kind. Aware of what that meant, Harvey made a snap decision. "Millburn,

I'm going down to finish the job. You're in charge if anything goes wrong."

"The hell with that, Frank. You've done enough."

Harvey's incensed shout shivered the air waves. "Do as you're told, Blue Leader. Get over to the island and see if you can plug the vent with your Highballs. We lost our bombs when Pulford and McMaster went down. Green Section, give me cover."

At that moment the message came that Harvey had feared and expected for minutes. "Bandits, Barracuda Leader. We'll try to hold 'em but watch your backs." A quick glance upwards confirmed Dent's warning. Mustangs and enemy fighters were milling about like gnats on a summer day. Cursing, Harvey dipped a wing and went slicing down, giving orders to Martin on the way. "Keep your eyes on that bombsight and don't take 'em away whatever happens. I want another bomb slap in the middle of that tunnel."

His face pale, Martin nodded. Heading west, Harvey banked on a wingtip over Buchansee village and hugged the railway track towards the saw mill. Seeing him flash over it and then sink down towards the valley, enemy crews cocked their guns and waited. In that brief moment, less than a few seconds, everything became very vivid to Harvey, the powerful thudding of his heart, the pulse of blood in his neck, the tension in his arms and legs. As Harvey knew only too well, a healthy man never feels so alive as when death is near.

The guns opened out a few seconds later. Luminous arcs of shells criss-crossed the valley, forks of tracers speared out and tried to impale A-Apple. A shell burst outside the cupola, making both men jerk back in their seats. Another explosion almost turned the Mosquito over. LMG fire hammered along her fuselage and Harvey felt his right leg jerk upwards as if it had been kicked. Not daring to take his eyes off the smoking track ahead, he forced A-Apple back on course, only for another hail of LMG fire to ricochet from the half exposed Highball in the bomb bay. Bathed in sweat, Harvey drove A-Apple on, his big hands white on the control column, his cheek muscles prominent on his rugged face. Halfway along the valley a Mustang dived out of the smoke and flashed over the cupola. With Dent's fighters strafing the gunposts and Van Breedenkamp's

Mosquitoes trying to draw fire, collision was as great a threat as gunfire.

But Harvey could see the tunnel entrance now, a wraithlike structure appearing out of the smoke. Below him the track was unfolding like a roller coaster. Seeing the tree trunk straddling the smouldering ground, Harvey waited until it flashed beneath him and the tunnel entrance filled his windshield. A second more, then he gave a yell. "Now!" As the Mosquito jerked, he heaved back on the control column. Rearing up, A-Apple seemed to the breathless crews above to claw her way up the very facade of the shattered stonework. As she levelled out over the lake, Harvey turned to Martin. "Was it a hit?" There was no need for the shaken navigator to reply. Confirmation came in a dozen excited voices. Ignoring the flak still reaching up to him, Harvey stared down intently at the sullen expanse of lake. For a full ten seconds he could see no change. Then the stretch of water near the tunnel entrance shivered as if a sudden squall was crossing its surface. A moment more, and ripples began to extend from an epicentre some two hundred yards from the entrance. As the ripples grew into waves, the entire configuration began to turn around its epicentre like the water pouring out of some enormous bath. As the rotation increased, waves ruffled the surface and swept up on the nearby beaches. Alongside Harvey, Martin gave an awed gasp. "My God, skipper. The water's broken through."

Harvey's brusque voice interrupted him. "Send Maelstrom to Waterloo! Do it now."

After their initial excitement, there was little jubilation from the crews. They had seen too much death that day to revel in the thought of hundreds of men drowning in an underground tomb. Nor was there time for reflection. As Harvey gazed down and saw the leg of his flying suit was soaked in blood, a yell of warning rattled his earphones. "Bandit, Barracuda Leader! Eight o'clock high."

Only training and reflex action saved A-Apple. As Harvey swung instantly to port, a harmonised burst of cannon shells ripped past his starboard wing. As he searched for the fighter that was attacking him, he caught sight of a twin-engined aircraft shooting skyward with the speed of a rocket. Martin sounded shocked. "What the hell was that, skipper?"

Harvey knew only too well. Before he could speak he heard Dent's breathless voice. "Barracuda Leader, get your ships together and make for the clouds. They're using a couple of ships we've never seen before and they're sensational."

"Can you handle them, Gettysburg Leader?"

"Yeah, we'll handle them as long as there aren't any more. Get your guys into the clouds. We'll give you all the cover we can."

It was not Harvey's way, nor to his liking, to accept Dent's invitation. But with almost every Mosquito carrying some damage, he knew the danger of structural failure would be great if they tangled with the enemy fighters. His task now was to save what remained of the Squadron. For Harvey his words of appreciation were lavish indeed. "Thanks, Gettysburg Leader. I reckon we owe you a pint or two."

"As long as the beer's cold, Barracuda Leader, we'll enjoy your company."

Harvey turned to Martin, who had noticed the blood seeping through his flying suit. "Find a piece of string or a strap of some kind and put a tourniquet on this leg." As Martin climbed from his seat, Harvey addressed his crews. "Check your damage and drop the rest of your Highballs. Then formate behind me. We're going home."

Chapter 30

Staines gave a grunt of relief as he lowered the receiver. "It's O.K. Dent's boys got them. Apparently they ran out of fuel and were destroyed before they could land."

Davies, who had almost danced with joy and relief on hearing the codeword Maelstrom, now showed concern. "Did any more arrive?"

"No. There were only two. My guess is they were being put through tests somewhere else in Krautland and when your boys attacked their research base, they were diverted there. I guess you could call it an act of desperation."

Davies's expression was heartfelt. "Thank God they didn't arrive any sooner."

"You can say that again, although I guess the radar cover my B-17s gave your boys accounts for the delay. According to Dent they were some ships. They got five of my Mustangs before they ran out of gas. If the Krauts had ever got them into series production, they'd only have needed a few hundred to put us right out of business."

Adams could not help asking the question he knew must be worrying the others. "I suppose there's no possibility they've built others and can use them as prototypes?"

From the look Davies gave him, Adams felt he had asked a question of dubious taste. Staines answered him. "It's always possible, Frank, but I like to think we've stopped their research just in time. Although those ships were deadly enough while they were flying, their running out of gas so quickly suggests the fuel tank problem hasn't yet been solved."

Simms nodded his agreement. "I think the general is right, Adams. When our boffins heard about the project, they said fitting fuel tanks into slim wings would be one of the major problems. It would need specialised wind tunnels and, with thousands of tons of lake pouring down under tremendous pressure into the centre, it's certain there will be nothing left there to salvage. Of course another centre can be built, but the time we've gained may be priceless."

At that moment the Signals corporal pressed the R/T receiver to his ear. A few seconds later he glanced at Henderson. "It's Squadron Leader Millburn, sir. He's asking for our crash wagons and ambulances to be put on alert."

Henderson grabbed the telephone from him. "What's your status, Millburn? And what's happened to Harvey?"

The others leaned forward to listen but could not make out Millburn's reply. The impatient Davies was about to order the loudspeaker to be switched on when Henderson handed the telephone back to the Signals corporal. "Well?" Davies snapped. "What's the news?"

"Apart from the losses already reported, Larkin and Van Breedenkamp have some damage and Beckenridge, Larkin's navigator, is dead," the Scot told him. "Naturally we'll have crash wagons and ambulances standing by. We always have."

Adams beat Simms to the question by a short head. "What about Harvey, sir?"

"He had to land at a satellite airfield along with Miller, whose navigator was wounded. Apparently Harvey lost a great deal of blood and only just made it."

Staines was frowning. "Is he badly wounded?"

"I don't know yet, sir. But the satellite field will phone us as soon as they have some definite news."

"That guy did a hell of a job," the Texan muttered. "No one could have done better."

Adams noticed that Davies made no comment. Instead the small Air Commodore glanced at Staines and Simms. "I'm going to the Control Tower, gentlemen. Will you both come, or don't you have the time?"

Staines heaved his massive bulk from the bench. "Yeah, I'll come and see your boys back before I leave."

The Brigadier also rose. "It's the least we can do, Davies. They've done a magnificent job."

Davies turned to Henderson. "You coming, Jock, after you've put the station on alert?"

"Yes, sir. I'll join you there in a moment."

Adams watched the three men disappear from the Operations Room before turning to Henderson. "What's going to happen to Frank, sir?"

The Scot lifted his big shoulders. "God knows. He did break every rule in the book. I ought to court-martial him myself."

"But from all we've heard he saved the operation and got wounded doing it. At any other time he'd get a decoration."

"I know all that, Frank. But he's in His Majesty's Armed Forces, not in a bloody Biggles novel. He can't go about knocking out his Squadron Commander and leading a mission as important as this one without getting punished." When Adams opened his mouth to argue, the Scot put up a big hand. "Don't, Frank. I've heard you before. They should never have allowed a sentimentalist like you to join the Services."

"But Harvey didn't do it for glory, sir."

"I know exactly why Harvey did it. In his way he's as daft as you are. But he still can't take swings at his Squadron Commander and then have Davies and an American general shitting themselves for six hours in case a hugely important operation turns into a disaster." When Adams sighed, Henderson went on: "Anyway, it's not in my hands. Davies is the one who detailed Moore to lead the operation and if I know my man at all, Davies is the one who's going to punish him. Air Commodores don't like looking fools in front of American generals, and who can blame them?"

When Adams did not reply, Henderson clapped him across the shoulders. "Stop worrying about it, Frank. Come up in the Tower and watch the boys come home. There'll be time for your de-briefing later."

The Mosquito was lowering itself to the airfield as gingerly as a cat descending a hot tin roof. Flak had torn away half its port aileron and sprung the hinges on the rest, making lateral stability difficult. Naked spars were visible along its fuselage and a row of blackened holes disfigured its tail assembly. But Larkin's main problem was not the flying condition of his aircraft but the physical state of his navigator. A shell fragment had penetrated the cockpit and driven deep into the body of young Beckenridge, his navigator. The result was a corpse that rocked from side to side and sometimes obscenely nudged the New Zealander.

Larkin knew he ought to have landed at the satellite airfield along with Harvey and Miller. But, tough although the New Zealander was, the shock of seeing his young navigator so brutally killed had given him an illogical desire to return with his other colleagues to the comforting ambience of Sutton Craddock.

Still in some degree of shock, with his flying suit stained in Beckenridge's blood, he watched the airfield rising beneath him. He crossed the road that ran past the inn and from the corner of his eye saw a distant figure waving at him. He knew it was Maisie who had heard the Mosquitoes returning but the lateral unsteadiness of G-George allowed him no return salute. With throttles back and airfoils whining, Larkin sank lower and lower. Below, like shadows in the pale sunlight, a crash wagon and an ambulance were racing along either side of the approaching runway. With painful slowness the Mosquito sank and sank until at last it touched down with a scream of tyres. Instantly its port wing dropped and it ground-looped in a massive snapping of spars.

Up in the Control Tower Davies's party were viewing the scene with various degrees of dismay. Terrified the Mosquito was going to explode in flames and incinerate Larkin, Adams was urging the crash wagon on with every muscle in his body. To his relief he saw no fire and half a minute later G-George was being drenched with foam. At the same time asbestos-clad men armed with axes climbed into the wreckage and pulled out Larkin and the corpse of Beckenridge.

As the ambulance carried them away and a tractor worked feverishly to drag the wreckage from the runway, the Controller alongside Adams could he heard asking which Mosquito was next in line for an urgent landing. As another battle-scarred Mosquito ceased its orbiting and gingerly approached the airfield, Davies gave Henderson a wry glance. "618 Squadron are going to be happy when they see what we've done with their kites, Jock. There doesn't appear to be one without damage."

Although Henderson knew it was a remark intended to disguise Davies's feelings, the big Scot was in no mood for humour, however wry. "I couldn't give a damn about the aircraft, sir. I've lost nearly a third of my crews today."

Sizing up the situation, Simms was quick to intervene. "Your boys have done a wonderful job, Henderson. When my report goes in I wouldn't be surprised if the PM himself doesn't personally congratulate you."

"Amen to that," Staines said. He turned to Davies. "You know, Davies, if your squadron had cocked-up this operation, I'd have had no option but to tell Spaatz what happened here today. And that would have meant recriminations going right up the chain of command to Eisenhower and probably Churchill himself."

With the squadron he had created so much a part of his life, Davies hid his feelings well. "I realise that, sir. Might I know what you intend doing now?"

Staines paused to light himself a cigar before replying. "I guess I still ought to say something. But, goddam it, how can I put in a bad report about a bunch of guys who've done what your boys have done today? I'm forgetting all about it, Davies. In fact I'm putting in a report that the mission was superbly led and directed. After that, what you do to that guy Harvey is your own affair."

Adams followed the others out on to the airfield. Mosquitoes were still coming in to land, their scars betraying the ordeal they had endured. As he paused to watch them, Adams knew that in a few minutes their crews would be joining him. As they talked and laughed to disguise their relief at having survived, and as they drank the hot sweet tea WAAFs brought them, Adams knew he would experience his old envy at not being one of the chosen few whose missions brought hope to the enslaved people of Europe.

But he also knew that feeling would only last until he saw the empty chairs in the Mess that evening. Then a great wave of revulsion would sweep over him at the monstrous obscenity of war. Nor would it be only for the young friends he had lost that day. German lives were as sweet to their loved ones as Allied lives, and when the heady moments of victory died away, Adams could sorrow for the enemy too. To Adams death seemed to emphasise the universal brotherhood of man. The curse of violence that plagued his kind showed only in the living.

Davies' somewhat high-pitched voice broke into his sombre thoughts. "I'll be attending your de-briefing, Frank, as soon as the General has gone. In the meantime get every detail you can from the boys. They'll be wanted by the Yanks as well as ourselves."

Adams nodded and started across the oil-stained tarmac. Wishing for the hundredth time he could understand himself, he entered his Confessional and with Sue Spencer in attendance prepared to hear the profit and loss details of a victory.

Davies paused on the steps of The Queen Mary Hospital in Highgate and turned to the three men alongside him. "Now remember, watch how you behave in there. I don't want him to get the idea he's being forgiven for all he's done."

Adams exchanged a glance with Moore who, along with Henderson, made up the rest of the party. The Scot, Adams noticed, was about to say something but then changed his mind. When no one spoke, Davies grunted something and led the way up the steps again.

A week had passed since the attack on Buchansee and word had reached Sutton Craddock that Harvey had recovered enough to be transferred to a local hospital. After some deliberation Henderson had put a call through to Davies, who had snapped that he wanted to know the moment the transfer was made.

Harvey had arrived by ambulance the previous afternoon. Henderson had wanted to see him at once but Davies had issued orders that no one was to visit him until he, Davies, was present.

That morning Davies had arrived at Sutton Craddock in his staff car. At first he had given only Henderson permission to accompany him, but after the Scot had told him Moore and Adams also wanted to see the wounded man, Davies had reluctantly agreed. "After all, Moore, you're the one he slugged, so I suppose you've a right to give him a rollicking. But none of you will say a word to him until I've had my say."

Davies was now leading his party down a long corridor. As a nurse approached them, Davies checked her. "Nurse, you had a

Squadron Leader Harvey brought in here yesterday. Do you know what ward he's in?"

"Yes, sir. He's in Ward 16." The nurse's eyes travelled over the party. "Have you got permission to see him, sir?"

Davies ignored the question. "Where is Ward 16?"

The nurse pointed down the corridor. "You take the first corridor to the right. Ward 16 is halfway down." Looking worried, she re-jigged her question. "Have you spoken to the Matron, sir? You must get permission before you can see a patient."

Motioning the others to follow him, Davies began marching down the corridor again. Startled, the nurse turned and ran into a glass-fronted office. A moment later a stentorian voice boomed out. "You men! Just a minute! Where do you think you're going?"

Turning, Adams saw a huge woman in a blue uniform bustling towards them. "Who's in charge here?" she demanded.

Davies frowned at her. "I'm in charge. We've come to see Squadron Leader Harvey who was brought in yesterday."

The formidable figure stiffened. "Have you indeed? Just like that. This is a hospital, man, not a dance hall. Why haven't you asked my permission?"

Adams had never seen Davies so taken aback. "I didn't know we needed permission."

The woman's massive bosom heaved. "You didn't know? What sort of an officer are you? Do you let any Tom, Dick or Harry walk unchallenged into your airfield? If you do, then God knows how we're ever going to win this war."

Davies scowled. "I'm sorry, Madam."

"Matron. You address me as Matron."

By this time Adams' sides were aching with his efforts to suppress his laughter. Alongside him Moore's lips were twitching and Henderson looked almost hysterical as Davies's scowl deepened. "All right. Matron! What do you want me to do? Go down on my knees?"

The formidable figure stiffened. "Don't compound your offence, sir. I expect you to behave like an officer and a gentleman. Is that too much to ask?"

Davies's effort to control himself could be felt. "Are you going to let me see Squadron Leader Harvey? He's an officer of mine who was wounded in action."

Still breathing hard, the woman stopped a young nurse who was approaching them. "Nurse Gibson! Is Squadron Leader Harvey fit to see these men?"

"Yes, I think so, matron."

"What do you mean, you think so? Is he or isn't he?"

The girl's nervousness grew. "He's still quite weak, matron, but I think he's well enough to see them."

Dismissing the nurse curtly, the woman turned back to Davies. "You can have ten minutes with him. Not a second more. Now off you go and don't you ever come in here again without my permission?"

With that she turned on her heels and, like a galleon under full sail, stormed back to her office. As Davies muttered "Bloody old cow!" Henderson gave a stifled sob. Davies glared at him. "What's so funny, Jock? The woman's a gorgon."

They entered Harvey's ward a minute later. The Yorkshireman was in bed and Adams saw him start and try to sit upright. As a middle-aged nurse, standing at his bedside, tried to restrain him, Davies frowned and strode across the ward. "All right, Harvey. Lie back. This isn't a tribunal. At least not yet."

The Yorkshireman stared up at Davies, his pale, drawn face showing both defiance and contrition. "Hello, sir. I didn't expect you so soon."

"Why not? Did you expect to lie here for the rest of the war without getting the clobbering you deserve?"

From Davies's tone, Adams feared the worst. He watched Harvey's resigned eyes move from Davies to the other three men. As they paused on Moore, he gave a wry grin. "Hello, Ian. How's your jaw?"

Moore rubbed his jaw and smiled. "It aches. You nearly knocked my teeth out."

Relief flooded into Harvey's eyes at the young Squadron Commander's reaction. "I'm sorry, Ian. But I had to do it."

It was a reply that darkened Davies's scowl. "What the hell do you mean, you had to do it? Do you realise what would have happened if you'd cocked up the operation? High Command would have disbanded the Squadron and Jerry would have shot us out of the sky in the New Year."

Henderson made a brave effort to calm him. "But it didn't happen that way, did it, sir?"

Davies's concession was hard won. "No, but that's not the point, is it? We can't have officers bashing one another to take control of an operation. Anyway, what are you doing defending him? As his Commanding Officer it's your job to have him court-martialled."

"As it was your operation I thought I'd leave that to you, sir."

With a grunt of disgust, Davies turned back to the Yorkshireman. "What the hell am I going to do with you, Harvey? I can't deny you did a good job over there."

Harvey wasn't listening to him. "Have you any news of Anna, sir?"

Davies scowled at his own sentimentality. "Yes. She's one reason I'm here today. Brigadier Simms told me last night she was safe with our Forces in France. With any luck she ought to be back here in a few days."

Adams had never seen such relief flood into a human face. As Harvey's eyes closed, Adams could almost believe he saw the glimmer of tears beneath the Yorkshireman's lashes.

Moore had also given a start at Davies's words. "Is it true, sir?"

"Of course it's true. You've never known Simms give us false information yet, have you?"

After believing Davies' visit had only punitive purposes, all three men were staring at him in astonishment. By this time Harvey had recovered himself. "Thank you, sir. It's good of you to come and tell me."

Davies frowned. "As her husband, you had a right to know. But I still don't know what to do with you." He swung round. "Has anyone any suggestions?"

With tension beginning to relax, Henderson took a deep breath and then grinned. "You could ground him, sir."

Davies's reply exceeded all expectations. "What? After he threw my promise into my face? One thing is for certain, Jock. If I don't court martial him, he goes back on flying duties."

Believing by this time that the unbelievable had happened, Adams took his courage in both hands. "Why don't you leave it to Moore, sir? After all, he was the one who took the beating."

Davies slapped his thigh. "That's it! You always were the one with good ideas, Frank. All right, Ian. What's it to be?"

Moore smiled. "I think he ought to have the worst punishment a Yorkshireman can have, sir. He has to stand the entire Mess a round of drinks when he's back with us."

For a moment Davies looked like a malicious hobgoblin. "Bloody good idea, Ian! That'll teach the sod to act like Attila the Hun."

Adams remembered little that was said after that. It was only afterwards, when he entered his Confessional, that he realised what the morning had done to him. Sue Spencer, who knew of old the effect heavy crew losses had on him, showed her surprise. "You sound happy, Frank. Have you had some good news?"

Adams looked surprised at her question. "How did you know that?"

"You were humming when you came in. That's not the way you usually behave after one of Davies's operations."

Frowning, Adams took off his glasses and wiped them. "You're right. After all that happened last week, it does seem wrong to feel like this. But the truth is, this is the first time I've known one of Davies's operations have a happy ending."

She was showing intense curiosity now. "A happy ending? After all those casualties?"

"Yes. Perhaps a small one in the great scheme of things. But not small to the people involved."

By this time Sue's attractive eyes were huge and pleading. "You're going to explain, aren't you? You must now."

Adams, who could never resist the girl's requests, sighed, then drew up two chairs before the coke stove. "I suppose there'll be no peace until I do. All right, Sue. Sit down here and I'll tell you all about it."

THE END

If you enjoyed this book, look for others like it at Thunderchild Publishing: https://ourworlds.net/thunderchild_cms/

Made in the USA
San Bernardino, CA
19 April 2018